Royal
Protector

CAITLIN CREWS

DANA MARTON

CATHERINE MANN

MILLS & BOON

First Published in Great Britain 2019
By Mills & Boon, an imprint of HarperCollins *Publishers*
1 London Bridge Street, London, SE1 9GF

ROYAL PROTECTOR © 2019 Harlequin Books S.A.

Traded to the Desert Sheikh © 2015 Caitlin Crews
Royal Captive © 2010 Dana Marton
His Pregnant Princess Bride © 2016 Catherine Mann

ISBN: 978-0-263-27602-2

0519

MIX
Paper from
responsible sources
FSC® C007454

This book is produced from independently certified FSC™ paper to ensure responsible forest management.

For more information visit: www.harpercollins.co.uk/green

Printed and bound in Spain
by CPI, Barcelona

USA TODAY bestselling and RITA® Award-nominated author Caitlin Crews loves writing romance. She teaches her favorite romance novels in creative writing classes at places like UCLA Extension's prestigious Writers' Program, where she finally got her MA and PhD in English Literature. She currently lives in California with her very own hero and too many pets. Visit her at caitlincrews.com.

Dana Marton is the author of more than a dozen fast-paced, action-adventure romantic suspense novels and a winner of the Daphne du Maurier Award of Excellence. She loves writing books of international intrigue, filled with dangerous plots that try her tough-as-nails heroes and the special women they fall in love with. Her books have been published in seven languages in eleven countries around the world. To find more information on her books, please visit www.danamarton.com. She loves to hear from her readers and can be reached via e-mail at DanaMarton@DanaMarton.com.

USA TODAY bestselling author **Catherine Mann** lives on a sunny Florida beach with her flyboy husband and their four children. With more than forty books in print in over twenty countries, she has also celebrated wins for both a RITA® Award and a Booksellers' Best Award. Catherine enjoys chatting with readers online—thanks to the wonders of the internet, which allows her to network with her laptop by the water! Contact Catherine through her website, catherinemann.com, find her on Facebook and Twitter (@CatherineMann1), or reach her by snail mail at PO Box 6065, Navarre, FL 32566.

The Royals

COLLECTION

Royal Affairs – January 2019
Royal Sins – February 2019
Royal Temptation – March 2019
Royal Babies – April 2019
Royal Protector – May 2019
Royal Weddings – June 2019

TRADED TO THE DESERT SHEIKH

CAITLIN CREWS

CHAPTER ONE

She had no warning.

There had been no telltale men with grim, assessing eyes watching her from the shadows. No strange gaps in conversation when she walked into the small coffee shop in a tiny lakeside village in British Columbia. There hadn't been any of the usual hang-ups or missed calls on her latest disposable mobile phone that signaled her little noose was drawing tight.

She had a large mug of strong, hot coffee to ward off the late-autumn chill this far north, where snow was plastered across the Canadian Rocky Mountains and the thick clouds hung low. The pastry she chose was cloyingly sweet, but she ate all of it anyway. She checked her email, her messages. There was a new voice mail from her older brother, Rihad, which she ignored. She would call him later, when she was less exposed. When she could be certain Rihad's men couldn't track her.

And then she glanced up, some disturbance in the air around her making her skin draw tight in the second before *he* took the seat across from her at the tiny little café table.

"Hello, Amaya," he said, with a kind of calm, resolute satisfaction—while everything inside her shifted into one great big scream. "You've been more difficult to find than anticipated."

As if this were a perfectly casual meeting, here in this quiet café in an off-season lakeside village in a remote part of Canada she'd been certain he couldn't find. As if he weren't the most dangerous man in the world to her—this man who held her life in those hands of his that looked so easy and idle on the table between them despite their scars and marks of hard use, in notable contrast to that dark slate fury in his too-gray eyes.

As if she hadn't left him—His Royal Highness, Kavian ibn Zayed al Talaas, ruling sheikh of the desert stronghold Daar Talaas—if not precisely at the altar, then pretty damn close six months ago.

Amaya had been running ever since. She'd survived on the money in her wallet and her ability to leave no trail, thanks to a global network of friends and acquaintances she'd met throughout her vagabond youth at her heartbroken mother's side. She'd crashed on the floors of perfect strangers, stayed in the forgotten rooms of friends of friends and walked miles upon miles in the pitch dark to get out of cities and even countries where she'd thought he might have tracked her. She wanted nothing more than to leap up and run now, down the streets of the near-deserted village of Kaslo and straight into the frigid waters of Lake Kootenay if necessary—but she had absolutely no doubt that if she tried that again, Kavian would catch her.

With his own bare hands this time.

And she couldn't repress the shiver that swept over her at that thought.

Much less the one that chased it, when Kavian's sensually grim mouth curved slightly at the sight of her reaction.

Control yourself, she snapped. Inside her own head.

But Kavian looked as if he heard that, too. She hated that some part of her believed that he could.

"You seem surprised to see me," he said. "Surely not."

"Of course I'm surprised." Amaya didn't know how she managed to push the words out of her mouth. A list of things she needed to do—right that second, if there was any hope for her to escape him again now that he'd be fully expecting her to try—raced through her head. But she couldn't seem to look away from him. Just like the last time she'd met him, at her brother's palace to the south of Kavian's desert kingdom, for the occasion of her arranged engagement to this man, Kavian commanded her full attention. "I thought the last six months made it clear that I didn't want to see you, ever again."

"You belong to me," he said, with that same sheer certainty that had sent ice spearing through her at the celebration of their betrothal in the Bakrian Royal Palace half a year ago. That same spear felt even colder now. "Was this moment truly in doubt? I was always going to find you, Amaya. The only question was when."

His voice was deceptively calm, something like silken in the quiet of the small café. It did nothing to lessen the humming sort of threat that emanated from that lethal body of his, all harsh muscle and a kind of lean, austere maleness that was as foreign to her as it was oddly, disruptively fascinating. He looked nothing like the local men who had been in and out of this very café all morning, wreathed in hearty beards and thick plaid jackets to fend off the northern cold.

Kavian wore unrelenting black, relieved only by those furious slate-gray eyes he didn't shift from her for a single moment. Black trousers on his tough, strong legs, utilitarian black boots on his feet. What looked like a fine black T-shirt beneath the black bomber jacket he wore half-zipped that managed to show off his granite-hard chest rather than conceal it in any way. His thick dark hair was shorter than she remembered it, and the closer-cut style accentuated the deadly lines of his brutally captivating face, from that warrior's jaw with the faintest hint of his dark beard as if he hadn't bothered to shave in days, his blade of a nose and cheekbones male models would have died for that nonetheless looked like weapons on such a hard-hewn face.

He looked like an assassin, not a king. Or perhaps a king in hiding as some kind of nightmare. *Her* nightmare. Either way, he looked catastrophically out of place here, so far across the planet from Daar Talaas, where his rule seemed as natural as the desolate desert and the stark, forbidding mountains that dominated his remote country.

Or perhaps the only catastrophe was the way her heart thundered inside her chest, louder by the second. He was like a shot of unwanted, far-too-tactile memory and adrenaline mixed into one, reminding her of the treacherous, unwelcoming desert where she'd been born and where she'd spent the first few years of her life, wrapped up tight in all that sweltering heat, storming sand and blinding, terrible light.

Amaya hated the desert.

She told herself she wasn't any fonder of Kavian.

"You are quite enterprising."

She didn't think that was a compliment. Not exactly. Not from this man, with his harsh gaze and that assessing way he looked at her, as if he was sizing her up for structural weaknesses he could then set about exploiting for his own ends. *That's exactly what he's doing*, she told herself.

"We almost had you in Prague two months ago."

"Unlikely, as I was never in Prague."

That crook of his mouth again, that made her breath feel choppy and her lips sting, and Amaya was certain he knew full well that she was lying.

"Are you proud of yourself?" he asked. She noticed then

that he hadn't moved in all the time he'd sat there. That he remained too still, too watchful. Like a sentry. Or a sniper. "You have caused untold damage with this pointless escapade of yours. The scandal alone could topple two kingdoms and yet here you sit, happy to lie to my face and sip at a latte in the wilds of Canada as if you are a stranger to your own responsibilities."

There was no reason that should hit Amaya like a blow.

She was the half sister of the current king of Bakri, it was true. But she hadn't been raised in the palace or even in the country, as some kind of royal princess draped in tiaras and expectations. Her mother had taken Amaya with her when she left and then divorced the former king— Amaya's father—and Amaya had been raised in her mother's painful whirlwind of a wake. A season here, a season there. Yachts in the south of France or Miami, artistic communes in places like Taos, New Mexico, or the beach resorts of Bali. Glitzy cities bristling with the rich and famous in their high-class penthouses and hotel suites, distant ranches ringed with fat, sleek cattle and more rustic interpretations of excessive wealth. Wherever the wind had blown Elizaveta al Bakri, wherever there were people to adore her appropriately and pay for the privilege, which Amaya had come to understand was her mother's substitute for the love her father hadn't given her, that was where they'd gone—as long as it was never, ever back to Bakri, the scene of the crime as far as Elizaveta was concerned.

That Amaya had returned to the country of her birth at all, much less because Rihad had prevailed upon her after their father had died and somehow gotten into her head with his talk of *her birthright*, had caused a distinct rift between Amaya and her mother. Elizaveta had been noticeably frosty to her only child since the old king's funeral, which Amaya had attended and which had been, in Elizaveta's view, a deep betrayal.

Amaya understood. Elizaveta still loved her lost king, Amaya was sure of it. It was just that Elizaveta's thwarted love had grown more than a little gnarled and knotted over all these years, becoming indistinguishable from hate.

But there was no point thinking about her complicated relationship with her mother, much less her mother's even more complicated relationship with emotions. It solved nothing—especially not Amaya's current predicament. Or what Kavian viewed as her *responsibilities.*

"You're talking about my brother's responsibilities," Amaya said now, somehow holding Kavian's hard warrior gaze steadily as if she weren't in the least moved by his appearance before her. It she did it long enough, maybe she'd believe it herself. "Not mine."

"Six months ago, I was prepared to be patient with you." His voice was soft. It was the only thing about him that was. "I was not unaware of the way you were raised, so ignorant of your own history and the ancient ways, forever on the run. I knew this union would present challenges for you. Six months ago, I intended to meet those challenges as civilly and carefully as possible."

The world, so still already since he'd sat across from her, shrank down until it was nothing but that flame of sheer, crackling temper in his dangerous gaze. Gray and fierce. Piercing into her, beneath her skin, like a terrible burning she could neither control nor extinguish. It seared through her, rolling too fast, too unchecked, too massive to bear.

"How thoughtful you were six months ago," she said faintly. "It's funny how you didn't mention any of that at the time. You were too busy posturing and grandstanding with my brother. Playing to the press. I was nothing more than a little bit of set dressing at my own engagement party."

"Are you as vain as your mother before you, then?" His voice turned so hard it left her feeling hollow, as if it had punched straight through her, though he still didn't move at all. "That is a great pity. The desert is not kind to vanity, you will find. It will strip you down to the bone and leave only who you really are behind, whether you are ready to face that harsh truth or not."

Something flickered behind that fierce gaze of his, she thought—though she didn't want to know what it was, what it meant. She didn't want to imagine who he *really* was. Not when he was so overwhelming already.

"You paint such a lovely picture," she threw back at him. She didn't understand why she was still sitting there, doing nothing but chatting with him. *Chatting.* Why did she feel paralyzed when he was near? The same thing had happened the last time, at their celebration six months ago. And then far worse—but she refused to think about that. Not here. Not now, with him watching her. "Who wouldn't want to race off to the desert right now on such a delightful voyage of self-discovery?"

Kavian moved then, and that was worse than his alarming stillness. Far worse. He rose to his feet with a lethal show of grace that made Amaya's temples pound, her throat go dry. Then he reached down, took her hand without asking or even hesitating and pulled her to her feet.

And the insane part was that she went.

She didn't fight. She didn't recoil. She didn't even *try.* His hand was calloused and rough against hers, hot and strong, and her stomach flipped, then dropped. Her toes arched in the boots she wore. She came up too fast and once again, found herself teetering too close to this man. This stranger she could not, would not marry.

This man she could not think about without that answering fire so deep within.

"Let go of me," she whispered.

"What will you do if I do not?"

His voice was still calm, but she was closer to him now, and she felt the rumble of it like a deep bass line inside her. His skin was the color of cinnamon, and heat seemed to blast from him, from his hand around hers and his face bent toward her. He was bigger than she was, tall enough that her head reached only his shoulder, and the fact that he'd spent his whole life training in the art of war was like a living flame between them. It was written deep into every proud inch of him. She could see the white line of an old scar etched across the proud column of his throat, and refused to let herself think about how he might have come by it.

He was a war machine, this man. *Kavian is of the old school, in every meaning of the term*, her brother had told her. She'd known that going in. She couldn't pretend otherwise.

What she hadn't realized was how it would affect her. It felt as if she were standing too close to a wicked bonfire, her face on the verge of blistering from the intense heat, with no way to tell when the wind might change.

Kavian tugged on her hand, bringing her closer against his chest, then bending his head to speak directly into her ear.

"Will you scream?" he asked softly. Or perhaps it was a taunt. "Cry out for help from all these soft strangers? What do you think will happen if you do? I am not a civilized man, Amaya. I do not live by your rules. I do not care who gets in my way."

And she shook, as much from the sensation of his breath against her ear as the words he used. Or maybe it wasn't either of those—maybe it was that he was holding her against that body of his again, and she was still haunted by what had happened the last time. What she hadn't done a single thing to stop—but that was desert madness, nothing more, she told herself harshly.

She had no choice but to believe that. It was the only thing that made any sense.

"I believe you," she hissed at him. "But I doubt that you want to end up on the evening news, uncivilized or not. That would be a bit too much scandal, I think we can agree."

"Is this a theory you truly wish to test?"

She yanked herself back from him, out of his grip, and it wasn't lost on her that he let her go. That he had been in control of her since the moment he walked into this café—or before, she realized as her stomach flipped over inside her again and then slammed down at her feet. It must have been before.

Amaya looked around a little bit wildly and realized—belatedly—that the café was unusually empty for the early afternoon. The handful of locals who remained seemed to have studiously averted their gazes in a way that suggested someone had either told them to do so or compensated them for it. And she could see the two brawny men, also in head-to-toe, relentless black, standing at the front door like sentries and worse, the sleek black SUV idling at the curb outside. Waiting.

For her.

She jerked her gaze back to Kavian. "How long have you been following me?"

His dark eyes gleamed.

"Since we located you in Mont-Tremblant, all the way across this great, wide country in Quebec ten days ago." Kavian was calm, of course. But then, he'd already won.

Why wouldn't he be calm? "You should not have returned there if you truly wished to remain at large."

"I was only there for three days." She frowned at him. "Three days in six months."

He only gazed back at her as if he were made entirely of stone and could do so forever—and would, if it was required. As if he were a monolith and as movable.

"Mont-Tremblant was your favorite of the upscale ski resorts your mother preferred whenever her winter tastes ran to cold weather and ski chalets. I assume that played a part in why you opted to go to university in Montreal, so you could better access it in your free time. I've long suspected that if you were likely to return to any of the places your mother dragged you over the years, it would be there."

"How long have you been *studying* me?" Amaya managed to scrape out, her heart right there in her throat. She was surprised he couldn't see it.

And Kavian smiled then, a quirk of his absurdly compelling mouth that made her doubt her own sanity. But there was no doubting the way it wound in her, tightening the knot in her belly, making her feel unsteady on her feet.

She had the strangest notion that he knew it.

"I don't think you're ready to hear that," he told her, and there was something else, then, in those slate-gray eyes. Inhabiting that warrior's face of his, stone and steel. And he was right, she thought. She didn't want to hear it. "Not here. Not now."

"I think I deserve to know exactly how much of an obsessed stalker you are, in fact. So I can prepare myself accordingly."

He almost laughed. She saw the silver of it in his gaze, in the movement of that mouth of his, though he made no sound.

"What you deserve is to be thrown over my shoulder

and bodily removed from this establishment." She'd never heard him sound anything but supernaturally calm and almost hypnotic in his intensity, and so that rough edge to his voice then shocked her. It made her jolt to attention, her eyes flying wide on his. "Make no mistake. If I'd caught up to you in a less stuffy place than Canada, we wouldn't be bothering with polite conversation at all. My patience ran out six months ago, Amaya."

"You threaten me, and then you wonder why I ran?"

"I don't care why you ran," he replied, ruthless and swift, and she'd never heard him sound quite like that, either. "You can walk outside and get in that car, or I can put you there. Your choice."

"I don't understand this." She did nothing to hide the bitterness in her voice, the anguish that she'd walked into this trap six months ago thinking her eyes were open, or the fear that she'd never get out of it again. "You could have any other woman in the world as your queen. I'm sure there are millions who lie awake at night dreaming of coronations and crowns. And you could certainly ally your country to my brother's if that was what you wanted, whether or not your queen was related to him. You don't need me."

Again, that smile, dangerous and compelling and world-altering at once. The essence of Kavian, boiled down to that small quirk of his too-hard mouth.

"But I want you," he said, deep and certain. So very certain, like stone. "So it amounts to the same thing."

Kavian thought for a moment she would bolt, despite the obvious futility of another such attempt.

And that wildness that was always a part of him, the desert that lived inside him, untamed and unconquerable and darker than the night, wished that she'd try. Because he was not the kind of man she'd known all her life. He was not pallid and weak, Western and accommodating. He had been forged in steel and loss, had struck down treachery and rebellion alike with his own two bloodstained hands. He had made himself what he most hated because it had been a necessary evil, a burden he'd been prepared to shoulder for the good of his people. Perhaps it had been too easy a transition; perhaps he *was* the darkness itself—but those were questions for a restless soul, a long, dark night. Kavian had never been a good man, only a determined one.

He would not only chase her to ground; he would enjoy it.

Something of that must have showed on his face because she paled, his runaway princess who had evaded him all this time and in so doing, proved herself the very queen she claimed she didn't want to become. The very queen he needed.

And then she swallowed so hard he could hear it and, beast that he was, he liked that, too.

"Run," he invited her, the way he'd once invited a challenger to attempt to take his throne. With untrained hands and an unwieldy ego. It had not ended well for that foolish upstart. To say nothing of the traitorous creature who had struck down Kavian's father before him. Kavian was not a good man. The woman who would become his queen should have no doubts on that score. "See what happens."

He didn't know what he expected her to do, but it wasn't that defiant glare she aimed at him, her hands fisted on her hips, as if she was considering taking a swing at him right there in public. He wished she'd do that, too. Any touch at all, he'd take.

She was so pretty that she should have been spoiled and delicate, a fragile glass thing better kept high on a soft, safe shelf—and he'd thought she was. He would have worshipped her as such. That she was *this*, as well—with the ingenuity to hide from him for this long and the sheer strength to stand before him without shrinking or collapsing when many grown men did not dare do the same—came far too close to making him…furious.

Well. Perhaps *furious* was not quite the correct term. But it was dark, that ribbon of reaction in him. Supple and lush. And it gripped him like a slick vise all the same. He imagined it was a kind of admiration. For the fierce and worthy queen she would become, if he could but tame her to the role. Kavian had no doubt that he could do it, in time. That he would.

Had he not done everything he'd ever set out to do, no matter how treacherous the path? What was one woman next to a throne reclaimed, a family avenged, the stain on his soul? Even if it was this one. This woman, who fought him where others only cowered.

God help him but he liked it. The angrier she made him with her defiance, the more he liked her.

Her beauty had been a hammer to the side of his head from the start, taking him by surprise. His first inkling that he, too, was a mortal man who could be toppled by the same sins as any other. It had not been a revelation he had particularly enjoyed. He could remember all too well that meeting with Rihad al Bakri, the other man at that time merely the heir apparent to the Bakrian throne.

"You want an alliance," he'd said when Rihad was brought before him in the grand, bejeweled throne room in the old city of Daar Talaas that had been hewn into the rocks themselves and for centuries had stood as a great stronghold. Kavian wanted to make certain it would stand for centuries more.

"I do."

"What benefit is there in such an alliance for me?"

Rihad had talked at length about politics and the drums of war that beat so long and so hard in their part of the world that Kavian had started to consider it their own form of regional music. And it was far better to dance than to die. Moreover, he'd known Rihad was correct—the mighty powers around them imposed their rule by greed and cunning and, when that did not work, the long-range missiles of their foreign-funded militaries. In this way, the world was still won, day after bloody day.

"And I have a sister," Rihad had said, at the end of this trip through unsavory political realities.

"Many men have sisters. Not all of those men also have kingdoms in peril that could use the support of my army."

Because Daar Talaas might not have been as well funded as some of their neighbors, nor was its military as vast, but they had not been beaten by a single foreign force since they had ousted the last Ottoman sultanate in the fifteenth century.

"You strike me as a man who prefers the old ways." Rihad had shrugged, though his gaze had been shrewd. "Surely there remains no better way to unite two families, or two countries, than to become one in fact."

"Says the man who has not offered to marry my sister," Kavian had murmured, lounging there on his throne as if he hadn't cared one way or the other. "Though it is his kingdom that hangs in the balance."

Rihad had not replied with the obvious retort, that Kavian had no sisters and that his brothers had been taken out much too young in the bloody coup Kavian's predecessor had led. Instead, he'd handed over a tablet computer and had pressed Play on the cued-up video.

"My sister," he'd said. Simply enough.

She'd been pretty, of course. But Kavian had been surrounded by pretty women his whole life. Supplicants presented them to him like desserts for him to choose between, or simply collect. His harem had been stocked with the finest selection of feminine beauty from all over his lands, and even beyond.

But this one was something else.

It was the perfect oval of her face and that lush, carnal mouth of hers as she'd talked back to Rihad in a manner that could only have been described as challenging. Defiant. Not in the least bit docile, and Kavian found he liked it far too much.

It was the thick, lustrously dark hair she'd plaited to one side and thrown over one of her smooth shoulders, covered only by the faintest thin straps of the pale white tank top she wore that drew attention to her olive skin even as it was perfectly clear that she'd given her appearance little to no thought. It was the crackling energy and bright, gleaming light in her faintly Eurasian eyes, the color of bittersweet chocolates ringed in fancifully dark lashes, that inspired a man to look again, to look closer, to do what he could to never look away.

And it was what she was saying, in that slightly husky voice with an unplaceable accent, neither North American nor European, not quite. She'd used her hands for emphasis, and animated facial expressions besides, instead of the studied, elegant placidity of the women he knew. She'd talked so quickly, so passionately, that he'd been interested despite himself. And when she finished, she'd laughed, and it had been like clear, cool water. Sparkling and bright, washing him clean, and making him thirsty—so very, very thirsty—for more.

"Let me guess," she'd said, her voice dry and faintly teasing in a way that had shot straight to the hardest part of him—forcing Kavian to remind himself that she hadn't been speaking to *him*. That what he'd been watching was a taped video call between this woman and her brother. "The mighty King of Bakri is not a Harry Potter fan."

She had been a hard blow to his temple, making his head spin. The effect of such an unexpected hit had coursed through his body like some kind of ferocious virus, burning away everything in its path and leaving only one word behind:

Mine.

But he'd only smiled blandly at Rihad when the video finished.

"I am not at all certain I require a wife at present," he'd said languidly, and the negotiation had begun.

He'd never imagined it would lead him here, to this inhospitable land of snow and ice, pine trees and heavy fog, so far north he could feel the chill of winter like a dull metal deep in his bones. He admired her defiance. He craved it. It would make her the perfect queen to reign at his side. But he also needed a wife who would obey him.

Men like his own father had handled these competing needs by taking more than one wife—one for each required role. But Kavian would not make his father's mistakes. He was certain he could find everything he needed in one woman. In this woman.

"Listen to me," Amaya was saying, her hands still on her hips, her defiant chin high, as if this were another negotiation instead of a foregone conclusion. "If you'd listened to me in the first place, none of this would have happened."

"I have listened to you." He had listened to her back in Bakri, or he'd intended to listen to her anyway, and then she'd run. What benefit was there in listening any further? Her actions had spoken for her, clear and unmistakable.

"The next time I listen to you, it will be in the old city, where you can run your heart out for miles in all directions and find nothing but the desert and my men. I will listen and listen, if I must. And it will all end the same way. You will be beneath me and all of this will have been a pointless exercise in the inevitable."

CHAPTER TWO

KAVIAN TURNED THEN and started for the door, aware that all the exits were blocked by his men on the off chance she was foolish enough to try to escape him one last time.

He still hoped she would. He truly did. The beast in him yearned for that chase.

"We are leaving, Amaya. One way or the other. If you wish me to force you, I am happy to oblige. I am not from your world. The only rules I follow are the ones I make."

He yanked open the door and let the sharp weather in, nodding to the guards who waited for him on the other side. Then he looked back at this woman who did not seem to realize that she'd been his all along.

That all she was doing was delaying what had always been coming, as surely as the stars followed the setting sun. As surely as he had assumed the mantle of his enemy to defeat the murderous interloper and reclaim his throne, no matter the personal cost or the dark stain it left behind.

Her hands had dropped from her hips and were balled into fists at her sides, and even in the face of her pointless stubbornness he found her beautiful. Shockingly so. He could still feel that resounding blow to the side of his skull, making the world ring and whirl all around him.

And this despite the fact that she still wore her hair in that same impatient braid, a long, messy tail pulled forward over one shoulder as if she hadn't wanted to bother with it any further. At their engagement party, she'd worn it up high in too many braids to count, woven together into some kind of elegant crown. And here he stood on the other side of the world, still itching to undo it all himself and let the heavy, dark length of it fall free.

He wanted to bury himself in the slippery silk of it, the fragrant warmth. In her, any way he could have her. *Every* way.

It didn't even matter that she was dressed in a manner that did not suit her fine, delicately otherworldly allure—and was certainly not appropriate for a woman who would be his queen. Jeans that were entirely too formfitting for eyes that were not his. Markedly unfeminine boots. Both equally scuffed and lived in, as if she were still the university student she'd been not too long ago. A bulky sweatshirt that hid her figure, save those long and slender legs of hers that nothing could conceal and that he wanted wrapped around him. And the puffy jacket she'd thrown over the nearest chair when she sat down that, when she wore it zipped up to her chin, made her look almost like a perfect circle above the waist.

Kavian wanted to wrap her in silks and drape her in jewels. He wanted her to stand tall beside him. He wanted to decorate her in nothing but delicate gold chains and build whole palaces in her name, as the ancient sultans had done for the women who'd captivated them. He wanted her strength as much as her beauty.

He wanted to explore every inch of her sweet body with his battered hands, his warrior's body, his mouth, his tongue.

But first, and foremost, he wanted to take her home.

"Is it force, then?" he asked her, standing in the open doorway, not in the least bit concerned about being overheard by the townspeople. "Will I throw you over my shoulder like the barbarians of old? I think you know I will not hesitate to do exactly that. And enjoy it."

She shuddered then and he would have given his kingdom, in that moment, to know whether it was desire or revulsion that swept through her at that thought. He hated that he didn't know her well enough, yet, to tell the difference.

That, too, would change. And far quicker than it might have had she come with him as she'd been meant to do the night of their engagement party, when he'd been predisposed toward a gentler understanding of her predicament. But there was nothing gentle left in him. He had become stone.

Amaya swept her big coat up in one hand and hung the ratty bag she carried over one shoulder. But she still didn't move toward him.

"If I come with you now," she said, that husky voice of hers very even, very low, "you have to promise that you won't—"

"No."

She blinked. "You don't know what I was going to say."

"What can it matter? I made you a set of promises upon our betrothal. You should not require anything further. You made me promises, too, Amaya, which you broke that very same night. It is better, I think, that you and I do not dwell on promises."

"But—"

"This is not a debate," he said gently, but he could see the way the edge beneath it slapped at her.

Her lips fell open, as if she had to breathe hard to get through that slap, and he couldn't pretend he didn't approve of the way she did it. She even stood taller. He liked that she was beautiful, of course he did. Kavian was a man, after all. A flesh-and-blood king who knew full well the benefits of such beauty when he could display it on his arm. But his queen had to be strong or, like his own fragile and ultimately treacherous mother, she would never survive the rigors of their life together. She would dissolve at the first hint of a storm, and he couldn't have that.

Life was storms, not sunshine. The latter was a gift. It was not reality.

Kavian was a warrior king. Amaya had to be a warrior queen, in her own way. No matter how little she liked the lessons that would make her into what he needed.

He was certain he, at least, would enjoy them.

"There are no caveats, no negotiations," he told her. Perhaps too firmly. "You have no choices here. Only an option regarding the delivery method toward the same end."

He thought she would argue, because it seemed she always argued—and, of course, when he'd elected to quiet her in the only other way he knew, she'd bolted for six months. He could admire it now that it was over. Now that she was in his possession, where she belonged.

But today, his warrior queen lifted her head high and walked toward him instead, her dark chocolate gaze cool on his.

"That sounds ominous," she said. Still, she walked through the door of her own volition, out into the moody light of this cold northern morning. "Will you throw a potato sack over my head? Keep my mouth shut with duct tape? Make this a good old-fashioned sort of kidnapping?"

Kavian probably shouldn't have found that amusing. He was aware that was begging for trouble, but he couldn't help it, especially not when she walked out in front of him and he understood, at last, the true benefit of a tight pair of jeans on a fine-figured woman.

His palms ached with the urge to test the shape of

that bottom of hers, to haul her against him the way he had done but once, six months ago. It hadn't been nearly enough, no matter how many times he'd replayed it while scouring the earth for her trail.

"It is a relatively short helicopter flight to Calgary," he said. "Then a mere fifteen hours or so to Daar Talaas. It is entirely up to you if you wish to dress in sacks and tape. I can drug you, if that will appeal to your sense of victimization. Whatever you wish, my queen, it shall be yours."

She stopped then, on the street in this small little Western town in the middle of so much towering wilderness. She turned slowly, as if she was still processing that dry tone of his, and when she met his gaze her own was solemn.

"I can't be your queen," she said quietly. "You must know that. Surely that, if nothing else, became clear to you over all these months."

He didn't try to keep his hands off her, then. He pulled that thick plait into his palm and let the warm silk gently abrade his skin. It wasn't lost on him that if he wished it, he could tug her closer to him, hold her fast, use that braid to help him plunder that plump mouth of hers. The specter of that possibility danced between them and he knew, somehow, that those dark, greedy moments in her brother's palace hung there, too. Steaming up the cold air. Making her cheeks bloom red and his blood heat.

"You promised yourself to me," he reminded her. "You made oaths and I accepted them. You gave yourself into my hands, Amaya. You can confuse this issue with as many words as you like—forced betrothal, political engagement, arranged marriage. Whatever way you hedge a bet in this strange place and pretend a promise need not be kept. In my world, you belong to me already. You have been mine for months."

"I don't accept that," Amaya whispered, but he was attuned to what she didn't do. She didn't weep. She didn't pull away. She didn't so much as avert her gaze. He felt all of those things like caresses.

"I don't require your acceptance," he said softly. "I only require you."

There were no direct routes into the ancient desert city that comprised the central stronghold—and royal palace—of Daar Talaas. It had been a myth, a legend, for many centuries, whispered about by traders and defeated challengers to its throne, incorporated into battle songs and epic poems. In these modern times, satellites and spy drones and online travelogues made certain there was no possibility of truly hiding a whole city away from the rest of the world, but that didn't mean the old royal seat of the warrior kings of Daar Talaas was any more accessible for being known.

The roads only led an hour or so into the desert from any given border, then ended abruptly, unmarked and nowhere near the city itself. There was nothing but the shifting desert sands in the interior of the country, with secret and hard-to-find tunnels beneath the formidable mountains that the natives had used to evade potential invaders for centuries. There were other, somewhat more modern places in the country that appeared on all the maps and were easily approached by anyone insane enough to consider the wide, empty desert a reasonable destination—but the ancient seat of Daar Talaas's power remained half mystery, half mirage.

Almost impossible to attack by land.

Much less escape.

She might not ever have wanted to end up in this place, Amaya reflected as she stepped out of the small, sleek jet into the bright, hot desert heat and the instantly parching slap of the wind that went with it, but that didn't mean she hadn't studied up on it. Just in case.

Kavian moved behind, shepherding her down the stairs toward the dusty tarmac as if he imagined she really might fling aside her jet lag and race off into the treacherous embrace of the shifting, beckoning sand. And after fifteen hours in an enclosed space with all that sensual menace that blazed from him like a radiator in the depths of a Canadian winter, Amaya was almost crazed enough to consider it.

"I won't even send my guards after you," he murmured, sounding both much too close and entirely amused, as if reading her mind or the longing in that glance she'd aimed at the horizon was funny. "I'll run you down myself. I'm not afraid to tackle a woman, particularly not when she has proved as slippery as you have. And imagine what might happen then?"

She didn't have to imagine it. She'd spent a large portion of her time and energy these past six months doing her best to cast the memory of that night at her brother's palace out of her head.

"That will never happen again," she assured him.

His hand curled around the nape of her neck as her feet hit the ground. He didn't release her as he stepped into place beside her; if anything, his hand tightened. He leaned in close, letting his lips brush against her cheek, and Amaya was certain he knew exactly what that did to her. How the heat of it rushed over her as if she'd dropped off the side of the parched earth into a boiling sea. How her skin pulled tight and her breasts seemed to swell. How her breath caught and her core melted.

Of course he knew. He remembered, too. She had no doubt.

"It will happen often," he said, warning and promise at once, "and soon."

Amaya shuddered, and she couldn't convince herself it was entirely fear. But he only laughed, low and entirely too lethal. He didn't let go of her until he'd helped her into the waiting helicopter and started to buckle her in himself.

"I'm not going to fling myself out of a moving helicopter," she gritted out at him, only *just* stopping herself from batting at those fascinatingly male hands of his as they moved efficiently over her, tugging here and snapping there, and managing to kick up new brush fires as if he'd used his teeth against the line of her neck.

He eyed her in that disconcertingly frank way of his that made something low and hot inside her constrict, then flip.

"Not now, no," he agreed.

It was a quick, dizzying ride. They shot up high into the air in a near-vertical lift, and then flew over the nearest steep and forbidding mountain range to drop down in a tumultuous rush on the other side.

Amaya had a disjointed, roller-coaster sense of a city piled high along the walls of a deep, jagged valley, the stacked buildings made of smooth, ancient stone that seemed almost a part of the mountains themselves. There were spires and minarets, flags snapping briskly against the wind, smooth domes and thick, sturdy walls that reminded her of nothing so much as a fort. She had the impression of leafy green squares tucked away from the sprawl of the desert, of courtyards bursting with bright and fanciful flowers, and then they touched down and Kavian's hands were on her again.

She started to protest but bit it off when she looked at the expression on his hard face. It was too triumphant. Too darkly intent.

He'd promised her months ago that he would bring her

home to his palace, and now he had done so. Her throat went dry as he herded her off the helicopter with him—she told herself it was the desert air, though she knew better— as she wondered exactly how many of his promises she could expect him to keep.

All of them, a small voice deep inside her intoned, like a death knell. *You know he will keep every single promise he ever made to you.*

She had to repress an involuntary shiver at that, but they'd stepped out onto a breezy rooftop and there was no time and certainly no space to indulge her apprehension. Kavian wrapped his hard fingers around her wrist and pulled her along with him as he moved, not adjusting his stride in the least to accommodate hers.

And she would die before she'd ask him to do so.

They'd landed on the very top of a grand structure cut into the highest part of this side of the valley, Amaya comprehended in the few moments before they moved inside. And then they were walking down a complicated series of sweeping, marbled stairs and through royal halls inlaid with jaw-droppingly beautiful mosaics, lovingly crafted into high arches and soaring ceilings. Though they'd gone inside, there was no sense of closeness; the palace was bright and open, with light pouring in from all directions, making Amaya feel dizzy all over again as she tried to work out the systems of skylights and arched windows that made a palace of rock feel this airy.

People she was dimly aware were various members of his staff moved toward him and around him, taking instruction and carrying on rapid-fire conversations with him as he strode deeper and deeper into the palace complex without so much as a hitch in that stride of his. They all spoke in the Arabic she'd learned as a child, that she still knew enough of to work out the basic meaning of what was said around her, if not every word or nuance. Something about the northern border. Something about a ceremony. An aside about what sounded like housekeeping, a subject she was surprised a king—especially a king as inaccessibly mighty as Kavian—spent any time thinking about in the first place. Each aide would approach him, walk with him briefly and deferentially, then fall back again as if each were a part of the royal wake he left behind him as he charged through his ornate and bejeweled world, never so much as pausing as he went.

That was Kavian. She'd understood it six months ago, on a deep and visceral level. She understood it even more clearly now. He was a brutal force, focused and unstoppable. He took what he wanted. He did not hesitate.

It took her a shuddering sort of moment to recognize it when he finally did stop walking, and even then, it was only because he finally let go of her arm. She couldn't help putting her hands to her stomach as if she could stop the way it flipped and rolled, or make her lungs take in a little more air.

First she realized they were all alone. Then she glanced around.

It seemed as if they stood in an enormous cavern, lit by lanterns in the scattered seating areas and sconces in the stone walls, though she could see, far on the other side of the great space, what looked like another open courtyard bathed in the bright desert light. It took Amaya another moment or two to notice the pools of water laid out in a kind of circle around the central seating and lounging area where they stood. Some steaming, some not. And all the fountains that poured into them from a dragon's mouth here, a lion's mouth there, carved directly into the stone walls.

"Where are we?" she asked.

Her voice resounded in the space, coming back a damp echo, and smaller, somehow, than she'd meant it to sound.

And Kavian stood there before her, his arms crossed over his magnificent black-covered chest with the gleaming pools all around him, and smiled.

"These are the harem baths."

There was something sour in her mouth then. "The harem."

"The baths, yes. The harem itself comprises many more rooms, suites, courtyards. A whole wing of the palace, as you will discover."

"It's empty." Amaya forced herself to look around to confirm that, and hated that she was afraid she was wrong. She didn't particularly want his attention anyway, did she? What did it matter if it was shared with the other women who must surely be around here somewhere? Her father had been the same kind of man. She'd lived the first eight years of her life in his palace, with his other women in addition to her mother, each one of them one more lash of pain Elizaveta still carried with her today. *Loving a man like your father is losing yourself,* her mother had taught her, *and then watching him lavish his attentions on others instead, while what remains of you shrivels up and dies.* Amaya shouldn't have been surprised, surely, that Kavian was cut from similar cloth. "Surely it can't be a harem without…a harem."

Again, that dark, assessing look of his that she worried could separate her flesh from her bones as easily as it bored inside her head.

"Do you not recall the conversation we had in your brother's palace?"

She wished she didn't. She wished she could block that entire night out of her head, but she'd tried. She'd tried for six months with little success. "No."

"I think you do, Amaya. And I think you have become far too comfortable with the lies you tell. To yourself. To me."

"Or perhaps I simply don't remember, without any grand conspiracy." But her voice was much too hoarse then and she saw that he knew it. Those eyes of his gleamed silver. "Perhaps I didn't find a conversation with you all that interesting. Blasphemous, I know."

"You told me, with all the blustering self-righteousness of your youth and ignorance and many years in North America, that you could not possibly consider marrying a man with a harem, as if such a thing was beneath you when you were born in one yourself. And I told you that for you, I would empty mine." His mouth crooked again, but she felt it like a dark, sensual threat, not a smile. "Does that jog your memory? Or should I remind you what we were doing when I made this promise?"

Amaya looked away, blindly, as if she could make sense of this. What he'd told her then, when she'd been shooting off her mouth to cover the tumult he'd caused inside her. What he appeared to be telling her now.

"I didn't think you really had a harem." She didn't want to look at him again. She didn't want to see the truth on that face of his that had yet to soften a single blow for her, and she really didn't want to question why she should care either way. "My brother doesn't have a harem."

"Neither do I." He waited until, despite herself, she looked at him again as if magnetically drawn to him. As if he controlled her will as easily as he controlled her body. "I haven't had a harem for the past six months. You are welcome."

Amaya blinked, and tried to process that. All its implications.

As if he saw some of that internal struggle on her face,

Kavian laughed, which hardly helped anything. He moved away from her, toward the nearby seating area that dominated the central expanse in the middle of the pools, all stone benches and bright floor pillows around graceful round tables covered in trays of food she didn't want to look at, because she didn't want to eat anything. She didn't want to be here at all.

Amaya had read entirely too many ancient myths in her time. She knew how this went. A few pomegranate seeds and she'd find herself forced to spend half her life trapped in the underworld with the King of Hell. *No, thank you.*

She refused to accept that this was her fate, like her mother's before her. *She refused.*

So she didn't follow him. She didn't dare move a muscle. She was afraid that if she did, the graceful, high ceilings would crash down and pin her here, trapping her forever.

Or maybe she was afraid of something else entirely—and of naming it, too, because she knew exactly where this ended. She'd witnessed it as a child. She'd lived through its aftermath. It didn't matter how hard her heart beat. She knew better.

"How many women did you keep here?" She meant to sound arch and amused, a great sophisticate who could handle what was happening here and the fact of *a harem*, but that wasn't at all how it came out. She felt the searing look he threw her way, though she didn't dare look over at him, felt it sweep over her skin, making her wish she hadn't discarded all her winter outer layers on the plane. Making her wish there was some greater barrier between them than the simple, too-sheer T-shirt she wore.

"Seventeen."

"Seven—you're messing with me, aren't you? Is this your version of teasing?"

"Do I strike you as a man who teases?" he asked, mildly

enough, yet she could hear the heft of his ruthlessness beneath it, the deadly thrust of his intent, like the rock walls all around them.

"You kept seventeen women locked away here." She felt as if she were in the helicopter again, that wild ride like a slingshot across the mountains. "And you—did you—at night, or whenever, did—"

She couldn't finish.

"Did I have sex with them?" he finished for her, his voice smooth and dark, and it moved in her in all the worst possible places. It made her feel greedy and panicked, exactly the way she'd felt in that terrible alcove in her brother's palace when she lost her mind. And everything else. "Is that what you want to know, Amaya?"

"I don't care," she threw at him. "I don't want to know anything. I don't care what you do."

"Do not ask questions if you cannot handle the answers, because I will not sugarcoat them for you." His voice was so dark, so harsh. Inexorable, somehow, as it wrapped around her. "This is no place for petty jealousies and schoolgirl insecurities. You are the queen of Daar Talaas, not a concubine whose name is known to no one."

She jolted at that, as if he'd electrocuted her. "I'm not the queen of anything!"

And it was as if her body only then realized it could move if it liked and that she wasn't trapped here—not yet—and so she whirled around to face him again.

A mistake.

Kavian had stripped down to boxer briefs that molded to his powerful thighs and made Amaya's head go completely, utterly blank. No harems. No concubines. Nothing but him. *Kavian.*

And when she could think again, it wasn't an improvement. There was still nothing but that vast expanse of his steel-honed chest, ridged and muscled in ways that defied reason, that made her mouth water and her knees feel wobbly. He was beautiful. He was something far more intoxicating than merely *beautiful*, more overwhelming than simply *hard*, and yet he was a harsh and powerful male poetry besides.

Her mouth fell open. Without realizing she'd moved at all, Amaya found her hands clamped tight over her heart as if she was afraid it might burst from her chest.

She was, she realized. She was afraid of exactly that.

"I hope you are finished asking these questions I suspect you already know the answers to, Amaya," Kavian said with that dark, quiet triumph in his voice that washed through her like a caress and made her body feel like someone else's. As if it belonged to him, the way it had once before, and she hated that she couldn't get past that. That she felt indelibly marked by him. Branded straight through to her soul. *Owned* whether she wanted to be or not, no matter that she knew better than to let herself feel such things. "Now take off your clothes."

CHAPTER THREE

AMAYA COULDN'T POSSIBLY have heard him correctly.

"I would strip down all the way myself," he was saying, his eyes never leaving her face as he started toward her again. "But I imagine that if I did so, you would faint dead away. And the marble beneath your feet is very hard. You would hurt yourself."

"I would not faint." She cast about for some way to convince him, then settled on the easiest, most provocative lie. The one most likely to repel a man like him. "I've seen battalions of naked men before as they paraded in and out of my bed. What's one more?"

"No," he replied as he closed the distance between them, and there wasn't the faintest hint of uncertainty on his face, in his hard-edged voice. "You have not."

Amaya's shoulders came up against one of the great stone arches, which was how she realized she'd backed away from him. She'd been too lost in his dark gaze to notice anything else. And then he was in front of her and it took every bit of self-preservation she had left not to let out that high-pitched sound that clamored in her throat, especially when he didn't stop stalking toward her until he was *right there*—

If she breathed out, she would touch the golden expanse of his skin. That glorious, warrior's chest with all those fascinating planes and stone-carved shallows that begged for her fingers to explore. That she hungered to *taste* in ways that made her head spin.

But then, she could hardly breathe as it was.

"I told you to remove your clothes, *azizty.*"

His mouth was so close then. She could feel his breath against her lips, particularly when he said the unfamiliar word she was terribly afraid was some kind of endearment. She was more afraid that she *wanted* it to be an endearment, that she was starting down that slippery slope. She could taste him if she only tipped forward—and she would never know how she managed to keep herself from doing exactly that.

She wanted it as much as she feared it. The push and pull of that made her feel something like seasick, though that certainly wasn't *nausea* that pooled in her. Not even close.

"I'm not very good at following orders," she managed to say.

There was the faintest suggestion of a curve to that grimly sensual mouth, entirely too near her own.

"Not yet, perhaps," he said. "But you will become adept and obedient. I will insist."

Time stopped, taut and desperate in that tiny sliver of space between them, and the past tangled all around the present until she hardly knew what was happening now as opposed to what she remembered from the night of their betrothal ceremony.

She could feel his hands in her hair, holding her elegant upswept braids in his palms, holding her head still as he'd taken her mouth like a starving man, again and again and again in that private corner of the Bakrian Royal Palace where they'd gone to "discuss" the very formal, very public promises they'd made to each other. She could feel him again as she had done so then, hard against her as the rest of the world ignited. She could feel that catapulting passion as it had eaten them both alive and made her into someone wholly new and entirely ungovernable, could feel the way he'd hitched her up between his tough, strong body and the alcove's hard wall, and then—

But that had been six months ago. This was here, now, in a great room of bathing pools and echoes, the ghosts of seventeen harem girls and that silvery awareness in his slate-gray eyes.

Amaya thought he would simply bend forward and take her mouth again, the way he had done then, with that low, animal noise that still thrilled her in the recesses of her own mind, still made her nipples draw tight and her toes curl even in memory—

He didn't.

Instead, he shifted and knelt down before her, making what ought to have been an act of some kind of submission feel instead like its opposite.

She should have felt powerful with him at her feet. Bigger than him at last. Instead, she had never felt more delicate or more precarious, and had never felt he was larger or more intimidating. It didn't make sense.

And her heart stopped pretending that what it was doing was *beating*. It wasn't anything so tame, so controlled. It tried to rocket straight out of her chest.

It took her a confused, breathless moment to realize that he was removing her boots, one at a time, and then peeling off her socks, as well. The cool stone beneath her bare feet was a shock to her system, making her remember herself in a sudden rush, as if Kavian had thrown open a window in all this stone and let a crisp wind in.

She reached over to shove him away from her, or that was what she told herself she meant to do, but it was a mistake. Or maybe she hadn't meant to do anything but touch him, because her hands came up hard against those powerful shoulders, and she couldn't describe what she did then as a *shove*. She couldn't seem to *think*. She couldn't seem to do anything but hold on to all that heat, all that fiercely corded strength, and when he tipped his head back to fix her with one of those unsmiling looks of his that wound deep inside her like some kind of spiked thing, laying her bare, she didn't say a word.

She didn't tell him to stop.

His hands moved to the waistband of her jeans, and the denim was shoved down around her thighs before she took another breath, then around her ankles. And she still didn't tell him to stop.

"Please," she said as his big hands wrapped around her ankles, when it was much too late. "I can't."

But she didn't know what she meant. And he wasn't caressing her; he was undressing her with a ruthless efficiency that stunned her into incoherence. He surged to his feet and pulled her against him with an arm banded low around her hips—not an embrace, she realized as every nerve inside her sang out in something a little too much like exultation, but so he could kick her jeans out from beneath her. And when he was done, her palms were flat against his gloriously bare chest and she could feel that great, scarred hand of his at the small of her back, and she thought she really might faint, after all.

"Can you not?" he asked her in that low, stirring voice of his, his head bent as if he was moments away from another one of those drugging, life-altering kisses that had ripped her whole world apart six months ago, so far apart even half a year on the run hadn't put it back together. "Are you certain?"

And she didn't mean to do it. She didn't know *why* she

did it. But she arched her back as if she couldn't help herself, and her breasts were so close then, so very close, to pressing against him the way she remembered they had that once, that delirious pressure that had undone her completely.

Kavian let out a small, indisputably male laugh then that did nothing at all to soothe her, and then, unaccountably, he let her go.

She stumbled back a step, and might actually have crumpled where she stood had that cool stone pillar not been right there behind her. She dug her fingertips in to it as if it were a life raft and still, her breath was as shallow as if she'd run a marathon or two.

"Take off the rest of your clothes, Amaya," Kavian said, and there was no mistaking the royal command. The powerful imperative. Or that surge of *something* inside her that wanted nothing more than to obey him. At once.

"I can't think of a single reason why I would do that." She managed to meet that gaze of his. Hold it. "More important, I don't want to take the rest—*any* of my clothes off."

"That is yet another lie. Soon there will be so many they will block out the desert sun above us, and I have no intention of living in such a darkness. Know this now."

That had the unpleasant ring of prophecy or foreboding, or perhaps more than a little of both, and it was as if her pulse had gotten too hard, too loud. It hammered at her.

"It's not a lie simply because it's something you don't want to hear," she threw at him, forcing her knees to lock beneath her, to stop their wobbling. "You don't own the thoughts in my head. You can't order me to think only the things you like."

His gray eyes gleamed, and there was not a single part of him that was not hard, unflinching. Tempered steel.

Barely contained power. She'd seen softer, more approachable statues littered about the sculpture gardens of Europe.

"It is a lie because you do, in fact, wish to take off the rest of your clothes." His voice was so quiet it almost disguised the cut of his words, the way they sliced into her. Through her. "More than that, you wish to give yourself over to me the way you did before, but this time, not in a sudden rush in a hidden alcove. You wish to run like honey against my palms and shake apart when I claim you. Again and again."

"No." But she scarcely made a sound.

"You are mine, Amaya. Can you doubt this? You shake even now, in anticipation."

"I was never yours. I will never be yours. I will—"

"Hush." An expression she might have called tender on another man, one not carved directly from stone and war and the cruel desert all around, crossed his brutally handsome face. He reached over and fit his hard palm to her jaw, cradling her too-hot cheek. "I did not know you were an innocent, Amaya. I would never have taken you like that, with so little consideration for anything but passion, had I known. You did not have to run, *azizty*. You could have told me."

And something yawned open inside her then. Something far more terrifying than the things he made her feel when he was autocratic and overbearing. She was drawn to him even then, yes. More than simply *drawn to him*. But this… She shoved the great sinkhole of it away in a panic, afraid it might spill out with that hectic heat she could suddenly feel behind her eyes. Afraid it marked her as weak and disposable, like her own mother before her.

Amaya jerked her cheek back, out of his hold, as if his palm had scalded her.

"I…" She felt too much, all at once, buffeting her from

all sides. Her memories and the present wound together into a great knot she couldn't begin to unravel—and was afraid to poke at, lest it fall apart and show him too much. She lied again, hoping it would push him back into temper, or put him off altogether. Anything but that hint of softness. *Anything but that.* "I wasn't innocent. I was the Whore of Montreal while I was at university. I slept with every man I could find in the whole of North America. I ran because I was bored—"

Kavian sighed. "And now I am bored."

She didn't know what he would do then and felt oddly bereft when he only stepped back from her. His dark gaze pinned her to the pillar behind her for a long, uncomfortably assessing moment that could easily have lasted whole years, and then he simply turned and dove into the nearest great bath.

It should have been a relief. A reprieve. She should have taken it as an opportunity to regroup, to breathe, to figure out what on earth she was going to do next as that solid, smooth warrior's body of his cut through the water and briefly disappeared beneath it.

But instead, she watched him. That marvelous, impossibly strong body could not possibly have been the product of a fleet of personal trainers or hours on modern gym equipment. He used every part of his intense physicality in everything he did. He was a smooth, powerful machine. And he fit here, in this age-old place. A weapon carved directly from the mountains themselves, beautiful and graceful in its way, but always, always deadly. Lethal in every particular.

Kavian surfaced in the middle of the pool and slicked his dark hair back from his face, his gaze like a punch, even from several feet away. Then he reached up with one perfectly carved arm and threw something toward the far end of the pool. It arced through the air and landed with a wet *splat*, and Amaya felt drunk. Altered. Because it still took another few moments to realize what he'd thrown was his boxer briefs.

And another jarring *thud* of her misbehaving heart to realize what that *meant*. That he was naked in all his considerable glory. Right there. Right in front of her.

She had to get a hold of herself, she thought sternly, or she was at definite risk of swallowing her own tongue and expiring on the spot. Which the Whore of Montreal would have been unlikely to do, surely.

"I don't understand what's happening," she said, forcing herself as close to an approximation of *calm* as she could get.

"Do you not? And yet you claimed you were no innocent. I'd have imagined that a woman of so much sordid experience would scarcely blink at the sight of a naked man in a pool."

He was no longer touching her. He was no longer caging her between his masterful body and that pillar. He was no longer even *near* her. So there was absolutely no reason that Amaya should have been standing there at the edge of the pool, staring at him as if he were holding her fast in one mighty fist.

"Is this—do you really want to—right here? You dragged me straight off the plane without any discussion or—"

He was pitiless. He said nothing, only watched her as she cut herself off and sputtered off into nothing as if she really were the artless, naive little girl he seemed to think she was already. She hated it. She hated herself. But she stood there anyway, as if awaiting his judgment. Or his next command.

As if it didn't matter what she felt, only what he did.

You know where that goes, she reminded herself with no little despair. *You know exactly where that leads, and who you'll become, too, if you let this happen.*

But all the vows she'd made to herself—that she would never lose herself so completely, that she would never disappear into any man until she could not exist without him the way her mother had done, until the loss of his affection sent her staggering around the planet like some kind of grieving gypsy with a thirst for vengeance and a child she resented—didn't seem to signify as she stood there in nothing but boy shorts and a T-shirt in the harem of the sheikh who had claimed her.

"This is a bath," Kavian said evenly. Eventually. Long after she was forced to come to several unfortunate conclusions about how very much she was like her mother, despite everything. "I dislike flying. I want the recycled air washed off my skin as soon as possible. And I want the last six months washed off you."

Amaya shivered, visibly, and Kavian tamped down the roaring beast in him that wanted nothing more than to put his hands on her and drag her to him, and who cared that she was anxious? He needed to be inside her. He needed her—and he had long since stopped *needing* a damn thing.

But he would not leap upon her like a feral thing, no matter the power of will it required to keep himself from doing so. This was no pretty diversion he was trying to lure into his bed for the night, not that he had ever needed much more of a lure than his name or his mere presence. Amaya was his queen. She would bear his sons, stand at his side, raise his heirs. She deserved what passed for a courtship here in this hard place he loved with every part of himself despite what he had done for it and no matter that there was only one possible, foregone conclusion.

This was a long game he played, with clear objectives. Like all the games he'd played in his time. And won.

So Kavian waited. He, who had not had to wait for much of anything since the day he reclaimed his father's throne. He, who had already waited for this woman for half a year, unaccountably. He, who was better used to women throwing themselves at him and begging for his notice.

He, who had never had a woman run from him in his life, before now. Before Amaya.

It was of little matter. She was here. She would stay here, because he willed it so. The world would return to the shape he preferred and do his bidding besides, and he would be inside her soon enough.

"Each pool is a different temperature," he said in the faintly bored tones of a tour guide, as if that fire in him didn't threaten to consume him whole despite the water he stood in. "There are any and all bathing accessories you could possibly require, from handmade soaps crafted here in the old city by local women to the finest luxury products flown in from Dubai."

She was beautiful even when she was obviously nervous, standing there in a small white T-shirt that she obviously wore nothing beneath and those stretchy little shorts that made her hips look nothing short of edible. Her legs were even longer than he'd imagined, and perfectly formed, giving her a bit more height than the average woman—which meant he would not dwarf her in bed or out. Her narrow feet were pale and delicate, and she'd painted her toes a cheerful, bright blue that made his chest feel tight and hit him as critically important, somehow. Though he knew that was foolish.

"Come in, Amaya," he said, invitation and order in one. "You will be the happier for it."

Her head canted slightly to one side. "Do you promise not to touch me?"

He let his gaze move over that full mouth of hers that he'd dreamed of, these past months, more than he cared to admit. That thick, dark hair he wanted to see swirling around her shoulders and that he wanted to feel slide across his own skin. Those small, proud breasts and the peaks he had yet to taste that he could see poking against the sheer fabric of her T-shirt, perhaps an invitation she didn't mean to extend. The hint of that smooth, olive expanse of her belly between her panties and her shirt, which he wanted to spend a very long time learning with his mouth. And that tempting triangle where her legs met, that he wanted to lick his way into until he forgot his own name.

Kavian took his time dragging his gaze back up her tempting body, noting the goose bumps that marked her arms as he did, and then smiled when his gaze tangled with hers again.

"No," he said. "I certainly do not."

Her lips parted as if that threw her off balance, but then she moved—and not away from him, as he'd expected. Instead, she walked along the edge of the pool toward the wide steps that led down into it from one side.

"Well," she said, with a certain primness that reminded him of that way she'd laughed at her brother in that long-ago video, and coursed through his veins like that same sweet wine. "I have nothing against hygiene, of course."

"Merely against sheikhs?" Perhaps, he thought with some surprise, he had it in him to tease after all. Only Amaya. Only alone.

"Sheikhs and kings and desert palaces," she agreed, her gaze touching his, then moving away again as she made her way down the wide stairs and on into the water, still wearing that shirt and those sexy little shorts as if they were some kind of swimming costume. "Awful things, I think we can all agree."

"Your misfortunes are vast, indeed. Of all the princesses I have chosen to become my queen over the course of my life, your burden is by far the heaviest."

Amaya moved farther into the water until it lapped at the sweet indentation of her waist, and skimmed her palms over the surface of the pool on either side of her, as if testing the water's temperature. She kept herself out of his reach, which Kavian could not abide a moment more. He moved toward her.

She watched him with as much enthusiasm as if he were an approaching shark. It shouldn't have been quite so entertaining, he supposed, but her various forms of defiance...delighted him. If that was what that sudden bright thing inside him was. He hardly recognized it.

"How many have there been?" she asked. When he didn't speak, when he only closed the distance between them, she swallowed in a way that belied that light tone she used. "Princesses that you've turned into queens? Am I the last in a long line? A parade?"

He didn't answer her. He liked the question too much, and what it told him of her, and she seemed to realize that. She danced back from him, then dropped abruptly, dunking her head beneath the water. For a moment she was a shimmer, the inky darkness of her hair obscuring her limbs from his view, and then she shot up again.

And the beast in him roared.

Her T-shirt was soaked through, showing him every contour of those glorious breasts, every mouthwatering detail. And better still, her hair had finally tumbled out of its braid and the dark mass of it coursed over her, framing her and presenting her like some kind of slick mermaid fantasy.

His mermaid fantasy, which Kavian hadn't realized he had until that moment.

She was swiping water from her face and she let out a sharp, high noise when she opened her eyes and found him there, much closer to her than he'd been when she submerged—which he also found entertaining.

He slid his hands over her hips, those sweetly rounded hips that had been seared into his memory, so deep that the tactile memories had kept him awake some nights. And then he pulled her toward him with his pulse a wild thunder in his veins, almost in pain, his need for her was so intense.

She gulped, but she didn't say a word, not even when he lowered his head and put his mouth *just there*, almost against her lips. *Almost*. He felt the fine tremors move through her, like an orchestra of *want*—a music that only she could hear. But Kavian could feel it. He felt the heat of her, let her scent—honey and rain—move in him like a blessing.

"I don't think I can kiss a man who kept seventeen women," she said, and he could feel each word against his mouth the same way he could feel the taut points of her nipples against his own chest, and neither was even close to enough. "I don't think I can reconcile myself to it, whether you emptied your harem or not."

"Then by all means, do not sully yourself," he said against the lush seduction of her mouth. "You can stand there and suffer. I do not mind at all."

And then he slid his hands up into the thick, wet glory of her hair, indulging himself. He dragged that smart mouth of hers the remaining millimeter toward his, and then finally, finally, he took her mouth with his.

CHAPTER FOUR

HIS KISS WAS like a bomb.

It detonated inside her, she burst into a shower of light and all the need and want and haunting desire that had been chasing her across the months she'd run from him slammed into her.

Amaya clung to him. She didn't think. She didn't *want* to think.

She kissed him back.

Just like six months ago, his kiss stormed through her. He wasn't gentle. He wasn't particularly kind. His kiss was carnal and dark, a blistering-hot invitation to a wickedness she'd experienced but once and still only vaguely understood.

But she wanted it. Oh, the things she *wanted* when this man took hold of her as if he had every right to her. As if her presence was all the surrender he required.

His hands moved from her hair to slide sleek against her skin, and she shuddered against him as he fit his hard palms to her breasts the same way he had done earlier to her cheek. But this was nothing like tender. This was pure, uncontainable wildness.

And it thrilled her, low and hot, dark and deep.

Amaya had never considered her breasts one way or the other. They were small, incapable of creating cleavage without help, and she'd have thought they weren't the least bit sensual or enticing. But that low growl in Kavian's throat, the one she felt inside her as he continued to take her mouth as if he truly did own her, made her think otherwise for the first time in her life.

Made her feel something like beautiful and cherished, all at once, which was as bright as another flame. And as dangerous.

When he pulled his mouth from hers, she let out a moaning noise she knew she'd later regret, which she almost regretted even as it happened—but in that moment, she didn't care. She couldn't.

There was that bright hot fire, dancing inside her. Whispering that she was as beautiful as he was, as powerful. Telling her that she was his. His mate, his match. *His*.

Amaya didn't even care when he let out that very male sound of laughter, of sheer and unmistakable victory. She felt the same thing shudder through her, as if the more he won this intimate battle of theirs, the more she did, too. She only shook when he pressed his open mouth to the column of her throat, and then she simply gave herself over into his talented hands.

The way she'd done once before. He made her mindless with longing. He made her shake with need.

He made her feel more alive, brighter and wilder and hotter and *right*, than she'd imagined was possible.

And Kavian knew exactly what he was doing. He bent his head to her breasts and this time he took one taut peak in his mouth. Then he lifted her against him with another matter-of-fact display of his superior strength, settling her so that she straddled his leg. The bright hot center of her was flush against the rock-hard steel of his thigh, and she could tell by the way that his hands moved to press her there that it was no accident.

And then he sucked her nipple in, deep and hard despite the T-shirt she wore, and the world disappeared.

Heat. Delight. That impossible blaze she'd half convinced herself she'd made up over all these long months alone and on the run—

He never removed her T-shirt, and that made the whole thing feel more illicit, more wild. Amaya could hardly breathe. Her thoughts crashed into each other and flew apart, and there was only him.

Only Kavian. Only this.

He toyed with her through the sheer material, using his hot mouth, the edge of his teeth, his remarkable hands, all the while keeping her in place against his hard thigh, where she couldn't help rocking herself with increasing intensity as the sensations stormed through her.

It was like being caught in a lightning storm, struck again and again and again.

Amaya couldn't imagine anyone could survive this— and she didn't care if she did. It was worth it, she thought. It was all worth it—

Harder and harder she moved herself against him, shameless and mindless at once, wanting only to *do something* about that wild need that shook through her and centered in her core. Wanting nothing more than *him*.

Kavian made a harsh noise, and that only lit her up all the brighter.

"You will be the death of me," he growled, low and intent, as if he read her mind.

As if, she managed to think with no little wonder, she had the same affect on this hard, wicked man as he did on her.

He took one nipple deep into the heat of his mouth again while his fingers rolled the other between them, lazy and sure. The twin assaults were like a new flash of light, a new storm. He did it once, then again, her core molten against his thigh.

"Now, Amaya," he ordered her, his mouth against her breast.

And Amaya shattered all around him, only aware that she screamed as she toppled straight over the edge into a wild oblivion when her own abandon echoed back from the walls as she lost herself completely in his arms.

When she came back to herself, Kavian had swept her up, high against his sculpted chest, and was carrying her out of the pool toward the central seating area. He wrapped her in a wide, soft bath sheet and sat her down on one of the lounging chairs. Amaya couldn't breathe—but then he left her there while he claimed his own bath sheet and tucked it around his lean waist, which only seemed to call more attention to the mouthwatering perfection of his glorious form.

She should say or do something, surely. She told herself she would, just as soon as her head stopped spinning. Or when he came back over here and claimed her once again, as he was surely about to do.

But he didn't.

Instead, Kavian went to the low table and the trays of food laid out for his pleasure. He took his time filling his plate with various local delicacies, and then sat in a lounge chair facing her where he could watch her as he ate.

Amaya didn't understand what was happening.

Her heart still pounded. She could feel it in her temples, her throat, her belly. And hot and soft between her legs.

"Aren't you going to...?"

She trailed off into nothing, irritated with herself. Why did this man turn her into the blushing, stammering fool she'd never been at any other point in her life? Why did he make her feel so foolish and so young with only the merest crook of his dark brow?

"If you cannot say it, Amaya, it does not exactly inspire me to do it," he replied mildly. Almost reprovingly, she thought.

And then he carried on eating, as if he hadn't left her in a spineless heap only moments before. As if that had all been a demonstration of some kind and he was entirely unaffected by the lesson he'd decided to teach her.

She didn't know why that made her furious, but it did—in a shocking, searing wave from her head all the way down to her feet. And if the rush of temper felt like some kind of relief, she told herself that hardly mattered. She struggled to sit up, ignoring the aftershocks of all that pleasure that still stampeded through her, as if he really had made her body his own.

She didn't want to think about that. She *refused* to think about that.

"I'm not a two-year-old," she threw at him instead. "I have no idea what your expectations are. We had sex once, by accident, and you chased me all over the planet for six months. You rant about how I'm *yours* and how I *gave myself to you.* But then you give me an orgasm and break for a quick snack. Right here in a subterranean bathhouse where you kept seventeen women under lock and key until recently, or so you cláim. I have no idea what *reasonable* is under these circumstances. I have no idea what you're capable of doing." She pulled in a breath that felt much too ragged. "I don't have the slightest idea who you are."

That gaze of his took on an unholy gleam, but he only lounged back in his seat, looking otherwise unperturbed. Remote, as if she were looking at a carving on the side of a temple, not a man. She thought of ancient kings and actual thrones, feats of chivalry and strength and drawn-out, epic battles better suited to Tolkien novels, and found her throat was dry again.

"No one was held here under lock and key," he said after a moment, when she could feel anxiety like pinpricks all up and down her body, and was afraid she'd actually broken out in hives. "This is neither a prison nor a work of overwrought fiction."

"I'll keep that in mind the next time you start thundering on about promises."

Something far too dangerous to be amusement moved across that face of his and did not make her feel in the least bit secure. It occurred to her then that she was wearing nothing but a soaked-through T-shirt and panties, and a towel. And that this man had absolutely no qualm using her body against her when he felt like it.

But he didn't move toward her and prove that all over again, as she was far too aware he could. He stayed where he was, and Amaya couldn't understand how that was worse. Yet it was.

"And this might come as a great surprise to you," he said, his voice like smoke and temptation, "but thus far you are the only woman I have ever encountered who was not delighted at the prospect of sharing my bed."

"As far as you know, you mean." She glared at him, trying to be as furious with him as she should have been. Furious with herself that she was not. "People lie, especially to terrifying kings of the desert who threaten the very air they breathe."

"Ask yourself why I am so sure," he encouraged her, in a tone that made her stomach swoop toward the ground, though he could not have seemed more relaxed as he said it. No matter that glittering silver thing in his gaze. "Ask yourself how I can know this."

Amaya had absolutely no desire to do anything of the kind. Because she could think of several ways a man could be that certain, and he'd already demonstrated it to her twice. Six months ago in an alcove of the Bakrian Royal Palace and right here in the large pool today.

And she had no idea what must have showed on her face then, but Kavian only smiled, an edgy and dangerous crook of that hard, hard mouth of his she could still feel, as if he were still touching her when he was not.

That didn't help.

"You do not have to wonder about my expectations," he said, the way other men might comment on the weather. Their favorite sports team. Unlike with other men, whole armies he could command with a wave of his hand lurked beneath his words and settled around her neck like a heavy choke collar. "I do not traffic in subterfuge. I will tell you what I want. I will tell you how I want it and when. You will provide it, one way or another. It is simple."

"Nothing about that is simple." But he only gazed back at her, implacable and resolute, and she felt a searing kind of restlessness wash through her. Hectic. Almost an itch from deep within. She couldn't name it. But she couldn't sit still, either, and so she let it take her up and onto her feet. "I don't want to be here. I want to go home."

"If you wish it," he said amiably enough, and everything stopped. Her breath. Her heart. Had he truly agreed—and so easily? But that smile of his was not the least bit encouraging. It made her feel…edgy. *Edgier.* "Which home do you mean?"

Amaya thought in that moment that she might hate him. That she might never recover from it. That it was stamped deep into her bones, like a different kind of marrow, as much a part of her as her own.

It had to be hatred. It couldn't be anything else.

"You can return me to Canada," she bit out. "Right where you found me. I'll take it from there."

"Canada is not your home." Still he lounged there, as if this were a casual conversation. As if he weren't holding her between his hands like a giant, malicious cat, and toying with her because he could. Because he felt like it. Because he enjoyed using his damn claws. "You were born in Bakri. You lived there until you were eight years old. Then you and your mother wandered for the next decade. Here, there. Wherever the wind blew her, that is where you went. The longest you stayed anywhere in that time was fifteen months at a family-owned vineyard in the Marlborough wine region of New Zealand's South Island. Is that the home you mean? It pains me to tell you that the gentleman you stayed with then moved on from your mother's much-vaunted charms some time ago and now has a new family all his own."

Amaya remembered crisp mornings in a late New Zealand winter then, walking through the corridors of rich dirt and gnarled vines with the friendly man she'd imagined might make Elizaveta better. *Happier*, anyway—and he'd seemed to manage it, for a time. She remembered the long white-capped mountain range that stretched out lazily alongside her wherever she went, reaching from the vineyard she'd called home that year toward Blenheim and the sea in the east. The skittish sheep and curious lambs who marked her every move and bounded away from any signs of movement in their direction, real or imagined. The stout and orderly vineyards, set in their efficient lines all the way north to the foothills of the Richmond range.

Most of all she remembered the thick black, velvety nights, when the skies were so filled with stars they seemed messy, chaotic. Magic. Weighted down, as if, were she to blink, all that fanciful light might crush her straight down into the rich, fertile earth like nothing but another seedling. And yet somehow they'd made it impossible for Amaya to believe that she could really be as terribly alone as she'd sometimes felt.

She hadn't thought about that period of her life in a very long time. Elizaveta had moved on the way Elizaveta always did and Amaya had stopped imagining anyone could fix what her father had broken. She felt something crack inside her now, as if Kavian had knocked down a critical foundation with that unexpected swipe—but he was still talking. Still wrecking her with every lazily destructive word.

"Or perhaps you are referring to your years at university in Montreal?" He didn't wait for her to answer. "While it appeared to be a city you enjoyed, in many respects, you left it as often as possible during your studies. You went to the mountains, as we have established. But also to Europe. To the Caribbean for sun in the midst of all those relentless winters. And you left Canada altogether shortly after your graduation for Edinburgh, where you took up a very unsuitable job in a local pub while you made the most feeble of gestures toward a master's degree in some or other form of literature at the university there."

Amaya wanted to make a gesture toward him that was anything but feeble, but restrained herself. Barely. She felt the prick of her own nails against her palms, and wished she could sink them into him instead.

"It's not up to you to decide what feels like home to me. My life is not something that requires your input or critique." She fought to keep her voice even. "You can tell because I didn't ask you for either one."

"Unfortunately for you, it is indeed up to me." Kavian shrugged, and it was not a gesture of uncertainty on a man like him. It was another weapon, and Kavian, she was beginning to understand all too well, did not hesitate to use the weapons he had at his disposal. "You do not have a home, Amaya. You never have. But that, too, has changed now. Whether you are prepared to accept that or not is immaterial."

She couldn't breathe. She felt as if he'd thrown her down a staircase, as if she'd landed hard on her back and knocked all the air from her lungs, and for a moment she could do nothing but stare back at him.

"I want to be somewhere you are not," she managed to grate out, finally.

"I am sure you do. But that is not among the choices available to you."

"This is a huge palace. There has to be a room somewhere you can stash me, far away from everything and everyone. I don't care if it's a dungeon, as long as it's nowhere near you."

Where she could figure out how to breathe through this, recover from this. If that was even possible.

Where she could work out what the hell she was going to *do*.

"There are many such rooms, but you will be staying in mine."

He only watched her, utterly without mercy. And she didn't know which was worse, the wet heat threatening to spill from her eyes, the simmering flame deep in her core that she wanted to deny, the shaking she couldn't quite seem to control now he'd upended the whole of her life in a few short sentences or the fact that he'd trapped her here. In every possible way, and they both knew it.

"No," she said.

But it was as if she hadn't spoken. It made her wonder if she had.

"I apologize if this distresses you, but I am not a particularly modern man," Kavian replied. He did not sound remotely apologetic. Nor did he look it. "I do not trust what I cannot touch. I want you in my bed."

Bed. The word exploded inside her, ripping through her with a trail of white-hot images that centered on his mouth, his hands, that body of his above her and around her and in her—

"I don't want to be anywhere near your bed. You've already done as you like with me in an alcove, a pool—why can't we leave it at that?" She sounded hysterical. She felt hysterical. "Why can't we just *leave it*?"

Kavian, by contrast, went very, very still, though his dark eyes burned.

And she felt another foundation crumble into dust at that look on his face.

"The next time I take you, Amaya, two things will happen," he said softly. So very softly. It was a whisper that rolled through like a battle cry. "First, it will be in a proper bed. I may not be civilized, precisely, but I do have my moments. And I wish to take my time. All the time in the world, if necessary." He waited for her to shudder at that, as if he'd expected it. Then he nearly smiled again, which was its own devastation. "And second, you will use my name."

"Your name?"

"You have yet to utter it," he pointed out, and she could see that though he still lounged there, though his voice was almost as languid as he looked, there was absolutely nothing *mild* about him at all. That *mildness* was an illusion he used to do his bidding, nothing more, like everything else. "I assume this is yet another attempt on your part to maintain distance between us. Is it not?"

"I have no idea what you're talking about. I say your name all the time, usually as a curse word."

"You will use my name." He didn't rise. He didn't have

to. It was as if he held her tight between those hands of his even as he reclined in his chair. She was sure she felt the press of his palms, like all those New Zealand stars when she'd been thirteen, crushing her deep into the earth. "You will sleep in my bed. You will give yourself to me. There will be no distance between us, Amaya. There will be nothing but my will and your surrender."

"Followed by my suicide, as quickly as possible, to escape you," she threw back at him to hide the pounding of her heart that told her truths she didn't want to face.

But Kavian only laughed at her, as if he could hear it. As if he knew.

CHAPTER FIVE

AMAYA HADN'T MEANT to fall asleep.

The smiling, almost too deferential attendants had been waiting for her when she'd pushed her way out of the baths, still reeling from all that had happened with Kavian. They'd surrounded her as they'd led her through the gleaming labyrinth of a palace, and Amaya hadn't been able to tell if they were deliberately taking her on a confusing route to her rooms or if the palace really was that difficult to navigate.

Either way, they'd deposited her in a rambling suite of rooms that clearly belonged to the king himself. And had pretended they didn't understand her when she demanded to be taken elsewhere.

"I don't want to stay here," she'd told them, again and again, until she'd finally had to take it up with the two intimidatingly ferocious guards who stood at the doors.

They'd only stared back at her, without any of the sweet smiles or pleasing laughter of her attendants.

"I need my own rooms," she'd said stubbornly. "This is a mistake. I'm not staying here."

The guards had only stared back at her, for what had seemed like an inordinate amount of time, especially when Amaya realized she was wearing nothing but the robe the attendants had wrapped her in.

"You may take that up with the king if you feel it is your place to question him," the larger of the two guards replied eventually, in a tone that suggested this conversation was itself scandalous and inappropriate—or perhaps, Amaya had realized belatedly, it was simply that *she* was. After all, from this man's perspective, she wasn't the unfairly trapped woman who deserved to make her own choices in life no matter whose blood ran in her veins—she was the princess who had been exalted by his beloved king's notice only to throw her good fortune in the sheikh's face by running away.

She'd been certain she could *see* that very sentence run through the man's expression like a tabloid ticker at the bottom of a television screen. That—and the fact that he and his compatriot looked as if they'd have relished the opportunity to chase her down in the corridor like an errant fox—made her retreat into the suite and shut the door.

Amaya had stood there for a long moment, breathing much harder than she should have been, her back against the door that represented her only path out of Kavian's rooms, her bare feet cold against the chilly marble floor of the sheikh's grand foyer.

That was when she'd decided that her best bet wasn't to run. That should have been obvious. He'd already caught her once, in the most remote place she'd known. Her only option now was to hide.

Surely Kavian couldn't be *that much* a barbarian, she'd told herself stoutly as she wandered from room to room in the rambling collection of gorgeous chambers on two floors that composed His Majesty's royal suite. There were two or three elegant salons, making clever use of the many stacked terraces and the sweeping views down into the hidden, protected valley. The marble foyer opened into a private courtyard with a graceful fountain claiming its center.

Several sitting rooms were scattered here and there along with a media center, a well-stocked library, even a formal dining room dressed in silk tapestries and golds.

She'd kept looking for a hiding place. Kavian might have talked a big game there by the bathing pools, but the reality was that he'd never forced her to do anything, as shameful as that might have been to admit. The truth was that she'd agreed to marry him in some pathetic attempt to please her brother and possibly her dead father, and then she'd melted all over Kavian every time he touched her.

Amaya didn't fear him physically. She feared herself. She feared the depth of her own surrender and how much a part of her wanted nothing more than to sink to her knees and exult in Kavian's claim over her. To let him keep every one of those dark, delicious promises he'd made to her. To learn precisely what he meant when he told her she would learn *obedience*...

Stop it, she'd snapped at herself as she moved from room to room. She was a liberated woman, damn it. She might have been born into a society like this one, she might even have been briefly nostalgic enough to let her brother talk her into returning to it after their father's death a few years back, but her heart wasn't here. Her heart had never been here.

It can't be here, she'd assured herself. Because she'd seen what leaving a heart behind in a harsh place like this could do to a woman, hadn't she? She'd spent her entire childhood handling the aftermath of her ever more brittle mother's broken heart.

But that particular organ was all too traitorous, she'd realized then, when she walked into a gilt-edged room that Kavian clearly used as a private office and saw the portrait of the man himself hanging there on the wall, in thick oils and bold shades that made him seem a part of the very desert he commanded. And her heart had thumped at her. Hard.

Too hard, as if it had its own agenda.

She'd rubbed at her chest, annoyed that the attendants had taken her clothes from her and given her nothing to wear but a silky thing she refused to acknowledge was some kind of negligee and a raw-silk wrapper to ward off the complete lack of chill in the air. She might as well have been laid out on a silver platter, trussed and bound for Kavian's pleasure—

That was not a calming image. She'd shoved it out of her head, but not before her entire body had broken out in goose bumps. *Damn him.*

She'd finally settled on Kavian's dressing room. It was a vast space, much larger than the dormitory rooms she'd lived in while in halls at university and probably bigger than the whole of the flat she'd shared with three other postgraduates during her brief time in Edinburgh. She'd ignored the rows of exquisitely cut suits that had clearly been made in the finest couture houses for Kavian alone, the traditional robes in the softest and most gorgeous of fabrics that she couldn't help touching as she passed, all the trappings of a great man who could dress to kill in any scenario he chose.

She'd ignored the somersaults her heart and belly did at the sight of all that sartorial splendor that summoned him to her mind as if he'd stood there before her, those slate-gray eyes gleaming silvery and lethal.

And then she'd crawled into the farthest, darkest corner and curled up amid a selection of what appeared to be stout winter boots and dark wool overcoats, hiding herself from view.

She'd meant to wait him out. To see what he'd do when

he returned to the suite—as he'd do soon, she had no doubt, because she'd been quite certain he'd meant every word he said to her near the bathing pools—and if maybe, just maybe, the fact that she'd been moved enough to hide from him would impress her position on him with far more emphasis than mere words.

But she hadn't planned to fall asleep.

She jolted awake with a terrific start, but for a panicked moment she couldn't figure out what was happening. Kavian loomed above her, and the world spun drunkenly and by the time Amaya understood what was going on, he'd hauled her out of her hiding place and into his arms.

"You have the mark of my boot upon your face," he said, his voice cool and yet with all that power of his seething beneath it, like the darkest shadows. "How very dignified you are, my queen."

Amaya would have said she wasn't particularly vain, that there'd been no point with a mother like Elizaveta, who had been a model in her youth, and yet her hand moved to her cheek anyway. It felt nothing but hot, and the way he gazed at her while he held her against that steel-hard chest of his didn't help.

"It should tell you something that I'm willing to go to such lengths to avoid you," she said, hating the rasp of sleep in her voice. She tried to pull herself together despite the fact that he'd started to move—but every step he took made her far too *aware*.

Of him. His strength. His heat. The hardness of his chest, the granite bands of his arms around her. And of herself, too. The way the silk moved over her skin. The lick of flame that followed every soft, sleek shift of the fabric against her belly, her hips, her breasts.

"It tells me a great many things," he agreed, in what did not sound like a particularly sympathetic tone of voice.

He shifted her, which had the cascading effect she most wanted to avoid, a spinning sort of caress that sank deep into her core and was nothing short of a full-body betrayal. She sucked in a breath audibly. He glanced down at her as he moved through the door, out of his dressing room and into the larger sitting area that lay between it and the actual bedroom she hadn't wanted to investigate too closely earlier.

She could see sunlight on the far side of the sitting room, drowning the terrace that ran the length of it in all that golden desert light, and she couldn't have said why that made her breath catch. As if she'd imagined he could only come after her in the dark? But she'd known better, surely. Kavian didn't play by any rules. Ever.

But she kept trying to make him. What other choice did she have?

"Does it tell you that you are a monster?" She knew it was dangerous to poke at him when he was holding her like this, when there was no possibility of escape. But she couldn't seem to stop herself. "That you are so overwhelming and so unreasonable that I was forced to hide in a closet to try to get through to you?"

"That," Kavian said. "And the fact that you are desperate. I suspect you think that if you act like a child, I might be tempted to treat you like one instead of the woman we both know you are."

There was no reason that should have stung. "I've never claimed I was a child."

"That is wise, Amaya, as the definition of a *child* is markedly different in my country. We, for example, do not coddle our young well into their twenties, then welcome them into our homes again until such a time as they feel sufficiently inspired to begin an adult life. We expect them to assume their duties far younger, and then take responsibility for the choices they've made. I myself was a soldier at thirteen and something far less palatable when I was barely twenty. I was never treated like a boy."

"If you think either one of my parents coddled me in any way, at any point in my life, you're insane."

She hadn't meant to say that, certainly, and could have bitten her tongue once she did. Kavian only gazed down at her for a brief, electric instant—but that glimmering moment of contact seared through her.

"I know exactly who and what you are," he said as he strode through the far door into his bedchamber, a stately affair in dark woods and richly masculine shades of red and gold. "Whether you stage melodramatic displays in my closet or race across the planet in a bid to humiliate me in front of the world, it is all the same to me. It will all end right here."

And then he set her down on his bed.

As punctuation.

Amaya expected him to leap on her, but of course he didn't do that. He simply stood there before her, a part of the magnificence of the room, the palace—and at the same time its intensely masculine focal point. He'd donned a pair of very loose white trousers that flowed around him and somehow made him look even more like the desert king he was than anything else she'd ever seen him in. And that was it. He folded his arms over the golden expanse of that carved and battered chest of his that shouldn't have been half so appealing, and watched her.

And she wanted to run. In her head, she threw herself to the side, she scrambled across the slippery gold coverlet and leaped from the mattress, she threw herself off the side of the terrace into thin air to escape him—

But in reality, she did none of those things. She was frozen into place. She was too tense and she couldn't quite

breathe and she *hurt*... Except she realized, one shuddering, shallow breath after the next, that it was a very specific
kind of ache, located in a very particular place.

And worse, that the knowing expression on his hard face
and that silvery awareness in his gaze meant he knew it.

How could he know it? But he did.

"You didn't have to chase me." Amaya hardly knew
what she was saying. "You could have let me go."

His hard mouth flirted with the possibility of a curve.
But then didn't give in to it.

"Are you wet?" he asked.

For a moment, Amaya didn't understand. The baths
had been hours ago and she'd dried off with the towel—

Then she got his meaning, and she simply *ignited*.

The flush lit her up, inside and out. She was certain she
was bright red, searing and glowing, *neon*, and she could
neither pull a full breath into her lungs nor look away from
him. Much less control the surge of desire that pooled between her legs.

"I will take that as a yes," he said, sounding darkly
amused and something far more dangerous besides. "You
already came apart in my hands today, Amaya. Do you
doubt that you are mine? I wasn't even inside you."

She should have leaped to her feet then. Slapped him.
Screamed at him. Made it clear to him that this kind of
behavior was completely unacceptable—that he couldn't
treat her like this. That she wouldn't *let* him.

But Amaya did none of those things. She only stared
back at him, that ache in her growing hotter and more desperate by the moment.

"I want you naked," he said, and there was a certain
gruffness to his voice then. A certain edge that told her
that perhaps he wasn't as unaffected by this as he was pretending he was.

"I don't want—"

"Now, Amaya." That gruffness turned to granite and pounded through her veins. "I already stripped you once today. Don't make me do it again." His gaze moved over her face, and she was sure there was something wrong with her, that she should feel it like a caress. That she should long for more. "Show me, *azizty*. Show me you are as proud of your beauty as I am."

Something shifted deep inside her, then turned over. It was like a dream, she told herself. And the truth was, she'd had this dream. Again and again. This, or something like this, all across the long months since she'd fled the Bakrian Royal Palace on the night of their betrothal. It always starred Kavian in some or other state of undress, so that part was familiar, though he was far more magnificent in reality. And it always involved this same roller-coaster sensation inside her, hot and then cold, high and then low, a longing and an ache and a *need*.

This is just another dream, she assured herself.

And in a dream nothing she did mattered, so she could do as she liked in the moment. It had no meaning. It held no greater significance. She could lose herself in that calm, ruthlessly patient gray gaze of his as if it was a way home. She could let that become what mattered instead.

So that was what she did.

Amaya pulled the wrapper off her, letting it slide over the skin it bared, in an almost unconscious sensual show. Then, before she could question her motives, she pulled the silken little scrap she wore beneath it up and over her head, tossing it with the wrapper so they sat there in a slippery heap of deep blue against the gold coverlet.

Then she swallowed, hard, and simply sat there.

Completely naked, as he'd commanded.

And she knew that it didn't mean anything. That it was

nothing more than a psychological trick to imagine it was the crossing of a very serious line. She'd lost her virginity to this man in a shocking rush six months ago. He'd had his mouth and his hands on her in the palace pools only today. But both of those times, she'd had clothes on.

It was amazing how different it was to sit before him, utterly naked, for the very first time.

"Why are your shoulders rounded like an ashamed teenager's?" he asked her, so mildly that she'd have thought that he hadn't noticed her nudity at all were it not for that near-hectic glitter in his gaze. "Why are you slumped before me as if you do not know your worth? Is this how you offer yourself to me, Amaya? In apology?"

"I'm not apologizing." She didn't think she was offering herself to him, either, so much as following his orders for reasons she didn't care to examine too closely—but somehow that part got tangled on her tongue and stayed in her mouth.

"Are you certain? I have seen more tempting sea turtles, tucked away in their shells where no one can see them." As if he'd said that purely to make her flush with temper, his mouth curved slightly when she did. "Sit up. Arch your back as if you are proud of your breasts."

"I think we both know perfectly well that they're nothing to be proud of. Why flaunt what I don't have?"

"I am not interested in your opinion of them." His eyebrows edged higher on his forehead, as if he was amazed at her temerity. "I am recalling how they felt in my mouth. More, please."

She hadn't realized that she'd done as he asked until then. But she had. She'd sat up and let her back arch invitingly. That presented her breasts to him, yes, and it also made her hair move around her shoulders, and she knew, somehow, that he liked that, too.

And for a long moment—it could have been years, for all she knew—he simply looked at her.

It should have been boring. She should have felt awkward. Exposed. Embarrassed. Cold, even.

But instead, Amaya burned. She ached. She *wanted*.

"Look at you," Kavian said softly. "Your breath comes faster and faster. You are flushed. If I were to reach between your thighs, what would I find?"

She couldn't answer him.

"It would take so little," he continued, his voice almost soft. "Your nipples are so hard, aren't they? Think of all the things I could do with them. Think how it would feel." She shifted against the bed beneath her, pressing herself against it and hardly aware of what she was doing, and he laughed. "None of that. You will come for me or not at all, Amaya. Remember that, if you please."

She knew, distantly, that there were a hundred things she should say. She should challenge him. She should fight him. She should refuse to act like this simply because he wanted her to do it—but she knew, of course she knew, that he wasn't the only one who wanted it. And she wasn't sure she could face what that said about her, what it made her.

So perhaps it was easier to simply do as he asked instead.

"Kneel up," he told her in that same low, knowing voice, as if he was already inside her. As if he was in her mind, as well. As if he knew all those dark, twisted things she couldn't admit to herself. "Right where you are."

"I'm not going to kneel before you and beg you for—for anything," she threw at him. But she didn't sound like herself and he didn't look particularly moved by her outburst.

"Of course not. You are so appalled by all of this, I am sure."

"I am."

"I can see that." His head canted slightly to one side, and those slate-gray eyes gleamed silver. "Kneel up, Amaya. Do not make me ask you again."

This, right here, was the moment of truth. She didn't entirely comprehend why she'd taken her clothes off when he told her to, but she couldn't unring that bell. But this, here, *now*—this was where she had to draw the line.

It was simple. All she needed to do was stand up. Climb off this bed and walk away. Kavian was many things, but she didn't believe he was truly a brute. Hard, yes. The hardest man she'd ever met. But she understood on some deep feminine level of intuition she hadn't known she possessed that while he might merrily shove away at her boundaries, he wouldn't actually force her into anything. All she needed to do was get off this bed.

She moved then, though her body hardly felt like hers. She could feel every part of her skin, as if every square inch of it was alive in a way it never had been before—a way *she* never had been until now. She felt so highly sensitive it was as if the air around them were a thick, padded thing, massaging her.

Maybe that was why she didn't really notice what she was doing until she'd already done it. And then she was kneeling there before him, precisely as he'd commanded her to do.

That was bad enough. Worse, when he only looked at her, she arched her back again, pulling her shoulders back and presenting him with her breasts as he'd asked her to do before. Not only her breasts—her whole body. Right there before him.

This *was* the silver platter, she understood then. She'd climbed up onto it and undressed for it and arranged herself on it, all for him.

Her pulse skittered through her body, wild and erratic and much too fast.

He waited.

She didn't know how she knew he was waiting, but she did. He was.

And the air between them seemed charged. Spiked. She couldn't see anything but that hard, oddly patient gaze of his. She couldn't *feel* anything but hunger. A deep, dark, consuming hunger that made her knees feel so weak she was deeply, wildly grateful that she wasn't trying to stand.

She wanted him to touch her. She wanted him to take her the way he had done that night six months ago, the way he had today in that pool. She wanted *him*.

"Then you must say the word, *azizty*, and you will have me," he murmured, and Amaya realized to her horror that she'd said all of that out loud.

Her throat was as dry as if she'd inhaled the whole of the desert outside. She shook, over and over, and she didn't think she'd stop. She understood that this was a line she could never uncross. That there would be no returning to who she'd been before. That if she was honest, it had already happened six months ago and she'd simply been trying her best to deny it all this time. Running and running and ending up right back where she'd started.

Worse, this time, because she knew not only what she was doing, but what he could do, too.

"Please," she whispered. But that wasn't what he was looking for.

"Say it," he ordered her, his voice tight.

She didn't pretend it wasn't a full and total surrender. But in that moment, she wasn't sure she cared.

You will use my name, he'd told her. Perhaps the begging part had been implied, even then.

Amaya didn't care about that, either.

"Please," she said again. "Kavian, *please*."

Kavian smiled. It was very male. Dark and satisfied. It made her whole body light up and burst into flame.

And then he reached for her and made it all that much worse.

CHAPTER SIX

KAVIAN WANTED TO throw her down and sink deep inside her in that instant. He wanted to slake the white-hot burn of *hunger* inside him, made all the worse for the uncharacteristic restraint he'd showed these past months while he scoured the planet for her.

He'd found to his great surprise that after he'd had Amaya, even in such a blind rush, no other woman would do.

She would pay for that, too.

But first he would bind her to him in a way she'd never untangle. First, he would make certain she saw nothing else in all the world but him. He would make her need him more than air and maybe then she would stop looking for exit strategies. He wanted to own her, body and soul. But first, he would worship her.

Kavian told himself they were the same thing.

And if the idea of having her completely at his command—the way she should have been since the day of their betrothal—made that tight thing in his chest feel easier, well, he told himself it was the conquest that fired his blood, nothing more. That tightness was about the injustice and sheer insult of the way she'd kept herself from him, that was all. She was his. It was time she behaved as if she knew that at last, as if she finally understood her place.

Because Kavian was king of this harsh land, not a blood-hound who could roam the earth forever in search of his runaway bride. He had won back his father's throne with his blood, his strength. He ruled Daar Talaas with his own cunning and his commitment to defend what was his no matter the cost. He'd had no choice but to chase down the woman who had tried to shame him in the eyes of his people.

More than that, he'd wanted her. He thought he would always want her. *She was his.*

But it was past time he got back to the intricate business of running this ancient, desert-hardened place, or he would lose it to someone who would do so in his stead. That was the law of Daar Talaas. That was the price of power—it belonged only to the man who could wield it.

His relationship with this woman could be no different. He would not allow it.

Kavian took Amaya's sweetly rounded chin in his hand and held her there, though he knew he could hold her as easily with his gaze. He could feel the way she shivered at his touch. He could see emotion and longing in those dark eyes of hers, and he reveled in both. He could smell the delicate scent of her soft skin and the sweet fragrance that rose from the masses of her dark hair she finally wore down around her pretty shoulders.

And beneath it all rose the far richer fragrance of her arousal.

The only thing he'd ever wanted more, in all his life, was the throne he'd won back through his own fierce determination. He'd found the darkness within him; he'd become it. He'd used it to do what was necessary. He'd been raised on vengeance and he'd finally taken his when he was barely twenty. And even that—the achievement of his life—seemed far off just now, with Amaya naked and obedient before him, her gaze fixed to his.

This is the way back to reality, he assured himself. *Conquer her here, now, and you will never need to risk the throne for her again.*

He'd known that he wanted Amaya from the moment he saw that video of her. And he'd known precisely how he would take her, and how she would thrill to it, the moment he met her in her brother's palace. He'd suspected then that she would fit him perfectly.

Now he knew it as well as he knew his own name.

Six months ago, the wild passion between them had been a burst of flame, unexpected and all consuming. They'd met for the first time when Kavian arrived with his entourage at the Bakrian Royal Palace to claim her as his betrothed and begin the official alliance between their two countries. It had been a formal and very public greeting of political allies, an elegant affair in a majestic salon, surrounded on all sides by ministers and aides, ambassadors and carefully selected palace reporters who could be relied upon to trumpet the appropriate information into all the correct ears.

There had been all those contracts to sign, all those oaths to take, and this woman he'd agreed to marry had been dressed in a fine, formal gown that made her look every inch the untouchable desert princess. They'd talked with excruciating politeness while surrounded and closely observed on all sides. They'd been feted at a long, formal dinner ripe with too many speeches from what seemed like every Bakrian noble in the whole of the kingdom. And for all that they'd sat next to each other during the endless evening, they'd never been out of that too-public fishbowl for even a moment. There had been no real conversation, no chance of anything but the loosest connection.

Then they'd had their betrothal ceremony the following day, in the grand ballroom of the palace that had been draped in every shade of gold in the glare of too many cameras to count. Cameras and gossips and a parade of aristocrats to comment on every last bit of it. Like carrion crows, pecking away at them.

"In my country," Kavian had told her as they'd made their formal entrance together, touching only in that stiffly appropriate manner that befitted their respective ranks on such an occasion and before so many judgmental eyes, "there is no need for a wedding ceremony. It is the claiming that matters, not the legalities that follow. A wedding is all but redundant."

"My brother's kingdom may not sit at the forefront of the modern age, exactly," Amaya had replied, and he'd been lost in the bittersweet chocolate gleam in her eyes, the sweet lushness of her lips, that kick of deep, dark need that had haunted him since the moment he saw her face. To say nothing of the unscripted, less than perfectly polite thing she was saying then and that flashed in her gaze, giving him a hint of the woman beneath the high-gloss Bakrian princess adorning his arm. A glimpse of that defiance of hers that sang to him. "But he does prefer that any royal marriages be legalized. As do I, I will admit."

"As you wish," Kavian had murmured. In that moment, he'd thought he'd give her anything she asked for another glimpse beneath her surface. His name, his protection, that went without saying. His kingdom, his wealth, his lands, certainly. His blood. His flesh. His life. Whatever she desired.

But she'd kept her gaze trained on the ceremony, not on him.

He'd hated it.

They'd exchanged their initial vows, there before the kings of the surrounding realms, sheikhs and rulers and sultans galore. Officials and ministers, the ranks of Bakrian aristocrats and the high-placed members of his own cabinet. Her brother. His men.

And then, once it had been finished and all the rest of the formal speeches about unity and family had been made for the benefit of their enemies in the region, Kavian took his betrothed aside so they could finally, *finally*, have a moment to themselves.

Merely a moment, he'd thought. He hadn't had anything planned. He'd only wanted a little bit of privacy with her, with no eyes on them and nothing but their real faces. He'd wanted to see what was between them then, when there was no one but the two of them to judge it, pick over it, analyze it.

He had congratulated himself on his magnanimity, proud of himself that he was not like his own forefathers, that he had every intention of winning this woman slowly and carefully—instead of throwing her over his saddle and riding off into the desert with her like the Bedouin chiefs of old who made up a sizable portion of his family tree. He'd had absolutely no intention of playing the barbarian king to a deeply Westernized woman like Amaya, who no doubt had all sorts of opinions about what *civilized* meant. Oh, no. He'd planned to wine her and dine her like all the urbane sophisticates he'd imagined she'd known all her life, in all the cities she'd visited in all those concrete and glass places he abhorred. He'd planned to do what he had to do, whatever it took, to bind her to him in every way.

She'd led them to that alcove, tucked away out of sight in a far-off corner of the ballroom's second-floor balcony while the rest of the assembled throng moved about far below, reveling in Rihad al Bakri's lavish hospitality. Kavian had stared down at her when they were finally alone.

He hadn't smiled. He'd been trying to see inside her, trying to match her exquisite beauty in person to the image he'd carried around with him in his head. He'd been trying to process the fact that she was well and truly his already, no matter *how* he approached her.

It had felt like sunlight, deep inside him, warm and bright. He hadn't known what to make of it.

"Well," she'd said with false brightness. "Here we are. Officially betrothed and still total strangers."

"We are not strangers," he'd corrected her, with far more gruffness than he'd intended. He hadn't meant to speak. He'd found those intricate braids that she'd worn like a crown of her own glossy hair an enchantment, and he'd been deep in their spell. He'd felt her gaze like a caress, an incantation. "I will soon be your husband. You are already mine."

"I'm not yours yet," she'd said, and then she'd lifted her chin in a kind of challenge that he'd only understood, in retrospect, had been a bit of foreshadowing he should have heeded. Back then, he'd simply enjoyed it. "And you should know that I can't marry a man with a harem. A betrothal for political purposes is one thing, especially if it helps my brother, but a marriage under such circumstances? No. I refuse."

Kavian had only continued to watch her, as if it was a deep thirst he felt and she the only possibility of ever quenching it. Most people caved under his regard, and quickly. Amaya had only squared her shoulders and held his gaze.

He'd liked that. Far too much, truth be told.

"For you," he'd said, as if she had any choices left, as if she hadn't just signed herself over to his keeping in full view of two countries and by now, the better part of the world, "I will empty mine. Is that what you require? Consider it done."

He'd stopped restraining himself then. He'd looked at her with all that fire, all that dark longing, right there on the surface. He hadn't hidden a single bit of the beast inside him. He hadn't tried.

And Amaya had done the most extraordinary thing. She'd flushed, hot and red and flustered—but not frightened. Not horrified. Not even particularly scandalized—all of which he'd expected, on some level. Just…*hot*. Then she'd looked away as if the heat was too much. As if *this* was too much. As if he was.

As if she felt exactly as he did.

Everything in him had roared, approval and acknowledgment.

Mine, he'd thought, with every cell in his body. With every breath.

And he'd taken her head between his hands, those braids warm and soft beneath his palms, and he'd tasted her for the first time. It had changed everything.

It had blown them both up, right then and there.

That flame had only intensified in all the months since, while he'd had nothing to do while he chased her but imagine her right here, naked before him in his very own bed, the way she was right now. *Finally*.

"Why are you staring at me like that?" Amaya asked, and he could hear the nerves in her voice. The hunger and the heat.

He'd been right about her—about this magnificent chemistry between them—six months ago. He was right now, too.

"I keep telling myself I am going to take this slow," he said, dropping his hand from her chin but moving closer to her. "Act like the sophisticated gentleman I am not. But that is unlikely, *azizty*. Very, very unlikely, the longer you look at me with those big, innocent eyes of yours that are nothing but a temptation."

"My eyes aren't innocent." It was as if she couldn't help herself, when she must know he knew she lied. "They're wicked. As dirty and debauched as the rest of me. I keep trying to tell you."

He only gazed back at her until he saw that flush again, warming her skin, prickling over all the soft flesh on display before him. Just as he recalled it. Then he smiled. Slightly.

"I want you to take it slow," she whispered.

"No," he said, gathering her into his arms and pulling her against the wall of his chest, exulting in the way she slid against him, then melted into him, as if she really had been made to his precise specifications. "You do not."

And then he settled his mouth over hers, at last, and let the fire break free, searing both of them.

Kavian *consumed* her.

There was no other word for it.

His kiss was a slick addiction. A wild, impossible ride, and she couldn't get enough. He held her against him and he angled her head where he wanted it and he simply *feasted*.

And Amaya loved it.

The more he took, the more she gave, meeting every slide of his tongue against hers. She arched into him, pressing her aching breasts against the dizzying wonder of his hard chest, reveling in the sensation of that strong hand of his on her bottom, kneading her. Guiding her.

Driving her crazy with need.

He pulled his mouth away from hers, letting out a very

male sound of satisfaction at the small, disappointed noise she couldn't keep herself from making.

"Be patient, *azizty*," he said in that dark way of his, and she didn't know how she knew that he was teasing her. That he was deliberately drawing this out to make that ache in her intensify.

Or that he would continue to do it until he felt like stopping; that what she wanted would have nothing to do with it.

She loved that, too. She had the sense he'd known she would.

Kavian took his time, lazily tracing a path down her neck to taste every inch of her collarbone. Then he dropped his head to play with her breasts again, making her moan and shake against him as he tested the plumpness of each of them, then tasted and tugged each proud peak.

This time, he didn't let her topple over that edge. This time, he had more on his agenda. He swept her up and then he laid her out on that big, wide bed, stretched himself out beside her, and kept going.

He licked his way over her navel, then lower, laughing as she bucked against him, lost somewhere between desire and delirium, and she didn't much care which as long as he kept touching her. Tasting her. Making her feel more beautiful, more precious, than she'd had any idea she could feel.

"Kavian." She didn't mean to say his name. She hardly knew what she was doing as he took her hips in his big hands and held her there before him as if she truly were a feast and he was nothing but hungry. "Please."

"I like that," he said approvingly, and she could *feel* his voice against that most private part of her that was molten and aching and already his. It made her shudder, deep within, the feeling radiating out everywhere, coursing in her veins and washing over her whole body. "Beg me."

And then he licked his way straight into the core of her.

Amaya exploded.

She thought she screamed his name, or maybe that was only what it *felt* like inside her, and either way she was lost in the storm of sensation. Lost completely. It swept her away. It altered her very being.

It was like dying, and the crazy part was how much she loved it. All of it.

She felt like someone else entirely when she came back to that bed with a jolt and found Kavian propped up above her and entirely naked, holding his weight on his elbows while the hardest part of him probed at her entrance.

He looked harsh. Unsmiling, as ever. And incredibly, impossibly beautiful.

Amaya couldn't seem to breathe. She was falling, she realized—tipped off the side of the world and tumbling end over end without any hope of stopping, washed out to sea forever in that dark gray gaze of his.

He looked at her as if he wanted to eat her alive. He looked at her as if he already had done so.

She wanted to say a thousand things. She wanted to tell him of that mess inside her that was all his doing, that she hadn't known could exist. She *wanted*, and yet she couldn't seem to do it. Instead, she held that terrible and wonderful gaze of his, and she only reached up and slid her hand along his proud jaw, holding his lean cheek in her hand.

His gaze burned. And then he pushed himself into her, easy yet ruthless at once, sheathing himself to the hilt.

For a moment—or a year, a lifetime, more—they only stared at each other, stretched out to near breaking on the edge of all that impossible sensation.

"Last time, I hurt you." His voice was gruff. Raw. Not apologetic in any way and yet it made a wet heat prick the back of Amaya's eyes. She pressed her hand that little bit harder against his face.

"Only for a moment," she whispered, as if he'd asked for her forgiveness. As if she was giving it.

And more, it was true. It had only been an instant of pain, easily forgotten and soon forgiven in the wild tumult that had followed. Even if she still didn't understand how any of that had happened. One moment they'd been talking while officially betrothed; the next their mouths had been fused together as if there was no other possibility, and the moment after that her skirts had been pulled up to her waist and he'd been buried deep inside her.

Inside her.

Amaya had understood with a vivid shock that she had no control around him—over *herself.* She'd managed *not* to have sex for twenty-three years because she'd never felt that kind of connection with anyone, and then Kavian had come along and wrecked that in a day and a half. She'd been as shocked at herself for allowing it as she had been at what had actually happened.

He was inside her again now, and this time she was far less shocked. But no more in control of either one of them. He waited, still propped there on his elbows, an enigmatic curve to that hard mouth of his.

"Go on," he murmured, as if he knew that she didn't know what to do with herself and didn't know *how* to do it anyway. Any of it. Last time had been like careening over the side of a cliff into a brilliant, cataclysmic explosion. This was no less vivid, no less overwhelming. But the explosion hovered out of reach. She thought perhaps that was his doing. His iron control. Because it certainly wasn't hers. "Find out what feels good to you, *azizty.* I want to know."

Dimly, Amaya thought that she should find this all deeply embarrassing. He seemed to read her far too well. He seemed to know too much.

He always has, a little voice whispered. *He always will.*

But Amaya ignored it, and took him at his word. She circled her hips, tentatively at first. Then, when Kavian growled in stark male approval, with more deliberation. It made a whole new fire sear its way through her as she tested out the deliriously hot sensation, the drag and the friction. She ran her hands along those delectable ridges in his torso, learning the flat, hard muscles and the carved perfection of his form, crossed here and there with scars that spoke to a life of action, lived hard. She tested the shape of his strong neck, teased his flat male nipples and licked the salt from his skin.

She pulled back, then surged forward, testing his length deep inside her, so hard in all her quivering, melting softness. Again and again and again. Until she shivered all over with a new crop of goose bumps, and looked to him, feeling something like helpless. Vibrant and electric, and still unsure.

"Allow me," Kavian said then, his voice hoarse and dark, and rich with satisfaction.

And then he dropped down closer to her, slid his hands beneath her bottom and took over.

It was the difference between the light of a candle and the blaze of the desert sun.

He took her the way he'd kissed her—all-encompassing, almost furious, dark and sweet and *necessary.* And Amaya could do nothing but wrap her arms and legs around him, hold him as tightly as she possibly could and surrender to the glory of it.

He reached between them and pressed hard at the juncture of their bodies, right where she needed it most, and she thought she heard him laugh as she shattered all around him.

But then he followed after her, right over the side of the world, and the only thing Amaya heard him call out then was her name.

CHAPTER SEVEN

IT SHOULD NOT have surprised Amaya that Kavian was a man of very definite opinions, all of which he had no trouble sharing with her as he saw fit. After all, he'd never pretended otherwise.

What Amaya should wear, and when, and with whom. How she should spend her time in the palace when he was not with her, and certainly what she should do when he was. What she should eat, how often she should take walks in the extensive, terraced gardens, how much coffee she should drink and so on. There was no detail too small to escape his attention. Not because he was so controlling, he'd told her, but because they were making her his queen. A role that would be dissected by the masses of his people and a thousand tabloids the world over, so they could not gloss over the details.

"You can't really care about that," she'd said one afternoon, a bit crossly.

He'd come upon her in one of the gardens, bursting with bright pink-and-purple blossoms beneath the blue fall sky, and told her flatly that he didn't like her hair up in a ponytail. That he preferred the braid she wore over one shoulder sometimes or it loose and flowing around her as she moved.

He'd reached over and pulled the elastic from her hair

himself, then tucked it into one of his pockets, as if he couldn't bear to so much as look upon the offending ponytail a moment longer than necessary. "Can I not?"

"You have a country to run, Kavian." She'd scowled at him, and had wondered as she did where the courage to defy him so openly came from. When he still made her quake deep within. When it took everything she had. "What I'm doing with my hair should be the least of your concerns. Literally, the very least."

"I find nothing about you insignificant, *azizty*." That hint of a smile on that hard mouth of his, and it spilled through her like the desert sun above them, hot and bright, and made her think she'd do anything to see it again. Stand up to him, run, submit—whatever it took. The rush of that realization had stunned her. "None of it is beneath my notice. You are my queen."

And then he'd taken her in his arms, right there in the gardens, and kissed her until she'd decided that she had no particular allegiance to wearing her hair in a ponytail after all.

But it occurred to her—as she sat with the group of advisers who were tutoring her each day on a selection of subjects Kavian felt it was important his queen know, like proper palace protocol and the intricate social hierarchies of Daar Talaas—that she always gave in. Or he caught her and then she gave in. That it wasn't only Kavian—that her life was a series of similar surrenders that had led her straight here.

Because it had always seemed easier to bend than cause a commotion.

"You don't have the right to make that decision for me," she'd told her own father some years back. She'd wanted to take a few years off from her studies; he'd wanted her to get her degree—and he'd wanted her to stay in one place so that he'd be able to more closely monitor her, she'd suspected. She'd been very brave indeed on a mobile phone from Paris, far away from him. Polite, yet firm.

"I beg your pardon," the old sheikh had replied, and his voice had boomed down the phone line as if he'd been delivering a new edict he'd expected would become law within the hour. "I am your father and your king, Amaya. More than this, I pay your bills. Who has the right if I do not?"

And she'd acquiesced. She'd told herself that she'd simply made the practical choice. That she'd done what she had to do in the space that she'd been given. That she'd always done so as a purely rational survival tactic.

Or perhaps it's that you are a weakling, she'd snapped at herself back then, more than once, and again now as the dry and surpassingly dull vizier in front of her launched into a lecture on the importance of learning the appropriate address for visiting ambassadors. *Or you'd stand up for yourself.*

But the only person she'd openly defied in all her life was Kavian when she'd run from their betrothal—and she couldn't understand how everything had gotten so twisted since then, that she could still want to defy him with every atom in her body, fear him as much as hunger for him with every breath and yet melt at his slightest touch.

And worse, feel all that as if it was no contradiction at all.

Kavian was like all the other men in her life. Worse. They expected instant obedience not only from her, but from the whole world—and usually got it, like her late father. Her older brother, Rihad, the new king of Bakri, had been crafted from the very same mold. Even her lost brother, Omar—who'd died in a car accident while Amaya was on the run but had long been the black sheep of the

Al Bakri family because he'd refused to dutifully marry on command like the rest of them—had very much lived his life on *his* terms, no one else's.

It was only Amaya who bent. Or was it only Amaya who had to bend? It seemed the longer she spent in Kavian's intense, commanding, addictive presence, the less she knew the answer to that question.

"You are not made of rubber," Elizaveta had told her not long after her father's funeral, which Elizaveta had expected Amaya to boycott. She'd been furious that Amaya had defied her and gone to pay her respects anyway. "What happens when you cannot bend? When instead you break?"

Amaya had so desperately wanted to say, *You didn't break me, Mother. If you didn't, who could?* But she hadn't. Because it had been easier not to fight. Easier by far to simply bend.

Amaya al Bakri didn't break. She bent and she bent, and then, when she could bend no more, she ran away. There was another word to describe that kind of behavior, she often thought as she plotted escapes from Kavian's palace she knew she didn't dare attempt. *Coward.*

But she didn't feel like a coward. She felt as courageous as she felt overwhelmed every time she surrendered herself to Kavian's sensual, demanding possession, the days blending into the nights and all of it focused on his masterful touch. Was that bending? Or was she simply allowing herself to sink deep into a dizzying world of hunger and want she hadn't known existed? Where need and desire were all that mattered—despite how deeply each terrified her?

Surely the ease with which she'd given herself over to this man who'd claimed her and brought her here against her will should worry her, she thought then. She nodded along with the vizier as he gestured wildly and made points in rapid-fire Arabic that she understood more and more of by the day. Surely Kavian himself should trip every last one of her alarms.

She'd been opposed to men like him her whole life. Autocratic, overbearing, dangerous and very, very sure of themselves in all things. From what they wished to have for breakfast to what they thought Amaya should do with her life. From ponytails to polygamy.

That was why her mother had left her father, she knew—because he'd had no intention of curtailing his extramarital activity both in and out of his harem. He'd been offended when Elizaveta expressed her dismay. And that was why Amaya had spent the better part of her time on the run, furious with her brother Rihad for ordering her to marry Kavian in the first place. He had never once indicated that he understood how difficult it was for her to marry a complete stranger when he should have, having done so twice himself.

It was why she'd been certain she had to escape Kavian within moments of meeting him. Because he was *that much worse* than all the rest of them put together. That eternal, relentless imperiousness he wielded so offhandedly. That dictatorial need of his to issue commands at will and his arrogant astonishment when said commands were not immediately obeyed. That intense focus on every last, seemingly insignificant detail of *everything.* She should have been horrified by him after spending these weeks with him—as overwhelmed and trapped as she'd felt the night of their betrothal.

The trouble was that when it came to Kavian, every time he put those hard hands of his on her it was pure magic.

Maybe all men were equally magical, she reasoned. Maybe all sex was exactly the same, exactly like this. She told herself that what happened between them was probably run-of-the-mill and boring—she simply had no context by which to judge it. Because Kavian was the only man Amaya had ever known this way, ever touched this way, ever *surrendered to* in this way. Or at all.

And the truth was that she didn't find his bossiness and sheer male certainty as upsetting in the bedroom as some part of her, deep inside, insisted she should. Quite the contrary, in fact, no matter how her heart pounded at her or her head swam at the thought of him. Then again when he touched her. No matter that sheer, stunning drop into pure sensation that terrified her in retrospect and yet seemed to disappear when he hauled her against him and—

"Are you following, my lady?" The vizier's voice was an unpleasant slap back into the here and now and Amaya had to force a polite smile to cover it. "I cannot stress to you the importance of official palace protocol. It is—"

"All we have left when the world crumbles around us," Amaya finished for him, trying to sit up straighter and focus, glad she'd paid enough attention earlier to parrot that back at him. "Please, continue. I assure you I'm hanging on your every word."

The following morning Kavian rose before the sun, which Amaya had learned he did religiously. A man in his kind of peak physical condition did not happen into it by chance— he subjected himself to a rigorous fitness regime every day without fail. For hours, with what appeared to be half of his army and all their hardcore military drills.

And then, also without fail, he came back to their bed and woke her in his typically inventive, wicked style.

Sometimes with his hands. Sometimes with his mouth. Sometimes in other imaginative ways altogether.

Today he took her as she lay sprawled on her belly, one of his big hands beneath her to prop her up and hold her hips at the precise angle he wanted them, the other flat against the mattress beside her and his mouth hot on the nape of her neck.

It was blisteringly hot, wild and fast, and almost too much to bear.

"Come," he ordered her in that dark voice of his when he'd held her there on the brink for what seemed like a lifetime. When she'd lost herself completely in that desperate world of intense sensation he built so effortlessly around them, where she didn't care who was surrendering or what that might mean. "Now."

And he'd taught her so well in the weeks they'd been together. It took only that rasped command and she was gone. She wept out some kind of plea or prayer as she shattered into too many pieces to count, her face in the pillows and her hands curled into fists beside her. Then Kavian shouted out his own release and nearly threw her over once more.

He kissed her again, right there on the nape of her neck until she shuddered from the sweet kick of it all over again, and then he murmured something she didn't quite hear before he left her lying there to begin his day in earnest. It didn't matter, she thought then, dreamily suspended in that delicious in-between state where there was nothing but that sweet heat thrumming in her body. Whatever he did, however he did it, it felt like another caress.

It took her a while to rise from the bed. It took her longer to find her way into the walk-in shower that could have comfortably fit the whole of the harem he'd discarded—though that wasn't a topic she cared to think about too closely, as it led nowhere good. She stood under the hot spray and let it work its way beneath her skin.

When she was finished she wrapped herself in a silken robe so she could join him at breakfast in the sunny room directly adjoining the bedroom suite. It was the finest of his private salons, all wide-open doors to his secluded terrace and vast, sweeping views of the mountains and the desert beyond, and it struck her as she hurried into it that she was something very much like...eager.

That was a jarring thought. She told herself they'd fallen into a routine, that was all—or more accurately, he'd set one for them. He'd insisted they share these mornings from the start.

"I never know where my day will lead me," he'd said that first morning in the palace, when Amaya woke with a start to find herself draped over his chest as if she'd always shared his bed. His voice had been gruffly possessive, and he'd held her gaze to his with her hair wrapped tight around his fist, holding her head where he wanted it. "I want to know exactly where it will start, and who with."

At first she'd acquiesced because she'd been so swept away by him, by everything that had happened since she looked up to see him standing over her in that faraway café. Or that was what she'd told herself—that it was far better to lose a battle than the war. That it had nothing to do with the softness that had washed through her when he said something that might have been very nearly romantic, had he been another man. Had they been other people.

Today she recognized another truth wrapped up in that eagerness that she wanted to deny but couldn't, quite: that there was a large part of her that wanted nothing more than to sink into this life he'd laid out for her after all her years of following her mother's changeable whims and broken heart all over the planet. It was much too tempting to simply dissolve into this place, into this man, into the vision he had of her and into this life he obviously ran as smoothly and as ruthlessly as he did everything else.

It was more than tempting. It was something very much like comforting.

It feels like safety, something inside her whispered. *Like home.*

Like a note of music, played loud and long.

But she couldn't let herself think those things.

Amaya slipped into place at the glass-topped table where Kavian sat, his newspapers spread around him and his laptop open before him. Nothing about this man was safe. She knew that. Not when his gray eyes sparked silver as he gazed at her. Or when he showed her that small, dangerously compelling crook in the corner of his mouth that had become everything to her.

Though she was careful not to think of it in those terms.

"Today you will tend to your wardrobe at last," he told her, by way of greeting. "I've flown my favorite dressmakers in from Italy and they await you in the yellow parlor even now. They've brought some ready-to-wear pieces, I imagine, but will also be taking your measurements."

It took a moment for all that to sink in. Amaya jerked her attention away from his temptation of a mouth and back across the hearty breakfast Kavian preferred after his intense morning workout, set pleasingly on an array of gold and silver platters as befit a king.

"What's wrong with my wardrobe as is?" She blinked down at herself, wearing nothing but a silk wrapper and the desert breeze in her wet hair. "I don't mean this."

"I like you like this." That dark gray gaze. That responsive flip inside her chest that boded only ill. "But I would kill anyone else who saw you dressed in so little."

And she felt it again. That deep flush of pleasure, as if his *liking her* was the only thing that mattered to her—and as if he was being romantic when he said such things. It almost diverted her attention from the fact that he had *favorite dressmakers* in the first place.

"How many dresses have you had made, exactly?" she

asked him, raising her gaze to his slowly. Very slowly. "Seventeen, by any chance?"

Kavian sat there in his favorite chair with the golden morning light cascading all around him, and his slate-gray gaze seemed deeply and darkly amused the way it often did these days, though his mouth had lost that curve she craved.

"Do you truly wish me to answer that?"

"My wardrobe is perfectly adequate as it is, thank you," Amaya said quickly, as much because she really didn't want him to answer her question as because that was true. Her brother had shipped over all her things months ago, long before Kavian had caught up to her in Canada and brought her here. She'd woken up that first morning in Daar Talaas to find a separate, equally vast second closet off Kavian's sitting room stocked with everything she'd left behind in Bakri, from the gowns she'd worn to formal affairs at her brother's palace to her favorite pair of ripped black jeans from the university that she doubted Kavian would find at all appropriate. "What fault can you possibly find in it?"

"None whatsoever, were you still slinging pints in a pub in Scotland. Alas, you are not. I can assure you that while your duties will inevitably vary here, according to the needs of the people, they will never include tending a bar."

"It was a perfectly decent pub. And what do you care where I worked?"

"You were a royal princess of the House of Bakri." He had never looked like more of a king than he did then, royal and arrogant, that gaze of his a dark fire as he regarded her with some kind of astonishment. "Aside from the fact that it involved parading yourself before crowds of drunken Scotsmen every night, which your father must have been insane to allow, such a job was quite literally beneath you."

Which had been the appeal of the job, not that she was foolish enough to admit that now. Or that both Rihad and her father had read her the riot act about it, the latter almost until the day he'd died. As rebellions went, hers had been a tiny one, but it had still been hers. She couldn't regret it. She didn't.

But she'd also been relieved, somehow, when Rihad had called her to Bakri after her father died and told her it was time she took on a more formal role. She'd never had much defiance inside her. Only Kavian seemed to bring that out in her. Even now.

"You and Rihad rant on and on about my being a princess," she said then, not quite rolling her eyes at him. "It's embarrassing at best. It's nothing but a silly title from a life that was only mine for a few years when I was a child, and then again recently for my brother's political gain." Amaya shrugged. "I'm no princess. Not really. I never have been."

She couldn't read the look on his face then, and ignored the small trickle of sensation that worked its way down her spine. She didn't want to read him anyway, she assured herself as she poured out a steaming mug of coffee from the carafe at her elbow and stirred in a healthy dollop of cream. He would do as he liked either way.

It was unfortunate that she found that appealing rather than appalling.

"It is a silly title that you will no longer suffer to bear, you will be happy to learn." It was amazing that he could sound so scathing when he was still so irritatingly calm, she thought, and not for the first time. She stirred her coffee harder than necessary. "You are now a queen, Amaya. My queen, should that require clarification."

"Officially, I am only your betrothed." She shouldn't have said that, of course. That level, considering stare of his made everything inside her go still, as if she'd roused the predator in him again and was fixed in its sights. "I've been learning a great deal about the traditional Daar Talaas palace hierarchy in the classes you've made me take."

"They are not classes." His voice was as dangerously soft as his gaze was severe. "You are not a fractious adolescent who has been dispatched to some kind of summer school in place of the detention she clearly deserves."

She really did roll her eyes then. "Lectures, then. Is that a better term?"

"You are meeting with your aides and advisers to better understand and shape your role as queen of this great land." The way he arched those dark brows at her dared her to contradict him. "Just as you are practicing your Arabic so you may converse with the subjects under your rule whenever appropriate."

He meant *when fully vetted by my men*. When it came to any issue that could be construed as pertaining to her physical safety, Amaya had found that Kavian was utterly inflexible. Unlike the rest of the time, when he was only *almost* utterly inflexible. Which should not have amused her, surely. Where was her panic?

What happens when you cannot bend? her mother had demanded, and what did it matter what Elizaveta's motivations for asking had been? *When instead you break?*

"The point is that the role of 'princess,' whatever that means, was never one I learned to play," she said instead, because she couldn't sort out was happening inside her. Because she was afraid this was what *broken* looked like, this absurd idea that she could be safe with a man this elemental, this raw and powerful. "I was never treated as a princess of anything anywhere we went after my mother and I left Bakri."

Quite the opposite, she thought then as the memories she usually kept locked away rushed back at her, thick and fast. There had been a long stretch of years when Elizaveta would fly into one of her cold furies at the very sound of the word *princess* and punish Amaya for it whether or not she'd been the one to say it out loud.

She took a sip of the thick coffee and tried to swallow the unpleasant past down with the dark Arabian brew. "If anything, my mother downplayed it as much as possible."

That shrug of his was still a cool, harsh weapon, and then he turned his attention back to the papers before him, which only made it worse. "Because you outrank her."

The shrug was a weapon and the words a blow.

For a moment, Amaya simply reeled. She placed her mug back down on the glass table very, very carefully. She blinked.

"My mother doesn't care about rank," she said, and she couldn't have said why her voice sounded like that, as if there were rough and terrible things simmering there beneath the surface. "She walked away from Bakri of her own volition. If she cared about rank she would have stayed in the place where she was queen, not taken off into the big, bad world where she had no means of support."

"No means of support?" Kavian shook his head when she frowned at him in confusion. "She had a walking, talking bank account at her disposal. She had you."

That sensation of reeling, of actual spinning, only worsened. "What are you talking about?"

"You," he said very distinctly, his gaze a fierce shot of intense gray in the bright room, "are the daughter of a king. Your mother did not live by her wits or her charm or even her looks, Amaya. She lived off the trust your father set up in your name, for your support."

Amaya couldn't speak. Or move. She felt as if he'd hammered a giant nail straight into her and pinned her to her chair.

She thought of all the times Elizaveta had lectured her about her *expectations*, her terrible *entitlement*. She remembered the many, many times her mother had embarrassed her in front of others by claiming that Amaya was "her father's daughter," in a manner meant to suggest Amaya always selfishly wanted far more than her share, that she was greedy and ill-bred, that she was entirely, deliberately heedless of reality. She'd excused these things, one after the next, because she'd understood where her mother was coming from, what Amaya's father had done. She'd assumed these things came from her mother's panic at having to find ways to support them all on her own.

"I treat you like an adult because you would otherwise grow up coddled and spoiled like every other member of the Bakri line," Elizaveta had said when Amaya was perhaps eleven. "The truth is that we have nothing. We are dependent on the kindness of friends."

She'd meant her many lovers, the men who she'd never stayed with for too long, because they had always required such careful handling to put up with a woman with a sulky daughter in tow. Or so Elizaveta had always claimed.

"I don't expect you to be as grateful as you should— that's your father's influence in you, I'm sure—but you must comprehend what there is to lose if you don't do as I say." Elizaveta had glared at Amaya as if she'd expected her daughter to argue, when Amaya had long since learned the folly of that kind of thing. Even then, even as a child, she'd known it was better to bend to those who could not. "We'll lose everything. The roof above your head and the clothes on your back. Is that what you want?"

That had not been what eleven-year-old Amaya had wanted. The very idea had given her nightmares. And Elizaveta had never been a perfect parent, certainly. Life with her had always been complicated, but Amaya had been sympathetic because she'd understood that her mother hadn't said those things to be cruel. Amaya's father had broken something inside her, and sometimes it came out as poison. Amaya had learned not to take it personally... Or anyway, she'd tried her best not to take it personally.

"You are mistaken," Amaya said to Kavian now when she could speak without that rough-edged thing inside her taking over and revealing too much. "I don't know where you heard such a thing."

"Had she married any of the men she found, she would have had to return you to your father and worse, to her way of thinking, give up her access to your money." Another shrug, which made her want to throw her plate at him. A flicker in that gray gaze made her think he knew it, too. "This is not an attack, Amaya. This is simply a fact. I did not hear this through some grapevine or other—I've seen the paperwork."

Amaya shook her head, so hard it almost hurt, and noticed her heart had started to kick at her, almost as if she was panicked.

"My mother was a self-made woman. She had nothing when she left Ukraine. She talked her way from minor dance halls into the fashion houses of Milan. She had nothing *but* her wit, her charm and her looks. That was how she entered her marriage to my father, and that was how she left it. If anything, I was a complication."

It was only when she was finished speaking that Amaya realized her voice had risen, as if every sentence were a plate thrown, a blow landed on his wholly impervious form.

"She also had ambition," Kavian said softly. He was so much more dangerous the quieter he got, she knew. She sucked in a breath against it. "Never forget that. She left Bakri because she was losing the sheikh's favor. Better to leave and tell a sad tale across the years to a thousand receptive audiences. Better by far to hold the king's daughter as ransom than to remain in Bakri as a neglected, forgotten wife. The sheikh would have banished her to one of the outlying residences, far away from the palace where she would wither away into irrelevance, and she knew it. That, *azizty*, did not suit your mother's ambitions at all."

Amaya stared at him, willing herself not to react in the way she suspected he wanted her to do. Her lips felt bloodless. Her stomach twisted—hard. "You don't know anything about my mother. She was not ambitious. She was in love."

She shouldn't have said that. She shouldn't have uttered those words. Not to him, not here. Not out loud—and she didn't dare ask herself why that was. But Amaya couldn't take them back, no matter how much she wished she could. She couldn't make that taut, near-painful silence between them disappear, or do anything about that sudden arrested look on Kavian's austere face. She straightened in her seat instead, and forced herself to meet that edgy gray gaze of his straight on as if she felt nothing at all.

"My father was a convincing man when it suited him." She heard that catch in her throat and she knew Kavian did, too, but she pushed on. "He convinced a woman who had been born with nothing and raised to expect little else that he adored her. That he worshipped her. That he would remake his world in her honor."

She didn't point out how familiar that sounded. Just as she didn't give that searing blast of temper in Kavian's dark gaze a chance to form into harsh words on his lips.

"He lied. Maybe he meant it when he said it—what do I know? But my mother believed him. That was why she thought there was something she could do to regain his favor, to win back his attention once it drifted. Anything to make him love her again. But what my father truly loved was collecting, Kavian. He was always looking for his next acquisition. He didn't lose much sleep over the things he'd already collected and shunted aside."

He didn't speak for a long, cool moment that careened around inside Amaya's chest, leaving jagged marks. She tilted up her chin and told herself she could handle it. *Him.* Or survive it, anyway.

"Is that what you're afraid of?" he asked.

She would never know how she held his gaze. How she managed to keep herself from reacting to that terrible, infinitely destructive question. She only knew that she did it. That she stared back at him, stone to his stone, as if her life depended on it.

"Are you talking about your mother, Amaya?" Kavian pushed at her in that quiet way of his that nonetheless made every bone in her body ache. She fought to restrain a shiver. "Or yourself?"

"Don't tie yourself in knots looking for comparisons that don't exist," she managed to bite out at him, still channeling stone and steel and *calm.* "I'm nothing like her."

"I am aware. If you were, you would not be here." She hated the way he looked at her as if knew all the things she carried inside, her memories and her dreams and her darkest secrets alike. As if what Kavian enjoyed collecting was every last piece of her soul. And once he had them all, she couldn't help wondering then in a panic, what would become of it? Or her? "And as fascinating as this conversation is, it doesn't alter the fact that you require an entirely new wardrobe. You must look like my queen whether you feel like it or do not. Especially at our wedding ceremony, which, I hesitate to remind you, is in a matter of weeks."

"I don't want a ceremony."

"I didn't ask you what you wanted. I told you what

was necessary and what I require." His gaze glinted with amusement then, and that was much worse. It moved in her like heat. Like need. "Shall I demonstrate to you why you should begin to learn the distinction between the two? And the consequences if you do not?"

But Kavian's consequences always ended the same way—with Amaya stretched out naked on the edge of some or other gloriously intense pleasure she worried she might not survive, begging him for mercy and forgetting her own damn name. So she only picked up her coffee again and took another sip, schooling her features into something serene enough to be vaguely regal and ignoring that wicked crook of his hard mouth as she did it.

"A new wardrobe fit for a queen?" she murmured, her voice cool and smooth. Stone and steel. Just like him. "How delightful. I can't wait."

"I am so pleased you think so," Kavian said in the very same tone, though his gray eyes gleamed. "We leave for your first public appearance as queen tomorrow morning. I'm thrilled you'll be able to dress the part at last."

"As am I," she said dryly. Almost as if she couldn't help herself—couldn't keep herself from needling him. "I have worried about little else."

"Ah, *azizty*," he murmured, sounding as close to truly amused as she'd ever heard him, "when will you understand? I am not a man who does anything by halves."

CHAPTER EIGHT

IF HE WAS a good man, Kavian reflected the following day, he would not have set up his betrothed for this particular day of tests. He would not have tested her at all. Had it been about what he wanted, he simply would have kept her in his bed forever. He would have lost himself there in the sweet madness of her scent, the addiction of her smooth skin. The glory he'd found in her arms that shook him far more than he cared to admit.

But this was Daar Talaas and Kavian had never been good. He'd never had the chance to try. He was the king, and thus he did what was necessary for his people. If that happened to align with what was good, so be it. But he would not lose sleep over it if it did not.

He would sleep like an innocent, he assured himself, whatever happened in the desert that had forged him. It would be the making of Amaya, too, he knew. There was no other way.

After all, she had already taken the news of her mother's true treatment of her in stride. Kavian dared to allow himself a shred of optimism that she would rise to whatever occasion presented itself.

They'd left the palace in the morning, taking a helicopter out to the stable complex on the far side of the treacherous northern mountains. They'd stood together in the center of the courtyard while his men, a sea of servants and stable hands, and a selection of his finest Arabian horses hurried all around them.

"Do you ride?" he'd asked, almost as an afterthought.

She'd been dressed like a Daar Talaasian noblewoman, in an exquisite dress that adhered to desert custom with her arms and legs covered and her head demurely veiled. It only made her every graceful movement that much more intoxicating, to Kavian's mind, because he had the pleasure of knowing what was beneath. All her soft skin, the temptation of her hair, the sweet taste of her, woman and cream. But there'd been no veiling that cool gaze of hers, dark chocolate mixed with ice as it met his.

"I've ridden a horse before, if that's what you mean. I'm sure you already know that my mother and I spent several summers on a ranch in Argentina."

What he knew was far less interesting to him than what she chose to tell him. "Did you fall off a great deal?"

She stiffened almost imperceptibly, and those marvelous bittersweet eyes of hers narrowed. "Are you asking me if I've suffered a head injury?"

He'd kept himself from smiling by sheer force of will, and it was much harder than it should have been. Much harder than he could recall it ever having been before. "I am asking if I can expect you to topple off the side of a horse while you are meant to be riding it."

"Not on purpose," she'd retorted, and it had only occurred to him then that they weren't in private any longer. That his men stood around him, closely watching this exchange with the scandalous woman who had evaded him for months—whom he had clearly not yet subdued. "Do you plan to ride me out into the desert, throw me to the sand dunes and then *claim* I fell off?"

They had been speaking in English, which was lucky

as very few of his men understood a word of it. The fact that he'd been nearly smiling at her in obvious indulgence, however, was less lucky. Any softness, any hint of a crack in his armor, would be exploited as a weakness by his enemies. Kavian knew that all too well.

He couldn't have said why he cared so much less in that moment than he should have.

He'd given the order then. It had taken only a few moments for the small party to mount up, and when he'd looked back down at Amaya she'd been standing there, doing an admirable job of keeping herself from frowning at him. He'd seen the effort she expended in the way her dark eyes crinkled in the corners.

"Did you ask me all those questions for your own amusement?"

"Yes," he'd replied dryly. "I am a hilarious king. Ask anyone."

And then he'd simply reached down from the back of his horse, clamped an arm around her middle and hauled her up before him.

He'd felt more than heard the tiny noise she made, somewhere between a gulp and a squeak, and he knew that had he found her pulse with his mouth, it would be going wild. Yet she only gripped the arm he'd banded around her abdomen and said nothing.

"Courage, *azizty*," he'd murmured, his voice low and for her ears only. "Today you must prove you are the queen my people deserve."

"But—"

"Whether you wish it or do not. This is about Daar Talaas, Amaya, not you or me."

He'd felt the breath she'd sucked in and he'd thought she'd planned to argue further, but she hadn't. She'd been quiet. Perhaps too quiet, but there'd been nothing he could do about it then—or would have done if he could, if he was honest with himself. A test could hardly matter if it was without some peril. So instead, he'd given the next order and they'd ridden out into the desert, deep into the far reaches of the desolate northern territories.

It was not an easy ride by any means, but Amaya did not complain, which pleased Kavian greatly. She did not squirm against him, nor divert his attention any more than the simple fact of her there between his legs, her pert bottom snug against the hardest part of him as they rode, distracted him.

He found it impossible not to notice that she fit him perfectly.

They reached the encampment by midafternoon, after hours spent galloping across the shifting sands, racing against the sun itself at this time of year. Fierce men on bold horses met them some distance away and led them the rest of the way in, shouting ahead in their colorful local dialect. The collection of tents that waited for them had the look of a makeshift traveling camp instead of a permanent settlement, despite the goats and children who roamed in and around the grounds and told a different tale. Kavian knew that it was all a deliberate, canny bit of sleight of hand. The truth was in the quality of the horseflesh, the presence of so many complacent and well-fed camels, the fine, sturdy fabric of the tents themselves.

It could have been a scene from any small village out here in the desert, unchanged in centuries, and there was a part of Kavian that would always long for the simplicity of this life. No palace, no intrigue. No political necessities, no alliances and no greater enemy than the harsh environment. Just the thick heat of the desert sun above, the vastness and the quiet all around and a tent to call his home.

Though he knew that was not the truth of this place, either.

"What are we doing here?" Amaya asked as they rode into camp, and he wondered what she saw. The dirt, the dust. The sand in everything. The rich, dark scent in the air that announced the presence of the tribe's livestock, horses and camels. The suspicious frowns from the people who could see at a glance that she was not one of them. The lack of anything even resembling an amenity.

There was no oasis to cool off in here, because it was another fifteen minutes or so farther north, fiercely guarded and zealously protected for the use of this tribe alone—but Amaya couldn't know that. The women who clustered around the fire, beginning their preparations for the evening meal, eyed them as their party approached but made no move to welcome them, and Kavian imagined how they must look to Amaya. But he knew what she could not—that their seeming poverty was as feigned as the rest.

Nothing was ever quite what it seemed. He came here as often as he could to remember that.

"I have come a very long way to have a conversation," Kavian told his betrothed, and that, too, was only a part of it.

"To settle a dispute?" Amaya asked. She didn't wait for him to confirm or deny. "The king himself would hardly ride out to discuss the weather, I suppose."

Kavian pulled on the horse's reins, bringing the Thoroughbred to a dancing stop in front of a line of stern-faced elders, all of whom bowed deep at the sight of him. He inclined his head, then swung down from the horse's back, leaving his hand resting possessively on Amaya's leg as he stood beside her.

He greeted the men before him, introduced Amaya as

his betrothed queen and then they all performed the usual set of formal greetings and offers of hospitality. It went back and forth for some time, as expected. Only when the finest tent belonging to the village's leader had been offered and accepted, as was custom, did Kavian turn to Amaya again and lift her down from the horse.

"That wasn't the Arabic I know," she said, in soft English that sounded far sweeter than the look in her eyes. "I caught only one or two words in ten."

He didn't laugh, though he felt it move in him. "Let me guess which ones."

"Did you accept the man's kind offer of a girl for your use?" she asked, and though her voice was cool, her eyes glittered. "They must have heard you'd gone from seventeen concubines to one. A tremendous national tragedy indeed."

He could have put her mind at ease. He could have told her that the girl, like so many of the girls he was offered in these far-off places that never advanced much with the times, was little more than a child. He had taken many of them back to the palace, installed them in his harem and given them a much better life—one that had never included his having sex with them. He could have told Amaya that such girls accounted for most—though not all, it was true; he had never been a saint by any measure—of the harem he'd kept. He could have told her that there had never been any possibility that he would take a young girl as his due tonight and more, that the elders had known that, hence the extravagant effusiveness of their offers.

But he did not.

"They approve my choice of bride and have offered us a place to stay," he replied instead, his voice even. "More or less. It will not be a palace, but it will have to do."

She blinked as if he'd insulted her. Perhaps he had.

"I'm not the one accustomed to palaces," she reminded him, her voice still calm, though he could feel the edge in it as if it were a knife she dragged over his skin. "I keep telling you, I was only ever a princess in name. Perhaps you should be worried about how you'll manage a night somewhere that isn't drenched in gold and busy with servants to cater to your every need. *I* have slept under bushes while hiking across Europe, when it was necessary. I've camped almost everywhere. *I* will be fine."

He wanted to crush her in his arms. He wanted to take that mouth of hers with his, and who cared what was appropriate or who was watching or what he had to prove? He wanted to lose himself inside her forever. But he could do none of those things. Not here.

Not yet.

"I will also be fine, *azizty*," he said, his voice blunt with all these things he wanted that he couldn't have. Not now. "I grew up here."

Kavian strode off and left Amaya standing there, all by herself in what was truly the middle of nowhere, as if he hadn't dropped that bomb on her at all. He didn't look back as he disappeared into a three-sided tent structure with a group of stern-faced men. He didn't so much as pause.

And for a wild moment, Amaya's pulse leaped and she thought about running again now that she was finally out of his sight—but then she remembered where she was. There had been *nothing*, all afternoon. Nothing but the great desert in every direction, which she'd found she hadn't hated as she'd expected she would. But that didn't mean she wanted to lose herself in it.

She had no idea how Kavian had located this place without a map today, just as she had no idea what he'd meant. How could he have grown up *here*? So far away from the world and his own palace? Her brothers had been raised in royal splendor, waited on by battalions of servants, educated by fleets of the best tutors from all over the world before being sent off to the finest schools. Amaya supposed she'd thought that all kings were created in the same way.

It occurred to her, standing there all alone in the middle of the vast desert that Kavian was clearly bound to in ways she didn't understand, that she didn't know much about this man who had claimed her—even as he seemed to know her far too well. And better every day whether she liked it or not.

You do like it, a small voice whispered. *You like that he notices* everything. *You like that he sees you.* But she dismissed it.

Kavian had marched off with those men as if he was a rather more hands-on sort of king than her brother or father had ever been. Amaya assumed, when she shifted to see the women watching her from their place by the central fire, that she was meant to be the same sort of queen. No lounging about beneath palm trees eating cakes and honey, or adhering to the stiffly formal royal protocols in place at her brother's palace. No disappearing into the tent that had been set aside for them and collapsing on the nearest fainting couch. All of those options were appealing, and were certainly what her own mother would have done in her place, but she understood that none of them would win her any admirers here.

You run, she reminded herself. *That's who you are. Why not do that here? Or do the next best thing—hide?*

But she hated the notion that that was precisely what Kavian expected her to do. That he believed she really was some kind of fluttery princess who couldn't handle herself. It was so infuriating that Amaya ignored the waiting tent, ignored what her own body was telling her to do. Instead, she made her way over to the group of women and set about making herself useful.

When Kavian finally returned to the center of camp with that same cluster of men hours later, Amaya found she was proud of the fact that the evening meal was ready and waiting for him, as the encampment's honored guest. It wasn't the sort of feast he'd find served in his well-appointed salons, but she'd helped make it with her own hands. There was grilled lamb, a special treat because the king had come, and hot, fresh flatbread the women had made in round pans they'd settled directly in the coals. There was a kind of fragrant rice with vegetables mixed in. There were dates and homemade cheeses wrapped in soft cloths. It was far more humble than anything in the palace, perhaps, and there was no gold or silver to adorn it, but Amaya rather thought that added to the simple meal's appeal.

The men settled down around the serving platters and ate while the women waited and watched from a distance, as was the apparent custom. It was not until the two old men who sat with Kavian drank their coffee together that the village seemed to relax, because, one of the women Amaya had come to know over the long afternoon told her in the half Arabic, half hand gestures language they'd cobbled together as they'd gone along, that meant the king had settled the dispute.

Amaya ate when the women did, all of them sitting on a common mat near one of the tents, in a kind of easy camaraderie she couldn't remember ever feeling before. Out here in the desert, they didn't have to understand every word spoken to understand each other. It didn't take a common language to puzzle out group dynamics.

Amaya knew that the older woman with the wise eyes whom the others treated with a certain deference watched her more closely than the others did. She knew exactly when she'd gotten *that* woman to smile in the course of their shared labors, and she hadn't been entirely sure why she'd felt that like such a grand personal triumph. Or why she'd laughed more with these women she'd only met this afternoon and only half understood than she had in years.

The night wore on, pressing down from all sides—the stars so bright they seemed to be right there within reach, dancing on the other side of the fire. It reminded her of that winter in New Zealand, but even there the nearby houses had cast some light to relieve the sprawl of the Milky Way and its astonishing weight up above. Not so here. There was no light but the fire and the pipes the men smoked as they talked. There was nothing but the immensity of the heavens above, the great twisting fire of the galaxy. It pressed its way deep into Amaya's heart, until it ached as if it were broken wide-open or smashed into pieces. Both, perhaps.

"You did well," Kavian said when he came to fetch her at last. He reached down and pulled her to her feet, making the other women cluck and sigh, in a manner that required no translation.

"They think you're very romantic," she said, and she didn't know why she felt something like bashful, as if she thought so, too. Or worse—wistful.

"They think we are newly wed," he corrected her. "And still foolish with it."

"It's the same thing, really." She tilted her head up to look him in the eye as best she could in all the tumultuous dark. "Either way, it's not expected to last."

She thought he meant to say something then, but he didn't, and she didn't know why it felt like a rebuke. She had to repress a shiver at the sudden drop in heat as he led her away from the group, the flames, the laughter. She felt a sharp pang as she went, as if she was losing something. As if she would never get it back—as if it was so much smoke on a Bedouin fire, curling its way into the messy night sky above them. Lost in the night, never to return.

Amaya made herself breathe. Told herself it was the thick night, that was all, making everything seem that much more raw and poignant than it was.

There were lanterns guiding their way through the cluster of tents, and Kavian's strong body against the impenetrable darkness that pressed in like ink on all sides, but that didn't change the way she felt. It didn't help that ache inside.

If anything, it intensified it.

"I am told you impressed the women," Kavian said as he pulled back the flap and ushered her into the unpretentious tent that was theirs for the night. She felt as nervous as she had in the baths that first day in Daar Talaas, Amaya realized. She walked ahead of him, running her gaze over the bed flat on the floor but plumped up high and piled with linens, the serviceable rug that looked handwoven, the fine pillows scattered on the floor to mark a cozy seating area and a collection of lanterns that made it all seem deeply romantic. And she was astonished at how much she wanted it to be. "That is no easy task."

"Did you imagine I would cower in the tent?"

"I accepted that was a possibility. You did once secrete yourself amongst my shoes."

"One of the gifts of having moved somewhere new every time my mother felt like it, is that I'm good with groups of strangers," Amaya said. She made herself turn and face him, and she was surprised at how hard that was with so much tumult inside her. "It's that or no one speaks to you for months on end."

"There is being friendly and then there is helping cook a meal for the whole camp." Kavian still stood near the entrance, his gray eyes searching hers. "They are not the same thing."

"You told me I was to act as your queen."

"And you take direction, do you? How novel." He eyed her, but she couldn't let herself respond. Not when she had no idea what it was that held her in its grip. "Does a queen normally tend a cooking fire and sit in the dirt with strangers?"

"This one did," she retorted, not sure why she was trembling. Why she couldn't stop. His hard mouth crooked slightly. Very slightly. It didn't help at all.

"I am a man of war, Amaya," Kavian said softly. "I need a queen who can get her hands dirty. Who is not troubled by palace protocol when the palace is nowhere in sight. You please me, my queen. You please me deeply."

Something turned over, deep inside her. "I'm not your queen."

"Now you contradict yourself."

"I think you're confused because I cooked for you. Like a real person."

That gleam in his eyes turned them a polished silver in the soft light. And she couldn't tell him that what had really happened was first that she'd wanted to defy his low expectations—and then that she'd wanted to make him proud.

Here, today, she'd *wanted* to be his queen. She couldn't *say* that. She couldn't admit it to him when she could hardly accept it herself.

"Are we not real?" he asked. Almost gently.

Her throat felt too tight. "Things aren't the same in the palace, are they? It's a *palace*."

"A palace is a building made of carefully chosen stone and the concentrated artisanship of hundreds of loyal subjects across decades," Kavian said quietly. Intently. "It is a monument to the hopes of my people, their desire for unity and strength against all that might come at them. As am I. As are you, too. It could not be any more real than that."

"But you said you grew up here, not there."

He moved farther into the tent and she watched as he unwrapped his traditional headdress, then shrugged out of his robes, stripping down until he wore nothing but a pair of boxer briefs low on his narrow hips. He should have looked like a normal, regular, everyday man, she thought with something like despair. He was in his underwear in a tent in the middle of nowhere. Surely that should...*reduce* him, somehow.

But this was Kavian. And today, she'd wanted to please him. To be the queen he wanted. Looking at him here, she understood that suicidal urge.

He better resembled a god than any mere man. It was as if he'd been hewn from the finest marble and then breathed into life. His skin gleamed like old gold in the lantern light and she couldn't read a thing on his face as he came toward her. Nor when he reached for her.

He unwound her scarves from her as if he was unwrapping a precious gift. Slowly. Reverently. He combed his fingers through her hair when it tumbled down, then helped her out of the long, traditional dress she'd been given yesterday by his dressmakers. When she wore nothing but her slip, a basic thing that wasn't meant to be at all alluring, his gaze heated, but still he did nothing but gently rake his fingers through her hair.

It was almost as if it calmed him as much as it did her.

"My uncle was the king of Daar Talaas when I was born," he told her, so softly she thought at first he hadn't meant to speak at all. "He was a good ruler and the people loved him, but despite the wives he took and the many concubines he kept, he had no sons. So when he died, the throne passed to his younger brother. My father."

He wasn't looking at her. His attention was on the thick fall of her dark hair that he wrapped around and around his hand instead, then let unravel again. Yet Amaya found she could hardly breathe.

"My father was a young man with two wives, one renowned for her fertility, the other for her beauty." His gaze was dark when it met hers. Something like tortured, she'd have said. "His first wife had given him four sons already, my half brothers. The people were pleased, for my father and his wealth of sons ensured that the throne would remain in the hands of our family, come what may. That meant stability."

"What about you?" she asked. "Were you considered part of that wealth?"

He did not smile. If anything, his gaze darkened.

"My mother was a fragile woman who had nothing but her beauty and, perhaps because of it, a great envy for all the things she felt she was owed," he said, in the cool tones of someone who was telling a distant myth, a legend. Not his own family's story. *His* story. That shook through Amaya, but she didn't move. She didn't speak. "She was far more pleasing to my father in bed than his first wife had ever been, but even when she had me, she could not compete with the simple fact of her rival's four healthy heirs. My father's first wife was a simple woman, without my mother's looks or cleverness, but none of this mattered. She was the queen. She was revered. My mother came second, and I, her only child, fifth."

Amaya might have realized only today that there were a great many things she didn't know about this man, but she did know that he didn't have any family. Everyone knew that. Which made her heart stutter in her chest, because this story could be headed only one horrible way.

She reached over and pressed her hand against the hard plane of the muscle that covered his heart, and her breath began to shake when he slid his hand over hers and held it there.

"You don't have to tell me this story," she said, and her voice was barely a whisper. "I didn't mean to dredge up bad memories."

"My mother took a lover," Kavian said by way of reply. His voice was so dark, leading them inexorably toward a terrible end. She could see that much on his face. She could feel it in the air around them, crushing her in a tense fist, but she made herself stand tall. If he could tell it, she could take it. She promised herself she could. "He was one of my father's ministers, ambitious and amoral. But he was not content to simply defile my father's wife. He wanted the throne."

"How could he take it? Was he related to you?"

"The throne of Daar Talaas is held by the man who can hold it." Kavian did not so much say that as *intone* it. "So it is written in the stones on which the throne itself sits. So it has always been."

Amaya had to press her palm that much harder against him, to remind herself he was real. Flesh and blood, not a statue in a palace hewn from rock. Not etched stones beneath an old throne. Far more than the story he was telling her. Far more than the darkness that was pouring from him now, his eyes and his voice alike.

"I don't know what that means." It was more that she didn't *want* to know. But she didn't look away.

"It means that while families often hold on to the throne for some generations, this is because they tend to consolidate their power, not because there is a blood requirement."

He shifted, which made his previous stillness seem that much more extreme by comparison. "My mother's lover was no fool. He knew he could not take the throne by force. The Daar Talaas army cannot be manipulated. They serve the throne, not the man."

He had never looked as distant as he did then. Bleak and uncompromising. He stepped back, Amaya's hand fell to her side, and she thought she'd never felt so empty.

Yet Kavian kept going. "He slit my father's throat as he sat at the dinner table, in a place where there is meant to be only peace, even between enemies. Then he killed my brothers, one by one. Then both of my father's wives, including my mother. Especially my mother, I should say. Because even the man she colluded with hated that she was traitorous enough to betray her own husband. Her own king."

"Why did he spare you?" She hardly recognized her voice.

That wasn't a smile he aimed at her then. It was far too painful. It cut too deep.

"My mother had a servant girl who she did not so much trust as fail to notice. The girl knew of my mother's lover and enough of the plans they made that when the first alarm sounded, she ran. She took me out of the palace and claimed I was her own."

Amaya knew who he meant immediately. "The woman with the wise eyes. All the other women looked to her today."

"She is the wife of the chief here," Kavian said, but there was a flicker in his gaze that told her she'd impressed him, and it warmed her. It more than warmed her. "Back then, however, she took a terrible risk in bringing me to her father's tent, alone and unwed, with a toddler she could not prove was the king's missing son. The elders might not have believed her. She risked her life and her family's honor to save me."

"But they believed her."

"They did." He studied her face. "And they are simple people here, not aristocrats with agendas. Good people who follow the old ways. Blood begets blood, Amaya. They raised me to avenge my family, as was my right and responsibility as its only remaining member."

Amaya couldn't speak for a long moment. She thought of a tiny boy who'd lost everything and had been given only vengeance in return, out here in this harsh, desolate place without a single hint of softness. It made her heart hurt, as if he were the great sky pressing into her, as impossible and as far away. As beautiful and as untouchable.

He had been a lost child and they had made him into a stone. And now he thought it was a virtue.

"I'm sorry," she said softly. "That seems like an undue burden to place on a child."

"You misunderstand me." His gaze was too dark. His eyes glittered. "I am not telling you this story because I regret what happened to me. What is there to regret? I was lucky."

"You are also now the king."

"I am."

"Does that mean…" She searched his face, but he might truly have been made of marble then. He was that unyielding. "Blood begat blood?"

"It means that I grew up," Kavian said quietly. With a deep ferocity that tugged at her in ways she didn't understand, as if his story was changing things inside her as he told it. Shifting them. "It means that I dedicated myself to becoming the necessary weapon to achieve my ends. And it means that when I had the chance, I exacted my vengeance, and know this, Amaya, if you know nothing else about me. My single regret is that the man who murdered my family could die but once."

CHAPTER NINE

IT WAS A TEST, Kavian reminded himself harshly. The most important one.

This had all been a test. The long ride into the most remote part of the Daar Talaas Desert, abandoning her to see what she would do under the watchful eye of the woman he'd long considered his real mother. Then this. Throwing out the bloody truth of his family and his own dark deeds to see what she would make of them.

To see what Amaya was made of, after all. Who she really was when there was nowhere to run. If she was, truly, the one woman who could embody all he wanted.

Kavian stood there, stone-faced before this woman he had chased across the world, and awaited her reaction. It would determine the whole of their future.

He told himself he didn't care either way. That his heart was as much stone as he knew his expression was. There were some who had found his pursuit of vengeance unforgivable. There were others whose interest in his past had always seemed *too* avid for his comfort. This was nothing but a test to see where Amaya would fall on that spectrum.

It would set the stage for how he handled his marriage going forward, nothing more. Either she would prove herself a worthy queen, a woman like his foster mother, who was braver than most men, *his queen*—or she would simply be a wife with a lofty title who would eventually give Kavian his heirs.

It matters little which way she goes, he told himself then.

But he found that he was frozen in place, awaiting her judgment, all the same.

Amaya swallowed hard, but she didn't shift her gaze from his. She still stood tall before him. The warm light from the lanterns made her look gilded, standing there with her glorious spill of dark hair all around her and her perfect breasts visible beneath that silky little shift she wore. She was still so pretty it almost felt like an attack. An assault. It rolled over him and flattened him. It took out his defenses like a kick to the knees.

But he had no intention of showing her that.

"You obviously expect me to clutch at my pearls and faint," she said after a long, long moment.

"Aim for the bed," he advised her. "The rug is not as soft as it appears."

"Did you torture him?" she asked.

He hadn't expected that. He considered her more closely.

"No," he said at last. "He was the butcher. I wanted only what he took. If not my family, then the throne."

"Did it change you?"

He blinked, and ignored that heavy thing inside his chest that seemed to bear down hard at that, as if his heart was still wrapped in those same old chains.

As if he was.

"No," he said after a moment, when that harsh pull inside him faded. Or became more bearable somehow. "The change you mean happened much earlier. When I accepted that I would become what I hated in order to do what I must. I do not regret avenging my family. I regret only that I share anything with the man who killed them—that in order to honor my family I became a murderer, just like him."

"No." Her voice was fierce then, immediate, and her eyes glittered. "Nothing like him. You could never be anything like him. He killed children for his own selfish gain. All you did was take out a monster."

And Kavian had not realized, not until that moment, how very much he'd needed to hear her say that. How much he'd needed proof that she was who he'd thought she was from the start. He didn't want to analyze it. He didn't want to consider the implications. To hell with all that.

She was looking at him as if he was some kind of hero. Not the monster he'd long ago accepted he'd had to become because he'd had no other choice. She was looking at him as if—

But he couldn't let himself go too far down that road. He couldn't risk it.

"Come here," he gritted out at her, and he didn't smile when she jerked slightly at the harsh command, or even when she obeyed. He crossed his arms over his chest and peered down at her as she drew near. "Kiss me."

Amaya swayed toward him, the light playing off the silken shine of her shift and the smooth intoxication of her skin. She hooked one hand over his forearm where it crossed the other, and then she went up on her toes and slid her other hand along his jaw as if she sought to comfort him. And he felt the wholly uncharacteristic urge to lean into her palm, as if she was sunlight and he could bask in her a while.

Just a little while, something in him urged.

"Does this mean I passed your test, Kavian?" she asked him, a smile in those dark chocolate eyes and teasing the corners of her lips. "Or are there more hoops I must leap through tonight?"

He smiled then. Triumph and need and that heavy thing in his chest that made his heart beat too fast, too hard. He didn't want to name it. He refused.

"It means I want you to kiss me," he said, as if hunger for her weren't tearing at him, deeper and more ravenous than any he'd ever felt before. As if he could stand here all night, ignoring it. "I do not believe I was unclear."

"A kiss is my only reward for hours on a horse and hard labor by the fire?" She was teasing him again. Kavian understood that, even though he rather thought she took her life in her hands when she dared do it. Or maybe that was his life she held, and she was squeezing it much too hard as she went. So hard, it was almost a struggle to breathe. "That hardly seems equal to the effort I put out today to please you. Shouldn't you be the one to please me for a change?"

"Kiss me," he suggested, darkly, "and you will find out exactly how pleasing I can be, *azizty*."

She didn't laugh, though he felt it there in the air between them, music and magic, as if she had. She hooked her other hand around his neck and stretched herself up toward him, and he let her. He waited.

Amaya hovered there for a moment, her mouth a scant breath from his, her dark gaze solemn. Kavian remembered, suddenly, their first meeting. That same look in her eyes as they'd met his for the first time. The promises she'd made him then.

And that next morning, when her brother had come to tell him that she had fled the palace, her whereabouts unknown.

"If you break another vow, Amaya, I will not be quite so forgiving." He hadn't meant to speak. He hardly knew his own voice when he did.

But her lips curved slightly, only slightly, and she didn't pull away. "Has this been your version of forgiving?"

He could hardly hear her over the thunder of his own heart.

"You'll understand if I find that confusing."

"You are the only living creature I have ever forgiven anything."

It was a confession, gruff and unexpected. And he should not have made it to her, Kavian knew, but it mattered to him that she had not looked at him with horror drenching those lovely eyes once he'd told her his story. It mattered to him that she'd sought to defend him instead.

He could not for the life of him understand why it *mattered*.

Why she did.

Only that she had from the start. That she made him believe he could have a different sort of ending than the one he was certain he deserved.

"I'm honored," she said quietly now, like nothing so much as another promise, one more solemn vow, and then she kissed him.

She was as sweet as she was enticing, and he drank her in. He let her explore him, tasting him and teasing him, kissing him again and again until he could feel the catch in her breath.

And then, when he couldn't take it any longer, he slid his hands deep into her hair, he hauled her against him and he took control.

If the tent had ignited around them, he wouldn't have noticed.

He simply lifted her to him so that she wrapped her long legs around his hips and her arms around his neck, and still he plundered her mouth. He angled his jaw and he took the kiss deeper, kissing her as if his life depended on it. As if he could kiss her forever. As if time had stopped for precisely this.

And then, when she was making those wild little sounds in the back of her throat that were more precious to him than all the jewels in his possession, in the whole of his treasury and all of his museums besides, he carried her over to the bed and laid her down on the soft cloud of linens.

He stretched out above her, pressing her deeper into the bed and taking her mouth again. And he kept on kissing her. He could not seem to taste her enough. He could not seem to slake his own thirst.

Her hands moved all over him as if she was learning him with her fingertips, soaking him in. He shifted, slipping a hand down to cup the sweet heat of her in his palm. He held her there until she moaned, and only then did he move, slipping beneath the lacy underthings she wore and thrusting his fingers deep into her molten core.

It was his name she cried when she shook around him, and Kavian hoarded that to him like another vow. Her voice against the night, brighter than the lanterns that lit the space around them, etched deep inside him like letters carved into the stone of his own heart.

He was filled then with a kind of wild desperation he'd never felt before. He needed to be inside her, or die of it, and he hardly knew what to make of it when he saw his hands shook slightly as he rid her of her little slip and those lacy panties she wore, then peeled off his own boxer briefs.

Nothing mattered but that slick initial thrust, so deep inside her they seemed more like one, and even that was not enough.

It will never be enough, a voice within him whispered.

And just then, he didn't care.

He gathered her close. His arms wrapped around her,

her mouth against his neck. And he rocked into her, slow and easy. A pace he kept even when she started to shift, to writhe. To move her own hips against his, trying to buck at him and make him go faster.

He laughed, a dark jubilation that seemed to come from every part of him, while she dug her fingers so hard into the skin of his back that he could feel her nails.

And still he held that torturous pace. A slow thrust in, a long drag back. Again and again, driving them both insane.

"Please," she began to whisper. "Please, Kavian. *Please.*"

She was flushed red. Her whole body went stiff and she threw her head back, and Kavian had never seen anything so beautiful in all his life. He pounded into her, his own promise and his own solemn vow, over and over, like a prayer.

And when she burst into flame again, white-hot and endless, she took him with her.

The ride back across the hot sands was different.

Everything is different, Amaya thought.

She sat between Kavian's legs again, with all his lean strength and male heat wrapped around her, hard against her back as the sleek Arabian stallion galloped so smoothly south. She couldn't understand the things that moved in her without name, making her feel as if she hardly knew herself any longer.

The desert stretched out before them and around them, shimmering in the heat, immense and treacherous. Amaya had always hated the desert. The stifling heat. The sheer barrenness and lack of life. The profound emptiness. Its inescapable presence, vast and creeping closer all the time…

Yet that was not at all what she felt today. She wanted the desert to go on forever, vast and unknowable, as immense and beckoning as the sea. Or maybe it was this trip that she wanted never to end. And she had no earthly idea how to feel about that. About any of it. About what had happened out there between them, making the world itself feel altered around them.

It had something to do with how Kavian had woken her that morning, lifting her into his arms and then settling them both into a great tub she hadn't seen the night before, tucked away behind a screen in the far reaches of the tent. She'd winced as she tried to move in the warm, fragrant water, and he'd made a low, rumbling sound that had not quite been a growl.

"Behave," he'd ordered her. "You must let your muscles soak or you will find the ride back sheer agony."

And she'd tried to behave. Truly she had.

But he'd been so hot and hard behind her, his strong arms so perfectly carved as they'd stretched out along the high sides of the bath. The hardest part of him had been like steel, pressed tight against her behind. She'd only shifted position once. Then twice, without really meaning it. Then again, to test the little thrill that had washed through her, before he'd let out a sound that had been something between a laugh and a curse. Both, perhaps. His big hands had gripped her around the waist and he'd lifted her up before settling her on him again, but this time he thrust hard and deep inside her while he did it.

He'd angled them both back again into their original positions, so she'd been lying sprawled over his chest again, her back to his front. And his hardness buried so deep inside her she almost climaxed from that alone.

And then he'd done nothing.

"Is that better?" he'd asked mildly after a moment, and it had been exquisite, to have him so deep within her and to *feel* his voice like that, a rumble against her spine, the tease in it like a drug. "I plan to sit here and soak myself, Amaya. If you wish to do anything else, you must do so all on your own."

But even as he'd said that, his big hands, even warmer now from the water, moved to cover her breasts, sending a kind of delirious electricity rocketing through her as he cupped them, then brushed his thumbs over the tight peaks.

Amaya had tipped her head back so it had been cradled on his wide, hard shoulder, the urge to poke at him as impossible to ignore as his hardness snug inside of her. "I thought you liked to be in charge. That you insisted upon it. I thought that went with the kingly territory."

"I think I can handle a single bath," he'd assured her in that dark, stirring way that made her stomach flip and her core clench hard against the length of him deep within her. "Do as you like, and we'll test that theory."

So that was what Amaya did.

She'd quickly discovered that he'd severely limited her range of motion—but that maybe that was the point. The delicious challenge of it. She'd moved her hips in a sinuous, rocking motion that had them both breathing hard in only a few strokes, and then she'd given herself over to it. She'd learned the beauty in the sweet, slow slide. The lazy circle, all white-hot sensation and endless pleasure.

And all the while his wicked hands had moved between the tight peaks of her breasts and the hot center of her need, helping her build that fire between them, and pouring his own kind of gas on the flame. Until she hadn't been sure who was in charge and who was simply reveling in the heat between them, or why such a thing should matter.

Until she'd forgotten to care.

She had ridden them both to a slow, hot, shattering finish that she'd been sure had left her completely boneless.

Destroyed inside and out. And she'd been fiercely glad that they hadn't been facing each other, because she was terribly afraid Kavian would have seen too easily all the ways she was ripped wide open. That her vulnerability was written right there across her face.

But she thought he knew, even so.

When it had come time to climb back on the horses and head south toward the palace, she was grateful. It had meant long hours for her to put herself back together before anyone could study the ways she'd fallen apart. Before she had to admit it to herself, how broken she'd become out there. Or, far worse, how much she'd liked it. Hours to hide herself away again, behind a mask she hadn't understood she was wearing until he'd torn it off.

"I've never understood the appeal of the desert," she said now, forgetting to censor herself as the sprawling royal stables came into view before them. Was that relief she felt that this ride—this odd interlude—would soon be over? Or something far more complicated?

"Never?" He made that low sound that was his form of laughter, that she found she craved all the more by the day. "But you are the daughter of a mighty desert king. It is deep in your blood whether you understand it or not. It is your birthright."

"I've never cared much for sand," Amaya said.

"Is this where you try to put up all your walls again, *azizty*?" His mouth was right there at her ear, and his voice was a dark flame that lit her from within, that dark current of amusement ratcheting the heat in her even higher. "How many ways must I take you before you understand that there will be no walls between us? There will be nothing but surrender. It would be better by far if you accepted this now."

"Or perhaps I simply do not care for sand," she said, and

she laughed, then felt his hard muscles tighten all around her in reaction. "Not everything is a conspiracy, Kavian. Some things are simply statements."

"And some statements have consequences." His eyes would be gleaming silver if she could see them, she was sure. "As I have been at some pains to show you."

"Is that what you call it? I rather thought you were putting on a grand show. Hauling me into the harem baths, then off to play queen of the desert tribes with no warning. It's almost as if you don't really want a queen at all, so much as a plaything."

"Surely not having to choose is a benefit of royalty," he said, and there was no denying the laughter in his voice then. "I will have to consult the manual upon our return."

Amaya felt that as a victory, the rumble of laughter in his chest behind her. From the man who'd stood before her like marble to tell her the worst of himself, to this man who laughed with her, and it was all her doing. There were darker things that batted at her then, but she ignored them. She would bask in this, even if only for a moment. That she could do this for him. Take a stone and make him a man again. Even if only for a moment.

Even if only for her.

Kavian didn't speak as they rode into the great courtyard. He swung from the horse's back as they entered and led her the rest of the way toward the waiting stable hands. He lifted her from the saddle the way he had before, lowering her to the ground in a manner that only called attention to his superior strength.

And made her wish they were alone so she could feel the drag of his mighty chest against hers again. Like the addict she knew she was.

"We marry in two weeks, Amaya," he said, the vastness of the desert in his voice and silver in his gray eyes, and she felt it like a caress. All of it. His command. His authority. Like a long, hot, drugging kiss. It made her feel alive.

"Perhaps if you didn't keep saying that like it was a dire threat, you'd get a better response," she said, tipping her head back to meet his gaze.

Her reward was that crook of his hard mouth. That gleam in his dark eyes.

"You prefer the threat, I think," he said, and ran a fingertip along the line of her jaw. There was no reason it should echo throughout the rest of her, making even the blood in her veins clamor for more. "You rise to meet it every time. You'll make me an excellent queen, *azizty*."

And when she didn't argue that away for once, when she only met his gaze and let her mouth curve instead, Kavian smiled.

Amaya felt it deep inside her, warm and bright, like a song she told herself she'd let herself sing for a little while.

Just a little while longer.

CHAPTER TEN

WHEN THE WEEK of their wedding dawned, Kavian insisted upon greeting all of their guests in the most formal manner possible, and he didn't much care that the idea of such pomp and circumstance made Amaya balk.

"We're not really going to sit in thrones and wave scepters about, are we?" she asked, her voice as baleful as her gaze as she stared at him from across the length of her dressing room. He'd instructed her attendants to prepare her for court, and the scowl on her face did nothing to take away from the breathtaking new gown she wore or the hair she wore up in a marvelous sweep of combs and braids, exactly as he'd wanted it. She looked exquisite. Deeply, irrevocably regal. The perfect queen.

But Kavian thought he knew this woman well enough by now to know better than to point that out to her. She might have stepped into her role in the desert. But he wasn't fool enough to think she'd accepted it entirely. He needed to marry her, tie her up in legal knots, make sure she understood what he'd known since their betrothal: this was for life. There was no escaping it, for either one of them.

"There is only one throne," he told her mildly. He remained where he was in the doorway as the women fussed over her skirts, his gaze trained on her lovely face and the hint of emotion he could see on her cheeks. "I sit in it. But if you wish to wield a royal scepter, I am certain we can have one made for you."

"Don't be ridiculous." Kavian knew the exact moment she realized that was, perhaps, not the best way to address him in the presence of others. She straightened. Her dark chocolate eyes gleamed with more of that hectic emotion he'd seen more and more of the closer they got to their wedding date. "I don't need a scepter. I have no desire whatsoever to play queen of the castle."

"That is the problem, *azizty*. No one is playing, save you. Because you are, in fact, the queen not only of this particular castle but of all the land."

Her scowl deepened as she dismissed her attendants and walked to him, and he took a moment longer than he should have to admire her. To soak her in. It wasn't merely that she was so beautiful, or how she looked every inch a queen today. It was how perfectly she fit here. In this life. On his arm. At his side.

Did she truly fail to see that? Or was this merely another one of the games she liked to play—her way of teasing him to a distraction? He reached over when she drew near and wrapped his hand around her upper arm, enjoying the way she swallowed. Hard. Because she could deny a thousand things, but never that fire that raged between them. Never that.

"And if you look at me like that in the throne room, in public, in the presence of our guests," he said softly, "you will regret it. I am only as civilized as it suits me to be. That can change in an instant."

She was warm beneath his hand, her skin supple, and he was tempted to ignore the people waiting for them and simply back her up against the nearest wall and—

"You say that as if I do not regret everything already,"

she murmured, but he heard a teasing note in her voice. He could see the sheen of it in her gaze. "Whether you threaten me with it or not."

"I don't make threats, Amaya. I make promises."

She smiled. "And it should worry you, shouldn't it, that one is indistinguishable from the other?"

He dragged his thumb up, then down, enjoying the friction almost as much as the way her lips parted slightly at the sensation. She was his, he thought then, on every possible level. She was surely running out of ways to deny that—and their wedding would put an end to it, once and for all.

But there were miles to go first. Kavian had the suspicion they might be the hardest yet, like any long siege in its final hours. Better to concentrate on the details and assume the rest would fall into place. He reminded himself of the reason he'd come into her dressing room.

"Your mother arrived at the international airport in Ras Kalaat and is en route to the palace," he said, watching her face.

Amaya flinched slightly, so very slightly that had he not been studying her, he might have missed it entirely. She swallowed again, and he saw the pulse in her neck leap, though her face went blank. Panic? Fear? He couldn't tell.

He hated that he still couldn't tell.

"Now?" she asked.

"She will be here in the palace within the hour." He released her arm, straightening in the doorway, frowning down at her. "Were you expecting her? You have gone pale."

"I expected she would attend my wedding, yes," Amaya said. Carefully, he thought. Much too carefully. He was reminded of the mask she'd worn when he'd first met her and it was like a howling thing in him, the urge to tear it

off. "I'm her only child, after all, and she is my only remaining parent."

She blinked too hard, then looked around as if she was
casting about for an escape route, and it hit him. He'd seen
that look on her face before, heard that exact same note in
her voice. It had been the night of their betrothal ceremony.

And in the morning, she'd been gone.

"What you did not expect, if I am to read between the
lines, was that *this* wedding would ever come to pass," Kavian finished for her. He wanted to touch her again, but
didn't, and it hurt like a body blow. "Someday, Amaya, I
hope you will come to understand that I keep the promises I make. Always."

She stepped back from him and he felt it like the deepest
cut. It took everything he had not to haul her back where
she belonged. He watched her pull in a deep breath, as if
readying herself for battle.

"It should matter to you that this is not what I want,"
she said.

It was laughable—and yet Kavian did not feel the least
bit like laughing. "You don't know what you want."

"That's astonishingly patronizing. Even for you."

He shrugged, never shifting his gaze from her face.
"You ran, I caught you. I will always catch you. That is
the end of it."

"It should make a difference that I didn't *want* to be
caught," she bit out, as if sobs lurked just there behind her
eyes.

"Did you not? It seems to me that if that were the case,
you would not have returned to Canada at all, and certainly
not to Mont-Tremblant."

Amaya jerked her gaze away from his then, but he didn't
stop.

"And, of course, you could have fought me. Showed

me how opposed you were to this union instead of merely making announcements."

"I've done nothing but fight you from the start."

"Yes," he said, and she shivered at his tone. He almost smiled at that. "That is precisely how I would categorize the way you melted in my hands at our betrothal ceremony. And then all over me in that alcove. And then again, how you walked straight into the pools here to join me, wearing almost nothing. What fighting tactics were those, exactly? And to what end?"

She couldn't seem to make herself look at him, but he could see the impact of every word he said. They moved over her, making her tremble, and he'd already confessed his sins. She already knew he was a terrible man. He could not regret this. He did not try.

"You seek my touch and respond to it, always." His voice brooked no argument. It was a statement of flat, inconvertible fact. "Meanwhile, you have not been held here under lock and key or even under special guard. You were left to your own devices out in the desert. You could have made an attempt to leave at any time, yet you have not."

"You would have caught me."

"That is an inevitability, I grant you, but it is a question of where. After all, it took me six months the first time. Yet you have not tried."

"Do you *want* me to make an escape attempt, Kavian?" She turned to glare at him. "Because I thought the point of this was that you wanted a biddable little wife to live out her life at your beck and call."

He felt himself go still.

"That is the first time you have used my name when I have not been touching you, Amaya," he pointed out, and she shuddered. "Who knows? Someday you may even address me as if I am a man with a name, not a strategy to be employed toward your own increasingly convoluted ends."

"Isn't that the point of this?" she asked, and he hardly recognized her voice. "We are nothing but strategies for each other. Cold and calculated. Surely that's the point of an arranged, political marriage."

"You did not have to prove yourself to the villagers out in the northern territory. Where was the calculation there?"

"It was politically savvy on my part, nothing more."

"You could have complained about your treatment here to your brother at any point over these last weeks and caused a major diplomatic incident."

"He is newly married with a small child." She tipped that chin of hers up into the air, because this was what she did. She fought. She never simply surrendered. He admired that most of all, he thought. That indomitable will of hers, like the desert he loved. "He is somewhat busy, I imagine."

"You could have called me a monster when I showed you who I am," he said quietly. She jerked at that, as if he'd hit her. "Others have before you. Will you call the fact that you did not political, too?" He did not let himself think about what he might do if she did. But her eyes were slick with misery and she didn't say a word. "Do you know what it is you want, Amaya? Or do you fear that you already know?"

"None of that means I want to marry you," she whispered.

"Perhaps it does not," he agreed. "But it does suggest that the chances are very good that you will anyway."

"If you remove all the threats from this relationship," she replied now, her voice revealingly thick, "we don't actually have one."

"I will keep that foremost in my thoughts, *azizty*, the next time I am deep inside you and you are begging me for your release." Kavian kept his voice low, because it was the only thing keeping his hands from her, and his court waited for them even now. "I will hold you on that edge until you scream and then I will remind you that we have no relationship. No relationship, no release. Is that what you had in mind?"

He could hear her breathing, too loud and too fast. And her gaze was wild as it met his. But when she spoke, her voice was flat. Almost matter-of-fact.

"They are waiting for us in the throne room," she said.

He didn't believe her apparent calm for a moment. But once again, he admired her courage. The way she stood up to him, the way she gathered herself when he could see the storms in her. The more she kept trying to prove they did not suit, the more perfect he found her.

"They can wait a little while longer." He raised his brows. "Until we arrive, it is only a very large room with a dramatic chair no one is permitted to touch. By law."

"That I get to stand behind, yes," she bit out. She moved then, sweeping past him toward the door, her spine rigid and her head high. "What a joyous experience that will be, I am sure. I can hardly wait."

He let her go, following behind her as she made her way from their suite and into the grand corridor that led toward the public wing of the palace and the ancient throne room that sat at its center. His aides converged upon him as they walked, and it was not until they'd entered the room and taken their places on the raised dais that dominated one end of the ornate hall that he focused on her once more.

"You stand beside me, not behind me," he told her. He could not have said what moved him to do so. That she was still pale. That her sweet mouth was set in a hard line no matter that defiant angle to her fine jaw. That she still seemed to imagine that this was something other than foregone conclusion. "A strong king holds the throne, Amaya, but a strong queen beside him holds the kingdom. So say the poets."

He saw something flicker in her gaze then. "And do you rule with poetry? That doesn't sound like the man who dragged me out of that café in Canada."

"You walked out of that café in Canada of your own volition," he reminded her. "Just as you walked into that encampment in the desert and just as you will walk down that aisle in a few days. My queen obeys me because she chooses it. That is her gift. It is my job to earn it."

An expression he couldn't define moved over her face then, as the guards stood at attention down the length of the long hall and announced the series of guests who awaited their notice, and her mother's arrival. Kavian eyed her as her mother's name rang out, taking in Amaya's too-stiff posture. The way she gripped her hands before her, so hard her knuckles hinted at white.

"You are afraid of your own mother," he murmured. "Why is that?"

But the great doors were opening at the other end of the hall, and she didn't answer him. Because her mother was walking in and Amaya sucked in an audible breath at the sight, as if she couldn't help herself. As if she truly was afraid.

Kavian turned slowly to gaze upon the person who could bring out this reaction in the only woman he'd ever met who had never seemed particularly intimidated by *him*.

Elizaveta al Bakri looked like every photograph Kavian had ever seen of her. She appeared almost supernaturally ageless. She was an icy blonde, her hair swept back into a ruthless chignon and her objectively beautiful face flawless, with only the faintest touch of cosmetics to enhance the high, etched cheekbones she'd passed on to her daughter. Her blue eyes were frigid despite the placid expression on her face, her carriage that of a prima ballerina. She looked tall and willowy and effortless as she strode down the long hall toward the throne, quite as if she hadn't flown halfway across the world today, and yet as far as Kavian was concerned she was little more than a reptile.

Much like his own, long-dead mother.

"Breathe," Kavian ordered Amaya in a dark undertone.

He felt more than saw her stiffen beside him, then he heard her exhale.

He kept his attention on the snake.

Elizaveta made a beautiful, studied obeisance when she came before the throne, sweeping deep into a curtsey and then rising in a single, elegant motion that called attention to her lovely figure. But then, most snakes were mesmerizingly sinuous. That didn't make them any less venomous.

"Your Majesty," Elizaveta murmured, her voice threaded through with the faintest hint of an accent that Kavian suspected she maintained simply to appear slightly exotic wherever she went. Then she shifted her attention to her daughter. "Amaya. Darling. It's been too long."

"You may go to her," Kavian said in an indulgent tone. It was over-the-top even for him and Amaya glanced at him, startled—but he trusted that the look in his eyes was savage enough to keep her from saying anything. Hers widened in response.

Challenge me, he suggested with his gaze alone. *I dare you.*

But Amaya merely moved toward Elizaveta, and Kavian was aware of too many things at once as she went. It was the same overly focused attention to detail that he experienced before an attack, whether while practicing the martial arts he'd trained in all his life or in an actual physical skirmish. The vastness of the great room as it echoed around his betrothed. The rustle of her long skirts as she descended the wide stairs. And the way this woman who was meant to be her mother looked at her as she waited, her expression still something like serene yet with nothing but calculation in her chilly gaze as far as he could tell.

The hug was perfunctory, the highly European double-cheek kiss a performance, and Kavian wanted to throw the older woman across the room. He wanted her hands *off* Amaya, that surge of protectiveness coming from deep, deep inside him, and it took all of his considerable self-control to keep himself from heeding it.

"I'm so glad you came," Amaya said to her, quietly.

And Kavian reminded himself that this was still her mother. Amaya actually *meant* that. It was the only reason he did not throw this creature from his palace.

"Of course I came," Elizaveta replied, bright and smooth and still. It wedged beneath Kavian's skin like a blade. "Where else would I be but by your side on your wedding day?"

"Your maternal instincts are legendary indeed," Kavian interjected, like a dark fury from above, his gaze the only thing harder than his voice. "The world is a large place, is it not, and you have explored so many different corners of it with Amaya in tow. An unconventional education for a princess, I am sure."

Elizaveta inclined her head in a show of respect that Kavian was quite certain was entirely feigned. Amaya stared back at him, stricken. And he could not hurt her. He could not.

"But I welcome you to Daar Talaas," he said then, for the woman who would be his wife. His perfect queen. He waited for the older woman to raise her head, and then he nearly smiled. "I do so hope you will enjoy your stay in my palace. What a shame it will be so brief."

* * *

"He is rather Sturm und Drang, isn't he?" Elizaveta asked Amaya when they were alone hours later, after a long day of formal greetings and diplomatic speeches. She sounded arch and amused and faintly condemning besides. As if this were all a terrific joke but only she knew the punch line. "Even for a sheikh. I'd heard rumors. Is he always *quite* so…commanding?"

Amaya was certain *commanding* was not the word her mother had been about to use just then. They sat in the charming little garden that adjoined Elizaveta's guest suite with hot tea and a selection of sweets laid out before them. Amaya shoved an entire almond pastry into her mouth with a complete lack of decorum, because it was far safer to eat her feelings than share a single one of them with her mother.

"He is the king of Daar Talaas," Amaya replied once she'd swallowed, aware that her mother had probably counted every calorie she'd just consumed and was mentally adding them to Amaya's hips. With prejudice. *She can't help who she became*, she reminded herself sharply. *This isn't her fault. It probably took her more to come here than you can imagine.* "Commanding is simply how he is."

Elizaveta leaned back. She held her tea—black, no sugar, of course—to her lips and sipped, never shifting her cold gaze from Amaya.

"Tell me what you've been up to," Amaya said quickly, because she could practically see the way her mother was coiling up, readying herself to strike the way she always did when she felt anything, and Amaya didn't think she could take it. "We haven't talked in a long time."

"You've been so busy," Elizaveta said, in that light way of hers that wasn't light at all. "Traveling, was it, these last six months? One last hurrah before settling down to this marriage your brother arranged for you?" She didn't quite frown—that would have marred the smoothness of her forehead, and Amaya knew she avoided that at all costs. "I hope you enjoyed yourself. You must know that a man in your betrothed's position will demand you start having children immediately. As many babies as possible, as quickly as possible, to ensure the line of succession. It is your foremost duty."

"There aren't any lines of succession here," Amaya replied, because concentrating on dry facts was far preferable to thinking about other things, like the total lack of birth control she and Kavian had used in all this time. Why hadn't they thought about that? But even as she asked herself the question, she was certain that *he* had. Of course he had. He thought of everything. She trained her gaze on her mother, because she couldn't fall down that rabbit hole. Not now. Not while Elizaveta watched. "Not in the classic sense."

"Every man wants his son to rule the world, Amaya, but none so much as a man who already does." Elizaveta smiled, which only made a chill snake its way down Amaya's back. Had Elizaveta always been so obvious a barracuda? Or was this simply her reaction to being back in this world again—when she'd avoided it all so deliberately since leaving Amaya's father? "You are so very, very young. Are you certain you're ready to be a mother?"

"You were a mother when you were nineteen."

"I was not nearly so sheltered," Elizaveta said dismissively. She shook her head. "I cannot fathom how you could end up in a place like this, with all the advantages I provided you over the years. I had no choice but to marry your father when he appeared like some fairy story to spirit me away. You have nothing but choices and yet here you are. As if you learned nothing."

Amaya should not have felt that like a noose around her throat. It shouldn't have mattered what Elizaveta said. It shouldn't have hit her so hard, right in the gut.

"You told me my father swept you off your feet. That you were in love."

She sounded like the child she had never been, not quite. She couldn't help herself.

"Yes, of course I told you that," her mother replied, arch and amused again. "That sounds so much more romantic than reality, does it not?"

"Anyway," Amaya said tightly, because she didn't believe Elizaveta's sudden nonchalance on this topic after years of wielding her broken heart like a sword, "there's no point having this discussion. I'm twenty-three years old, not nineteen. I'm not even remotely sheltered. And most important, I'm not pregnant."

You can't possibly be pregnant, she told herself ferociously.

Her mother turned that cool blue gaze on her, washed through with something enough like malice to make Amaya's stomach clench. Despite herself, she thought of the things Kavian had said about her. That she had lived off Amaya. That she had lied about that—and who knew what else?

"That's clever, Amaya. Once you are you will be trapped with him forever."

Trapped was not the word that came to mind, which was more than a little startling, but Amaya frowned at her mother instead of investigating that. "Luckily, it's not up to him."

But Elizaveta only smiled again.

Stop making her out to be something scary, Amaya snapped at herself. *She's not a demon. She's nothing but an unhappy woman. This is her hurt talking, not her heart, and anyway, you don't have to respond.*

"Of course not, darling," Elizaveta murmured. She leaned forward and put her teacup back on its saucer with a click that seemed much too loud. "I've never seen you in traditional attire before. Not even when we still lived in Bakri."

Amaya had to order herself to unclench her teeth. To curve her lips in some rendition of a smile. "I am not in traditional attire. You can tell because I am not wearing a veil."

"I wonder if this is merely a stepping stone toward a more traditional arrangement." Elizaveta's shrug was exquisite. It somehow conveyed worry and a kind of jaded weariness at once, while also making her look infinitely delicate. "A sleight of hand, if you will. He lures you in by pretending to be a modern sort of man and then—"

"Mother." It was so absurd she almost laughed. "There is not one thing about Kavian that is the least bit modern. If that's the lure, he's already failed. Spectacularly."

Elizaveta moved to her feet and then wandered with seeming aimlessness around the small courtyard, as if she was taking in all the green and the riot of bright flowers. As if she'd never beheld their like before. "What a charming suite. I adore all these flowers. What part of the palace is this?"

Amaya understood where she was going then. Perhaps it had been inevitable from the start, given how furious her mother had always been at her father. Given how hurt she still clearly was.

"The guest part," she replied. Grudgingly.

Her mother smiled over her shoulder, but her gaze was hard. "Is that its formal name, then? How strange."

She watched her mother trail her always elegant, always red-tipped, always diamond-studded fingers along the petals of the nearest bougainvillea vine.

"I think you know perfectly well that this is technically

part of what was once considered the harem complex," Amaya said quietly. "But Kavian does not keep a harem."

Her mother glanced at her. "Not now, you mean."

"He kept a harem before we met, if that's what you're trying to tell me so subtly." Amaya was proud of how cool she sounded. How very nearly bored, as if the number *seventeen* were not flashing behind her eyes. "But then, he's never claimed to be a monk."

Her mother turned to face her, and Amaya was struck, as she always was, at how much she looked like the darker version of her mother's precise blond beauty. Where Elizaveta was like an ice sculpture, carved to sharp perfection, Amaya was so much softer. Blurrier.

Misshapen, she'd always thought. And yet today she found she was glad they weren't more similar.

"Did he give up his concubines for you?" Elizaveta asked, with that pointed smile that was her fiercest weapon. "That is enough to make the heart sing, I am sure."

Amaya had not spoken to her mother much in the six months she was on the run. There had been enough speculation in the papers that Amaya assumed Elizaveta had guessed that her daughter had run away from an arranged marriage, but Amaya had never confirmed it. Now she was happy she'd played it that way. That she'd confided nothing. That Elizaveta knew nothing at all about Kavian, or Amaya's relationship with him.

"Kavian is deeply romantic," she told her mother, giving her all to that lie. "He might not show it to you or the world. But he is a hard man who has only one bit of softness, and that's me."

Her heart skipped a beat at that, as if it was true. More—as if she wanted it to be true.

But her mother's cold eyes gleamed. "Is that what he told you?"

"I wouldn't put much stock in it if he'd *told* me," Amaya said, and even smiled. "I've learned one or two things from you, I hope. Actions speak louder than words, isn't that what you always said?"

"And when you are big and fat and ugly with his child, as you will be often," Elizaveta said, as if she was agreeing, "you must anticipate that he will see to his needs as he pleases, with as many other women as take his fancy. Men always do. That is their favorite course of action, Amaya. Always. Especially men like him, in places like this."

Amaya rose to her feet and skimmed her hands down her skirts, angling her head high. She wasn't eleven. She didn't have to listen to this. She certainly didn't have to believe it.

"I'm sorry if that was your experience, Mother," she said quietly. "It won't be mine."

And she hadn't understood until she said it out loud that she wanted that to be true. That more of her wanted to believe in Kavian than didn't.

She had no idea what to do with that.

"Does he love you, then?" Elizaveta asked, her voice so light. So terrible. "Or has he merely claimed you?"

Whatever she saw on Amaya's face then made her cluck in what sounded like sympathy. It washed over Amaya like something far more acidic, and wrenched at her heart besides.

"Darling." Elizaveta shook her head, and Amaya felt everything inside turn to ice. "They're not at all the same thing. And a woman must always know where she stands, or she will spend her life on her knees."

CHAPTER ELEVEN

KAVIAN KNEW THE MOMENT Amaya walked into their rooms as the afternoon edged toward evening that her mother had gotten to her. He could hear it in the heaviness in her step out in the foyer. The particular weight of her silence.

The pen he'd forgotten he was holding snapped in his hand and he muttered a curse, throwing the pieces into the wastebasket that sat beside his desk in his private office, the pen fragments making an oddly satisfying sound as they hit the metal sides.

He wished it was the poisonous Elizaveta instead.

"You are not truly planning to sneak past me, are you?" he gritted out, as if to the walls around him. As if to the ghosts that the locals claimed had plagued this place for centuries. "Do you imagine that is wise?"

A moment later, Amaya appeared in the doorway. She was still wearing the gown she'd had on in the throne room earlier, which displayed her femininity so beautifully and yet with such exquisite restraint that it made his throat hurt. That hair of hers that he was beginning to view as an addiction he might well succumb to completely was still caught up in all the braids and twists that he thought made her look something like ethereal. Something so much more than merely a bartered bride, his for the taking, though she was that, too. She was everything.

She was so lovely—so very much Amaya and *his*—it made his chest feel hollow. Scraped raw.

But it took her too long to raise her gaze to his and when she did, those chocolate eyes of hers were much too dark. Too troubled by far. He eyed her from across the span of the room, temper beginning to pound through him as if he were running flat out across the desert sands, straight on toward the enemy.

Amaya crossed her arms over her chest and he hated it. He hated the defensive gesture itself. He hated that she felt she had to make it. Even after he'd combed the whole of the earth for her. Even after everything he'd told her. Even though she knew the truth about him and it had not made her hate him.

Apparently only her mother could do that.

He wanted to throw back his head and howl, like some kind of wild thing, all claws and fangs.

"Why are you looking at me like that?" Amaya's voice was a scrape against the quiet and did very little to calm him.

"How am I looking at you?" he asked. Mildly. "As if I think you might be rationalizing a new way to betray me even as we stand here?" He studied her. "Are you?"

Something sparked in her dark eyes. "I can't betray you, Kavian. By definition. First I would have to pledge myself to you in some meaningful way, of my own volition."

"Careful, Amaya." His voice was rougher, deeper. "Be very, very careful."

The elegant column of her throat moved as she swallowed, but she didn't look away.

"Did you sleep with all seventeen of the women you kept here in your harem?"

He muttered something harsh in Arabic that he was quite certain she understood, but she only tipped that sweet chin of hers higher and let that mouth of hers go mulish. "It's a simple yes or no question."

"Ten of my so-called concubines were under the age of fifteen," he told her, and it was a remarkable experience for him. He had never explained himself to another living soul, as far as he could remember. He had never felt the slightest compulsion to do so. "They were gifts from each of the ten tribes who live in the great desert, as is tradition. I brought them here to educate them, to make them aristocratic women who could do as they pleased rather than chattel to be bartered and traded in the desert encampments. Most of them are currently studying abroad, or have made excellent marriages." He tried not to grit his teeth. "And, no, I did not sleep with these teenagers, Amaya. My tastes run to grown women, as you should know better than anyone."

She didn't crack. "Seven women, then."

"My predecessor kept a number of women. When I got rid of him I sent those with children to the far reaches of the desert, as I could not allow them to remain under my roof. It makes me look weak in the eyes of many of my subjects. Soft in ways that could hurt me." He shrugged. "As long as they dedicate themselves to living quiet lives free of political intrigue, they may do so safe from my interference."

"You mean, as long as they don't show signs of trying to wreak the sort of vengeance you did, you'll let them live."

He didn't back down. "Yes." He let his brows rise. "Does this offend you, Amaya? I have told you. Daar Talaas is not Canada. You may cringe from our brand of justice all you like, but that doesn't make it any less effective."

"I didn't cringe." She shifted. Swallowed again, as if against a lump in her throat. "But that doesn't mean I necessarily support it, either."

"Two of my predecessor's concubines remained in the palace after I took it back," Kavian told her. "But I never touched them. I merely allowed them to stay here after he was gone, as they had no families to take them in. It was widely considered an act of mercy."

She stared at him for a long while. Kavian felt a muscle in his jaw clench tight. His entire body tensed, as if he was moments away from launching an attack. Or perhaps warding one off.

"And of the five other women you kept here?"

He shook his head. "I am a king, Amaya. Should I have *dated* instead? I hear it is fashionable to do so online these days. Perhaps that would have worked. I could have put up an ad, I am sure. *Single sheikh seeks companion for sex on command, no possibility of marriage, yet many financial and residential perks.*" His voice was like acid. "I'm certain the tabloids would have loved that. They are so fond of me already."

Her gaze was hot and level at once. "And of the five—"

"I am not answering any further questions about the harem I disbanded when you asked me to do so. When I promised you I would, because of the two of us, I am the one who keeps promises." He watched her flinch at that, but he couldn't seem to modify his tone at all. "The harem I did without for six months while you led me on a merry chase across the planet. Do you truly wish to discuss this, Amaya?"

There was a glitter in her dark eyes he didn't particularly like. She stood tall and inescapably regal there in the door. "We haven't used birth control of any kind."

"No." He didn't avert his gaze from hers. "We have not."

"Is that how this works, Kavian? You think if you get me pregnant I'll be forced to stay here?"

He heard something far more ragged in her voice then, could see the echo of it in that storm in her too-dark eyes.

"Have I made my intentions unclear?" He studied her face then, wondering at that raw thing inside him. It seemed to grow larger by the moment. "Have I deceived you in some way? Is this what your mother came here to tell you?"

"Don't blame her. She's supposed to look out for me."

"Can you truly claim that was her goal?" He was incredulous.

But Amaya stared at him, openly defiant. "You took advantage—"

"Of your inexperience? Are we acknowledging that now? And I had grown so accustomed to the Whore of Montreal."

"You knew I was inexperienced. You knew I wasn't paying attention to the things I should have been. You used that against me." Her voice didn't shake. Her hands weren't in visible fists. And yet there was a certain sheen to her dark gaze that suggested both. "You want to keep me here against my will, no matter what it takes. Sex around the clock until I can't see straight. Barefoot and pregnant for the next ten years. Whatever works."

"Please remind me, Amaya, of any moment in all the time that you have known me when I indicated otherwise."

Kavian heard his own voice then, so rough and dark in the quiet room, he might as well have kicked down the walls. He was certain he could *see* the way it slammed into her. He saw the way she gulped in a breath. He even saw the way she adjusted her stance, as if her knees had suddenly weakened beneath her.

He didn't recognize the feeling that moved in him then. Thick, dark. A rich thread of an agony he could not name, balling in his gut and sitting there like a stone.

Shame, he realized after a stunned moment. And something like a keening hatred of himself and these battleground tactics on this woman who was no desert warrior, no matter how tough she appeared at times. He'd never felt anything like it.

He didn't much care to experience it now. He moved toward her, aware on some level that his careful veneers were cracking as he moved, the masks he wore shattering—

But he couldn't stop.

"And what will happen when you get what you think you want?" she threw at him, all the tears she was not crying audible in the thickness of her voice, and he hated himself more. "What happens when I give you everything I have and the thrill is gone? When you use me up and cast me aside? Will you consider that an act of mercy, too?"

"You should not listen to the rantings of a bitter old woman. I am not your father."

Her eyes swept over him, that bittersweet shine. "Are you sure about that? Because so far, the two of you seem very much the same."

He felt unchained then. Untamed. Wild beyond measure. And it did not occur to him to temper it at all as he moved toward her.

Kavian didn't stop until he was upon her, right there, looming over her until she stepped back and came up hard against the doorjamb.

"Do you want me to apologize, *azizty*?" It was a growl from the deepest part of him. "In this fantasy of yours, do I beg your forgiveness?"

"You wouldn't mean a word of it even if it was a fantasy."

He stroked the tender skin of her elegant neck, trailing his fingers over her satiny flesh and the tumult of her pulse. He felt the way she trembled, and he saw arousal edge into that darkness in her gaze, whether she wanted it—him—or not.

"No," he agreed, despite those too-dark things that still moved in him. "I would not."

"Kavian."

He knew what she was going to say. He could see the words form on her lips, see them scroll across her face.

"My mother—"

"I will have that snake of a woman removed from the palace within the hour. She—"

"She is my *mother*." Her voice was a shocked whisper.

"Do you think I cannot tell a bad mother when I see one? Can you have forgotten mine? Your mother is a viper. I want her and her poison gone from here."

"No." Amaya's voice was flat. Incredibly bold, for someone so much smaller than he was, so much more fragile, but she stared back at him as if she was unaware of those things. As if she was his equal in every way. As if she had every intention of engaging him in hand-to-hand combat if he didn't do as she asked.

As she commanded.

"I beg your pardon?"

"You heard me." Her chin rose fractionally. "You cannot throw my mother out because you don't like her. I don't *care* if you don't like her."

"*You* do not like her."

She frowned at him. "I love her."

"I cannot abide her." He felt that stone in him, dragging down, threatening his ability to stand before her. Threatening far more than that. "She is envious of you. She whispers poison into your ears. You fear her."

"I feel sorry for her." Her voice was even. Her chest rose and fell too quickly, he thought, and still she smelled of honey and rain and he wanted nothing as much as he wanted her. Nothing at all. "She was hurt a very long time ago, and hurt is what she knows. She can't help the way she lashes out."

He shifted, feeling his mouth flatten as he traced unknowable symbols along the elegant line of her neck, feeling the way she shuddered at his touch. "She is a grown woman who has spent the bulk of her life manipulating others to do her bidding. I do not dance to the tune of fools. Why should I suffer her presence here?"

He saw too many emotions chase each other across her face then, one after the next, and he felt them all like blows.

When she spoke, her voice was quiet. "Because I asked you to."

Kavian shook his head, a harsh negation that had more to do with the memory of Elizaveta's cold gaze, so much like the photographs he'd seen of his weak, vain, treacherous mother.

"Then you can't give me what I want. You can't *give* at all." She raised one shoulder, then dropped it, and he understood that she was not in the least afraid of him. Was that what roared in him, so much like desire? Like greedy admiration? "Don't claim you want a queen to stand beside you, Kavian, when what you really want is your own way in all things."

"I want exactly what I claimed from the start." His voice was practically a growl. "I am exactly who I have always been. More than that, *azizty*, I am exactly who you need."

"Then prove that. I've told you what I need." Her dark eyes searched his face. "I don't need you to understand, Kavian. I need to you listen to me for once."

He didn't recognize the thing that swelled in him then. He didn't understand why he felt as if he'd staggered blindly into a sandstorm and was being tossed this way and that. He only saw something unbreakable in her gaze. Tempered steel, forged in flames.

"If it is what you want," he said stiffly, because words of acquiescence were foreign to him and came slowly, thickly, "she can remain. She is your mother, as you say."

Amaya's eyes glittered. He felt that like another blow, and then her hand came up and slid over his jaw. He felt that touch everywhere. His toes. His sex. His throat.

"Thank you," she whispered, as if he'd given her a kingdom. All the jewels in his possession. "Thank you, Kavian."

That stone thing in him sank deeper. Grew harder. And he hated it all the more.

Kavian was finished talking. He hooked a hand around her neck and jerked her to him, noting with a fierce surge of satisfaction that her nipples were already stiff when they came into contact with his chest.

And then he bent his head and devoured her.

He kissed her with all the roughness within him. That wild thing that battered at him. That uncivilized creature that would have locked her away if it could have, that still thought it might. That great stone, that vast weight, that exploded into hunger the more he tasted of her. The man he could not be for her burst from him and into that kiss. He took her mouth like a storm, a great dark invasion, holding nothing back—

And she met him.

More than met him.

It was wild. Raw. Elemental.

He didn't know if she tore his clothing or he did. He knew he ripped open the bodice of her gown to get at her breasts, to worship them. He knew he sank his hands in the concoction of her hair, the great glory of it.

And God, the taste of her. It blocked out the world.

Then they were down on the floor, right there in his office, rolling and tearing at each other and wild. A hunger unlike any other roared in him, and in her, too. He could feel it as well as his own intense passion.

He thrust into her with more need than finesse. She screamed out his name, and he dug his fists into the thick rug beneath them, holding himself still while she clenched and shook around him and rode out her pleasure, her fingers digging hard into his back.

"Thank you," she whispered again, like the blessing he didn't deserve.

And that was when Kavian began to move.

The banquet the night before the wedding that was being fancifully billed in all the papers as East Meets West at Last—a rather theatrical name for what was, at the end of the day, a rehearsal dinner—seemed to drag on forever, Amaya thought. Dignitaries and aristocrats, many of whom had come in days before, lined the tables in the vast ballroom. A band played. Servants outdid themselves, a brace of belly dancers performed during one of the early courses and Kavian lounged there at the head of the high table with his slate-gray eyes fixed on her as if he expected her to bolt at any moment.

As if he could read her mind, even as she smiled and laughed and played her part for the assembled throng.

The meal ended after what seemed like several excruciating lifetimes and the worst part was, Amaya thought as she stood and dispensed her thanks to the guests, this was all her fault. There was something wrong inside her. Twisted. *Not right.* There was no other explanation. How else could she come to terms with the fact that she simply could not resist this man? Because if she'd had any kind of backbone, as he'd pointed out to her himself, she'd have attempted to escape him. She'd have done it, come to that. And she wouldn't have found herself standing here, poised to do the only thing worse than what she'd done to him six months back.

"Are you ready for tomorrow?" Her mother's voice sliced into her, but Amaya only smiled harder, hoping no one was paying too close attention as the crowd moved from the tables to the great room beyond, where desserts were to be passed instead of served, the better for the politicians to wield their trade as they moved from group to group.

Was she ready? How could Amaya still not know?

"Yes," she said, because she didn't want to second-guess herself. She didn't want to keep ripping herself apart.

"It's the right thing, darling. You'll see." But what Amaya heard was that thread of triumph in her mother's voice. That hint of smugness. "Men like him can only be the way they are. It never changes."

"Mother." She had to check her tone, remind herself where they were. "You don't actually know him. You know his title."

"I know men."

"You know what you want to know, and nothing more." Amaya glanced around, afraid someone might have overheard that tense tone in her voice, but most of the guests had moved toward the other side of the great hall and on toward the waiting courtyard. She and Elizaveta were as alone as it was possible to be in such a great crowd.

Her mother's gaze was as cool as her smile was polished. "I don't know what you mean, Amaya."

"It doesn't matter." Amaya's smile felt welded to her face. "This isn't the place to discuss it."

They would have all their lonely lives for that, she thought—and she felt hollow. Utterly empty and dark. But that was to be expected. She wouldn't be leaving Daar

Talaas unscathed. She'd be surprised if she even recognized herself.

"I don't think I care for your tone of voice," Elizabeta replied, her tone light. But her blue eyes were hard. "Is that the kind of disrespect you learned here? We can't get you away from him fast enough."

"Did we live off a trust my father set up for me when I was a child?" Amaya hadn't known she meant to fire that at her mother until she did it. And when Elizaveta froze, she wanted to grab the words back—except instead, she continued. "Is that how we survived those years? Because I must have misunderstood. I thought you told me we had to move around so much because we were destitute."

She saw the truth in her mother's face, so much like her own. She saw the glitter of it in her mother's gaze.

"Things were a good deal more complicated than you can possibly understand," Elizaveta said, her voice chilly in the warm room.

"That's all right, Mother." It wasn't until she spoke that Amaya heard the bitter edge to her words. That she felt it inside her, spiked and painful. "Lucky for you, I'm far more forgiving than you are."

She started to move away then, her emotions blinding her and her breath much too ragged, but her mother's hand on her arm stopped her.

"It's not forgiveness," Elizaveta said crisply. "It's weakness. Haven't I taught you the difference? Your trouble is, you make yourself a doormat for anyone who happens by and wishes to wipe their feet on you. That's the difference between us."

Something cracked then, so loud and so huge that Amaya was surprised she didn't hear screams from the crowd. It took her a stunned moment to understand that the palace hadn't crashed down around them—that something had instead toppled over inside her. She could feel the aftershocks, shaking through her.

She reached down and tugged her mother's elegant hand from her arm.

"I choose how I bend, Mother," she said. She might have shouted it, though she knew she hadn't—yet she saw the dazed look in Elizaveta's eyes as if she had. Amaya could only wonder what expression was on her face. She found she couldn't bring herself to care. "And to whom. I only kneel when I want to kneel, and that doesn't make me a doormat. I've spent my life catering to you because I love you, not because I'm weaker than you. You've spent your life prostrate to your feelings for a man who forgot you the moment you left him, if not long before, because you were never as strong as you pretended to be. That's the difference between you and me. I'm not pretending."

"You must be crazy if you think a man like Kavian thinks of you as anything but a conquest," Elizaveta hissed.

"Don't mention him again," Amaya said, with a certain finality that she could see made her unflappable mother blink. "Not ever again. He is off-limits to you. As am I."

"I am your mother!" Elizaveta huffed at her, as if Amaya had punched her.

"And I love you," Amaya said with a certain fierce serenity that reminded her of Kavian's desert. "I always will. But if you can't treat me with respect, you won't see me again. It's that simple."

For the first time in as long as she could recall, her mother looked old. Something like frail. But Amaya only gazed at her, and ignored the pity that made her heart clench tight.

"Amaya."

"This isn't a debate," she said quietly. "It's a fact."

She left her mother standing there, looking lost, for the

first time in her memory. It took a few steps to remember herself. To smile. To incline her head as regally as possible as she caught the eye of this or that noble personage. Amaya moved through the crowd as she reached the waiting courtyard, open to the night sky above with a series of decorative pools and fountains marking its center.

Kavian stood on the far side of the pools, that stark, harsh face of his intent as he listened to the two Daar Talaasian generals before him. As if he'd sensed her approach, or her eyes on him, his gaze snapped to hers across the night.

And for a moment there was nothing but that. Nothing but them. No crowd, no guests. No wedding in the morning.

His face was as brutally captivating as ever, and she knew it so much better now. She felt him deep inside her, as if he'd wrapped himself around her bones, taken her air. She felt him as if he was standing beside her instead of across a grand courtyard, as if they were alone instead of surrounded by so many people.

She thought she might feel him like this, as if they'd fused together somehow on some kind of molecular level, all the rest of the days of her life. Amaya told herself that what moved in her then, thick and harsh, was not grief. It couldn't have been.

"You do not look the part of the blushing bride to be, little sister."

Amaya started at the familiar voice at her ear, then controlled herself, jerked her attention away from Kavian and aimed her practiced smile at her brother.

But Rihad, king of Bakri, did not smile in return. His dark eyes probed hers, and Amaya had to look away, back to where the man who had scandalously kidnapped her from a café in a Canadian lake town stood there so calmly, as if he'd had every right to do so. Quite as if there weren't reporters everywhere, recording every moment of this night for posterity and dramatic headline potential, who wouldn't leap at that story if she'd chosen to share it.

If you marry him, scandals like that will seem like mountains made out of molehills, a small voice within told her. *If you do not, they will take over two countries and drown them both...*

She knew what she had to do if she wanted to survive. She'd set everything in motion. But that didn't make any of it easy. She cared a great deal more about what would happen in the wake of this decision than she had half a year ago.

Obviously. Or she wouldn't still be here.

"You look something very much like happy these days, Rihad," she said after a moment, "I don't think I realized that was a possibility."

For him. For her. For any of them.

He frowned. "Amaya."

But she refused to do this. She *couldn't* do this—and she'd already revealed too much. There was too much at stake.

"Not here, please." She forced another smile. "I will no doubt burst into tears at all your brotherly concern and it will cause a war, and I'll forever be known as that selfish, emotionally overwrought princess who caused so much trouble. There's a reason Helen of Troy doesn't have the greatest reputation. It's not worth it."

"Listen to me," Rihad commanded her, in that voice of his that reminded her that he was not only her older brother. He was a king. Her king.

Amaya remembered his own wedding to his first wife, which had come at the end of a week of celebrations in Bakri City. That, too, had been arranged. Amaya had been a small girl, in awe. She'd thought the fact of the wedding itself meant the bride and groom had loved each other. And in truth, Rihad had always told her that he and his first wife had gotten along well.

But it was nothing next to what was between him and Sterling, his second wife. That much had been obvious at a glance when they arrived the day before. Their connection crackled from the many tabloid articles that had been written about them, which in turn paled next to the sparks they struck off each other in person. Amaya didn't pretend to understand how that could be, when Sterling had spent a decade as their late brother, Omar's, mistress.

She only knew that she and Kavian didn't have the same thing. What they had was dark and physical. A terrible wanting that she was absolutely certain would destroy them both. It was not the calm affection of Rihad's first union. Nor was it the obvious intimacy of his second.

It was an agony.

"It will not be pretty if you fail to go through with this wedding," Rihad said in a gruff sort of voice. "I can't deny that. But I won't force you to the altar. I do not care what claim he thinks he has."

Amaya looked across the great courtyard to find Kavian again, and again his dark gaze met hers, so gray. So knowing. So fierce and hard at once, searing straight into her like a touch of his warrior's hands.

And she understood then.

It was the night before the wedding she'd been trying to avoid for more than six months. And Amaya was deeply and madly and incontrovertibly in love with the man she was meant to marry in the morning. She thought she had been since the moment they met, when those slate-gray eyes of his, so dark and so patient, had met hers and held.

Shifting everything else.

Changing the whole world.

She loved him. She understood with a certain fatalism, a shuddering slide that seemed to have no end inside her, that she always would.

And if she married him, she would become her mother. It was a one-way ticket to Elizaveta's sad life, no matter what Amaya might have told her earlier. If Amaya had Kavian's children, would she treat them the same way Elizaveta had treated her? Once he tired of her and cast her aside, would she spend the rest of her days wandering from lover to lover, playing out the same sort of vicious games and making everyone who came near her as unhappy and bitter as she was?

There were fates worse than death, Amaya thought then, her head thick and dizzy with this knowledge she didn't want. And that was one of them.

"Are you all right?" Rihad asked, the beginnings of a frown between his brows. "Amaya?"

She would never know how she managed to smile at her brother then, when inside her, everything was a great storm. There were no foundations left. She loved Kavian and she couldn't have him and all was ash. Ash and grief and a terrible darkness that scarred her even as it burrowed deep. Because he'd showed her who he was. How he was made. He'd showed her how much he could bend already—and it was so little. Too little.

What would happen when he no longer bothered to try?

"Don't be silly," she said to her brother, the king of Bakri like their father before him. The ruler who had traded her to this man she'd never escape, not really, not intact. She was already in pieces. She understood she would never really be anything else.

When she betrayed Rihad, Rihad and Kavian and two kingdoms between them, she imagined she would shatter even more. Turn to dust out there somewhere on that same lonely circuit, making history repeat itself in her mother's bitter wake.

And that was still better than staying with Kavian and loving him until it killed something in her. Better to love a brick wall, she thought miserably. It was far more likely to love her back.

But here, now, she widened her smile and tried to look as if she meant it. She thought from Rihad's expression that she almost pulled it off. Almost. "I've never been better in my life."

CHAPTER TWELVE

AMAYA FELT HIM behind her, as though he was a part of the shadows out on the terrace not long before dawn. Darker and more electric.

But she didn't look over her shoulder at him. She kept her eyes trained on the soft lights that spread out in the valley below her, making the old city sparkle in the lingering dark. The great immensity of the mountains rose on the other side of the ancient valley and beyond it, the great desert stretched out in all directions and had taken up some kind of residence in her soul without her knowing it until now.

Up above, the stars waited. A bright smear across what was left of the night, fading away by the moment.

"You're not supposed to be here," she said when she thought she could speak. When she thought she could push the words out around the heaviness that was turning her to concrete inside.

"Because you think I am bound by tradition or because you hoped to be halfway to Istanbul by now?"

Kavian's voice was soft. But so lethal there was no chance whatsoever that she might have missed it.

Still, Amaya took her time facing him. When she did, she had to catch her breath against that instant surge of sensation that almost took her from her feet. She had to reach back behind her and hold on to the railing that kept her from plummeting over the side of the high palace walls.

He was dressed all in black. Again. He looked like some kind of assassin, in the same way he had that day back in Canada that felt like lifetimes ago now. His strong arms were folded over his black T-shirt and he was barefoot beneath his black trousers, and her body shivered into that instant, near-painful awareness that she thought would never leave her. He was as much a part of her as the heart that knocked much too hard against her ribs. More.

"You told me at the party that I could have this one last night alone to—"

"Spare me the lies, Amaya."

She jolted at that. At that harshness in his voice, stamped all over his face.

"I haven't said anything," she heard herself say, as if from afar. "How could I have lied?"

"Did you pack a bag?"

Her throat went dry then. How long had he been watching her tonight? "No."

"You did. Not a suitcase, merely a rucksack, but I think you will agree that is splitting hairs at best."

Her heart was a riot in her chest. "Have you been spying on me, Kavian? The night before our wedding?"

"Our wedding." He let out a little laugh, entirely devoid of humor. "What I cannot figure out is why you are still here. Your mother was so explicit in her instructions to my men, who I believe she thinks she managed to turn against me. You were to sneak out through the palace kitchens. She would have transport ready to take you through the tunnels and spirit you out of my evil clutches at last, the better to humiliate me further in the eyes of the world."

Amaya wanted to die, right where she stood. She felt that dizziness return and with it, all that wet heat behind her eyes she tried desperately to keep at bay.

"I know you might not understand this," she said as best she could. "But she loves me, too, in her way."

The look he gave her should have set her on fire. Amaya felt singed as if it had. She straightened from the terrace and took a step toward him, but stopped when he lifted one of his hard, scarred hands.

"Do not come any closer to me." Dark and brutal.

"Kavian—"

But she couldn't finish. His gray eyes were the darkest she'd ever seen them. The night around them was edging into blue, but his gaze stayed much too black. And for the first time since she'd met this man, there was no glimmer in there. No relief.

"You conspired with a woman who is little better than a cobra to run from me, again, after you prevailed upon me to let her stay here when I wanted her removed," he said, as if he was rendering judgment. "But this time, I was to stand at the Western altar you insisted upon and wait for you. Is this not so?"

"Kavian."

"I do not know what it is you want that I have not given you." His voice was a dark throb then, as much inside her as it was in the air between them. "A kingdom. A throne. *Me.* I do not know what you think you will find out there."

Amaya didn't know when her arms had snuck around her own middle, only that she held herself tight as if, were she to let go, she would fall apart. And still she couldn't look away from him.

"I imagine you must want declarations, poetry. I am not that man. I am brute force poured into an old throne, masquerading as a man. I am not soft. I cannot shine the way others do, perhaps. But I would protect your life before my own. I would worship you all the rest of my days."

"You would keep me here."

"You like it here." He didn't precisely shout that last. He didn't have to. "I watched you for days before we picked you up in that lakeside town. You were miserable."

"I was on the run!" she protested, but she was shaken.

"You were lost and alone," he gritted out at her. "But then, I have met your mother, Amaya. You always were."

She sucked in a breath, and it hurt. All of this hurt. It always had.

"I hate it when you do this," she seethed at him. Maybe at herself. "You don't know anything about me!"

"I know everything about you," he threw back at her, harsh but certain. "That is what I have been trying to tell you. I do not know how to *date*. I am not romantic. But I saw your face, I heard your voice and I altered my world to have you. I have nothing else to give you but that."

"What if I don't want it?"

He moved then. He crossed the terrace like lightning and he hauled her against him, his tough hands wrapped around her biceps, yanking her up on her toes. He put his face directly in hers.

"You have never wanted anything more in your life."

Amaya pushed at him, but he didn't let her go, and the tears she'd tried to keep at bay poured over and ran down her cheeks. And Kavian was like an avenging angel towering over her, forcing her to face the things she most wanted to pretend she didn't see.

"I've told you from the start what I wanted," she threw at him, desperate and wild. Because she loved him, and she knew where that led. She knew who it would make her, what she would become. "Let me go, Kavian. Just let me go!"

She saw something rip across his face, too harsh and too dark to bear, and then he opened up his hands. Impossibly, he released her. She staggered back, catching herself against the railing again, unable to look away from him and unable to catch her breath.

Unable to believe he'd done it.

He was breathing as heavily as if he'd been running, and for a taut, electric moment, that was all there was. That and what was left of her heart.

"I will honor my military commitments to your brother," Kavian said, and for a long beat, then another, Amaya had no idea what he was talking about.

Then she did. And it was as if he'd extinguished the stars that easily.

"Hear me, Amaya," he said in that same voice, all command. All of him a king who had won his throne with the strength of his own hands. And more, the man who had conquered her with a glance six months ago, no matter what lies she'd told herself since. No matter her contortions. Her desperate pretense. "I will not pursue you. I will not come after you."

She couldn't speak. She told herself she should feel relief. She should. She was sure she would start at any moment, once it sank in.

"If you do not have a doctor forward the results of a pregnancy test exactly one month from now, I will send one of my physicians to you and have him administer it. If you are pregnant—"

"I can't be." Her voice hardly sounded like hers. It was too thick, too distorted. *Broken*, she thought. "I can't possibly be."

His eyes glittered in the strange, predawn light.

"Then you have nothing to worry about. I am sure you will find that convenient."

And she realized then that she'd never seen him look at her like this before. So cold. So remote. That he had never before seemed anything but fascinated with her, even when he was wild with rage, with passion.

This was a Kavian she didn't know. And that revelation smashed the remaining pieces of that broken heart of hers into smithereens. Until nothing remained but dust. And regret. And that loneliness she'd always carried deep inside her, like her own bones.

"Do you need me to sign something?" she asked.

He didn't appear to move, or even to breathe. Yet she thought she saw a muscle clench in his lean jaw.

"Why?" His voice was a dark lash. "You signed many things six months ago. Your word, your signature, your promises—these are all meaningless."

She wanted to reach out and touch him, but she didn't dare.

"Kavian—"

"You wanted to go, Amaya." His voice was so harsh it bordered on cruel then. "Go. You do not need to sneak off through the tunnels like a refugee. I will have the helicopter waiting, and the plane. You can take it wherever you wish. Just make certain you also take your mother."

"I thought…" She had no idea what she meant to say and she swayed slightly on her feet as if the ground buckled beneath her. "I thought you wanted…"

"I want you," he bit out. "But I will not force you and I will not play this game any longer, where you pretend that is what I am doing when it is what you want. Go, Amaya. Be free. But remember, I know you. This is the only real home you've ever known. *I* am."

And she knew he was right. Maybe that was why she fought it.

Maybe that was why she was still here. Standing here, almost as if she'd been waiting for him to find her.

Still, she fought. "It's a big world. There are a lot of places out there."

He shook his head. "You've seen them all. You've been dragged everywhere. There are no secrets out there, Amaya. You know them already."

"I don't belong here." She only realized she was whispering, raw and broken, when she saw a hint of that calm gray in his eyes again, edging out that awful blackness. That cold.

"Azizty," he said with absolute certainty, "this is the only place you belong. With me."

"You want my abject and utter surrender. You want me to kneel in front of you. You want me to beg."

"Perhaps," he said simply, "that is because you do, too, after you fight it for a time. You are simply too afraid to accept that we both want this. We both like this. This is what we were born to do, together."

"Kavian—"

But he shook his head, cutting her off.

"The sun is rising," he said. "The day is upon us. You have a decision to make, Amaya. I suggest you make it as quickly as possible. Then go, if you mean to go. I have a wedding to cancel and a terrible scandal to manage."

And then he turned on his heel and walked away from her.

She couldn't believe it. It didn't make any sense. He was not the one who left, she was. She couldn't *breathe*—

And then the desert sun peeked over the far hills, and the golden light bloomed, molten and bright, blinding her as it poured down into the valley. It washed over the palace, wrapped her in its instant warmth, transformed the world.

And Amaya understood, at last.

The lesson of the stars, of that great weight. Of the desert. Of the sun.

All of these things were love.

They did not bend, they simply were. They could not be altered or changed, they were far too immense. They were infinite. What did it matter what her mother said? What did it matter what the world said, for that matter? Or those voices inside her that told her what she *should* feel, not what she *did* feel?

The only thing that had ever mattered was love. And when she looked in Kavian's beautiful gray eyes, she'd always seen that greatness, that eternity, that sheer and shocking boundlessness.

Why *wouldn't* she surrender? Wasn't that the point?

And for a man like Kavian, who had done what he had, who ruled this stark and uncompromising place and had for more than a decade—what had his acquiescence to her on the subject of Elizaveta been if not the equivalent?

Amaya scrambled forward then, flinging herself into the great suite, her feet slippery against the marble floors. He wasn't in their bedroom. He wasn't in the grand shower. She raced down the long hall, frantically checking the salons as she passed, and was almost to the point of hysteria when she found him standing in his office again, a mobile phone in his hand.

She had the distant impression that he looked surprised, but she didn't wait to look any closer. She simply threw herself at him, trusting that he would catch her—

And he did.

He always did.

"I let you go," he said darkly as he set her on her feet,

and she watched him go still again as she kept going, sinking right down to her knees before him. More than that, she felt every single muscle in his body go taut beneath her hands.

"I love you," she said.

And for a long, long time, it seemed, ages and epochs, there was nothing but that arrested look in his eyes and that mad clamor in her chest.

"Yes, *azizty*, I know," he said at last, the arrogant man. "I have been trying to tell you this for some time."

It was better than love poems from another. Far better. And the words rolled out of her then, an unstoppable force, like the brand-new day over those old mountains all around them.

"It doesn't matter if you can't love me back," she assured him. She meant it, with every last part of her. "I don't want to be like my mother. I don't want you to sleep with a whole new harem when I get pregnant, every time I get pregnant. I don't want to share you with anyone. I don't want to disappear in you, bending and bending until there's none of me left." She pulled in a shuddering breath, tears slicking her vision, so he was nothing but a dark, blurry blade there above her. "But if that's the price, I can pay it. I will. Because you're right, Kavian. You're right." She was shaking, and she gripped the material of his trousers in her fists. "This is the only place I belong. With you."

She thought he would laugh then. Order her to remove her clothes so he could surge deep inside her, showing her precisely how they fit. Prove, once again, that he was a man hewn from stone, not flesh.

And she wanted that. She wanted him, however she could have him. There was no shame in that. There was only love.

But instead Kavian breathed in deep, then let it out. Long and hard, as if it hurt.

And then His Royal Highness, Kavian ibn Zayed al Talaas, ruling sheikh of Daar Talaas, sank down on his knees before her.

His mouth crooked in the corner at her thunderstruck expression. And then he reached over and took her face in his hands, cradling her as if she was infinitely precious to him.

"This *is* love," he said, his voice a deep rumble. "This is what it looks like. You haunted me from the moment I saw you. I hunted you across the world. You live in my body, you move in my veins, you are my blood. You are mine." He shook his head, his gray eyes stern, his mouth that unsmiling line she adored. "You will never be like your mother. She loves no one and she never will. You will never have to worry about me betraying you, pregnant or not. I do not share well. I do not expect you to be any more giving in that area than I am. And there is no price to pay, *azizty.*" He angled his head closer, brushing his mouth over hers. "There is only this."

He kissed her, and the world was made new. He kissed her, and he loved her, and Amaya felt as large as the desert, as bright as the stars, as golden straight through as the sunlight that danced through the room.

Kavian angled his head away, waiting until she opened her eyes and looked at him. That serious, warrior's face of his, harsh and tough. That hard mouth. Those ruthless gray eyes. He was stark and made of stone, and he was hers. He was all hers. She thought it might take her a lifetime or two to get used to it. At the very least.

"I love you, Amaya," he said, quiet and true. And it sang in her, like a great chorus with no end. His mouth shifted into that little crook that was his smile and lit her up from the inside out. "Marry me."

She smiled and snuck her arms around his neck, moving closer so they were flush against each other, still down on their knees. Together.

"Are you asking me?" she teased him. "Because that sounded a lot like another order. A royal command."

"I am asking you. I doubt such a thing will happen again." He slid one hand up into her hair, the other down to grip her hip, holding her close.

She smiled at him, holding nothing back. Surrendering everything, risking everything, and she'd never felt stronger in all her life. Or more sure.

"Marry me, Amaya." Those gray eyes of his gleamed. "Please."

Terrifying sheikhs did not yield to anything, Amaya thought then, and *this* sheikh least of all. He'd proved that a thousand times.

But it seemed even Kavian could bend.

Just a little.

Just enough.

"I will," she said softly. And she held his gaze, the way she hadn't done when they signed all those papers. The way she hadn't before she ran from him the first time. Because this time, she knew what she was vowing, and she meant every word of it. "I promise you, Kavian. I will."

And then she wound herself around him, pressed her mouth to his and showed him exactly how much she meant it.

Kavian claimed his queen in a grandiose ceremony that was reprinted in a thousand papers all over the world and broadcast on far too many channels to count. Bakri and Daar Talaas, united as one in the eyes of the world and against their common enemies.

His wife, his at last.

"This way," he told her with complete satisfaction when they were bound to each other in three languages, two religious systems and under the laws of at least three countries, "there can be absolutely no mistake. You are mine."

"I am yours," she agreed, with a smile that nearly undid him.

And she was. Finally, she was.

More than that, she was the queen he'd always dreamed she'd be. She was beautiful enough to stand at his side and make the nation sigh in wonder. And she was capable enough to do her good works, dirtying her hands when necessary, making the nation love her as he did. The people admired her as much for leading him on a merry chase as for her eventual surrender, and they called her *the strong queen*, like the old poems, as if they believed she was as much a warrior queen as he was her warrior king.

They loved her.

They loved her even more when she gave him his first son some eight months after their wedding, bringing Kavian's own bloody circle to a far happier conclusion. This son would not need to avenge his father. This son would not need to wonder what kind of man he was—he would know.

And they called for national holidays when Amaya gave him his first daughter a year and a half later, the prettiest little girl in the history of the world—according to the besotted king, who considered making that declaration into law.

Kavian made her the greatest queen in the history of Daar Talaas.

But Amaya made him a man.

She loved him fiercely and fully, and demanded nothing but the same in return. She fought him as passionately as she made love to him, and he learned how to bend. Just a little. Just enough. She forgave him and she redeemed him, every day.

She taught him. Every day, she taught him. He did not have her mother thrown in his prisons as he'd wanted, and he saw the benefit of that as the years passed. Elizaveta would never be warm or cuddly, or even, to his mind, tolerable—but she was a far better grandmother than she had ever been a mother.

"She has softened," he said to Amaya one day. They stood together in the old harem, watching Elizaveta and the children play in the desert sunshine that danced through the courtyard. The blonde woman laughed as she held his squirming five-year-old daughter aloft. When she was with their children, she was unrecognizable. "I would never have believed it."

"She's not the only one who has softened," Amaya said, and only smiled at him when he glared at her in mock outrage.

"I am a man of stone, *azizty*," he said, but he couldn't keep himself from smiling. Amaya didn't try. She laughed at him instead, and the world stopped. The way it had when he watched a video of her a lifetime ago. The way it would, he was certain, when they were both old and gray and addled.

"You are a man," she agreed, and surged up on her toes to kiss him, hard and sweet and fast. Kavian felt her smile against his mouth, and deep in his heart besides. "My man."

And then she took his hand in hers and led them out into the sun, and all the bright days of their future.

* * * * *

ROYAL CAPTIVE

DANA MARTON

With many thanks to Allison Lyons

Chapter One

The five men in the back of an unmarked van across the park from the Valtrian Royal Palace maintained radio silence. They were crowded by a wall of instruments, ignoring the dead body at their feet, watching the feed from a button camera that panned one checkpoint after another as its wearer passed through them.

Then the gilded, magnificent reception room of the palace came on the screen at last, looking exactly like the postcards vendors sold all over the city.

"Boss's in. We're good to go," the oldest of the men said, then clapped the rookie on the shoulder. "We'll be in an' out before they know what hit 'em."

The mood in the air was tense but optimistic as they checked their weapons.

"ANYONE BUT HER." Prince Istvan nestled the stash of two-hundred-year-old documents back into their leather pouch, then a ziplock bag and a protective box, careful not to damage the brittle paper. He shoved the copy he was making by hand into the inside pocket of his jacket. Every time he began work on the Maltmore diary, someone or something interrupted him. His office, located deep inside the palace, was supposed to be his sanctuary. He resented this latest intrusion, even if by his own brother.

Janos lifted a one-of-a-kind, eleventh-century medicine vial and turned it over, tapping the bottom with his fingernail while eyeing the rest of the curiosities on the desk. "She's already here. How was Brazil?"

"Loud." Istvan grabbed the artifact with his white-gloved hands and set it back on its special stand. He'd trained the staff to respect his wishes and keep their hands to themselves. But nothing was sacred to his brothers, who felt free to waltz in and rifle through centuries-old treasures as they used to ransack through each other's toy chests three decades back.

Janos—economist, two-time golf champion and superb yachtsman—was moving toward a side table and eyeing a medieval broadsword that had been brought in only that morning by a farmer who was digging a new well. A lot of discoveries were made like that. Istvan was itching to stop by for a look of his own. He had the farmer's invitation and full permission. All he had to do was find some time later in the week.

He could probably clear Friday morning, he decided as he came around his desk and deftly stepped between his brother and the sword.

Janos, older by a year, adjusted his impeccable tuxedo and fixed him with a look as he opened his mouth to speak.

Here it comes. The speech on how Istvan should pay as much attention to living things as inanimate objects. He heard that enough from his family to be able to recite it by heart. He shoved his hands into his jeans pockets, the only one of the royal brothers who would ever dress so low. He caught plenty of hell for it, too, the tabloids regularly mocking him as the worst-dressed of the princes. As if he didn't have bigger things to worry about.

"What are you going to do about her?" Janos asked, skipping the lecture, which was unlike him. He probably had the latest trouble in the financial markets on his mind.

"I'm not sending for her today." He'd decided that as soon as he had arrived that morning and was alerted to her presence at the palace. He was hoping to get out to the old palace wall before lunch to check on a small excavation there, one among two dozen projects he had going on simultaneously. "Maybe tomorrow. Or the day after."

His time was in even shorter supply than usual. The last of the summer sunshine poured in the oversize windows, reminding him that whatever excavations he wanted to finish this year, he better get on it. Soon the fall rains would slow all open-air digs to a crawl, then the winter freeze would stop surface work altogether until spring.

An amused look flashed across his brother's face. "I don't think she's the type to wait to be sent for."

"I know exactly what type she is," he muttered under

his breath then, watching Janos closely for any clues, asked, "Have you met her?" Janos was a fairly good judge of women, with experience that outpaced Istvan's by at least five to one.

"Have not had the pleasure. But I've been told she's already at work in the treasury. Seems very diligent. Certainly an interesting woman from what I hear." His brother moved on to the glass-front display cabinets. "Your office is starting to look like a warehouse again. Time to send a few boxes over to the museum. Learn to let go. Anyone ever told you that?"

Istvan was thinking about how long he could put off the meeting without appearing inexcusably rude, so his brain caught up with his brother's words a few seconds late. "What treasury?" His muscles jerked, and he nearly knocked over a vase by his elbow, a unique piece that had taken the better part of a month to piece together.

He steadied the copper coil stand, his jaw muscles tightening. "Who authorized it?"

"There's only one treasury at the royal palace. And I believe Chancellor Egon gave her the go-ahead. Did I tell you I finally got a golf GPS? Gives accurate distance to any key point on any golf course." He was grinning like a kid at Christmas. "You should get one."

Istvan strode for the door, his mind as far from golf as possible. "Come." He gestured with impatience when he was forced to wait for Janos to follow. Once they were both out, he turned the key in the door, then pocketed it—he didn't like the way Janos had been looking at that sword—then he took off down the hallway as if the devil was after him.

But the devil was ahead of him, in fact.

"It could be worse," Janos called out with undisguised glee. "The Chancellor could have brought her here to make you marry her."

He barely paid attention to his brother's words. The Chancellor had given up his mad quest to see all the princes married just to gain good publicity for the royal family. The unfortunate marital consultant who'd come all the way from New York City to see Lazlo settled had eaten poison meant for the prince and nearly died of it. All worked out well at the end; Lazlo married her in a stunning turn of events. But the Chancellor lost his taste for matchmaking after that.

Which meant the remaining three Kerkay brothers who were still single could breathe easy for now. Although, to be fair, Istvan almost rather would have been forced to marry than be forced to share his treasures with *that* woman. Because he didn't plan on falling in love again, an arranged marriage would have suited him fine. For certain, he wouldn't put up such a fuss as Lazlo had when his matchmaker arrived. When the time came for Istvan to take that blow, he'd take it on the chin and be done with it.

He strode across the reception room without looking in the floor-to-ceiling Venetian mirror, a gift to one of his ancestors from a sixteenth-century doge, but made a mental note that a minor repair job of the silver backing still had to be scheduled. He pulled off his white cotton gloves and shoved them into his pocket, exited the room and ran down the long hallway that led to the treasury—to hell with decorum.

The guards at the door snapped their heels together in greeting. He went through, nodding to the next set of guards in the antechamber. Then he burst through the door to the treasury proper, a large hall with tables covered in velvet, giant bank safes lining one wall, another hosting hundreds of secured deposit boxes.

Priceless rugs, left behind by the Turkish invasion four hundred years ago, were kept in a climate-controlled chamber, along with some elaborately studded and painted war chests. Artwork that wasn't on display at the moment in the palace was kept in a side room, exhibited there in all its splendid glory.

"Your Highness." Chancellor Egon came forward and made the introductions.

"Your Highness." The woman measured up Istvan as she did a rather understated curtsy. She wore white gloves meant to protect museum artifacts, identical to the ones he'd just taken off.

Probably so she wouldn't leave fingerprints. She wasn't fooling him. Once an art thief, always an art thief—he believed that with his whole heart. As far as he was concerned, Lauryn Steler was only one small step above a tomb raider, which had been her father's sordid occupation, in fact.

She and her kind stood for everything he spent his life fighting against.

"Miss Steler." Greeting her politely took effort, but

good manners had been hammered into all six princes at an early age. He did stop short, however, of telling her that she was welcome at the palace.

"Chancellor Egon was about to show me the coronation vault." She beamed, either not noticing the slight or choosing to ignore it.

Fury that had been rising inside him now bubbled dangerously close to the surface. "How kind of him." His voice had enough edge to cut through the seven-layer titanium alloy that still stood between her and his heritage, the sacred symbols of his country and his family.

The Chancellor stiffened and took a step back, giving him a worried look. "Your Highness, I was merely—"

"I'll take over here. You may leave."

"Certainly, Your Highness." The Chancellor backed out without argument. He'd lost a lot of his bluster and bossiness after the mishap with Lazlo. He wasn't exactly malleable, but he no longer butted heads with the princes over every little thing either.

The woman was still politely smiling. Her mouth was a tad too wide to be called aristocratic, but nevertheless, some people would have found her face pleasant. She didn't seem to have caught a single whiff of doom in the air.

"This is exciting," she said.

Either she was beyond belief impertinent or incredibly dense. Given her reputation, Istvan didn't think it was the latter.

"Isn't it?" He didn't bother forcing a smile, welcoming

or otherwise. "I imagine it's the first time you've seen something like this."

"Yes, yes, it is." Her green-gold eyes looked a little too wide with innocence.

Of course, she'd been in a treasury before. In Portugal, he seemed to remember now something he'd heard about her a while back. If half the rumors about her were true, she'd been the best art thief who had ever lived.

She certainly dressed like a cat burglar. A pair of tight-fitting black slacks covered her long legs, her black short-sleeved shirt leaving her toned arms bare. She was as perfectly proportioned as a painting by the grand masters, her eyes mesmerizing, her skin translucent, her lines magnificent. Her copper hair was pulled into a sleek ponytail to make sure it didn't get in her way.

The closer he looked, the easier he could see how she'd bewitched many of her victims in the past, even poor Chancellor Egon who'd been taken by her enough to open the treasury doors, of all things. *No fool like an old fool,* his father had been fond of saying.

Good thing Istvan was always a lot more interested in what lay below the surface of things. And in her heart of hearts, Lauryn Steler was a thief, the worst kind of villain. He didn't care if the whole world had forgotten that. *He* wouldn't.

"I've already seen a few pieces I would like to take," she told him as if she were at one of those abominable wholesale outlets of her country that sold mass-produced goods in batches.

"I'm sure you have."

If she weren't a consultant for the Getty Center in Los Angeles, one of the most respected museums in the world, his answer would have been, *Over my dead body*. But the board at the Getty had asked for a loan of Valtrian artifacts for a special exhibit. Then the treasure would embark on a trip, residing for three months each in the top-twenty most-prominent museums of the world.

Chancellor Egon had made cultural exchange his new quest. If he couldn't use another row of royal weddings to cheer up the people and raise the country's visibility abroad, then he would do it by parading Valtria's past all over creation. A very bad idea, Istvan had been saying from the beginning, but somehow the Chancellor gained the Queen's approval anyway.

Of course, as ill as the Queen was some days, the Chancellor could probably manipulate her into any agreement. Istvan had said as much to Arpad, but his eldest brother brushed off his concerns. The Crown Prince fully trusted the Chancellor.

Maybe he should have left the conference in Brazil and come back to the palace sooner, Istvan thought now, looking at the woman, still unsure what to do with her. She moved with sinuous grace as she considered the display cases, wandering away from him as if pulled by a magnet toward his country's treasures.

"Magnificent," she said with awe that didn't seem phony.

"And protected by state-of-the-art security," he mentioned in a note of forced nonchalance, not at all approving of that throaty, sexy voice of hers that didn't go with her sleek, crisp appearance.

Her voice belonged to a seductress swathed in silk in a candle-lit boudoir. He blinked that ridiculous image away. He didn't think Miss Steler spent much time reclining on satin pillows. He could, however, see her rappelling from high ceilings, or jumping roofs and disappearing with her latest loot strapped to her back, nearly invisible in the night.

He had a feeling that if quizzed, she could tell him the exact number and location of every security camera in the room, in addition to the content and worth of each display. The Getty sending her was a stunning oversight.

Their excuse was that none of her past transgressions could be proven. That they couldn't punish her for her father's sins. That even if she had a shady past once, she was reformed now, one-hundred-percent trustworthy and the best in the business.

"Shall we?" she was asking with unbridled optimism, nodding toward the safe door that protected the crown jewels.

He wished he could say, *When hell freezes over.* Instead, he stepped up to the iris scanner. "Istvan Kerkay," he said for the voice recognition software. And with a soft hiss, the hydraulic lock opened.

The lights inside came on automatically. He motioned for her to proceed first. As outraged as he was, he was still a gentleman.

She gave a soft gasp.

He didn't blame her. The sight had the same effect on him, and he'd been in here hundreds of times. In glass cases that lined the small chamber were the most important treasures of the kingdom. The crown without which there could be no coronation and no new king. The specter. The Queen's tiaras. A ceremonial sword with a gold-and-diamond handle that he remembered his father wearing when he'd been a kid. A robe woven from threads of gold, once worn at coronations but now put away for all prosperity as it had become too fragile to even touch.

There were other treasures. The most important of the Queen's jewels took up one long case. Another held the signet rings of all the old kings.

She moved to stand in front of the main case.

"None of those will be going anywhere, you understand," he told her. "There's a law forbidding any of the coronation jewels to leave the country." If the Queen traveled to visit other heads of state, she usually took one of the lesser crowns or a simple tiara.

She nodded, but seemed distracted, as if she'd barely heard him. From the corner of his eye, he caught her fingers twitching. She was flexing her hands inside her gloves.

Probably thinking that he'd open one of the cases and let her take something out for closer examination. *The temerity of her—* He stepped back, ready to get her out of the vault. Everything about her being in there shouted *wrong* and went against his most basic instincts. "So now that we're done here…"

That green-gold gaze flew to him, still filled with awe. Her delicate nostrils were trembling. "One more minute, please." She wasn't exactly begging, but she was close to it. There was a luminous quality to her all of a sudden, as if what she was seeing was lighting her up from the inside.

He understood exactly how she felt and resented having even this small thing in common with her. But he couldn't deny that he had felt like this dozens of times in the past when he stood over a new discovery. No amount of time would have been enough. And he wasn't about to indulge her, in any case.

"Maybe another time," he said, but thought, *Not as long as I live and breathe*.

She walked out as if leaving physically hurt her, moving as slowly as possible, glancing back frequently.

He sealed the door behind them and made a show of setting the locks, then pointed toward the back of the treasury. "I was thinking a few paintings and dresses." A number of those had been severely damaged over the centuries and had to be extensively restored. Save a few square centimeters here and there, little of them was original.

She looked back toward the vault and drew a deep breath before turning her attention to him. "I understand that you're reluctant to let anything go. But we have to keep in mind that whatever I take to the Getty will also be going around the world to represent your country."

She was making a play on his pride. Smart, but she

wasn't going to trap him as easily as that. "Be that as it may, the safety of the artifacts is my first concern."

"And mine, as well." Her chin came up, her eyes challenging him to bring up her past.

Of course, she could easily dismiss anything he said as malicious rumor. A prince did not stoop to repeating rumors in any case. He said nothing.

"I was thinking some of the artifacts left behind by the Brotherhood of the Crown," she told him after a moment, wiping the small, triumphant smile off her face so fast he might have imagined it. "They make a compelling story. Eight brothers, princes, coming together to save their country. They were brave and dashing. It's very romantic. I think their story is perfect to introduce Valtria to an American audience."

Definitely not artifacts of the Brotherhood. She was beginning to give him a headache. He'd returned from an overseas trip only that morning. He was tired and irritable, a dozen things clamoring for his immediate attention. He didn't have time for this.

"We have plenty of chances to discuss all that later. Now that you've seen the treasury, you should probably go and see the Royal Museum." Let her be somebody else's problem for a while. Her charm couldn't do much harm over there. She could ask for all she wanted, and the museum director could promise anything she could hoodwink out of him. All final decisions on the items that would go on tour were Istvan's. He could and would overrule any promise that felt injudicious to him.

She threw a disappointed, longing glance toward the

wall of safety boxes and the other vaults, then gathered herself. "Of course. The museum is on my itinerary." She looked around one more time. "Do you have some sort of an inventory of everything that's in here?"

"Color catalogs." A fine set. He'd put them together.

"I would love to take a look."

"I'll have them sent over to your hotel." After he decided which catalogs she could see.

He called a guard to escort her to the museum and stay with her. Then he took one last glance at the room, to make sure nothing was missing, before he headed back to his office.

But when he was sitting at his desk at last, ready to tackle his correspondence, he realized he was completely exhausted. He'd flown home on the red-eye from Brazil where he'd given an address at a conference as the head of the European Society of Social Anthropology. He could never sleep on anything that moved, forget the first-class fully reclining seats of the plane. He had motion sickness, worse than the plague for someone who traveled as much as he did.

He glanced at his watch. Maybe he could squeeze in thirty minutes of rest. He was used to taking short breaks like this when out in the field on a dig. They often had to work around the clock to beat collapsing tunnels or bad weather.

Going up to his suite would have taken too much time, so he simply let his head rest against the back of the chair, stretched his legs in front of him and folded his hands over his abdomen. But far from refreshing, his sleep was restless, his dreams disturbing.

He woke to desperate knocking on his door some time later, blinked hard while he ran his fingers through his hair, then adjusted the collar of his shirt as he sat up straight. Cleared his throat. "Come in."

Chancellor Egon burst through the door, breathing as hard as if he'd been doing laps around the grand ballroom. His eyes were wide with panic. "Miss Steler is missing."

"Is she now?" And good riddance. Things were looking up. She had probably assessed their security system, realized it was beyond her and given up whatever thieving plans she'd been nursing. Istvan's heart was suddenly lighter as he looked toward the upcoming week.

"We—" The Chancellor wrung his hands, apparently thinking this was some great tragedy. He was rather attached to the idea of the artifacts touring, his flying in for each opening and giving one of his interminable speeches on Valtrian glory. "We—"

"What is it?" Istvan glanced at the antique clock on the wall and realized he'd slept a lot longer than he'd meant to. His gaze slid to Amalia's photo in its silver frame under the clock, and his heart gave a painful thud as always. God, how he missed her.

He focused back on the Chancellor, who was still hemming and hawing. "Anything else?" He didn't have all day to waste on Miss Steler.

The Chancellor went pale as he said, "Your Highness, I'm afraid— I have to inform you—" He took a deep breath and spit it out at last. "I've come from the treasury. We can't find the crown jewels either."

Chapter Two

"I want the security tapes." Istvan paced the room. He wanted progress, and was getting anything but. No more than half an hour could have passed since he'd first received the news from the Chancellor, but, without answers, every minute of that time seemed unbearably long.

He was at the security offices on the basement level of the palace with Miklos, Janos and Arpad. Benedek was on a world tour with Rayne, his opera-diva wife, in South Africa at the moment. Lazlo was still on his honeymoon on some undisclosed Mediterranean island.

"There's no security footage." Miklos was seething, as well, ignoring the worried looks of some of the security personnel in the next room. He could be intimidating when angered, something that came from decades of army life. He could stare down a full platoon if needed. No doubt, he'd had already taken the staff to task.

"This wasn't a spur-of-the-moment thing. And if Miss Steler was involved, she didn't work alone," he said, and Istvan agreed.

That the bastards could take as much as they had in half an hour and seemingly turn into smoke was amazing. The crown jewels were just the tip of the iceberg, albeit the most important among the artifacts that had disappeared.

"The cameras went out?" he asked. "Don't we have backup?"

"We have an alarm that gets triggered if recording is stopped or if the tape is blank." Miklos's face hardened. "But recording kept going. We have half an hour of footage of Channel Three. Someone hacked into the system from the outside. That's not supposed to be possible."

"And the people whose job it was to watch the monitors?" Arpad asked.

"Killed."

The guards who'd protected the Royal Treasury had been murdered, as well. The mood in the office could not have been more grim.

"How sure are you that Miss Steler was involved?" Janos asked.

"One hundred percent. I showed her the treasury earlier. She begged Chancellor Egon to take her back there, telling him she needed to take more notes and think things over. She charmed him by asking for his help with the selection process." The whole story came out once the Chancellor had calmed down enough to talk. "When the Chancellor had to run off for a quick meeting, she convinced him to leave her locked in there so she could keep working until he returned. He left her with a guard."

"And when he went back, the guards were all dead, and Miss Steler and the loot were missing," Janos finished for him, still wearing a tux. He'd been pulled from a formal reception for the top economists of the nation. Istvan hated social obligations. Janos very much enjoyed that sort of thing.

"Lauryn Steler," Arpad was saying the name pensively, staring at the treasury's blueprint.

He should have seen it coming, Istvan thought. He should have fought harder to keep her from entering the country, or should have put her under heavy guard, or at the very least should have issued a preemptive order to forbid anyone from letting her near the treasury without his being present.

"When we find her, we'll find her team. Who is looking for her?" he asked, gathering his thoughts, pushing back on the regret and the anger. He needed to calm his mind to be able to think more clearly.

"The police and every man I have available. Every border station, airport, train station, bus station and shipping port has her name and picture," Miklos reassured him, but from the resignation in his voice it was clear that he knew how little those precautions meant in reality.

Someone like Lauryn Steler would have multiple passports and could switch between identities with ease. Hell, she could be anywhere by now, traveling as a gray-haired grandmother.

But she had to have left a trail, however faint.

Istvan reached a decision. "I'm going out there. I have contacts."

To break into the palace she had to have local help, and he knew most of the local bad boys in the stolen arts and artifacts world, and had helped to put some of them behind bars one time or another. Anybody hit one of his digs or cherished museums, he went after them with a vengeance. He knew exactly where to look, whom to pressure.

"We're going with you," his brothers said as one, moving closer together.

"A reassuring show of loyalty. Thank you. But it would only complicate things." A few years back, they had resurrected the Brotherhood of the Crown in secret, but in this case he was certain he'd be better off alone. "It'll be difficult enough for me to get out of the palace unnoticed and go around asking questions without attracting media attention."

Arpad looked as if he might argue the point, but then said, "A brief press conference about a security breach should keep the media busy in the press room. Nothing about the loss of the crown jewels, of course." He was always good at seeing the big picture and protecting others. All useful attributes for a Crown Prince.

"We have things on hand for undercover ops. Disguise." Miklos headed for the metal lockers in the back, the staff immediately clearing a path for him.

"I can distract your bodyguard while you leave the palace," Janos offered.

Due to prior attacks on the royal family, at least one

guard had to escort the princes at all times when they left the grounds, a recent royal order by the Queen that drove all of them crazy. They were all rather attached to their independence.

Miklos came back with a box. "While you're scouring the underworld for tips, I'll investigate how they got in and out. I already have a forensics team over at the treasury. Whatever they find should give us some clues to follow."

Janos and Arpad were heading off, clapping Istvan on the shoulder.

"Stay safe," Janos said.

"And bring the crown back," Arpad added. "If we can get everything back in a few days, nobody needs to know what happened. If we can't, we'll deal with it then."

They all agreed on that, given the sharp political climate and their mother's health. The Queen was feeling poorly again. Istvan swore he would solve this latest disaster before news could reach her and put more stress on her system.

His hands fisted at his sides. This wasn't just an attack on the treasury. This was a direct attack on his family and his heritage, the two things most important to him.

"I'll bring back the coronation jewels and see to it that Lauryn Steler pays miserably for taking them," he promised.

NIGHT HAD FALLEN BY the time he found the first usable clue. He'd dealt with thieves in the past and had a network of informants, one of whom came through half an hour earlier. The meeting left a bad taste in Istvan's mouth. Now he owed a favor he knew he was going to hate paying back. But he understood that sometimes he had to compromise on smaller issues to obtain something that was even more important.

The man had heard of something going down at the South Side shipyard tonight. A cousin of his worked there and blabbed about a recent bribe. Istvan had called in the tip and agreed with Miklos that a large-scale search would only draw attention and maybe even allow the thieves to escape in the confusion.

And he wasn't sure if anything would pan out here anyway. For all he knew, this could be some minor drug deal. He didn't want to pull Miklos's men who were doing random vehicle checks on the highways and had as much chance of finding something as he did. But he did accept the five corporate security guards Janos sent from his company.

Hungry and tired, he watched the shipyard, alert for any movement. Hundreds of metal shipping crates were piled in orderly rows, giant cranes towering over them. He was near the loading docks, but with the shipyard lit up, he could see even the dry docks in the distance and the small cruise ship that was currently under repair.

"Six vessels at the loading docks," came the latest intel through his headset.

"We'll split up," he ordered and moved forward to the first in line, a flat-bottomed riverboat.

Since Valtria had no seaport, they used these boats

to take cargo down through Italy to the mouth of the river. The shipping containers were then transferred to much larger ocean liners and made their way to various worldwide destinations from there.

He took the first boat and realized quickly that he'd made a mistake. The containers were all empty, damaged. They were probably going no farther than the factory four miles down the river where they would be recycled. He checked the crew's cabins and the engine house anyway, but found no one and nothing of interest. The boat was completely deserted.

He scratched his nose, his face itching under the disguise Miklos had concocted. At least the sun was below the horizon, so he was no longer sweating.

He sneaked back down the plank and caught sight of a small boat on the water, headed for shore. No lights. The motor wasn't going either, no other sound disturbing the night but the waves gently lapping the docks. The boat drifted, although clearly there was someone at the helm.

Istvan could think of only one reason why the man would want to remain unnoticed. He probably had something to hide. He could have come from the riverboat moored in the middle of the water. It must have been loaded earlier in the day and was still waiting for some permit and the go-ahead, but the captain had been kind enough to leave the loading dock so another vessel could take his place. South Side Port was often crowded.

The captain would get his papers first thing in the morning when the office opened and be off posthaste to

wherever he was going. Except, as Istvan watched, the
riverboat pulled up anchor and began moving with the
current. A quiet departure in the middle of the night.

His instincts prickled even as he realized that every
moment he hesitated, the riverboat would only move
farther away from him. He jumped without thought, hit
the cold water and came up for air, felt his pocketknife
slip from his pocket, grabbed after it, but couldn't find
it in the dark. Damn. At least he still had his gun. He
shoved it tighter into his waistband, then swam as fast
as he could, carried by the current, grateful that the man
in the boat didn't seem to notice him, hadn't heard the
splash.

All the princes were strong swimmers. Soon, he
caught up with the impossibly long boat and went around
the propellers, then grabbed on to a rope that had been
carelessly left to trail the water.

He climbed up with effort, his hands wet and slippery, but eventually he vaulted over the side and ducked
down just in time. A handful of men loitered on deck
ahead, around an open shipping container. He caught the
glint of a rifle, which helped him decide that he'd seen
enough to have Port Authority stop and search the ship.
Even if the crown jewels weren't on board, something
else most certainly was that shouldn't have been.

He reached for his radio to call in the information,
settling into a spot where he could remain unseen in
the meantime and keep an eye on the container and the
men.

But the radio was dead, water dripping from the

earpiece. Same with his cell phone. He should have called before he'd jumped into the river. Miklos would have thought of that. Arpad, too. But they were military. As much time as he spent in the field and even fancied himself an adventurer, Istvan was an academic, not a soldier.

But all was not lost, he thought, when the men were called to the pilot's cabin, leaving the container un-locked and free for him to search the contents. He would have specific information when he swam back to shore to alert Port Authority. Maybe slipping back into the water quietly, right now, would have been the smartest thing, but he couldn't be this close to the royal treasure and not know for sure.

He crept forward, keeping in the shadows, aware that he was leaving a wet trail on deck. The late summer night was warm with a slight breeze. With some luck, his tracks would dry before anyone came this way.

The possibility of a find drew him forward as it had many times in the past. He could hear voices up ahead, but didn't see anyone, and he was too far away to make out what they were saying. He kept an eye out for Lauryn, listened for her voice. If the crown jewels were on the ship, she had to be somewhere around, as well. Someone like her would never let treasure like this too far from her, not until she handed it over to her buyer. He didn't think that had happened yet. The stolen artifact business in Valtria was relatively small-time, thanks to his efforts. The more he thought about it, the more trouble he had picturing any of the known players with enough money to pay for something this big, even at devalued black market prices.

And if the buyer was foreign, Lauryn's fee would include delivering the goods safely to him, smuggling everything neatly out of the country.

Her face and figure floated into his mind unbidden, a mocking smile on her lips and the light of satisfaction in her eyes. She had to be laughing her behind off at how easy it had been to trick them all, to trick *him*. He pressed his lips together as he swore in silence to wipe that smile off her face at the earliest opportunity. The thing to remember was that she was even more dangerous than he'd thought. He wouldn't make the mistake of underestimating her again.

He made his way to the container without trouble, but other than carefully stacked crates, he saw little in the darkness. He pulled the gun, then stepped inside. At least the gun would work. Miklos had assured him that it was the latest and greatest military model and, among other things, water-resistant. Good thing, since he'd forgotten to consider that, too, before jumping in the water.

He tried the first crate. Nailed down. Ten minutes of looking around brought him no luck with the others, so he moved farther in, hoping he would find something to pry those nails loose with.

Nothing.

But he did find an open crate at the very end of the line. And the thirteenth-century war chest inside was more than familiar. His heart beat faster as he ran his fingers over the wood, polished by hundreds of hands through history, some of the paint worn off in places. For the first time since he'd laid eyes on Lauryn Steler, he smiled, because if the men on the ship had one thing from the treasury, then most likely they had the rest of the stolen treasure, as well. The coronation jewels *would* be recovered.

He opened the chest, not expecting to find much, but was rewarded by the sight of Lauryn's notebook and pen, further proof of her involvement. He left them there, trying the next crate but only the one with the war chest had been opened. Still, he was certain now that he had what he'd been looking for right here.

Part of him didn't want to let the crates out of his sight. Another part knew that to save them he had to get help. The sooner he made contact and had the riverboat stopped, the better. He headed out reluctantly, not looking forward to getting back into the night water, but ready to do whatever was required to stop Lauryn and her gang of criminals.

But then two things happened at the same time. He heard—but could not see from behind a stack of crates—men at the door, metal creaking as they worked to seal the container for the journey. And Lauryn Steler stepped out in front of him with something in her hands, cutting him unaware, hitting him on the head so hard that he staggered backward.

After that, he could neither see nor hear.

LAURYN LOOKED OVER THE man's prone body, her heart going a mile a minute. Not that she would let a little adrenaline rush shake her. She'd been in tighter spots than this and had escaped.

Being trapped here didn't scare her nearly as much as the implications of this whole incident. She'd sweated blood over the past couple of years to earn trust in the art industry, to change her reputation. If even a shadow of doubt fell on her regarding this heist, her new career would be over. Her new life as she knew it would cease to exist. She would lose everything.

And Prince Istvan would be the first to crucify her. He wouldn't care if she were guilty or innocent. She'd seen that look in his eyes. If he'd had his way, he would have had her arrested just for thinking of coming near his treasury. He was as judgmental as he was good-looking. Too bad, because she truly respected what he had achieved in his field. He was an amazing archaeologist and practically the patron saint of preservation. But he wouldn't give her the benefit of the doubt.

Nobody would after this.

Once again, she felt the tentacles of her past reach for her, wrap around her and squeeze. She shivered, as if her body was trying to shake them off.

She could see little; not much moonlight filtered in through the small rust holes on top. The man's shape was familiar, but his face wasn't. He had a dark mustache and a nose that looked as if it had been broken at one point. He was no threat to her. She'd taken off his belt and tied him up, gagged him with an oily rag she'd found in a corner.

The bad news was, she was now locked in the damned

container. The good news was, she had at least nailed one of the bastards and had his gun, although she hadn't the faintest idea what to do with it. But if things went badly, he might come in handy as a hostage.

She sat with her back against a crate and waited for him to wake. She didn't have to wait long.

His dark gaze found her and focused on her as soon as his eyes popped open. He struggled against his restraints. She let him. If he wanted to tire himself out, that was fine by her. She didn't worry about the belt giving. She knew a hundred ways to tie a knot, one for every purpose.

"Hmm." He made an unintelligible noise as he glared.

"Stay put and stay quiet," she told him. Then it occurred to her that he could be a source of information. Knowing who these people were and where they were heading might help her better engineer her escape.

Or, if he wasn't with those men, he could tell her who on earth he was. Because now that she thought about it, why would they send one of their own into the container and then lock him in? If they knew that this guy was here, wouldn't they have come looking for him when he didn't return?

She held the gun on him while tugging the gag free from his mouth with her other hand. The threat was implicit.

He understood and didn't shout. "I should have had you barred from the country," he said, enraged but keeping it at a low decibel level.

That voice, those eyes… And her heart about stopped. "Your Highness?" She reached for the mustache on reflex. It came away in her hand. She jerked back, knowing that in some kingdoms, the touching of a royal person without his or her permission was punishable by death. Not that she thought Valtria was that archaic, but truth be told, she wasn't comfortable with touching its hostile prince.

"The nose piece, too," he ordered, then added in a less angry voice, "It itches."

There was her permission. She felt his skin and found the ridge, pulled off an oddly shaped 3D bandage kind of something that blended in perfectly while changing the shape of his nose. Her mind was spinning like a whirligig, but couldn't come up with an explanation for his sudden appearance. "What are you doing here?"

"I could ask the same, but let's not pretend we both don't know the answer to that." He seemed to be choking with barely controlled anger. "This has been your plan all along. You pulled it off. Congratulations."

The accusation felt like a kick in the face. "Right. I plan a good kidnapping at least once a year. To others, it might be cumbersome, but to me, it's like a vacation," she snapped, hating that he would immediately think the worst of her, even if it was exactly what she'd expected.

"If you're not guilty of anything, then there's no reason for you to be scared of me. You can put the gun down and untie me." He struggled to a sitting position, taking over even though he was practically her prisoner.

He was tall and lean, wide-shouldered and dark-eyed like the rest of his brothers. According to the media, he was the least social of the princes, something of an introvert.

Now that they'd met twice, she could certainly see why. Probably nobody could tolerate his paranoia and temper. Too bad. She'd come to the country with nothing but respect for the man and his body of work.

"I'm not scared of you," she told him. Not that he wasn't physically powerful, but she had plenty of moves he hadn't seen yet. "But while I know I'm not guilty, you're too prejudiced and stubborn to believe that. And if you tried something…" He should know that she wasn't going to stand still while he steamrolled over her. "I've worked hard to change my reputation and achieve the standing I have in this business. I wouldn't want to ruin it by shooting a prince."

He swore under his breath in French.

"Hey, I understood that."

He glared. "So why don't you tell me your perfectly innocent version of events." His voice dripped with sarcasm. "Maybe you can convince me."

If only. But it wasn't as if she had anything better to do. A long tale might calm him enough so that she could untie him. She had to do that eventually. He was a prince. Despite what she'd said, she probably wouldn't shoot him. But she couldn't set him free until she could be sure that he wouldn't try to overtake her and tie her up in turn. One of them would get hurt. And because he was a prince, she had a feeling that whatever the outcome of such a struggle would be, it wouldn't be to her advantage.

"After you barely let me take a look at the artifacts in the treasury, I realized you were going to do your best not to let me back in there. I asked the Chancellor, who is a true gentleman by the way, to allow me some more time. I figured that was my only chance to do a thorough job and make sure I made the right choices." The treasury was simply breathtaking, the most amazing place she'd ever seen. She wished—for a multitude of reasons—that they were both still back there.

"How convenient that the Chancellor had to step out," he said with derision.

"Not at all. He was most helpful about the history of some of the objects. And he was very entertaining. A gracious host." Unlike the prince had been, she thought, but left that part unspoken. No sense annoying an already-angry lion, even if he was tied and she had a gun on him.

"Which probably wouldn't have stopped you from murdering him if he didn't have to leave. Are you aware that nine men were killed? Men with wives and children who grieve them. Or were you rushing too fast to count?"

The anger in his voice was like a physical force, overwhelming and real. She thought of the young guard the Chancellor had left with her, and drew a slow breath. The man had pimples, for heaven's sake. Couldn't have been more than early twenties. Now he was dead, and others, as well.

"Fine, so it's not fair that they died and I lived." She pressed her lips together for a second, feeling the guilt, hating the prince for placing more blame on her and adding to the weight. "I was in the enclosure with the carpets and the war chests. We heard a commotion in front of the door. The guard rushed toward it. I thought I heard something that sounded like a gun being fired with a silencer. I slipped into the nearest war chest just as the door opened."

He had the gall to laugh at that. "Oh, an innocent bystander. A victim even. Well done, Miss Steler. You're a very creative woman. If my hands were free, I would clap."

Keep it up and we'll never be free. "Fine. Think what you will." She stood and walked away from him.

"Thank you," he called after her, as arrogant and full of himself as ever. "I think I'll do that."

She checked the door. Locked, just as she'd suspected. If she had her old tools, it wouldn't have posed a problem, but she had nothing with her save a pen and a notebook that she'd left on the bottom of the chest in which she'd hidden. She'd figured whoever was breaking in would go for gold. How was she to know that they would take the war chest, too?

She walked back to Istvan. "Where are we exactly?"

"On a ship called *Valtrian Freedom*, heading south, not that you don't know that better than I do. Out of curiosity, who is your buyer?"

She shoved the gun in the back of her pants so she

could put her hands on her hips. She simply watched him for a while, trying to decide whether reasoning with him would be a waste of breath. It would be. But she found she couldn't help herself.

"First, I don't steal. Second, even if I did, I'd never be stupid enough to steal crown jewels. Not very low-profile, is it? And not marketable either. They're easily recognizable. As stolen artifacts, they'd be completely useless. The safest way would be selling the stones separately and melting down the gold, but that's such a small fraction of their value. And a good thief could easily steal gold and gems from a number of other sources with a lot less difficulty."

He stared at her without a response. Apparently, her words had given him something to think about. Not long enough. "Maybe it doesn't make sense, but it doesn't have to," he said after a while. "It could have been a crime of passion. You saw the coronation jewels and you couldn't resist them."

She shook her head. "You know it as well as I do that this wasn't a spur-of-the-moment thing. This was a carefully planned and meticulously executed heist. There are not that many people in the world who have crews that can pull off something like this. And I'm not one of them."

"No longer one of them?" he pushed. "Or are the rumors true and you always worked alone?"

She said nothing to that. She never discussed her past.

"You know these crews?"

Again, she remained silent.

"If you didn't do this, do you have any idea who did?"

She shook her head.

She'd thought about little else while she'd been hiding in the chest. She had plenty of time on the way over here, then while she waited for the men to walk away from the container. Then she finally opened the top, busted the crate's lid and climbed out. The container door had still been open. But she hesitated too long between escaping and staying with the royal treasures.

Then someone came in, and she thought it was one of the thieves, about to discover her. So she'd done what she had to. But while she was busy with him, the door had been sealed and she'd lost the option of leaving.

"Could you untie the belt? You may keep the gun," he said.

"Aren't you the magnanimous one? You're in no position to negotiate," she reminded him, but untied him anyway. He was considering other options at least and didn't look as if he would attack her on the spot.

He rubbed his hands over his wrists, closed his eyes for a second, and for a moment looked almost vulnerable. Must have been a trick of the shadows.

"Are you okay?" she asked anyway before she could stop herself. She did hit him over the head pretty hard back there.

His fierce frown was an immediate rebuke. "Fine."

"Let me look at you." She leaned forward to check

his irises, chancing that he might grab for the gun, but couldn't see much in the dark.

He drew back as if offended. "That's not necessary."

"Do you have any nausea? I could have given you a concussion." Considering the way he'd been treating her, she felt only mildly guilty.

"You didn't."

"You don't know that. Anyway, if you feel sleepy, try to stay awake."

"I do not have a concussion," he said, stiff-lipped.

His obstinacy was ticking her off on every level. "You're too tough to get a concussion from a girl, is that it?"

He came to his feet and strode away from her, stopped as far as the crate allowed, then stared back. An image of buffalo came into her mind, pawing the snow, blowing steam out of his nose. No need to share that with him.

She gave him a minute before she followed. "How far is the nearest seaport?"

"Trieste would be two hours at the most."

She considered options and backup options, trying to come up with an escape plan. "What do you think will happen when we get there?"

"If we're lucky, they'll open the container to transfer the stolen goods. That'll give us a chance to make a break for it."

"I don't believe in luck." She peered through the darkness and tried to map the place.

The prince gave a brief nod. "Me neither."

So for two hours they searched every corner, tried to find a weak spot where they could break out—there wasn't one—and made plans on what they'd do once the riverboat reached port and the container would be opened.

Except that it wasn't.

No sooner did the boat stop moving than they felt the container lift as a crane hoisted it in the air. She slid against the prince who in turn slid against the back wall, then shifted quickly to the side, saving them from being crushed to death by some unstable crates.

He wedged himself into the corner and held off what had to be a couple of hundred pounds with his bare hands. Then the container settled with a loud clunk and everything stopped moving.

"I take it this would be the ocean liner," she said, a little rattled, which annoyed her. She didn't like thinking that the prince might have just saved her. She prided herself on being a self-sufficient woman. She didn't want to owe anything to any stuck-up, prejudiced Valtrian royalty.

She handed his gun back to him, a kind of payback, she supposed.

"I'm not too keen on going on an ocean voyage at the moment." Prince Istvan strode to the front and pointed at the lock from the inside. "Are you sure you can't open this?"

"Not with my bare hands." That was as close to admitting her shady past as she was comfortable with.

"I have a tool for you." He pointed the mean-looking handgun in the general direction. "Show me where to shoot."

"It'll be too loud."

"Not if I shoot just as they rattle the next container into place."

She felt around in the near darkness, then grabbed the barrel of the gun and pressed it against the right spot. "Here."

He aimed. They waited. Then when they could hear chains creak and the corner of the next container bump against another, he squeezed off a shot. Inside the container, the sound seemed deafening. But she had a feeling that with all the machinery and the noise of the harbor outside, it had been barely noticeable. Still, they waited a few minutes. When no one raised the alarm and no one came to investigate, the prince drew back, then slammed his shoulder into the door before she could stop him.

That had to hurt. She winced.

"Patience." She stepped over to examine the damage to the lock. "You'll need at least one more shot."

Except that the crane seemed to move on to the other side of the ship. He waited on the spot anyway, in case the crane came back. It didn't. An hour or so later they felt the ship shudder, the engines start and the ground move under their feet. Istvan used that distraction to fire off his second shot, which did the trick at last.

This time when he shoved his shoulder into the door, it opened.

Four inches.

Just enough for them to see that they were blocked in by another container in front of them.

"Trapped." She closed her eyes for a moment against the disappointment and frustration. She could have banged her head against the metal. They should have done something much sooner, on the riverboat. But the prince had thoroughly distracted her, and now it was too late. The very reason she always worked alone. A partner was nothing but trouble.

"Going in an unknown direction on a strange ship," he thought out loud. His voice sounded off.

"A ship that's controlled by criminals." Not that she blamed all this on him. Maybe a little. If he'd let her do her work in the treasury earlier, she would have been done and gone by the time the thieves got there. He would have still suspected her, but she could have been dealing with that unfair cloud of suspicion at the five-star hotel where the Getty was putting her up, instead of here.

"Or your friends. Although, the two might not be mutually exclusive, I suspect." Apparently, he still harbored some mistrust of her.

"People we don't want to meet up with," she offered as compromise. "At this point, if they found us, they'd kill both of us. They sure didn't hesitate shooting the guards at the treasury." The memory turned her mood even more somber. "And they *will* find us. If not sooner, then when they come to get the loot."

The more she thought of that, the bigger that lead ball grew in her stomach.

And bigger yet when he said, "Just so we're clear, I still think that you're involved in this in some way. And when we get out of here and I return the crown jewels to the treasury, I *will* figure out what your role has been. And then I'll personally see to it that you're prosecuted to the full extent of Valtrian law, Miss Steler."

Chapter Three

His stomach rolled with each wave that the ship encountered and there was an endless supply of those. When he went on longer trips, he usually took a pill to counter his motion sickness. There'd be no relief here.

Istvan leaned back against a crate as he sat on the ground, his arms resting on his pulled-up knees. He was passing the time by mentally listing his theories about Lauryn. Either she was in the container because she stole the treasure and wanted to stay as close to it as possible. Or because she'd stolen the treasure and then had a falling-out with her partners who locked her in. Or she'd witnessed the treasure being stolen while she was looking for pieces for the Getty, the heist got her blood heated and she followed the treasure, thinking she could take it from the thieves and keep it for herself. He didn't give much credit to her claims of being completely innocent.

"Are you sure you don't have a concussion?" she asked him, sitting opposite.

He resented her concern, given that it was more than

likely that she had something to do with their current circumstances. "Quite certain."

That only kept her quiet for a minute.

"We have no food or water," she said, stating the obvious.

"A good thing, because we don't have a toilet either," he said just to torture her.

She pursed her lips as she stood. "That's it, then. I'm getting out of here."

She did have an indomitable spirit, he had to give her that. "How?"

"I'm going to think of something."

"Happy thoughts will give you wings?" he mocked her.

"You can't underestimate the power of positive thinking."

Or the power of self-delusion, he thought, hoping she wouldn't get going and give him a motivational seminar.

She was staring straight up, as if expecting inspiration to drop from heaven. "How many more bullets do you have left?" she asked after a few minutes.

Great, here came the brilliant idea. He checked his gun, not keen on handing it back to her. "Ten."

"Do you have any matches?"

"How about a lighter?" He didn't smoke, but he always carried one, along with a pocketknife. Now and then they came in handy at a dig.

"Can I have it with five of the bullets?"

"What for?"

"There's light coming in. Which means rust spots in the top of the container. Weakness. A small explosion could peel back enough for us to squeeze through." She eyed the crates.

He didn't think she was kidding. "You can build a bomb?"

She didn't respond, only held out her hand, as good as an admission—of her bomb-making skills and her past.

After thinking it over and realizing they had few other options, he counted out five bullets for her. "You might see why I was reluctant to put you in charge of a traveling exhibit of Valtrian treasures."

She closed her fingers around the bullets and the lighter. "The skills I have might yet save your treasures."

He couldn't argue with that, so he said nothing. He simply watched as she scaled the crates, a sleek shadow moving swiftly, higher and higher until she disappeared on top. He pulled his dropped chin back into place.

"Do you need help?" he asked belatedly. He wanted out of here and she seemed to want the same thing. Whatever hidden agenda she had, for now it looked as if they were working toward the same goal. They might as well work together. "I can help."

Now and then the setting of charges was necessary at an excavation, although, due to the high risk of damage, he employed that tool as rarely as possible and always had an expert handle it. But he wasn't uncomfortable around explosives.

"Stay covered in case there's flying shrapnel," she called down from her perch.

Shards of steel flying from the top of the container, he realized, were a definite possibility. He looked at the crates. The wood boards were thick enough to protect the contents, his first concern. "And you?" he asked as an afterthought.

"I'll deal."

He started forward. "Look, I—"

A small explosion cut him off, which did send some shrapnel flying and shook the tower of crates Lauryn had climbed.

"Are you okay?" he called up as the dust settled.

"Of course I am."

"They had to have heard that." He put his disguise back on, hoping he got the mustache straight. His swim over to the riverboat had washed off some of the glue. He'd have to be careful not to lose the damn thing completely.

"There're plenty of other noise with all engines going full-steam. And even if they heard us, it'll take them a while to figure out where the noise came from. They might think it was just two containers sliding against each other." She peeked down at him. "The way is clear. Whenever you're ready."

He wasn't one of those super-macho types, but the fact that *she* would be rescuing *him* rubbed him the wrong way. His masculine pride prickled as he climbed the crates. They swayed the whole time, which didn't help his motion sickness.

She was already halfway through the hole when he got there, her shapely behind dangling practically in front of his face. "Watch the edges. They're pretty sharp." She grunted. "I could use a hand here."

For a moment he hesitated, not sure where or how to touch her. He ended up bracing her thighs, which seemed to do the trick. Her muscles flexed against his palms. He ignored the way that made him feel.

She hoisted herself up at last. "Come on."

He tried. There wasn't enough room for his shoulders. But he was good at navigating tight spots. He'd spent a lot of time in underground funeral chambers, squeezing through impossible passageways. He twisted, angling one shoulder up, and turning the right way to be able to clear the hole without losing too much skin.

The cool night air felt like heaven on his face.

He sat next to the hole and drew a couple of deep breaths, hoping to steady his stomach. She was already moving along, going for even higher ground, easily climbing the side of another container. He went after her, only succeeding with effort even though he had the advantage of upper-body strength.

She was looking all around when he caught up with her. "Any idea where we are? I can't see the lights of the land."

Neither could he, which meant that swimming to shore now was out of the question. He looked up at the sky to get his bearings. "Heading southeast for now." Of course, that was pretty much a given. They had to get out of the Adriatic. "Once we reach the Mediterranean

Sea, we'll see if the ship is heading toward Asia, Africa or for the Atlantic."

"How soon will we know?"

"In a couple of hours." They were traveling at a good clip.

"Any idea what we could do in the meanwhile?"

He looked out over the vast rows of containers and could make out the bridge up front. He drew a deep breath. "We could try taking over the ship."

HER IDEAS HAD BEEN more along the line of jumping ship and swimming for shore, but she could see the white froth of the waves in the moonlight. The water was too rough, the mainland too far away.

"Look." She pointed toward the starboard side.

A half-dozen men were walking the ship with flashlights.

"Maybe they heard the explosion," Istvan observed.

"Or it's a routine check. To make sure the containers are all steady and well-secured. They'd want to know that before the ship goes out to the ocean."

The muscles in his cheeks seemed to tighten as she said *ocean*. And she noticed how tightly he was hanging on to the edge of the container as the whole ship swayed.

Several pieces fell into place. "Are you seasick?"

"Certainly not," he said with heat, which told her she'd hit a nerve.

She sat back on her heels as she examined him. She didn't picture him having any weaknesses. He'd been nothing less than formidable from the moment they'd met. She couldn't help a relieved smile.

"I'm always glad when I can use my misery to entertain others," he groused.

"Having weaknesses makes a person more approachable. You can be harsh, you know." She paused. "You probably do. You probably do it on purpose. I wasn't looking forward to working with you, to be honest."

He pulled up an eyebrow. "The feeling is completely mutual."

She smiled again, at his unflinching honesty, the first thing she liked about the prince.

"Do you always take so much delight in other people's misfortune?" he asked in a wry tone.

"Sorry." She reached back and unhooked her necklace, pulled the round eye hook off with her teeth, rolled off all the pearls save two. She stashed the free pearls in her pocket, then with four knots she secured the remaining two about three finger widths apart. "Give me your wrist."

"I don't wear jewelry."

"Please, you're royalty."

"I wear some symbols of the monarchy on ceremonial occasions," he corrected.

She held his gaze.

"I don't have a problem."

"This will help the problem you don't have."

After a moment of glaring at her, he held out his left hand. She fastened the string so the pearls would be on the inside of his wrist, pressing against the nerves there.

"What is this?" He examined her concoction dubiously, while she made a matching one for his other wrist.

"An acupressure bracelet. My father used to be seasick. He was terrible. You've never seen that shade of purple. He looked like a walking Monet painting when it hit him bad."

The darkening of his face told her that bringing up her father might have been a mistake. "He was a good man, in his own way," she added, feeling the need to defend the man who'd kept her fed and clothed, alive for the first part of her life.

He remained stoic. "Forgive me if I don't take your word for it."

After a moment of silence, he climbed from the top of the container onto the top of the row below them, then down several more levels to the deck. He strode forward between the rows, going pretty fast, pulling into cover each time he reached a gap between two containers.

He was probably trying to make sure the men who were checking the load didn't see him, she thought and copied him. Then they reached the last row and there was nothing but empty deck in front of them and the bridge about a hundred feet away.

He waited and watched.

"What are we looking for?" she asked from behind him.

"I want to know how many men are on this ship and

if they're all armed. Some of these ocean liners work with skeleton crews. Everything's computerized these days."

"That the men at the treasury could take out all those guards means they must have been armed to the teeth."

"Those men might not be here. They could have a connection in shipping who agreed to smuggle the goods out of the country. There could be only a handful of bad apples on this ship, the rest of the crew and the captain honest men. In which case, we can ask for their help. Maybe taking over the ship isn't our only option. It could be as easy as capturing and immobilizing a couple of bad guys."

He was talking as if he believed her innocence at last, but she noticed that he made a point of not turning his back to her. Still, at least he was willing to work with her. They could sort out the rest once they escaped. At least they were no longer locked in. She was feeling more optimistic by the minute.

But their hopes seemed unjustified when, a few seconds later, the patrolling seamen came into view, armed. Every last one of them.

She held her breath and pulled close to Istvan, the two of them sandwiched together in a small gap between two containers, her breasts pressed against his back as she peeked over his shoulder. This was the closest they'd been to each other, and she was suddenly aware of his well-built body, his wide shoulders, the strength of the man as he stood in front of her.

He had his gun in his hand, his other hand holding her back, his feet slightly apart. His body language couldn't have been clearer. If anyone wanted to get to her, they had to go through him. A strange feeling seeped through her, part indignation that he would assume she needed protection, part something else.

She wasn't used to feeling protected by men.

She'd certainly never been protected by her father who'd used her even as a small child as his "little helper" in his often dangerous business. Sure, she'd been sheltered and fed, but she'd had to earn that food and the roof over her head.

The men kept walking, talking too low for her to understand. She had half a mind to elbow her way in front of the prince, or at least right next to him, but the fact was, he had a gun and she didn't. And while she was a self-sufficient and independent woman, she was also smart enough to correctly assess the situation they were in.

"This way," Istvan said and moved to the right between the first row of containers and the second once the men passed.

They were hidden from view of the bridge, moving away from the men who were checking the deck. Regardless, he stole forward with caution.

And still neither of them saw the guy who'd been hiding between the containers until it was too late. He was seated, a bottle of booze in one hand, an AK-47 in the other. He immediately lifted the rifle.

Istvan jumped forward, knocking the rifle to the left

while pressing his own weapon against the man's chest and pulling the trigger. The body had muffled the sound, but it was still unmistakable.

"Come on." Istvan tossed the dead man's rifle to her, then ran, probably in case anyone had been close enough to hear the muffled shot and was coming to investigate.

The whole incident lasted less than thirty seconds, Lauryn thought bewildered, running after him, her heart still banging desperately against her chest. Violence always shook her. Even back when she'd made her living in ways less than one-hundred-percent honest, she never took a weapon to a heist, prided herself on being able to get in and out unseen, unconfronted.

The prince had been quick in a crisis situation, acted without hesitation, done well. Maybe too well, she realized suddenly, for a prince.

"Where did you learn all the cloak-and-dagger stuff?" she asked as they slowed.

"Basic self-defense training all the princes received."

She nearly laughed. "I wouldn't buy that at a two-for-the-price-of-one sale. Want to try again?"

"A couple of years ago, I led an expedition to the Middle East. I was searching for the remains of a caravan a Valtrian king sent to the Far East a few centuries ago. The whole caravan had perished. I was trying to find some trace of it and figure out what happened to them, but my crew and I ended up stumbling into the middle of some serious tribal warfare."

She looked at him and felt her lips stretch into a shaky smile.

"What is it?"

"You live a more interesting life than I gave you credit for."

He flashed a smile back, the first he'd ever given her. It transformed his face in the moonlight from handsome to dazzling, and she had to catch her breath.

She'd thought of him as a soft academic before who'd been bitten by the archaeology bug. Sure, he published a lot, but she always thought someone else did the lion's share of the fieldwork. She couldn't picture a prince with a shovel and a wheelbarrow, getting his hands dirty. But suddenly it looked as if there was more to him than being a high-born professor. Those princely manners hid a warrior spirit.

She couldn't say she wasn't fascinated by it.

"This changes everything," he said.

She blinked, afraid for a moment that he could read her thoughts. "What does?"

"The man I shot back there. He will be missed. A thorough search of the ship will be conducted."

"Maybe he was a stowaway."

"He was a member of the crew, sneaking off for a drink."

"Why? Those guys looked like nothing more than thugs. I doubt they'd frown on a little whiskey."

"Maybe he was Muslim, forbidden to drink. He can't very well do it in front of the captain or he'd be punished." He cheered up. "If the crew is Muslim, it could mean we're heading to one of the Muslim countries in the region."

"And why is that good?"

"We'll be there by morning."

As opposed to being stuck on the ship for days for a cross-Atlantic voyage to South America or the United States. She was beginning to see his point.

Hopefully, the rest of the crew wouldn't notice that one man missing until then. In the chaos of landing and unloading, the prince and she might be able to slip off the ship unseen and alert the authorities.

Not that life had ever been that easy for her, she reflected the next second as they came around the corner and ran right into the armed posse that was patrolling the deck.

Chapter Four

"Why are you on my ship?" the captain was yelling at them in Turkish, waving the gun his crew had gotten off Istvan. His eyebrows were like fat, hairy caterpillars, wiggling with each word on a face that was lined by age and weather. He had a thick nose and a blunt chin he thrust out as he narrowed one eye. "Are you spies? Are you police?"

They were on the bridge where the instrument panels took up most of the space. The open sea was visible through a bank of windows, stretching endlessly toward the horizon.

"Stowaways," Istvan responded in the man's own language, glancing at Lauryn, who probably didn't understand any of the conversation and was scared to death.

Not that she showed it. On the surface she looked as if she was holding up, which was good. He'd found that in situations like this, the key was not to show fear.

"Where did you come from?" Only the captain was asking questions. The rest of the officers worked the instruments. The posse that captured Istvan and Lauryn

contended themselves with pointing their guns and looking menacing.

Istvan kept his gaze on the captain, ignoring the half-
dozen weapons. "Valtria."

"Stowaways from Valtria." A bushy eyebrow went up.
"I ask you again, what are you doing on my ship?"

The fact that this crew was armed, too, like the one
on the riverboat had been, didn't necessarily mean they
were criminals. A lot of ocean liner crews armed themselves these days in response to the increasing pirate
attacks off the coast of Africa. But the interaction between the captain and the crew said they were hiding
something. And the captain was angrier than he should
have been at a couple of stowaways. His small, calculating eyes kept returning to Lauryn and not in a good
way.

"We're running from the law," Istvan said to distract
him. If the man was doing shady business himself, he
might sympathize.

"Why?" The captain pointed the gun straight at
Istvan, his full attention back on him.

Istvan gave a small nod to Lauryn to reassure her,
wishing she could understand what was going on, then
put his hands up in a capitulating gesture. Now that he'd
seen the crew and how well-armed they were, he had
to accept that his plan of taking over the ship had been
overly optimistic.

"You're a rich man. No criminal." The captain's eyes
narrowed.

And Istvan caught his mistake at once. Raising his

arms caused his shirtsleeve to fall back and reveal his gold watch. Getting caught lying could be the worst thing at the moment.

The man cocked the gun. He didn't look as if he was giving them another chance to explain.

But Lauryn rushed forth with an explanation anyway. "We only pretend to be rich. We're thieves," she said in near-perfect, unaccented Turkish.

Istvan stared at her. The woman was full of surprises. Definitely not one to be underestimated.

"When I was young, in my country thieves got their hands cut off." The captain's scowl deepened, but at least he wasn't shooting. He was measuring up Lauryn.

Istvan used the distraction and eyed the man on his right. He might be able to lunge for the man's rifle. He shifted his weight, getting ready.

"Lucky for us, you're not a policeman." Lauryn smiled with a hint of teasing.

The captain smiled back and Istvan did a double take.

"I wouldn't go as far as to say that you're lucky." He swept his gaze over her from head to toe. "You don't look like a thief."

"Let me reach into my clothes and I'll prove it to you," she challenged him.

Armed men stood behind them, their guns pointed and ready to shoot. The captain nodded to the goon behind Lauryn and the man moved his rifle barrel forward so that it would touch the back of her head.

She rolled her slim shoulders for a brief second before

she reached into her waistband and brought out a pock-etknife, tossing it onto the floor at the captain's feet.

"That's mine!" One of the armed men stepped forward, flashing her a dark look.

A watch came next from her bra, similarly claimed. Then some pocket change of Turkish currency from her socks, a lighter from her shoe, a blue medal of the evil eye—a common charm in the Middle East. By the time she tossed a small black book on top of the heap, the men looked ready to strangle her, but the captain was laughing, the lines around his small eyes crinkling with mirth.

"And he's a thief, too?" The man pointed at Istvan with the gun that he'd relaxed during the performance.

Istvan's muscles stiffened. Now they would expect him to put on a show like she had. Brilliant. Because, of course, he had absolutely nothing.

But Lauryn said, "Mostly I'm the thief and he's the muscle."

The man nodded at that, looking Istvan over one more time, his gaze settling on his left wrist. "The watch?"

"An excellent fake." He pulled it off immediately and held it out, an offering.

One of the men snatched it out of his hand and the expensive timepiece immediately disappeared.

Istvan didn't care about the watch. He kept stealing glances at Lauryn. When on earth did she have time to pick these men's pockets anyway? Their struggle when they'd been apprehended had been brief, had been kept brief purposely by Istvan because he didn't want her to get hurt.

The captain shoved the handgun into his waistband, a calculating expression coming to his face as he glanced from one stowaway to the other. "Maybe we'll be friends, eh?"

The rest of the men still had their weapons aimed. They weren't as amused by Lauryn's party tricks as their captain.

The man assessed the prisoners for another few seconds, then seemed to come to a decision when he turned away from them, looking out to sea. "Take them to one of the aft storage cabins. I'll deal with them when we reach Mersin."

The crew grabbed them and didn't worry much about bruising. They were shoved forward, taken down narrow hallways and stairs, a rifle barrel stuck between Istvan's ribs to guide him to their destination. He took note of every turn, the location of every door.

Then they were stopped and he was thrust forward into a small cabin. Lauryn came next, pushed with enough force to lose her balance. He caught her before she would have crashed into the metal shelving that nearly filled out their makeshift prison cell. She felt fragile in his arms, although he knew she was anything but a lost little lamb. He'd seen her in action.

The door closed and locked behind them before they could have turned and tried any trick for getting out of there. She stepped away without looking at him, brushed her clothes off and took a minute to survey the place. "Welcome to the presidential suite," she said in a wry tone.

Hardly. The storage cabin was barely three meters by three meters with a single porthole, which was their only source of light. The switch for the metal-mesh-protected bulb overhead was outside the door and the men hadn't cared enough to turn it on for their prisoners.

His stomach growled. He ignored it. He had a feeling it'd be a long time before any food came their way. Lauryn didn't exactly steal herself into the men's hearts when she'd picked their pockets.

Her performance was more than confirmation enough that at least some of the things rumored about her had to be true. But because her "skill" saved their lives, he couldn't very well hold that against her just now.

"You speak very good Turkish." He checked the shelves, but found nothing beyond spare parts for the ship's machinery.

"I traveled a lot with my father when I was younger."

Her father the tomb raider, lest he forgot. And he couldn't afford to forget where she'd come from and who she was for a second. She might have saved their lives back on the bridge, but they weren't partners. She might have clever words and clever fingers, but he couldn't trust her. "Did he teach you pickpocketing, as well?"

"I don't know what you're talking about," she said bland-faced.

And he felt the corner of his lips tug up at her bravado. He immediately schooled his features back into place. He was willing to accept that they were going to have to work together to get out of this mess, but he was *not* going to enjoy it. And he most definitely was *not* going to like her, under any circumstances.

He turned his attention to the porthole and fiddled with the latch. Locked. Because he'd already looked the shelves over, the points of interest in the room seemed pretty much exhausted. At least in the shipping container he'd been near his precious artifacts and had room to walk around, stretch his legs. Their grand escape so far was turning out to be anything but, taking them from bad to worse.

"Any ideas on how we could get out of here?" Having to ask for advice from her galled him to no end, but there it was. He'd seen enough by now not to underestimate her.

She smirked at him. "I didn't give back everything I took." The smirk turned into a full-blown smile as she pulled a fork from her pocket.

That was it? "I was hoping for a semiautomatic and a set of keys."

"Those who can't value the small things in life, don't deserve the big ones." The smile turned into a look of annoyance. Then her eyebrows went up as she caught him looking at her mouth.

Oh, hell. He focused on the damned fork. "Where did you get that from?"

"Found it on a tray on a side instrument panel. When we were on the bridge. Probably came with the captain's lunch." She examined the lock on the porthole. "What do we do once this thing is open?"

"See if there's a way up to the main deck. Maybe we could get our hands on a lifeboat and slip away before the sun comes up. Why did you take all that stuff anyway?"

"You never know what'll come in handy in an emergency. Anyway, there was no time to evaluate. I grabbed anything I could feel."

He shook his head.

The locking mechanism was nothing more than a hole, must have worked with some kind of a tool. She had to break off two of the fork's tines and bend the other two together to make it work. Her competence was impressive, even if it was competence learned from a profession he disapproved of.

Having the lock popped, however, didn't mean that they were home free. The porthole had been painted over and over again with thick white maritime paint and had stuck shut years ago from the looks of it. She went at it with the mutilated fork. He found a chunk of scrap metal under one of the shelves and helped. Even with the two of them working side by side, it took nearly an hour to set the window free.

But only the smallest metal circle that held the glass in the middle opened. The rest was apparently framing. He stepped back in disappointment. All that time and effort wasted.

She stuck her head out. "This might be beyond your considerable contortionist skills."

He tried anyway, once she stepped aside, not ready to give up yet. Other than a bruised shoulder, he got little for his efforts. And the window had been their only chance. The door didn't have a lock on the inside, nothing to pick. And this time he didn't have a weapon to shoot the lock apart.

He sat on the floor and braced his back against the shelving, cataloging the contents of the small space, trying to think of anything he could use to break out of the place. There had to be a way.

Lauryn hung her upper body out the porthole again to get a good look up. Then she looked to the front. "I think I see something on the horizon ahead of the ship."

He ignored the tempting curve of her hips that was framed by the window. "Probably another ship. Fifteen percent of all the world's shipping goes through here."

"Can we signal to them?"

"Not from this far." Although, the idea held merit. "If they come closer."

He wore a black sports jacket he could wave from the window. Lauryn had on a black shirt. He would have preferred her to be the one to undress for rescue's sake, frankly. With her leaning out and her shapely behind dangling practically in arm's reach, he was beginning to become aware of her as more than a possibly reformed thief. She blocked most of the light, but his brain was happy to supply details he couldn't see. Nothing had ever been wrong with his imagination, unfortunately.

"We need something white. Black won't stand out

against the ship's black side, especially in the darkness," she said, her mind on more practically issues.

Too bad he'd chosen a dark blue shirt to wear that morning.

"It's not a ship," she said after a while. "It's bigger."

"Could be one of the Greek islands. There are more than two hundred of them." Janos often went there yachting. He wished he had his brothers with him or that, at least, they knew where he was. There was no trouble the six of them couldn't manage together.

"I think I see lights."

That had potential. "About forty of the islands are inhabited."

She slipped back in. "I can fit through the porthole. If the ship sails closer to the island, I'll swim to shore and get help." Her voice brimmed with excitement.

He had a feeling her face would be lit up, too, if he could only see it. But with their only source of light outside, her features were shadowed.

"No."

"I'm a strong swimmer."

"No." To emphasize his point, he went to the window and sat on the floor right beneath it. The fresh air eased his seasickness and if she dived for the porthole to escape him, he could catch her.

"You don't trust me," she accused him after a minute, her initial excitement waning. "You don't think I'd send help."

He watched her for a while before he responded. "The

thought did cross my mind." Her criminal background didn't exactly spell *trustworthy*.

Because she'd turned to him, the moonlight was in her face. She looked as if she was ready to murder him. His gaze dropped to the fork, still in her hand. Looked like the perfect tool for skewering any number of body parts he'd be reluctant to sacrifice. He pulled up his knees.

"Of all the pigheaded—" She stepped to the left, then to the right, using up all the room available for pacing. "If you let me go, I might or might not bring help. If you don't, you're not going to get help, guaranteed. Isn't at least getting a chance worth the risk?"

"Not from where I'm sitting." Just because she didn't seem to be in league with the captain, it didn't mean she wasn't involved in the heist. She could have been part of the retrieval crew, while the captain was transport. They could be working for the same person without knowing about one another. She could have been locked in the container by accident, or on purpose, to guard the treasures until final delivery.

All right, so she'd helped them escape the container, and she'd helped to avoid immediate execution by the ship's captain, but Istvan still wasn't about to let her go until he was sure about her and had a crystal-clear picture of her involvement in the theft of the Valtrian crown jewels.

"So I'm what, your prisoner?" She huffed, her hands on her hips, a stance that only accentuated her exceptional figure, which could have been a conscious, distracting maneuver on her part.

He refused to be distracted. "More like a cellmate. We're both prisoners here."

"But I could escape! And help you," she added quickly.

"Too dangerous. The currents are pretty strong. And the ship won't go close to any of the smaller Greek islands. It'll stay in deep water. It'll go close to shore only if it's headed for harbor, and none of the small islands down here have a harbor large enough to accommodate a ship this size."

"I could try."

He was done explaining. She wasn't going anywhere. The end.

She sat down, her back against the door, and glared at him. "I can't believe I'm being kidnapped by a prince. There should be a code of honor, you'd think, with royalty."

He fought a sudden grin. Under different circumstances, he might have appreciated the fire in her, although, hitherto he hadn't been aware that he liked fire in a woman. Amalia had always been soft-spoken and accommodating. "Consider it more like protective custody."

She stuck her chin out. She had a pretty chin, delicately shaped like the rest of her. Her tumultuous eyes narrowed. "I could take you."

"Your trying would certainly make our journey more

interesting." He wouldn't have minded it a bit, provided that she put that cursed fork down already.

Her lips tightened. So did her fist around the fork.

He drew a deep breath, appreciating the cool night breeze that came through the porthole, helping his stomach to remain semi-settled. *The porthole...*

"You're looking at me funny," she was saying.

He stood as the puzzle pieces came together in his head and a plan gelled. "We need a place to hide."

"Ha!"

All right, he got her point. The storage room was insanely small, every corner instantly visible from the door even with the half-empty storage shelves. But there was Turkish writing and some symbols on one wall. He moved there and ran his finger over the metal sheeting until he found a screw head. "I think there might be an electric panel back here. Would you hand me that fork?"

She did so grudgingly.

The edge was too blunt, of course. He had to work it on the rough steel of the floor to sharpen it. He got the first screw out, then the next and another. Having to work by nothing but moonlight didn't make his job easier, nor did the rust. But finally he was able to lift the panel off and take a look at the jumble of electric cables that ran beneath it.

"What's this?" Lauryn asked from behind him.

"Room to hide." He pushed aside the cables and was able to create a small nook. *Room for one.* He looked around, his gaze settling on two cardboard boxes on a bottom shelf, and his decision was made. "You squeeze in here."

"Not a chance." She took a step back, as if to emphasize her words. She folded her arms in front of her, her shoulders stiffening.

"You're smaller than I am."

She eyed the hole warily. "Say I do get in there. Then what? I have no way to hold the panel in place from the inside."

He took a thorough look at the smooth metal. "I'll put the screws back in."

"You want to wall me up? I better touch up my makeup. Something must have smeared and made me look stupid."

She looked anything but, with her fine eyes throwing sparks as she faced him.

"This is what I'm thinking," he said, tamping down his untimely masculine appreciation. "We leave the porthole open. When they come to give us food or water or to get us for more questioning, they'll find the place empty. They'll think we jumped."

She considered him. "And because we've flown the coop, so to speak, there won't be a reason to lock the door when they go to report to the captain."

He liked her quick wit. "Exactly."

Her eyes narrowed. "How about if I wall you in?"

Did everything have to be a battle with her? "I wouldn't fit."

"I don't like electricity."

"It gives heat and light, what's not to like?" He was never going to understand women.

"I got shocked as a kid."

That explained things. "You won't get shocked now. Look, it's all completely insulated. Just stay still."

"And if you leave me behind?"

"You have to trust me."

"Like you trusted me to swim for help?"

He rubbed his nape for a second. "It's different."

"Because you're a prince and you think you can order me around." Her hands went to her hips again as she glared at him.

He wanted to kiss her. Utter nonsense. The swaying of the ship was scrambling his brain.

"That, too," he admitted. "Plus, I have the fork. And I'm not afraid to use it." Maybe some humor would disarm her.

A smile hovered above her top lip. Then she said, "I want it to be noted that I'm trusting you, even though you were completely unwilling to trust me."

Not entirely fair, to be certain. "Might I point out that between the two of us I'm not the one with a history of criminal activity?"

"I have no idea what you're talking about. I wish you would stop insinuating things," she told him.

He motioned toward the crevice, pitying every policeman who'd ever had to interrogate her. "Are you going to get in there before someone comes or would you like to wait and chat a little longer?"

She drew a deep breath and did an about-face. "Let

me see this." She arranged a few more wires, turned again and stepped in backward. Flattened herself. "And where will you be?"

"Leave that to me." He picked up the panel.

"Watch my nose," she snapped at him.

Unnecessarily. He was already watching the parts of her that stuck out. Mostly her breasts, but they stuck out farther than her nose anyway.

His gaze traveled up and met hers. She looked miserable. He couldn't blame her. On a rare impulse, he leaned forward and pressed a brief kiss on her lips, then gently put the panel in place to stop her in case she thought to retaliate.

"What was that?" she whispered furiously as the first screw slid into place.

Her lips had been incredibly soft. He could still feel the contact. "For good luck," he said. Not that he really knew what the hell he was doing.

"I thought you didn't believe in luck."

She had him there.

"Just because I don't believe in it, doesn't mean we don't need it." Which made little sense. He hoped she wouldn't notice.

He made quick work of the screws, made sure nobody could tell anything had been tampered with. Then he emptied the two cardboard boxes he'd noticed earlier, distributed their contents on the shelves so the extra parts wouldn't be too obvious.

Separately, neither of the boxes would have been large enough to hide him, but next to each other, with one side taken out of each and the holes fitted together, he could squeeze in and settle into a semicomfortable position.

Which was probably still a lot more comfortable than Lauryn was, he thought, not without some guilt. "Are you okay?"

"Hunky dory," came the muffled reply.

Probably one of those Americanisms. "And that means?"

"Fine. I'm fine." She sounded decidedly snappish.

He thought it might be better not to annoy her any further so he remained silent. They spent an hour or so that way. In the end, she was the first to speak.

"How long do you think it'll be before they come?"

"They'll check on us soon. It's almost morning."

The sun did rise after a while. It shined right on his box, making him sweat.

Nobody came.

Finally, he heard the door open and shouting ensued immediately, spiced with a lot of Turkish swearing. Someone kicked the shelf. Istvan held his breath. If they kicked his boxes and they slid apart…

But the man seemed to have already spent his anger. The sound of boots running down the hallway came next.

He lifted the top of the box that held his upper body and stole a look. Then sat up and climbed out, careful not to rip the cardboard. If the men thought Lauryn and he had escaped the ship, they wouldn't begin a search. If they figured out the prisoners' ruse and realized that the two of them were still on the ship, they'd mount a manhunt for sure.

He put everything back together, then went straight for those screws in the metal wall panel. "Just give me a second."

But whole minutes ticked by before he had her out of there, then even more time passed as he rushed to screw the panel back into place. She was stretching her limbs in silence as he worked. They could hear voices by the time he was done, one of them the captain's.

He stuck his head out the door. The hallway was empty. The men were still around the corner.

"This way." He grabbed Lauryn's hand and dragged her in the opposite direction.

Chapter Five

Lauryn held her breath as she squatted behind a barrel at the end of the hallway that held the crew's quarters. She hoped her growling stomach wouldn't give her away if anyone was in hearing distance. She hadn't had any food or drink in two days.

But the hallway seemed deserted.

"I'll go and see what I can find," she told Istvan behind her.

"I'll go with you," he countered.

It had been his idea to come here and look for food after they found the kitchen well-attended and impossible to get into without drawing attention. He seemed to think that the crew must have had at least some snacks in their bunks.

Ready to see for herself, Lauryn darted forward in a low crouch. The door of the first cabin was open. Nobody in there. She was inside the next second and moved to the side, keeping in cover of anyone who might step into the hallway from one of the other cabins.

Istvan was right behind her, pausing for only a

moment to survey their situation before heading for the bunks. Four were crammed into the small cabin, the bedclothes he turned over smelling stale, carrying the odor of unwashed men.

Lauryn saw something under one of the bottom bunks and went for that, came up with a half-empty bottle of cola. She searched through a canvas bag next and found a fancy chocolate bar, probably a gift from one of the crew to his sweetheart back home. He could bring her another one next time, Lauryn thought and lifted that, too. Hopefully, the crew would blame each other. She moved on, but no matter how carefully she looked, she couldn't find anything else.

She shot a questioning look at Istvan when she was through searching. He held up a bag of dried figs as he nodded toward the door, apparently ready to leave.

She followed him.

He couldn't have cut it as a cat burglar, but he had some good moves for his size, had excellent instincts and amazing upper-body strength. Definitely not a palace weakling. Not counting his ever-present scorn for her, he was all right so far, although she would have preferred to work alone. She wasn't used to having someone by her side, especially someone who didn't trust her. It threw off her stride.

Under different conditions, she could and would ditch him at the first opportunity. He might have thought he was keeping her with him, but she stayed of her own will. Because during the time she'd spent walled up in the electric panel, she'd realized just how much she needed him.

Like it or not, her name was now connected to the biggest heist of the decade, if not the century. Rumors of her past *would* resurface. Worse, details of her father's past would be dragged to light once again. Her newly legitimate position in the art world had been delicate to begin with. A shadow of doubt would be enough to ruin everything.

And that wasn't all. The deal she had made with the FBI was good only as long as she stayed on the right side of the law. All investigation pertaining to her had been suspended. But Agent Rubliczky warned her that if he had the slightest suspicion that she stepped over the line, or was even thinking about stepping over the line, all bets were off and he would come after her with a vengeance.

If he did, she would be out in the open, defenseless. A lot of her old friends had cut her off, feeling betrayed when she'd left the shady side of the business. She couldn't count on that world hiding her again. And not all of her new acquaintances trusted her yet. If she was under scrutiny, they might not want to associate themselves with her and come to her aid.

She was alone. She'd been alone since her father's death.

It was a definite advantage, she told herself, as she always did when the loneliness got to her. Prince Istvan didn't trust her. He'd prefer to see her in jail than anywhere else. Almost enjoying his company was the most outrageous foolishness.

Her thinking would return to normal once their paths separated.

But she couldn't separate them yet.

She had to be firmly and visibly on the side of good. Personally on the recovery team, if possible. She needed to be at Istvan's side when he brought the stolen treasure back into the country. She needed to be in the pictures, needed a seat behind the table at the press conference. She had to talk him into letting her be there.

But now was not the time. Voices came from the hallway.

She swore under her breath. The crew couldn't have numbered over two dozen, a group that should have been insignificant on a ship this size, but it seemed they were constantly around.

She immediately stepped to an open window, larger than the porthole they'd had to deal with before, slipped outside and stood on the window frame. "Boost me up."

To his credit, Istvan did so without asking any questions. He pushed her high enough to reach a trailing chain and hoist herself up on deck. Then she watched as he came up behind her. As much as they could, they stayed on top, not knowing the outlay of the warren of hallways, cabins and storage areas below. She didn't like the idea of being trapped down there.

She followed Istvan, who was already climbing the nearest container. They both preferred higher ground.

He kept going, not stopping until he was on top of the container that was on top of the first. From here, they had a fair view of the ship and the sea, but were nearly invisible as long as they lay flat and kept away from the edges.

She set the bottle and the chocolate between them, he put the figs out there, too, then pulled a chicken drumstick wrapped in a greasy piece of paper from his pocket.

"Protein."

"I'm a vegetarian."

He looked at her as if she were out of her mind. "But this is an emergency."

"Principles are still principles. Even in an emergency. *Especially* in an emergency." Of course, he probably didn't expect someone with her background to have any principles. She absolutely hated the fact that she was beginning to care what he thought of her.

She drank some cola first, wishing for plain water instead of the sugary liquid, then ate a handful of figs.

"Eat it all." Istvan pushed the bag toward her. "I'll have the chicken. If you're sure."

"Very." She tended to cling to her convictions, a response to a life that she sometimes likened to a leaf blowing in the wind.

Her father, the work they did together, had defined her in her childhood then as a young adult. The change she'd had to make after his passing, the bargain with the FBI, had been more difficult than she'd expected. She had to change her life, her actions, her thoughts, everything about her. It was the ultimate paradigm shift.

She liked the person she was becoming. But from time to time, she still felt as if the ground wasn't one-hundred-percent solid under her feet. One of the reasons why she sought to define herself with lifestyle choices, she supposed.

Istvan wouldn't understand. He was a prince. His whole life had been defined for him the moment he'd been born. His foundations rested on a six-hundred-year-old royal dynasty. He certainly didn't seem to be troubled with any existential questions as far as she could tell.

The morning sun was peeking in and out from behind the scattered cloud cover, warm, but not unbearably so, its heat further mitigated by the sea breeze. He took off his jacket and offered it for her to lie on. She accepted. The corrugated steel was none too comfortable, and she knew they could be up here for hours.

When she ate the figs and he finished the chicken, they split the chocolate, then drank the last of the cola. Sharing the bottle felt strangely intimate. They were almost like old friends, sitting in companionable silence. But they weren't, she reminded herself.

"What about your mom?" he asked out of the blue, reclining on his side, watching her.

"What about her?" she shot back, caught completely off guard.

"I was thinking about how a person turns out like you. I already know about your father."

Her spine stiffened. *People like her...* So much for the brief mirage of the two of them as friends. "I turned out just fine." She was working on it, dammit, every single day.

"I never implied otherwise." An amused smile played above his lip. "Maybe I meant you were self-sufficient and quick on your feet." The sunlight glinted off his dark hair. His wide shoulders were outlined against the endless blue sea. His powerful body was relaxed, his full attention on her.

The whole scene had a surreal quality, almost as if they were on some romantic picnic, which couldn't have been further from the truth. They were stowaways on a ship filled with armed criminals.

"My mom died when I was young." She shared that much against her better judgment.

"How?"

She had no intention of telling him. She'd never spoken of that time to anyone, never intended to. But the way he was looking at her made it clear that he wasn't going to let the matter drop, so she decided to give him a sentence or two to satisfy his curiosity.

"She was killed. I don't remember much." She wrapped her arms around herself. "I don't like talking about it."

Of course, that didn't deter him in the least. He leaned forward. "Did it have anything to do with your father's occupation?"

For a second she considered saying car accident,

hoping that lie would cut off further questions. Then she decided against it and simply nodded.

"What happened?" He pushed as she'd feared he would.

She was already regretting telling him the truth in the first place. "My father had something someone else wanted. They took me and mom. He tried hard to get to us in time, but he was late."

She braced herself for more questions, determined not to speak another word of what had happened. But instead, he simply swept the garbage from between them and silently pulled her into his arms.

The gesture startled her as much as the brief brush of his lips had back in their prison cabin before they'd broken free. She was convinced that he couldn't stand her, yet this was the second time he wanted to comfort her and did so with an intimate gesture.

She pulled back and looked up into his face. "Why are you doing this?"

For a moment it looked as if he might pretend not to know what she was talking about, but then he said, "Damned if I know. I didn't exactly plan it."

"So what, you took me into your arms against your will?"

He grinned at her. "I'm a handsome prince, aren't I? I'm used to beautiful women throwing themselves at me. Whatever I do, don't take it seriously. You looked forlorn."

"I'm a strong, self-sufficient woman. I don't look forlorn. On principle." She pulled farther away. "Don't do me any favors."

His grin widened. "I didn't say it was strictly a favor. I said I didn't plan it."

He was impossible. Impossible to argue with, impossible to ignore, impossibly handsome. Beautiful, cultured, high-born women probably did throw themselves at him on a daily basis. And there was no reason on earth why the thought of that should annoy her.

She turned to the sea. She needed to quit engaging him at every turn. It wasn't as if he'd come on to her. He'd offered a moment of solace. End of story. He probably had someone waiting for him back at the palace.

"Don't you have a girlfriend?" European tabloids were always full of their princes' exploits.

From the corner of her eye she caught as his body stiffen. She turned back to him. The grin faded from his face. She'd hit a sore spot, obviously.

"Not really."

"She left you?" Curiosity got the better of her. "I can't blame her. Must be tiresome to kowtow to a prince 24/7. I know I couldn't do it."

He said nothing, a shadow passing over his face.

"Hurts the masculine pride, doesn't it?" She smirked. He'd been in full control from the moment they'd met, prejudiced against her and judging her without apology, so she enjoyed turning the tables on him. "Let me guess, she's an actress or a dancer or something."

His gaze darkened.

"No, no wait. The debutante daughter of a nobleman. Did you meet at court?"

"We met in a pit of mud," he said the words on a low voice but distinctly.

For a moment, she thought he was joking but the way his lips flattened hinted otherwise.

She kept the tone light. "How romantic. I didn't know you were a fan of mud wrestling."

If looks could kill...

"She was an archaeologist, the most honorable woman I know." He looked at her pointedly, then added, "A member of the Royal Valtrian Academy of Sciences."

She almost said, *How boring,* but that *was* caught her attention and kept her quiet.

"We met at an excavation. Her find." Pain came alive in his voice.

She couldn't have spoken now if she wanted to. The sudden vulnerability in his eyes made him seem more real, more ordinary, more approachable than she'd ever seen him before. His guard was down, for the first time since they'd met. There was a moment of connection where none had existed before.

"Amalia died last year. A tunnel collapsed on her," he finished.

"Were you there?" she asked at last, after a stretch of silence.

He shook his head somberly.

And she understood that it was part of his pain. That he hadn't been there when Amalia had needed him.

She felt the same at times about her mother. She'd

been there, but had done nothing. Granted she'd only been six, but she could have thought of *something*. Her father had been on his way. All she would have needed to do was find a way to delay.

"I was there with my mom. They hooked her up to an electric cable and made her scream into the phone for my father. I don't think they meant to kill her. She had a bad heart that just couldn't take it. I got loose and rushed to her. My fingertips got burned. And the top of my ears." She rubbed one absently. "That's why I don't like electricity," she whispered.

"I'm sorry." He seemed completely subdued all of a sudden, his gaze—filled with nothing but sadness—steadfast on her face.

She drew a deep breath, then scooted across the distance that separated them and slid back into his arms.

"Why are you doing this?" he murmured into her hair.

"Damned if I know. I didn't exactly plan it."

His comfortable warmth, the pillow of the nook of his arms and the gentle swaying of the ship made her sleepy. She had only rested in fits and starts in the past two days, always surrounded by danger. She wished they were off the ship and someplace safe so she could sleep.

The sun was low in the sky by the time she woke and found him watching her with an unreadable look on his face.

She blinked. "Did I miss anything?"

"There's land ahead." He pointed when she pulled away.

"Close enough to swim to?"

"Not yet, but we seem to be heading that way."

"Turkey?"

"Too soon."

Her mind was still fuzzy from sleep, surprised that she had nodded off, could sleep so soundly in the prince's arms. A strange rapport seemed to have developed between them when she hadn't been looking. She sure hadn't seen that coming.

They watched the land grow larger and larger on the horizon as time passed. Neither of them spoke, each trying to figure out if this changed anything.

Then Istvan broke the silence at last. "We're getting too close."

"Isn't that a good thing?"

His eyes narrowed to slits as he considered the landmass ahead. "The captain talked about Mersin, a Turkish port. Of course, that doesn't mean they didn't have any scheduled stops before that."

"You think the ship is going to port right now, over there? On some island?"

"On a large island. Looks more likely by the minute." He pushed up to a squat. "Let's go."

He moved to the edge of the container and lowered himself. Lauryn did the same. They were close to the side of the ship so they didn't have much open deck space to cross. They got in cover and waited.

When they were close enough to make out the row

of hotels sitting on a sandy beach, Lauryn climbed over the railing. He hesitated behind her. She knew why.

"You're not abandoning the royal treasure. You're going to get help so everything can be retrieved." She didn't jump until she saw him nod. Then she pushed away, fell by a couple of portholes and prayed that nobody was looking out and saw her.

She hit the water hard, went under but broke the surface again soon and immediately began swimming to get away from the current the ship's giant propellers churned up. Soon Istvan was there by her side and keeping pace. When they were at a safe distance, they stopped to tread water for a moment. At least the water was nice, it being the Mediterranean Sea at the end of summer. The sun was about to set. On the shore the lights were turning on one after the other.

"What do you think it is?" she asked, gesturing toward the island with her head, spitting out salt water.

He looked up at the cloudless sky where the first stars were coming out, and seemed to be orienting himself. "Cyprus."

Another wave splashed her face, but couldn't wash off her optimism. She loved Cyprus. Her uncle lived on Cyprus. She could ask him for help.

"So we made it, right?" She could have shouted with joy, but although probably nobody on the ship would have heard her over the noise of the giant propellers, she figured it was more prudent to celebrate quietly.

"Unless the sharks or the currents get us," he said,

seeming immune to her exuberance. "Or they spot us from the ship."

As if to underscore his words, shouting broke out on deck. Followed by bullets peppering the water all around them.

So they *had* been seen from one of the portholes, she thought, then drew a deep breath and swam for shore.

Chapter Six

In the end, it wasn't the bullets that got them, nor the currents, nor the fearsome sharks, but the lowly jellyfish. Istvan's skin burned as he climbed to shore. Now he knew how his brother Lazlo must have felt when he'd been trapped in a burning wreck at a car race. He could swear he felt the licking flames.

"How can something so small cause so much pain?" Lauryn sat on the sand next to him, pulling up her pant legs and blowing on the forming welts. Her wet shirt stuck to her like a second skin.

He glanced toward the hotel. "I'll go call for help. Stay here." He hesitated for a moment. "You *will* be here when I return?"

"I let you lock me in an electric closet." She rolled her eyes. "I would like some of that trust returned."

He waited a beat or two as he considered. Then he nodded.

"I'll go soak." She gave a soft moan as she rolled her pants higher, then stood to stride into the water up to her knees.

Salt water was supposed to be good for the stings. He'd be joining her as soon as he got back. "Be careful."

The patch of jellyfish were a few hundred meters offshore, but that didn't mean the waves couldn't wash some closer. They liked coming up to the surface at night.

He ran his fingers through his hair and squeezed as much water out of his clothes as he could without taking them off, then strode barefooted across the sand, going around rows of beach chairs and umbrellas. They'd both ditched their shoes in the water to make swimming easier. His fake mustache was gone, too, along with the rest of his disguise. They hadn't survived this last bit of swimming.

He walked right into the plush lobby and straight to the front desk, ignoring the curious stares from the guests. He kept his face from them, but couldn't do that with the front desk manager, whose eyes went wide with recognition. The man's hand flew up to adjust his tie. His back straightened. He drew a long breath and opened his mouth, no doubt for a ceremonial greeting.

"I need help," Istvan said under his breath before the man could have spoken. "And your discretion."

"Certainly, Your—" The front desk clerk caught himself and lowered his voice. "Certainly, sir." Even his graying mustache seemed to stand to attention.

"I've had a boating accident with a friend. I'll be with her on the beach. I need you to call the Valtrian Embassy and arrange for a pickup. Also if your security could keep the guests off the beach until we vacate it, I'd appreciate it."

The man bowed. Caught himself too late this time. Glanced around nervously. "Yes, sir."

"And I need your ID badge."

The white photo card was handed over without question. "Let me give you some privacy," the man said, then raised his voice as he addressed the guests milling in the lobby. Some were coming from dinner, considering a walk on the beach, others were meeting with friends to go out for a night of partying. "Ladies and gentlemen, we have an open bar at the Roman Lounge on the first floor at the back of the hotel. All drinks are on the house. We are happy to have you here. For the next hour, all drinks are free."

People began to move toward the back of the lobby, looking pleased and more than willing to be distracted.

Istvan turned on his heels and strode out, grabbing a couple of beach towels from a cart by the door, keeping his head down, avoiding looking at anyone who might have lingered.

He was relieved to see Lauryn still where he'd left her. He hadn't expected her to run—she was injured, without money or any form of ID in a strange country— but he hadn't been one-hundred-percent certain. She was good enough and troublesome enough to pull it off if she really put her mind to it.

He wasn't ready to let her go yet. He told himself it was because he still suspected her and he wanted to keep an eye on her until he figured out whether she'd had any part in the whole sordid heist business.

"How are your stings?" He draped a towel around her shoulders, the other one around his own.

"On fire."

"Help will be here in a few minutes. Lift your leg." He squatted before her and helped her balance with one foot on his knee while he ran the edge of the ID card along her skin to shave off any adherent nematocysts. "All right, let's do the other one."

To do the job right, he had to touch her. Her skin was hot where she'd been stung. He could feel the shift of muscles in her calf when she moved slightly. There were a few stings even on her thigh, the thin material of her pants having provided little protection. His jeans had done a better job, as well as his jacket. But his shirttail had worked loose while he swam, so he'd been stung around the abdomen. He was feeling a lot less of that pain now, however, as he did his damnedest to focus on her injuries and nothing else, certainly not the way moonlight reflected off her smooth skin.

"Let me help you," she offered when he was done.

"I got it." The thought of her nimble fingers on his lower abdomen was more than he could handle. He scraped the skin with painstaking care, making sure he got everything. "Now there won't be any more toxins released, at least."

"Neat trick with the card." She patted down her hair and squeezed water out of the ends. "Where are we in Cyprus?"

"I didn't ask." His main goal had been to arrange for help and get out before any of the guests recognized him. He glanced around and saw hotel security higher up the beach, on the large patio, turning guests back inside. They must have also escorted inside the handful of guests who'd been lingering at the edge of the beach when Istvan and Lauryn had reached shore. They were now completely alone on the stretch of sand.

"Thank God for the weather." Her hair arranged to her satisfaction, Lauryn moved on to dabbing the towel over her clothes to wick some of the water away from her body. "If we had a storm or if the water was cold, this could have been a lot worse."

He resisted the urge to offer help. "We'll have food, water and medicine soon. Hang in there." He scanned the road. How soon help would arrive was anyone's guess. The Valtrian Embassy was in Larnaca, the capital city. For all he knew, they were on the other end of the island. He could see several restaurants and hotels from where he stood, but as luck would have it, none had the town in the name.

He was craning his neck, trying to catch something he might recognize, so absorbed in the task that he almost didn't notice the black limo pull up ten minutes later, displaying a diplomatic license plate.

A uniformed chauffeur stepped out, along with a bodyguard. Istvan helped Lauryn out of the water and walked to meet the men halfway.

"Your Highness," they said at the same time.

"Thank you for coming. Where are we?"

"Porto Paphos." The chauffeur was better trained than to show curiosity either at the question or the disheveled state of his would-be passengers.

Porto Paphos. Should have figured. One of the major ports on the north side of the island, but not anywhere near Larnaca. "How did you get here so fast?"

"The ambassador is in town with his wife for the international cat show. And he's giving a welcome speech for contemporary Valtrian art at one of the galleries tomorrow morning."

Probably set up by Chancellor Egon. "Good timing," Istvan said, catching from the corner of his eye as Lauryn worked to roll down her pant legs.

"Should I call an ambulance?" the bodyguard asked, apparently having seen the welts already.

Istvan looked at Lauryn.

She shook her head.

"That won't be necessary. Have a doctor dispatched to the Duke of Oskut's estate along with a half-dozen guards from the embassy." He walked to the limo and then, seeing that Lauryn was uncomfortable with the men, told the guard to ride up front.

"How far are we going?" Lauryn asked once the divider was rolled up and the car was moving.

"Not far. Relax if you can." He reached for the minifridge. "Champagne or something stronger?"

"Plain water if you have it. And maybe some ice for the stings."

He poured mineral water into two tumblers and handed one to her, gave her another glass with nothing but ice, then picked up the phone and called the embassy, identified himself. "There's a Turkish ship by the name of *Suleiman's Glory* probably docking right now at Porto Paphos."

Once they'd jumped, he'd made a point of looking at the name painted on the ship's side. "I want it stopped and searched. All hands are to be held along with the cargo. Nothing is to be removed from that ship until I get to it in the morning." He hung up and took a drink. He needed a shower, food and at least a couple of hours of sleep. His brain was barely functioning. Lauryn, too, looked dead on her feet.

"Must be nice to have all that power." She leaned her head against the back of the seat, her lips tightly drawn. Didn't look like the ice she held to her leg was helping any.

He knew how she felt. "Now and then it comes in handy." He put down his glass. "They won't be going anywhere tonight. We can rest. Then tomorrow I'll come back to the harbor and take care of everything."

She sat up and looked at him. "*We*'ll come back."

"Your presence won't be necessary. I'll go alone." She needed rest and healing.

Her gold-green eyes narrowed. "You still suspect me?"

He considered what to say, what he believed at this point. She wasn't what he had expected. There were issues he needed to rethink.

"I can't believe you have to think about it," she accused before he could have said anything, hurt and fury in her voice. "People were shooting at us. I could have been killed!"

"I noticed." Yet, he still didn't like the idea of her around the coronation jewels. Especially because she seemed to want to be near them so badly, which did make her look suspicious.

She set her glasses in the holders. "You should be grateful I want to help you. It's no cakewalk, with all your—" She snapped her mouth shut and made a sound of frustration in her throat.

He turned to her fully, raising his eyebrows. "I'm *not* difficult to work with."

She stuck her chin out. "Like somebody would dare tell you, Your Highness?"

He turned away from her and dialed the phone again. She was obviously in an unreasonable mood. There was no point in talking to the woman.

"This better be urgent. The runner-up to Miss Valtria is waiting for me in the hot tub out back," his cousin said in way of a greeting.

He had cousins only from his father's side, twelve boys and three girls from the four uncles altogether, all younger than Istvan, mostly in their late twenties and early thirties. The girls were charming, but the boys were rakes, every last one of them. They were removed enough from the throne to escape the worst of public scrutiny and media attention, and they made sure to live the combination of their wealth, title and relative freedom to its full potential.

"Only the runner-up?" Istvan couldn't help a jab. "What happened to the winner?"

"We dukes can't always get everything that falls so easily to you princes." Alexander gave a good-natured chuckle. "Want to walk away from wherever you're digging right now and join us? You could bring the beauty queen. She'd probably come if you called her."

"I'm somewhat busy at the moment, but thank you for the invitation. I was hoping for another favor."

"Name it and it's yours if you let me off this phone in the next thirty seconds."

"The use of your estate in Cyprus."

Alexander, the Duke of Oskut, was in the movie business, one of the main benefactors of Valtrian cinema. He had filmed a documentary at a Cyprus country estate just outside Porto Paphos a few years back, fallen in love with it and purchased it on the spur of the moment.

"When?" he asked.

"Right now. I'm there."

"Say it's not so you can dig up my backyard. Tell me there's a beautiful woman involved. I want confirmation of female companionship."

"Confirmed."

Alex hooted like a common rodeo cowboy. "I'll ring the housekeeper to open the gates."

"*Now* will you tell me where we're going?" Lauryn asked when he hung up.

And, of course, she found fault with the answer, so the rest of the trip was spent in the same bickering mood that she tended to adopt every time he naysayed her.

Clearly she was the kind of woman who expected to get what she wanted or there'd be hell to pay. He was missing soft-spoken Amalia more by the minute.

He was still unsettled by Lauryn after having arrived at the estate and instructing the maid to show her to a room on the top floor. As a first order of business, he went to see about some more help. He made sure she had immediate medical assistance, food and drink, clothes, whatever she needed. The only restriction he placed on her was that she wasn't to leave the house without his permission.

Knowing her as much as he did by now, he was glad he wasn't there when that bit of news was delivered to her by the twenty-something knockout housekeeper. Leave it to Alexander to fill every position around him with aspiring actresses and models.

While the doctor applied some local herbal salve on Istvan's jellyfish stings—after having finished with Lauryn—the prince arranged for money and weapons and an early transport back to the harbor. Then he put down the brand-new, secured cell phone he'd received when the guards from the embassy had arrived and absentmindedly fingered the motion sickness bracelet Lauryn had tied around his wrist. One had come apart when they'd swam to shore and was lost at sea. He'd meant to remove the other one when he'd changed his clothing, but it had slipped his mind.

"I'll remain on the premises in case you experience any further discomfort, Your Highness." The doctor backed toward the door when he was finished.

"I'm fine. But do keep checking on Miss Steler."

He looked around the spacious suite once the door closed behind the man. Alone at last. He called Miklos and filled him in on everything that had happened.

"Arpad has some state occasion he can't miss, but Janos and I will be there by morning. Wait for us."

"I will." He wanted to bring in as few outside people as possible for the removal of the crown jewels from the ship. He didn't even want the royal guard to know what was in those crates, let alone the Porto Paphos Port Authority. Everything would be easier if he had his brothers there.

Istvan wished good-night to Miklos, then hung up, stretched out on the bed and stared at the Greek fresco on the ceiling. He thought the day over, everything that had happened since the hit on the treasury, trying to come to some conclusions about Lauryn, but didn't get far before he fell asleep.

His dreams were dark and hot, prominently featuring a very intriguing ex-thief. He was pursuing her. She had something of his. At times he would almost catch her, touch her, but in the end she always slipped through his fingers.

He woke to the certain knowledge that he wasn't alone in the dark room. He wished the weapons the guards had given him were closer at hand, but he'd left them clear across the room on an antique chest of drawers. He stayed still, looked through a slit in his eyes without moving his head.

Nothing.

Then, after a long minute, a shadow shifted toward the bed. A hand reached out, held something. A weapon?

He reached out and clasped the would-be assassin's wrist, yanked the arm up and the body forward until the attacker was sprawled on top of him, his free hand holding the other wrist immobile.

He was ready to roll in a wrestling move he remembered from his college days when he found his nose pressed against a soft neck with a familiar scent. The squirming body on top of his was too light for a man, and the curves, too, were unmistakable.

"Lauryn."

"That's not necessary." They spoke at the same time.

He flipped her anyway, not willing to let her weapon hand go, but put his body weight on the other one so he could reach for the light on the nightstand.

The bright light blinded him only for a second, then he could make out the folded piece of paper he'd mistaken for a knife in the dark. She was still wearing the clothes she'd swam to shore in. His gaze slid to hers, to eyes that were calling down the wrath of all the ancient gods of the island upon his head.

He should have let go right then. But her lithe body stretched below his awakened all sorts of sensations in a remarkably short time. And brought back his dreams where she'd always been a step ahead of him, always slipping out of his hands.

I caught you now.

He bent his head and kissed her.

He'd brushed his lips against hers before on impulse when he'd walled her in behind that metal panel in the ship's cabin. Afterward, he had no idea why he'd done it, was certain it would never happen again, grateful that she didn't make a fuss over his lapse of judgment. It proved that she could be sensible when she wanted to be, when she could overcome her argumentative nature.

But this kiss wasn't like the one before. This one he meant.

Few things could have surprised him more than her kissing him back. Need surged immediately and lust. If the wall behind their bed collapsed to reveal the archaeological find of the century, it couldn't have drawn his attention from her.

He let go of her wrist and brought his hand down to tuck her even closer. Her arms went around his neck.

Her mouth was hot and responsive, every touch of her tongue sending a new wave of desire through him. The strength of the heat between them caught him off guard. He wasn't the type of man to seduce every hapless female he came across, like his infamous cousins, of which the Duke of Oskut was the mildest.

Istvan had always been more focused on his work. Even his relationship with Amalia had been a slow and comfortable affair. But at the moment he could barely remember her or anyone or anything else. Lauryn filled his senses and his hands.

Before he knew it, her shirt was open and his face was buried between her perfect breasts. He drew a nipple in his mouth, the most natural thing in the world, his body—too long denied—growing hard as she arched her back beneath him.

"Tell me this is what you came for," he whispered with urgency when he came up for air. He didn't want to stop. He wanted her full cooperation and agreement.

But she gave a pained laugh. "I came to leave a good-bye note."

That sobered him enough to pull up and look into her face. "You were going to sneak out." Understanding dawned, disappointment coming close on its heels.

"Obviously, my sneaking skills are rusty." She tried to make light of it.

"I was very specific in my orders that you should not leave without my approval."

"That's exactly why." She shifted from him. "I want to work with you on getting back what was stolen, but I will not be your prisoner."

The air was cooling between them. He didn't want that. He pulled her back. "Let's not argue."

"You mean, I should just serve your needs like a good little subject of the crown without raising any objections? I have news for you. I'm not a subject of the crown." She was deliberately misunderstanding him. Her gaze was sharp now, all the softness gone form her mouth.

"That's not what I meant." Although, if she felt in an obedient mood, he wouldn't have objected. He drew a long, frustrated breath. "You kissed me back."

She shrugged. "I figured that might be the quickest way out of here."

That stung. "How far would you have been willing to go?"

"As far as necessary." She didn't even blink as she said that.

His body still ached for her. He had half a mind to put her to the test.

"Sorry." She slipped out of his grip, out of the bed. "The gig is up, I'm afraid. What's this?"

She was holding a page of his handmade copy of the Maltmore diary. Water had soaked the copy through, so he had laid each page out to dry. The secrets of the Brotherhood of the Crown were set out on every available surface.

"An old document I'm working on." He moved to get the page she picked up, but she danced out of reach. "I'll have that back," he warned her.

She studied the writing by the light of the lamp. "What language is this?"

"I'm not sure."

"Let's see." She raised an eyebrow. "Not a natural language. Looks more like code. Who wrote in codes? Secret societies. Let me think of a Valtrian secret society that could have a book that a strapping prince like yourself might be interested in enough to copy by hand and carry in his pocket." She tapped her forehead theatrically. "I'm guessing it's some secret book of the Brotherhood of the Crown. How am I doing so far?" She looked pleased as anything with herself.

On the one hand, he found her quick thinking incredibly sexy, watching her mind work a thing of beauty. On the other hand, he couldn't say her guessing his secret so effortlessly didn't annoy him.

"What is it about?" She tilted her head, a sparkle in her eyes.

"I don't know."

"You can't decipher it?" The question was put forth with such belittling intonation as if to say she would have broken the code on a single lazy afternoon with a hand tied behind her back if given half a chance.

"Of course, I can read it," he said and realized too late that he'd given himself away, which had been exactly her purpose. His mind was still too steeped in lust to follow her quick thinking.

"Okay, then let's try this again. What is it about?" she asked with a smirk.

He decided to tell her. In equal parts because he didn't want her to leave yet and because none of the diary made any sense anyway.

"It's a collection of poems and sayings. Like the *Song of Solomon* and the *Book of Proverbs* in the Bible."

She held the page out for him. "What does it say here?"

He let his gaze run across the marks. "The wealth of a nation is in the head of the ruler."

"Makes sense. The smarter the king is, the better off the country will be."

Yes, in some way, but the gems of wisdom were no help to him whatsoever. When he'd found the diary he'd been hoping that the clues would lead him to the treasure of the Brotherhood.

The original Brotherhood of the Crown was made up of eight princes who put Casanova to shame. The only thing that outshined their deeds in battle had been their deeds in the bedroom.

When the country went through a particularly difficult period of foreign invasion, their lovers supposedly gifted the young princes with massive amounts of their jewelry, as love tokens and as support for an uprising. Except, the princes were betrayed and the treasure had disappeared.

Lauryn held the paper to the light. "Which one is the word for *wealth?*" she asked.

He pointed it out.

"And *ruler?*"

He showed her that, too.

"Then this is the letter *E,*" she guessed correctly. Then asked a few more words and within minutes, literally, had the entire alphabet decoded, by which time he regretted ever giving her any information.

"So it says, *The wealth of the nation is on the head of the ruler.*"

"*In* and *on* were interchangeable in the old language."

She nodded. "This is interesting. Can I take these back to my room to read through them?" Her head was tilted, the light playing on her slim neck, reflecting off alabaster skin. Mesmerizing.

He very nearly fell for it, but in the end came to his senses.

"Absolutely not." He held out his hand for the page.

Her eyes narrowed. He expected one of her biting remarks, but in the end, she stuck her tongue out at him. "You're no fun to play with."

A bolt of desire shot through him. "Didn't hear you complain a couple of minutes ago."

The reference to the passionate kiss they'd shared made her cheeks tinge. *Interesting.* She hadn't seemed shy when she was kissing him back. Urgent need resurfaced quickly at the memory.

"Lauryn—"

She backed away from him, an intriguing creature of the night that begged further investigating. "Good night."

He hated to see her go, something he needed to consider later. He was going to have to straighten out his thinking and his unexpected attraction to her the first chance he had.

"Fine. Go back to your room and stay there," he told her. "How are your stings?" he asked belatedly, more than ready to give her thighs a close inspection.

Her impertinent response was, "None of your business."

As soon as she was gone, he called security to meet her in the hallway, escort her to her room and stand guard in front of her door until he sent for her in the morning. Then he stretched out in his bed, his arms folded under his head.

He could still taste her on his lips.

He had a couple of hours left until dawn, but sleep didn't come easily. It didn't come at all, in fact. So he got up at five, washed and called for a car and armed escort, then left for Porto Paphos without breakfast. He would wait for his brothers on the ship. It would take hours before he had the whole thing searched anyway. Beyond recovering the royal treasure, he also wanted to find some clues as to who was behind the heist. He wanted the man who'd ordered it.

He called the estate just as his car rolled into the harbor. Port Authority was already there, waiting for him. He could make out the Turkish ship by one of the loading docks.

On the phone, he talked to the guard in front of Lauryn's room, asking him to check on her. He could hear knocking. Knocking again.

"Miss Steler?"

He heard the key being turned in the lock and the door opening. Then silence for a moment.

"I'm sorry, Your Highness. She doesn't seem to be here. I can't find her," came the worried, embarrassed reply from the other end.

Pretty much what he had expected.

Chapter Seven

He hated to be right about her. Right in some ways, in any case. Wrong in others. She'd turned out to be an exceptional woman, possessing a lot more than the criminal brilliance he'd first attributed to her. For a second, as he walked across the shipyard, Istvan imagined what it would be like to work with her on a dig, deciphering ancient messages carved in stone. Her mind would be flying a mile a minute, that rapture of discovery on her face...

To work with her like that would be nothing short of exhilarating, he thought, and felt guilty. He'd used to do fieldwork with Amalia and he'd never once thought of her in those terms. He appreciated the warm companionship Amalia had provided, but his head had never been as full of her as it was with Lauryn. Even now, steps from reclaiming Valtria's royal treasures, she was the only thing he could think of, the way she'd come to his room in the middle of the night, the way her face lit up at the sight of the Maltmore diary.

The things that could have happened between them under different circumstances…

He could still feel her lithe body under his, taste her mouth, hear her laugh, hear her repeat some lines of the text. "The wealth of the nation is on the head of the ruler," she'd said.

His mind ground to a screeching halt, as did his feet. His guards nearly ran into him because they'd been following so closely, but he paid little attention to the puzzled looks they gave him.

On the head of the ruler.

He'd corrected her last night, but now as he heard her say the words in his head again, he got stuck on that small difference. *On,* as opposed to *in.* What if she'd been right the first time around? What if the Royal Brotherhood left clues to their treasure right on the royal crown?

What better place to hide that message? The crown was always well-protected. No one but the royal family had access.

Until now.

At the moment, the royal crown was on the ship ahead of him. He broke out running, everyone following behind.

"The crew?" he asked the Port Authority official who came to greet him. Suddenly he felt as if he didn't have a second to waste.

"Held in the canteen on the ship, under armed guard, Your Highness."

He strode across the plank onto the ship, then straight

to the containers in the general area where he believed the one they were looking for was located. "You and you—" He pointed at two of the guards behind him. "Climb this stack, get as high as you can. We're looking for a container that has one of its top corners peeled back." The small explosion Lauryn had created to get them out of there also marked the container, making his job easier now.

They couldn't just look for a door with two bullet holes in it. Most of the containers were crammed too closely together to squeeze in and check the doors on every one of them.

The men immediately dispersed and did as he'd ordered. He couldn't help but notice how much slower and clumsier they moved than Lauryn.

He had to wait at least half an hour before one of the men shouted down. "I got it." Then he led the group on the ground to the right location.

The container in front of his had been moved somehow. As if to allow someone entry.

He was going to wait for his brothers with the opening of the container, but he was unable to hold back now. He threw open the doors and strode in, adrenaline pumping through him. He would get everything back. The treasure was all safe. He willed it so.

But he could see within two steps that the contents had been disturbed. The tops of several crates had been tossed to the floor. He jumped up on the first, his skin burning where his clothes rubbed against his abdomen.

He barely noticed the pain from his lingering jellyfish welts.

Empty. The realization echoed through his brain.

He smacked his fist into the wood. "Search every crate," he ordered the Valtrian guards, while motioning Port Authority back. He worked alongside his men.

"Empty," one called out.

"Nothing here," said another.

"Bare-root roses packaged in sawdust," came the first response that was different.

Valtria's signature purple roses, a common export item, the official contents of the container that the ship's captain had declared toward customs as cover, Istvan guessed.

"Keep searching," he said, although he knew by then that all the effort would come to naught.

He turned away in disgust. He should have come earlier. He should have come right away last night. But he'd been tired, and he knew Lauryn had been tired. He'd wanted to see her safe and settled.

Then a familiar shape caught his eyes, Lauryn sauntering across the shipyard, dressed in all black, self-possessed and full of confidence. Catwoman had nothing on her. He came off the ship to meet her, ordering his men to search the entire ship and get the crew ready for interrogation.

He caught some of the Port Authority officers on shore looking her over and didn't approve one bit, frowned at the gawkers. Normally that was enough of a warning for anyone to heed a prince's displeasure, but currently had no effect whatsoever. Next to her, nobody even noticed him.

"Everything's gone," he told her matter-of-factly, determined not to show that part of him was glad she'd come back even as he wondered why she did, or if she had anything to do with the treasure's disappearance.

He didn't know when she'd left the estate. He didn't know when the crates had been emptied. Her involvement was more than possible. But if she'd come to Valtria for the crown jewels and now she had them, she'd be on her way, wouldn't she?

There was no figuring the woman out.

"I got here an hour ago. Everything was already gone by then."

He didn't even bother asking how she'd gotten on a ship under full guard.

"They probably handed off the stolen goods before the ship pulled into port," she told him.

And he had to admit that the ship having had a rendezvous off shore seemed the most likely explanation at the moment. They might have had the transfer set up for Cyprus, but changed that when their prisoners escaped, suspicious that someone might be onto them. Then, because the ship's manifest included Porto Paphos, they had to pull into port anyway.

Lauryn sneaking on the ship at dawn was one thing. But surely the guards would have noticed if someone tried to remove a dozen crates' worth of treasures. It wasn't as if that war chest could have been smuggled off the ship in someone's back pocket.

But even if Lauryn wasn't part of the group who'd made off with everything, she *had* left the estate during the night and she *had* come here. She *had* sneaked onto the ship and *had* checked the container. All that didn't exactly help when it came to trusting her.

"The pickup team probably had a local fishing boat that could come to shore anywhere and wouldn't be subject to inspection," she was saying.

She was right. She was sharp and quick. The smart thing was to let her help. Frustration coursed through him as he considered their new situation. "Which means the things they took could be anywhere on the island."

They were both careful not to mention what exactly they were looking for. The Port Authority men stood too close. Although a press release had been issued about the break-in at the Royal Treasury, it had been played down and no specific items had been mentioned. Istvan preferred to keep the extent of the heist under wraps while he investigated.

He watched Lauryn, her eyes narrowed but unfocused, her mind probably going at the speed of light. He didn't trust her motivations, but he couldn't deny that she could be an asset to him.

So when she said, "I'm going to stick with you until we see this through. But don't try to lock me up again," he simply nodded.

THEY WERE HOLED UP IN a villa in Porto Paphos, owned by one of Istvan's cousins, the duke of something or other. Her rooms had an unobstructed view of the sea out front and of an amazing pool out back. The grounds were shaded by date palms and inhabited by more cats than Lauryn had ever seen in one place. She liked cats. They were all over the island, but seemed to especially prefer the estate.

Valtrian guards, borrowed from the embassy, took up residence on the lower floors, securing the building. The top floor was reserved for her and the prince. They each had a suite of their own, plus another to be used as a war room. It was already furnished with giant maps of the island, two computers and stacks and stacks of papers. They had received a list of art and antiquities dealers on the island—legitimate and illegitimate—the name of every cop who could be bribed, the location of every nook that could be used as a hiding place for someone trying to lie low with stolen treasure.

When a prince asked questions, people responded.

Everything and everyone responded to the prince. *Including her body.*

Those kisses in his bedroom—where they could have led... It didn't bear thinking about. Except that, despite her best efforts, she hadn't been able to stop thinking about it, about him. She'd run because her own response to the man had scared her. Her casual attitude to his touch, to his seduction, had all been pretense once she recovered from melting completely.

She'd also run because no matter how much he was getting to her, she couldn't allow him to get the upper hand. No man was going to control her, not in any way.

He needed to understand that, the sooner the better. Putting her under house arrest, indeed.

But then she saw him at the harbor. And felt his frustration, shared it. She could have started investigating on her own. But the truth was, she needed his help. And if she was totally honest, she liked working with him. And so she had walked up to the prince. She could only hope she wasn't going to regret it.

She listened to Miklos on the phone, on speaker. He and Janos had arrived earlier that morning, helped to search the ship, then arranged for a quick extradition of the crew to Valtria and took them back, along with the ship's captain. Miklos would be handling their questioning there. The princes were adamant about keeping as much of the case under wraps as possible.

"The crew is not talking. Yet," Miklos added with optimism. "I'm working with them. Janos found a couple players in Valtria with good enough teams, we think, to pull off the heist. One boss is the guest of Great Northern Penitentiary at the moment. We'll go after the others. Shouldn't take too long between the five of us."

"The twins are back?" Istvan asked with surprise.

"Lazlo cut his honeymoon a few days short," Miklos said as if it was no big deal. "Rayne got sick or something in South Africa, so Benedek was bringing her back anyway. My lovely wife says the kids are about to have a little cousin, but I can't get anything out of Benedek."

"Leave the men to me," Istvan responded with sudden

force. "Enough of our people died at the treasury. I will handle the investigation."

"The Brotherhood—"

"Is out of business," he cut Miklos off with a quick glance at Lauryn.

Which set off her radar. The brotherhood? What about the Brotherhood of the Crown? Istvan had been reluctant to share anything every time the subject came up. Why? The Brotherhood of the Crown had ended with those princes' deaths two hundred years ago. Unless… She turned to look at the maps to make sure her face didn't give her interest and suspicions away.

"I can fly back and forth," Istvan added.

"You're on Cyprus. Focus on the connection there. Unless you want us all to come back over and work from Porto Paphos together."

"No." His response was sure and immediate. "I'll take care of what needs to be taken care of here."

Stubborn, she thought. Wanted to do everything by himself. She would have loved to have siblings. She would have loved that kind of support, to have someone care about her problems. Maybe he was the type who could never admit that he needed help.

Then something in Istvan's face made her think. His voice had been brusque, but worry sat in his eyes.

He wants to keep his brothers safe.

Her heart softened with understanding. He wanted them out of harm's way. And harm was a near certainty with the investigation. She'd heard the gunfight in the treasury. She'd seen the rifles the ship's crew had carried.

"Be careful. Duty and honor, our lives for—" Miklos was saying.

Istvan grabbed for the phone and pushed the off button before his brother could finish.

Too late, she smirked to herself, keeping her face averted. *Duty and honor, our lives for the people and the crown* had been the oath of the Brotherhood of the Crown. Well, well, well. Was it possible that the Brotherhood had been resurrected? She put an ambiguous expression on her face as she turned to look at the prince.

He paced the war room, his brows knit in a frown.

"Why are you still here?" He stopped and addressed her suddenly.

She figured the question was coming. She didn't have any illusions. Most likely, the only reason he'd agreed to let her help was because he wanted to keep an eye on her and it was easier if he kept her close.

She thought about what he would want to hear. *You tell people what they want to hear and they'll believe you all day long*—a lesson her father had taught her. But as she looked into his dark eyes, which watched her closely, she decided to go with the truth.

"I need to be clearly, publicly, visibly on the right side of this one. I worked hard on building a reputation in this business. If there's even a shadow of a doubt that I had anything to do with this heist, my career is over and I can never get it back again."

He remained silent as she weighed her words.

"The world of arts and artifacts is my life. It's the only thing I know. After my father's death, I swore I wouldn't live on the dark side of this business. I sweated blood by the time I could make an honest living from it. If I lose that, I have nothing."

He was still silent, but she stopped there with her explanations. Either he chose to believe her or he didn't.

"All right," he said after a while. "We'll work together. But a word to the wise, Lauryn. I live and breathe for my country and family. Without that, I have nothing. I will do anything to protect our future as well as our heritage." He paused, his gaze reaching to her soul. "If I say you stay in your room, you stay in your room. Don't cross me again."

From the moment she'd set eyes on him, her image of him was that of the gentleman prince. But now she could see that there was a dangerous edge to the man. A thrill ran through her unexpectedly. She quashed it.

For too long, she'd liked thrill and danger too much. That was the lifestyle she'd inherited from her father, a lifestyle that had brought both of them to misery and ruin. These days she made a point of staying on a slow and steady path.

Even if she was contemplating a short side trip at the moment.

"Do you have any idea how we should proceed?" Istvan asked.

"Maybe," she said with caution. "I know someone on the island who's not on your list. Someone who would actually help us instead of running when he saw us coming."

"Who is he? Where can we find him?"

She hesitated. Their partnership was still tenuous. The prince was unlikely to respond well to her conditions. But she cared too deeply about the man she was talking about to reveal his identity without proper reassurance.

"I want your word that his identity will not be revealed to the authorities, nor will he be prosecuted for any involvement with the current heist or in connection to any information you might find out about any of his past activities."

Istvan stiffened. "I will promise no such thing. Who is this man? An old partner of yours? An old lover?" His words were clipped, his gaze hard.

"Your word that he will not be pursued in any way."

"Give me a name." He stepped forward, that warrior in him coming out again.

She stiffened her spine. "Not without your word."

"I could make you tell me," he threatened.

And she didn't doubt him. Even if she judged him to be too much of a gentleman to harm a woman, he *was* on a mission for his country, and he had plenty of men downstairs to do his dirty business for him. "Not even under torture," she said, just to make herself clear.

"I can't promise anything if he had a part in the theft." Istvan shoved his hands into his pockets, the vein in his neck pulsing with effort to restrain himself.

"He didn't."

"How can you know that with certainty?"

"He knew I was going to Valtria. He knew what I was going to be doing there."

"And he would never put you in any danger? He wouldn't chance that you might be implicated? Are you sure you're that important to him?"

She didn't need to think about that. "I'm sure."

He took his time thinking over her offer. "If he's not involved in the heist in any way, I'll guarantee his anonymity," he said at last.

She watched him, considering whether she should trust him. A fine team they made, neither trusting the other. Yet they must achieve their purpose. Too much rode on retrieving the royal artifacts for both of them not to try their hardest.

"You have my word as a royal prince," he added, reading her hesitation. "Now, where is this mysterious man?"

"I'll take you to him."

HE HATED WEARING A disguise. Istvan smoothed his index finger over the new fake mustache he'd acquired. To go out in public without it carried too much of a risk. He couldn't chance being recognized now. And he couldn't take a royal escort with him either. Lauryn had been adamant that only the two of them could go wherever she was taking him.

"How much farther?"

The car rattled as he drove down a dirt road through

the most breathtaking countryside Cyprus had to offer. They were heading south from Porto Paphos through fields of sparse vegetation, nothing but a few olive trees here and there and the odd group of goats as far as the eye could see. Rocky hillsides broke up the landscape that possessed a stark beauty.

"Almost there." She hadn't yet given him a name or a destination, informing him of each turn of the road only as they came to it.

Then, when he was beginning to think they would never get to wherever they were going, he went up a small rise and could see bigger hills in the distance, with plenty of green covering the sides and large crosses dotting the ridge.

"There it is." She pointed.

He had to lean forward to figure out what she was talking about. Then, finally, he saw it. Another mile or so ahead, an ancient-looking building complex was carved into the rocky hillside. Little more than caves on the very top, the structure grew more and more elaborate as it reached the foot of the hill and spread out. The domed tops of the attached buildings and the double cross on top gave it away, as well as the men in brown robes that he could make out once they got closer.

"Don't tell me you're taking me to a monastery."

Her smile grew. She picked up the cell phone she'd received from Istvan. "We'll be there in a couple of minutes. Can you meet us at the gate?" she asked whoever picked up the other end. "They don't let women inside the walls," she explained to Istvan after she'd hung up.

So her ex-boyfriend or partner or whatever joined the priesthood. If any woman had the power to drive a man to extremes, she was it, he had to admit. Although the thoughts she'd been inspiring in him of late were less than holy.

The potholes in the road kept his thoughts from going too far in that direction. The area must have seen some nasty rains in the past couple of days. Car traffic was probably negligible up here, so nobody had hurried to fix the problem.

They reached the monastery at last and he could see a man come through the wooden gate just as he pulled the car up to park. The guy was in his late fifties, dark-haired and, from what his rolled-up sleeves revealed, in excellent shape. He wore drab slacks and a simple shirt instead of a monk's robe. Women probably thought him handsome.

Istvan grunted, not the least happy when Lauryn flew from the car and straight into the man's arms. He swung her around in the air with a deep belly laugh. He hugged her tightly, not seeming to care one whit that he was way too old for her and entirely inappropriate.

Istvan stepped out of the car and cleared his throat with some force. And they turned to him at last, the man keeping his arm comfortably around Lauryn's shoulder, keeping her close to him.

"This is the friend I told you about over the phone," Lauryn said, in no hurry to pull away from the guy.

"Arnie." The man stepped forward and offered his hand.

"Istvan." He felt a ridiculous need to make his handshake firmer than usual but resisted.

"Let's go for a walk." The man finally moved away from Lauryn, but she immediately went after him and laced her arm through his as they started up a path that went around the monastery walls, higher up the hill, toward three giant crosses that looked over the valley.

"Lauryn said you lost something of significant value and high profile." The man looked at Istvan's face closely, the calculating look in his eyes indicating that he saw straight through the disguise. "I have a fair idea what it may be, but we don't have to spell it out if it makes you uncomfortable."

He found the man's words patronizing, although they were said in an easy enough tone. Best thing to do was to be courteous, considering that he depended on the guy's goodwill at the moment. He simply nodded.

"There aren't that many people who could pull off the job," Lauryn put in.

"And even fewer who could commission something like this. I'm leaning more and more toward the idea that it was a commissioned job. Nobody in their right mind would risk so much without already having a buyer," Istvan added, picking his steps carefully on loose gravel. "If we could figure out who the buyer is— I don't suppose you heard anything."

"I'm out of circulation these days," the man said noncommittally.

Istvan waited. Lauryn wouldn't have brought him here if she didn't think they could gain some valuable information. "Anything you could think of would be helpful."

Arnie seemed to be considering, so Istvan left him to it. As the path narrowed, there was no room for him to walk side by side with him and Lauryn, so he fell behind. A mistake, since his gaze was immediately captured by her lithe figure and the sinuous way she moved up the incline. She could thoroughly capture and hold a man's attention without half trying. The woman was nothing but trouble.

She had certainly captured Arnie's at one point in the past as the man had hardly let her go since they'd gotten here. Even when they reached the top and he sat by the foot of the tallest cross, he pulled Lauryn down close to him. "You trust this one?" he asked her.

"Until further notice."

"Don't overwhelm me." Annoyance surged through Istvan. Who was the ex-thief here anyway? That *she* would question *his* character went beyond belief.

Arnie turned to him. And the glint in his hard gaze said that if Istvan proved to be trouble, he could and would be taken care of before he had a chance to hurt Lauryn. Great. How did *he* end up being the bad guy all of a sudden?

He said nothing, knowing there was nothing he could say or do to make the man hurry. Arnie had to make up his mind on his own. All Istvan could do was wait. And as he did just that, sitting by the other cross and leaning his back against its base, peace filled him little by little. The valley spread out before him was an oasis of serenity. The monastery had an aura that seemed to blanket everything.

His breathing evened, his muscles went slack. He didn't even mind the flat looks Arnie gave him now and then as the man examined him from under hooded lids.

"There is someone I used to know," Arnie said at long last. "Seems like he backed out of a major deal unexpectedly a couple of days ago. Caused a few ripples. He's not the sort of man who does that. Could be that something better came along."

"Or he got spooked by something, or fell out with someone on his crew. Any number of things could have happened," Lauryn responded. "But you don't think that's it."

"You always hear gossip." Arnie shrugged. "On this one, I hear nothing. That has to mean something. He's not a crew boss, by the way. He's a middleman. He passes things along."

"How can we find him?" Istvan asked.

"You can't."

"Could *you* find him?"

The man shook his head. "Not anymore. I don't run with that crowd these days."

"Do you know anyone who could?" Lauryn asked and then stood and started pacing.

"Nobody who would help you, not even if I vouch for you. It's a tight club, you know that. They don't like outsiders." He picked up a pebble and turned it between his fingers.

He was still thinking. That was something. At least he didn't say, "Sorry, can't help," and walked away.

Lauryn stopped. "You have an idea."

Arnie dropped the pebble. "It's not worth articulating."

"Please."

He made a face, held up his palms as if to say he was washing his hands of this. "Fernando."

Lauryn looked as if she knew exactly who the man was talking about, but Istvan had to ask, "Who is he?"

"Nobody knows exactly. Very few people have ever seen him. He's a purchasing agent for the biggest buyers." Excitement stole into Lauryn's voice. "Reclusive."

"I happen to know that he's laid up for a while in Brazil. He had another one of his plastic surgeries. Facial reconstruction, fingertips lasered off again, the whole works. Not many people know about this."

"How can he help us?" The guy definitely sounded like a step in the right direction.

"He wouldn't. He'd have you shot if you so much as asked questions about him." Lauryn grinned.

"Glad to see the prospect of that makes you so happy," he groused at her.

"It's not that. You could be him!" She laughed out loud now, obviously thrilled with whatever idea she'd come up with. "Only a handful of people know what he looks like. And he's constantly changing his appearance to stay ahead of the authorities."

"If there was a one-of-a-kind heist, even if done on commission for a buyer that wasn't his, Fernando is the kind to want to take a look at the loot anyway. He's not the type to shy away from a bidding war if he sees something he wants."

"I'll be Fernando." He caught on at last. If nobody knew what the guy looked like and nobody knew that he was out of commission for a while, Istvan could enter the world of underground stolen artifact trafficking impersonating the man, find what he wanted and hopefully get out before anyone figured out what he was doing.

"Brilliant." He flashed an answering smile to Lauryn, her optimism rubbing off on him. "Can you set up some meetings for me, as Fernando, with the top people in the business on the island? I have a list," he told Arnie, not wanting him to think that they expected him to do all the work.

The man picked up another pebble. "Maybe."

"You know you can. You know everyone." Lauryn moved closer to the man, true affection reflecting in her clear eyes. "Everyone trusts you."

"Because I don't betray them," Arnie said in a sour tone. "If I do this. I'm going to have to leave here. I can never come back."

The smile slid off Lauryn's face. And Istvan understood that this was some sort of safe haven for the man, an escape he'd likely planned for years, a retirement he'd set up for when he would withdraw from the business.

"I know I'm asking you to risk your life," he told the man. "If you help, know that you have a place in Valtria and my protection." That was as close as he wanted to come to admitting who he was.

Arnie didn't look impressed. He looked ready to walk, in fact. But then Lauryn squatted in front of him, took his hands in hers and said, "Please."

His shoulders slumped as degree by degree the man gave up resisting. "I'll see what I can do."

Lauryn threw her arms around him in a warm embrace that twisted Istvan's guts for a second. He should have felt grateful and relieved. But he couldn't get past the annoyance at their frequent and ample display of affection. Could these two keep their hands off each other for a minute?

"You'll be Fernando." Lauryn stood at last and turned to Istvan, practically jumping with excitement. "I'll go with you. On the rare occasion when Fernando does business personally, he always travels with one of his mistresses."

"No," Istvan and Arnie said at the same time.

"You should stay at the village." Arnie nodded toward the two dozen small houses in the valley, white-washed walls and blue roofs, a postcard image of Mediterranean tranquility. "I can keep an eye on you here."

"On second thought—" Istvan turned to her. "I think it would be all right if you came with me. You could be of help. Definitely."

Chapter Eight

"I love banana fields."

They were on their way back to Porto Paphos, the car rattling over a road that looked like the moon's surface. Lauryn gazed out at the countryside, pointing out a shepherd or an old chapel now and then to keep the conversation going. Despite their first real breakthrough, the prince seemed to be in a mixed mood, saying little beyond cursing the deepest potholes.

"I don't think your Arnie likes me," he said absently, seeming unimpressed by the beauty of the banana fields.

They were in an SUV, a comfortable car with more than enough space, yet his physique and presence seemed to fill it to the brim. He was masculine without putting on any macho displays, handsome without seeming to be aware of it and intelligent without the need to show off his smarts at every second to impress her. He was also grumpy at the moment. And he could be bossy. Definitely a strong tendency there. Still, nobody could say he wasn't interesting.

"If he didn't like you, he wouldn't have helped," she told him.

"Maybe you didn't notice the way he was looking at me."

Maybe. But she'd certainly noticed the way the prince looked at Arnie. Of course, considering the business Arnie had been in prior to his retirement, perhaps Istvan's dark looks were understandable. "He doesn't like it that you're taking me into danger. I'm his only niece. He's allowed to worry."

The car slowed as Istvan turned toward her. "He's your uncle?" The look on his face was comical. It was the first time that she'd seen him truly confused.

"What did you think?"

He turned back to the road and accelerated. "Old partner or whatever. There isn't much resemblance."

Her uncle and her father had been dead ringers for each other. She took after her mother.

"Decent of him to help us. We'd be up the creek without a paddle if he didn't." He was beginning to sound appreciative. "Maybe he was right. You could stay. It'd be safer." He pulled onto the highway, the road much smoother here, and the car picked up more speed. "You could pack your things at the estate and I'll have a car bring you up to the village tonight. Looked like a nice place."

She actually did have things to pack. Before they'd headed out this morning, he had called a store and told them her dress size. They delivered an armload of clothes including accessories within the hour. Apparently, they were used to such calls coming from the Duke of Os-kut's estate.

Right now, however, there was too much going on for her to enjoy the thought of her new wardrobe. Like the prince's sudden newfound mistrust. She'd really hoped they were past this. "An hour ago, you thought it was a great idea for me to come with you. Now you don't trust me enough to take me along? You do know you're driving me crazy?"

"You've been through enough danger in the past two days. It wouldn't hurt to at least try to stay safe and get some rest while you're at it."

"I'm going."

He considered her for a second before returning his attention to the road. "You really shouldn't."

"Oh, well. We're past that now."

He looked back at her, his eyes narrowing.

"Don't even think about it." She bristled, her mood mirroring his.

"What?"

"Putting me under house arrest again."

He said nothing, obviously remembering how easily she'd sneaked out the first time. He didn't look pleased at the memory.

Tough cookies.

Long minutes passed in silence as he drove. There were plenty of tourists out on the main highway, not all of them used to driving on the left side of the road, judging by the guy who pulled out from a side street straight into oncoming traffic. Horns blared.

The prince cleared the obstacle with ease. Then he drew a breath of resignation. "So you'll be my mistress."

There was something in his voice as he said those words that didn't sit well with her. "We'll be pretending," she reminded him.

BY THAT NIGHT, THEY HAD an appointment with Geoffrey Bellingham, the man Arnie had told them about. Bellingham agreed to a breakfast meeting the following morning. Turned out the guy was a British expatriate who had his operations set up on the north side of the island.

Istvan and Lauryn moved into a five-star hotel as if only having arrived, and shared a suite. Two of the most beefed-up royal guards dressed in black suits and black shirts took the next room as bodyguards. Fernando traveled with staff, so that fit right into their cover. Istvan would have preferred his cousin's familiar estate which provided more room and privacy, but they would be checked out thoroughly by Bellingham's men. He needed to act like the man he was impersonating, and five-star resorts seemed to be Fernando's usual home away from home when he traveled.

His guards were in their own room at the moment, Istvan picking over the remains of dinner that had been delivered to the suite, waiting for Lauryn to come out of the marble bathroom that was on par with those at the Valtrian Royal Palace.

His cell phone rang. The call came from his cousin's

estate, from the men he'd left behind. While he was going after Bellingham, he put an investigative team on his other suspects on the island. He didn't dare contact local law enforcement for help. He didn't know who could be bribed, which officer the bad guys might have in their pockets—according to Arnie, most of them.

"We have initial results, sir."

"Proceed."

"Costas is in jail. Has been for four months."

That left four more to worry about if Bellingham didn't pan out. "How about the rest?"

"Petrov is visiting family in Russia. Nobody's seen him for a month. He's said to be attending his sister's wedding."

As good an alibi as any. "And the other three?"

"Halil is keeping a low profile. Has some trouble with his crew. His second in command made moves to overtake the business."

So maybe Halil had other problems now and wouldn't attempt a major job.

"How about Berk and Canda?" According to the preliminary reports, both were of Turkish origin and known for their part in the black market artifact trade on the island. That gave them a possible link to the ship.

"Can't find either of them."

"Look harder," he said as the bathroom door opened.

Lauryn wore sensible cotton pajamas, well-fitting but not revealing. Part of him wished she'd picked something sexier from the pile the store had sent over. He hung up the phone. At least she hadn't come out wrapped in a robe to her chin, although in hindsight, he should have known she wouldn't. A shy woman couldn't have worn those Catwoman outfits that seemed to be her favorite.

She was comfortable enough in her own skin to dress any way she pleased. He liked that about her.

"So you'll be pretending to be my mistress," he spoke aloud the thought that waltzed circles in his mind while he'd been waiting for her. "Can you act? If either of us takes as much as one misstep, our lives are over."

One perfect eyebrow slid up. "If you're going to try to use that cheesy excuse to talk me into *practicing,* I'll be seriously disappointed."

Protesting would have only served to make him look guilty. And he wasn't about to admit that, yes, there was a sense of expectation in the back of his mind, his body buzzing now that she was there in the room with him, the enormous bed within reach.

"We have to look and act the part," he said simply.

She watched him for a long second, assessed him. Then her lips curved into a seductive smile. When she moved, there was a world of promise in her undulating curves. Slowly, tantalizingly she walked up to him. She straddled his lap, ran her fingers through his hair, never taking her eyes off him. She took his face between her hands, dipped her lips to his and kissed him.

There was nothing shy, tentative or simpering about her. She knew what she wanted and she took it as if he belonged to her. He found the kiss the most erotic of his life, and for the first time considered that maybe his brothers were right and he should spend more time in the company of women than in the company of centuries-old bones.

They'd accused him on more than one occasion of passing through the sea of ladies always present at court like a sleepwalker, barely noticing any of them. He was well awake now, conscious and alert. His body responded fully, passionately, his hardness pressing up against her soft core. His hands went to her waist to hold her in place.

Practicing seemed like a brilliant idea all of a sudden. He was looking forward to lots and lots of practice. It was the only path to perfection after all, as his father had been fond of saying.

But she was pulling away already, looking unaffected save for the smirk on her freshly kissed lips. "I think we can both make it look authentic."

He took a moment to collect himself. If she could walk away from this, then so could he. "How are your stings?" he asked when his breathing was semi-steady.

His had stopped burning, but they still itched.

"If that's a pitiful attempt to get me out of my pajamas so you can check, it's not going to work."

He couldn't help a grin. "What can I do? You're too smart for me."

"And don't you forget it." She sauntered to the obscenely large bed and lay right in the middle, then tossed a pillow at him.

"What's that for?" He knew he was slow on the uptake, but he couldn't help it. His mind was still addled; all he could think of was joining her on that bed and finishing what they started. That was the last thing he should have wanted under the circumstances, considering who she was and why they were here.

"For you on the couch. I wouldn't want you to be uncomfortable. You need to be fully rested for tomorrow." She gave him a cheeky grin.

"YOU SHOULD HAVE STAYED at the hotel," Istvan told her.

They were on their way to see Geoffrey Bellingham, sitting in the back of a limo while his guards rode up front. Bellingham took breakfast appallingly early. Istvan stifled a yawn. He'd barely slept the night before. Lauryn was not easy to ignore when sharing the same suite.

"We've covered this. We'll do the social thing with this guy, but I'm sure I won't be invited to the negotiating table. While you're with him, I'll wander around and see what I can see."

"The hotel would be safer." While he'd been lying on the couch and staring at the ceiling, he'd had plenty of time to think about, among other things, the danger he was taking her into.

"You were fine with me coming when Arnie offered to keep me safe in the village."

He didn't respond to that.

She watched him closely. And her eyes went wide

after a few seconds. "You thought he was an ex-boyfriend, didn't you?"

Should have known that she would work that out sooner or later. She had an amused look on her face. She clearly enjoyed having fun at his expense. Needling him was quickly becoming a hobby of hers. He couldn't say he minded it. He rather enjoyed their usual irreverent banter.

He wouldn't, however, give her the satisfaction of admitting anything. "Of course not."

"You didn't want to leave me with him." She grinned.

"Don't be preposterous. I'm not jealous of your uncle."

"You didn't know he was my uncle." She watched him with a speculative glint in her eyes.

"I talked to Miklos again earlier while I waited for you at the car."

"All right." She shot him a knowing look. "I'll be a good girl and play along. What did he have to say?"

"The ship's captain killed himself before he could be interrogated."

The blood left her face. "Why wasn't he secured?"

"He was. Looks like he ran full force into the brick wall of his cell and cracked his own skull. It's the damnedest thing."

"Whoever he worked for, he had to be pretty frightened of the guy." She rubbed her temple. "The rest of the crew?"

"Scared stiff and not talking." A moment of silence

passed between them before he continued. "Miklos had information on our Fernando, as well." Information Arnie must have known, although Istvan couldn't blame the man for not revealing it. "Apparently, when he gets tired of a mistress, he's known to leave her behind at a negotiation as a gift to seal the deal."

She blinked. "You're making that up."

He looked her straight in the eye. "Not hardly."

"If you dare—" She drew a deep breath.

He could see as she gathered steam. But even as she opened her mouth to give him some of her undiluted opinion, the car came to a halt. "We're at the lion's den," he told her. "Time to go in and do the bearding."

Truth was, he couldn't picture himself leaving her behind anywhere, not in the near future. He enjoyed her company too much. But at one point, he *would* have to give her up, he reminded himself. He was a prince. She was an ex-thief.

One of his bodyguards opened the door. Istvan stepped out first, then held a hand out to help Lauryn. She put on her mistress persona without a pause, linked her arm through his, pressing herself against his side as they walked, the thunder on her face seamlessly converting into a coy smile.

And he immediately realized what a huge distraction she would be. Yes, he could use her sneaking-around skills, but he couldn't shake the feeling that bringing her along might turn out to be a dangerous mistake.

Chapter Nine

Bellingham's home looked like a perfect English manor house both on the outside and inside, including a mahogany library with a fireplace, which, Lauryn suspected, didn't see much use given the climate.

The maid poured their tea, then left without raising an eye to anyone present or uttering a single word. Their host didn't acknowledge her either, certainly didn't thank her. He'd acted the upper-crust English nobleman from the moment they'd arrived. Probably wanted to make a good impression on the elusive Fernando. She knew Prince Istvan could outclass him in manners and in every other way, but he held back and acted the wealthy South American black market genius with aplomb.

"It's nice coming here this time of the year. Hot, but not any hotter than at home," he was saying as he lifted his cup to his mouth.

Bellingham's movements were more measured as he took in Fernando and his mistress, his gaze lingering on the soft silk dress Lauryn had selected for their breakfast, nearly sheer and snuggled close to the skin to accentuate every curve. She'd long ago learned the power of a good distraction.

She sat close enough to Istvan so their thighs touched, and made a show of paying attention only to him. But while she glanced up at him coyly from under hooded eyelashes and flashed him one bedroom smile after the other, she cataloged the contents of the room with a focus that wasn't easily won.

Plenty of bookshelves, but save an ornamental antique desk—Louis the Fourteenth, original—she found few signs that the place was Bellingham's working office. No computer in sight, for one. And she didn't see any filing cabinets either.

"I've heard a lot about you," Istvan was saying, faking a South American accent as best he could. "I regret that we haven't met until now. I'm not one for the social scene."

"So I've heard." Bellingham chortled. "You have the reputation of a hermit." His eyes narrowed. "All the more intriguing that you would stop by on a visit."

Istvan put his left hand on Lauryn's knee, then lifted it away slightly, hovering an inch or two above before allowing a finger to make contact again and trailing it up her thigh. Her skin heated from his touch, caressed by both his fingertip and the silk. Need snatched her breath away for a second before she could steel herself. He gave her a meaningful smile as he drew his hand back, the kind that would pass between lovers, full of promises.

She rose, acting on his silent message. "I'll leave

you gentlemen to your business. I saw a garden in the back as we came in. Would you mind if I explored it?" she asked their host, toning down the open heat, but remaining sufficiently flirtatious.

"Make yourself at home." The man's gaze dipped to her cleavage. "You may explore anything you like for as long as you please.

"You're a lucky man." She heard him say as she closed the thick wooden door behind herself. She didn't catch Istvan's reply if there'd been any.

Istvan's two guards stood at one end of the hall-way, Bellingham's two men at the other. They looked her over, but didn't interfere as she walked toward the French doors that led to the courtyard in the back. She could still feel the prince's touch and cursed her attraction to the man.

Given her past, men in her life had been few and far between. She could never fully trust any, could never take anyone home to meet Daddy. She could never be sure if someone pursued her because he was an up-and-coming rival and wanted her secrets or an undercover cop trying to gain her confidence to collect evidence against her.

Both had happened.

She learned and never allowed more than a couple of dates, always stopped short of a true relationship where she would have had to share things that were personal.

Her dating habits left her lonely and frustrated, but she told herself she didn't have time for a man in her life anyway. First because her father had made sure her schedule was always full, and now because it took a hundred and ten percent of her energy to establish some kind of normal, legal career.

The last thing she needed was this unrequited attraction to the prince who'd just as soon see her tossed in jail than accept her help. She was walking the tightrope with him. She had to remember that. And the fact that his affection for her, so openly displayed in front of Bellingham, was all pretense.

Okay, not *all* pretense. He'd seemed plenty interested in her on multiple occasions when they'd been behind closed doors and not performing for anyone's benefit. His kisses… *Anyway.* Whatever attraction there was was none too deep. Most likely, he sought only to satisfy his baser urges.

She drew her lungs full of fresh air, pushing the prince and the way he made her feel out of her mind. She was famous for her razor-sharp focus. She called on that as she continued walking.

The garden walls threw enough shade in the morning to make the walk pleasant, so she followed the brick path that wound its way around palm trees and giant prickly pears, enormous bushes of flowering rosemary that had the bees buzzing. A marble fountain sprayed water in the center, the mist further cooling the air. She ignored the fountain and walked the perimeter instead, pretending to admire the plants while surreptitiously looking in every window.

She found the kitchen, a formal reception room,

storage rooms, bathrooms and, finally, the office. Little red dots indicated the cameras in the corner. The security system was on. No surprise there.

She didn't linger much longer, not knowing how long the prince's negotiations with Bellingham would take. She headed inside, right past the man's guards.

"I need to use the little girls' room." She smiled coyly, bending forward enough to let the neck of her dress gape. She drew the back of her index finger down her skin, toward the spot that grabbed the guards' attention. "It's getting hot out there. Would be nice to splash some water on my face."

One of the men gestured toward the end of the hallway, and she headed that way with a thankful smile. They didn't follow. They wouldn't move from the library door while their boss was in there with a stranger, she suspected. And they didn't have to follow her in any case. The hallway had its share of security cameras, giving a view of her activities to whoever was watching the monitors.

She walked into the bathroom as if she had no cares in the world, scanned it and was relieved that at least here privacy had been preserved. No cameras anywhere.

Which did seem kind of lax, considering that she'd seen them everywhere else in the house so far. She took a fresh towel and wet it, dabbed the cool cloth down her neck as she looked around, slower this time, pretending to enjoy freshening up a little.

She caught a suspicious dark spot in the painting that hung overlapping the mirrored back wall. She let her gaze glide right by as if she hadn't noticed. Then she wadded up the towel and placed it on the glass shelf below the picture, making sure it blocked the hidden camera's lens. She did one more sweep of the place, but couldn't find anything else.

The window was connected to a motion detector, but that was switched off, probably so the bathroom could be aired out if needed. She imagined they only turned the sensors on at night when they secured the premises. She looked out at the garden. The office she'd seen was right next door. If the window sensors were turned off during the day, she could climb out here and climb in there.

The garden stood empty, just as when she'd left it. The main danger came from being spotted through one of the other windows if anyone was watching. She made sure she checked every window she could see, but detected no shadows or movement behind any of them. The library was on the opposite side of the garden with Bellingham and Istvan, but Bellingham had been sitting with his back to the window when she'd left them.

In any case, this was her only chance, and the risks, such as they were, would have to be taken.

She opened the window, careful not to make a sound, and leaned out. She still couldn't see signs of anyone else. She vaulted out in one quick move, making sure she didn't tear her dress. Nobody shouted at her to ask what she was doing. She pulled the bathroom window closed.

A quick swipe at her bra produced a pick that helped

to open the office window. Then she was inside and closed this window behind her, too. Nothing should look amiss from the outside. The camera sensed motion and its red light blinked. She knew this model. Took about three blinks before recording started.

She dived forward and grabbed a handy little gadget from the other cup of her bra, held it up to the keypad and pushed a button. It temporarily overrode the circuits, tricking the sensors into believing that all was well in there. The red light on the camera stopped blinking.

She went to work immediately. Her gadget would work for only five minutes before the slight magnetic charge wore off. To use it a second time would risk permanently damaging the circuitry, which would be discovered once they left. She preferred not to blow their cover. They might need it again.

She went straight to the laptop on the desk, working in order of priority. She pulled a sticker from her bra with one hand as she turned the laptop over with the other. She pulled off the original barcode, stashed it and replaced it with her own. How many people ever checked the old factory stickers on the backs of their computers? Her sticker concealed a transmitter chip, a cloner. With the corresponding receptor, they'd be able to see everything Bellingham did on this laptop, now and forever.

Done with that, she tried the desk drawers. Locked. No match for her picking skills, however. She did a quick look-through, hoping to find a small artifact from the treasury, something Bellingham was possibly prepping for shipment or still evaluating. But there was nothing there.

The filing cabinets came next, yielding nothing relevant. Then she looked for the safe and found it cemented to the floor. There'd been a time when those floor vaults were very fashionable. She knew what to do, although this type wasn't one of her strengths. She ended up wasting precious seconds and found nothing but cash in several currencies and a half-dozen passports with Bellingham's picture but different names. She made sure to memorize them.

She was almost done when she heard footsteps outside the door. She glanced around with desperation for a hiding place as her heart rate tripled.

"Would it be for your private collection or for a client?" Bellingham asked in response to Istvan's hints that he was looking for something extraordinary, one-of-a-kind pieces that might be floating out there.

"A client." He tried to look calm while his blood pressure inched up. He'd seen Lauryn climb in a window, but she hadn't come out. "An old client had come into some money recently and he heard rumors of certain items that don't usually come onto the market."

"Items like that are retrieved for specific clients, on order. More often than not," Bellingham added, his attitude remaining nonchalant.

"But if another buyer surfaced? I've yet to see a bidding war that was bad for us agents." He gave a short, conspiratorial laugh.

Bellingham nodded, his lips tugging up at the corners. "What sort of artifacts would your client be interested in exactly?"

Istvan dragged out the moment as if reluctant to reveal even that much. "He fancies himself the king of the underworld. Don't they all?" He chuckled again.

Bellingham's eyes narrowed. "And what brought you to *my* door?"

"Your reputation for one. If there's anything out there, I thought you might have heard of it. But I'll be making the rounds elsewhere, as well. I've heard a rumor that something somewhere might have disappeared. Somebody has to know where it went."

"Let me see what I can find out." Bellingham stood. "I hear you're a fan of Cubist art. I have a collection upstairs if you care to view it."

Istvan's heart about stopped. Lauryn was finally climbing back out the window. And Bellingham could turn any second.

"A wonderful library you have," Istvan said quickly, pointing at the shelves opposite from the window to draw the man's attention elsewhere. "I have lately grown to appreciate rare volumes myself. Another vehicle for investment."

"Feel free to look around," Bellingham said with pride in his voice.

Agents also being collectors wasn't that unusual. They started with lots they couldn't sell, then invested in better pieces over the years, as well. Having inventory on hand didn't hurt when they had clients with predictable tastes. Orders could be filled that much quicker.

"Look all you want." He indicated the room with an outstretched hand, turning in a circle, just missing Lauryn as she closed the second window behind her.

"I ALMOST GOT CAUGHT at the end. Somebody was coming into the office, but I skipped out the window while they fiddled with the lock. I've never been so grateful for a stuck key. What do we have so far?" Lauryn asked from behind Istvan.

They were back in their hotel suite, watching the screen change on the laptop in front of them. They had remote access to Bellingham's files.

"Enough to put him away for life, but nothing that would connect him to Valtria's royal treasures. He put out feelers after we left. His e-mails are vague. He's fishing around. If he found the stolen artifacts first, he could get a commission and I've given him the impression that my buyer is a grateful man."

"So even if he's not our guy, he's at least working for us."

He smiled, a glint of excitement in his dark eyes.

She felt the same. The hunt was on. To pursue her goals to the end was a challenge that gave her energy. She enjoyed every moment of the job. And judging from the look on Prince Istvan's face, maybe they weren't so different after all.

He'd already set up another meeting for tonight, with one of the two men who looked like the best bets out

of the five black market bosses on the island. Berk was
originally from Mersin, the Turkish port where the ship
they'd taken to the island had been headed. It could be
a connection or nothing more than coincidence. A link
they planned to investigate, in any case.

"Dinner before we go?" Istvan asked her.

"Here?"

They'd been taking their meals in his suite, not wanting to take the risk that someone would recognize him
despite the disguise. Their seclusion also fit their cover.
Fernando was a man known to keep to himself.

He nodded, holding her gaze, and she had a feeling
that this invitation was different than the ones before.
She said yes anyway.

He made the call to the concierge and this time didn't
invite his guards to dine with them, although his suite
had a large enough dining room for a private party.
The table for twelve was made of mahogany, a crystal
chandelier overhead, the place also suitable to serve as
a meeting room in a pinch.

He took off his jacket and unbuttoned the top button
of his dark blue, tailored shirt, rolled the sleeves up to
under his elbows, then took the chair at the head of the
table and leaned back casually.

"I hope you don't mind if I don't sit on the other end."
She picked a seat halfway down the table from him.

"Not at all. In fact, I'd prefer you closer."

His voice tickled something behind her breastbone.
But his face was unreadable, and she couldn't be sure if
there was any hidden meaning behind his words, or if

he was simply stating that he didn't expect her to stand on ceremony.

She didn't have time to work out what all of it meant, the private dinner and his strange mood. The food arrived with super speed. Apparently, being rich enough to take the most expensive suite came with its privileges.

The waiter pushed a cart in, left it just inside the door without looking up once, as before, and was gone before they could have thought about a tip.

Istvan stood to serve them—one of his guards had done the job before. She jumped to head him off and take over the task. Her nerves seemed on edge suddenly, unreasonably. She wanted to move, do something that kept her busy.

She set the table and realized it'd be smarter to sit closer to him so they could both reach the platters they received. He made no comment, simply watched her, which made her nervous and then angry. She didn't get nervous under any man's gaze. She'd faced down Agent Rubliczky, for heaven's sake. Not to mention a number of rivals over the years, and even an amorous mob boss who hadn't taken kindly to being told no when he asked for a date.

She lifted the first silver lid. "Tava," she said as she recognized the dish, a stew of meats with onions and herbs, her uncle's favorite. The next dish was stuffed grape leaves.

"Vegetarian dolmades." He shook his head as if not knowing what to make of them. "Stuffed with seasoned tofu."

He hadn't asked her what she wanted, and she hadn't paid much attention when he ordered, her mind on other matters. That he remembered her preferences softened something inside. She lifted the next lid. A seafood platter with prawns and other delicacies, another thing she could eat.

"And kebabs for me," he said when she reached the last dish. "I dare say the service is as good as at the royal palace. Commandaria?" He picked up the sweet dessert wine from the tray, a treat that had been enjoyed on the island for centuries.

They had a few hours before they had to leave for their meeting. "Sure."

She started with the dolmades, he went for the kebabs. He ate as elegantly as he did everything else. The muscles of his lower arms moved sinuously as he put pressure on the knife. His skin was tanned. Looked as if he spent plenty of time outdoors.

He looked up. Caught her watching him. Held her gaze.

"How does one become a thief?" he asked after a few heated seconds.

Her back muscles stiffened. "I'd say one either chooses the life or is born into it."

"Still, even with the born-into-it thing, there'd be a choice, I imagine."

"When you were young, were you fully aware that you could choose to stop being a prince?"

His fork hesitated halfway to his sensuous mouth, lips that had at one point been enclosed around her nipples.

She drew a slow breath, forcing a nonchalant smile onto her face.

He took his time to consider the question carefully. "You mean abdicate the title?"

She inclined her head.

"I don't suppose. But one is a prince from the moment of his birth. He is what he is long before he has intellect enough to think about it. It cannot be such with a thief."

"Infants are used as decoys, their strollers and diaper bags are handy hiding places."

"But they don't actively participate."

"They see the life. It's their earliest memory. They see it before they know right from wrong. When right or wrong is decided by daddy."

"Even so." He didn't look ready to concede. "At some point, there's a conscious choice to participate."

"If by conscious choice you mean a four-year-old fully realizing what her father wants when he pushes her through a dog door and asks her to turn the lock to let him in."

Surprise glinted in his eyes, even as his face darkened. "Four years?"

"Or even earlier."

"What kind of parent—"

She cut him off, not wanting to go there. "Maybe one who was raised the same way."

He put food into his mouth at last and chewed methodically, not looking as if he enjoyed his meal the least even though it was prepared superbly. Not that Lauryn could enjoy hers. She hated to discuss her past, even in the impersonal way they were doing it now.

"And when that child grows up," he said after a while, "does she not rebel? Surely, at one point there is some understanding."

"By that point, rumors about her might make it impossible to switch to an honest line of work, certainly not in the art world. It's too small. Everyone knows everyone."

"And yet, apparently, it can be done." He looked at her pointedly.

"If law enforcement chooses to stop all investigation and wipe the slate clean. I'm guessing that doesn't happen to everybody." *Thank God, it happened to me. Thank God.*

He dabbed a satin napkin to his lip. "Why would they do such a thing?"

"For a price."

"Such as?"

"Information on the location of a lifetime of acquisitions. For the child to betray her parent." She set her fork down and pushed her plate away as a dark ache spread in her chest.

"And the parent?"

"Got to live the last few months of his life in a hospital under proper care instead of on the run or in prison."

She pushed her chair back and walked to the window, keeping her back to the prince. She didn't want him to see the moisture in her eyes, the guilt and conflict she still felt over some past decisions. "Somehow, I don't see you betraying your family, your brothers."

"No," he remarked quietly. "But neither would they break the law to such degree that the authorities would come to me offering deals."

Outside, storm clouds gathered on the horizon, the sea choppy. Waves crashed to shore in an endless line. She watched the water, trying to quell the storm inside. Then strong arms came around her and she was pulled against the prince's wide chest, his chin resting on the top of her head as he held her from behind.

"You surprise me. Perhaps I judged you rashly."

She blinked the moisture from her eyes, then gave an unladylike snort, which didn't seem to put him off.

He turned her in his arms gently, held her gaze. His attention on her was full and undivided, mesmerizing. His head dipped.

She stood still, needing this, needing him, refusing to think of any of the hundreds of reasons why she should move away.

The moment their lips met, heat flooded her. She felt like she had when they'd swum to shore in Porto Paphos after escaping the bullets and the jellyfish field, reaching the safety of land—immense relief and rightness, a sense of security and gratitude for having found a safe haven.

For a while, she had no coherent thought in her head, and getting lost in him was bliss. But eventually the questions came. What on earth was she doing here, with this man? What did she expect to come of this? Where did she think they were heading? Sure as anything, it wasn't some fairy-tale happy ending.

She would have thought she had more sense than to become a momentary play toy for the rich, but she was proven wrong when her mouth defied incoming instructions from her brain and opened to him.

He tasted like sweet wine and felt like heaven.

She recognized danger when she saw it.

She liked him too much, that was the trouble. Really liked him, far more than any of the others. Honor was woven deep into the fabric of him. He drew her against all reason, and the strength of that frightened her as much as it thrilled her.

She pulled back, working hard to produce some righteous anger. She needed *something* to put between them. "Just like a man. Now that you want me, you're ready to forget my past and forgive everything."

Better to have him mad at her than have him in his current mood. He was dangerous when he was bent on seduction.

"I want you. I'm not going to apologize for it," he said evenly. "You don't have to be scared of this," he added.

Her chin came up. "I'm not scared of anything."

Even as he lifted an eyebrow, a smile hovered over his upper lip. He unceremoniously pulled her back into his arms for another kiss.

Chapter Ten

It had been a long time since he'd held a woman like this. And what he remembered hadn't been this raw, this urgent. Lauryn had blasted into his life like a comet, turning everything upside down, setting him on fire.

They'd fought for their lives together, outwitting thugs on that ship, even spent a few quiet moments here and there, talking about excavations on the island and the diary of the Brotherhood, shared a couple of meals, a couple of kisses. He wanted more. More of what they already had—minus the running-for-their-lives part. She *was* the most self-sufficient woman he knew, but he still hated to see her in danger. He wanted a prolonged, full-fledged affair.

He liked her and he didn't want to let her go. It was that simple for him. But knowing women and the way they couldn't help but make everything out to be more complicated than it had to be… The key was not to leave her too much time to think.

So he deepened the kiss, drinking in her sweetness as he lifted her into his arms and carried her to the bedroom, to the bed they hadn't yet shared. Now was the time. He laid her down gently and gave his hands free rein.

Running his seeking fingers and lips over her body nearly drove him out of his skin with need. She had sleek muscles, soft curves in other places, a delicious contrast.

But his appreciation for her went far beyond his appreciation for her body. He'd begun respecting her resilience on the ship and during their escape. He'd seen her intelligence numerous times since. And now he was beginning to understand some things about her, about her past. His old prejudices were fast disappearing, leaving something new behind, a yearning for companionship with someone who was very much like him in some regards and completely different in others.

But all that was still too new for him to fully comprehend let alone articulate. For now, he was content to let his body speak. And his body and hers were definitely speaking the same language.

Her silk dress practically slipped out of the way of his hands. Her breasts arched into his palms. He'd wanted to do this all day. Her nearness, her familiar behavior with him to keep up their ruse, had gotten to him on every level. She'd smiled at him as a mistress, touched him as a mistress and tantalized him beyond endurance.

Tension had gathered all day as they were together but always in the company of others. Now they were alone. And they were like two live wires placed near each other, electricity arching between them.

His haze of need was punctured only by a sharp object drilling into his hand. "What's—"

"Sorry." She pulled a metal lock pick from her bra and placed it on the nightstand. Then gave him a small, embarrassed smile and went on to retrieve various other objects. A small, sharp-looking switchblade came from her panties, and he winced thinking the injury that could have caused him.

"Where did you—" He bit off the rest of the question when the answer came to him. No doubt, she'd gotten her tools either from her uncle or she'd acquired them that morning when she'd sneaked out of his cousin's estate and left him behind.

A small pile gathered by the time she was done.

"Wearing a weapon in the presence of a royal person is against the law and carries the charge of treason," he observed drily.

She shrugged with a grin, never one to be intimidated. "You already thought I was a born criminal."

He didn't like the reminder. He might have been a fool to have judged her before they even met. He didn't play the fool often, so the thought didn't sit well with him. "Never mind. Anything else?"

She shook her head. "You?"

"Completely unarmed. But feel free to check my pockets."

She laughed.

He slid his hands up her thighs, dragging the material of her skirt up as he went. He felt the same sensation as when he was looking at a new site, getting to know the lay of the land, anticipating peeling off the layers one by one until he found what he was looking for.

Anticipation coursed through him. He had no doubt that there was treasure in front of him, a nagging feeling that he might discover in her something more beautiful, more profound, more valuable than he'd ever expected. He took her mouth and kissed her deeply, couldn't stop kissing her.

She didn't protest. Instead, she arched her back so he could reach the clasp of her bra more easily. And there they were, her amazing breasts about to spill out for him to see, to touch, to taste.

His body hardened even more, if that was possible. He moved his head closer. He was beyond ready for her.

The phone rang, bringing a frustrated curse to his lips. Under other circumstances he would have ignored it—or smashed it against the wall—but it was his secured cell phone and they were in the middle of important and dangerous business.

He grabbed the cell from the nightstand with one hand, holding on to her with the other. Having to push the answer button pained him. "What is it?"

"News on the investigation," his brother Miklos said. "The break-in had help from the inside, as we suspected."

"Do you know who?"

"Partial recording of one of the video cameras we've overlooked has been restored. Chancellor Egon's son, Zoltan, was on it, along with an unidentified male."

He was too stunned to process his brother's words at first. Then things slowly began to fall into place. The Chancellor's son was a spoiled brat, a man who rose in the ranks due to his father's merit rather than his own. Maybe he was jealous of the amount of time and effort his father spent on the princes since he'd been chosen Chancellor.

"What does the father say to this?"

"Crushed."

He would be. Chancellor Egon took his job very seriously, to the point of being overzealous about it, which annoyed the princes on occasion, even if they appreciated his dedication for the most part.

"What else?"

"Benedek said Zoltan was definitely the voice in the catacombs."

For a moment he didn't know what Miklos was talking about, then he remembered Benedek being trapped with Rayne in the catacombs under Palace Hill after the siege of the opera house the year before. He'd always maintained that one of the rebels he overheard had a familiar voice, but could never put a name to it. They'd suspected one of the staff and backgrounds had been checked and rechecked, two men dismissed.

"So we let people go unfairly."

"Benedek is making retribution. He's in a mood because he didn't make the connection to Zoltan earlier. It clicked the second he saw the guy on the video, but—well—"

He knew what his brother wasn't saying. If Zoltan

were caught earlier, lives could have been saved. But Benedek was not at fault.

"Nobody would have suspected Zoltan. He's like a distant cousin. His father has become a pillar—"

Lauryn slipped away to lie on the bed next to him, distracting him momentarily. He focused back on the latest developments in the investigation with effort.

"So if Zoltan was involved in both the attack on the opera house and in this heist that links the theft of the crown jewels to the Freedom Council." The clandestine group of unidentified business tycoons had been working to bring down the monarchy for ages, planning to carve the small kingdom up and divide it among themselves.

Not if he and his brothers had anything to do with it, Istvan thought and said, "This explains so many things. If there's no crown, a new king cannot be crowned and confirmed." And their mother was ill enough that Arpad becoming king someday soon was a very distinct possibility.

As Lauryn had said, taking one-of-a-kind, easily recognizable artifacts like the crown jewels made little sense for their gold and gem value alone. But the theft made a world of sense if the purpose was to disrupt the monarchy.

And the crown held other power, too. Like the key to the Brotherhood's treasure, a find of historical significance, which he didn't want to go into over the phone. He didn't even want to think about the kind of war that it could finance if it fell into the wrong hands.

"Any developments there?" his brother asked.

Istvan filled him in, getting up to pace the room as he did so.

"And how is the princess of thieves?" Miklos asked at the end, after all his other questions had been answered.

Istvan walked from the bedroom to the living room and closed the door behind him. "Don't call her that."

"What would you like to call her, plain *princess?*"

He shook his head silently. The one drawback about having a close-knit family was that they felt free to stick their noses into his business anywhere, anytime. "It's not like that between me and Miss Steler."

The connection was purely physical. And intellectual. But that was it. Nothing he couldn't walk away from at the end. Not that he'd told his brothers about the physical part even. None of their meddling business.

"Because of Amalia?" Miklos asked. "Still?"

He said nothing. Because the truth was, he thought about Amalia less and less.

"You were never in love with Amalia. You know that, right?"

"I was. You go too far. Being married doesn't make you an expert on the subject," Istvan responded with some heat.

"Why didn't you marry her?"

Why didn't he, indeed. He'd thought about that many times in the aftermath of her death. "The time wasn't right." Among many other things. "And there were obstacles. She was a commoner. Divorced. There would have been a bloody fight at the palace over it. The Chancellor would have had a stroke. Mother would have had a heart attack." The reasons that seemed to have had all kinds of power in the past, suddenly sounded weak, even to his own ears.

"Here is a piece of unsolicited advice from your big brother—the time is always right with the right woman."

"If there's nothing else you have for me on the investigation, I'm signing off here." Istvan closed the phone before his brother could have pushed further.

He longed for the days when they used to share hunting stories and sword-fighting tips. Now that Miklos and Benedek and Lazlo were married and more in touch with their emotions, whatever that meant, God help the rest of them.

Janos and Miklos had met Lauryn when they'd come and taken the ship's crew back to Valtria with them. Both liked her, which made no sense at all. Janos, maybe, but Miklos ran palace security—he'd lost several of his men to the heist. He should not approve of an ex-thief so thoroughly.

Not that his disapproval would have been better. Istvan felt defensive just thinking about anyone disapproving of her. She scrambled his brain like no other, he thought as he walked back to her.

She stood next to the bed, her dress back in place, looking as if she, too, had sobered in the few minutes that had passed. She glanced at the bedside clock. "It's time for us to leave."

For the next meeting with the next criminal. And the stakes were higher than ever. "You should stay."

She gave him a stubborn look. "We've already done that song and dance."

"These people are more dangerous than I thought." He told her what he'd found out from Miklos, told her a little about the Freedom Council. "We're not facing a simple gang of thieves with a wealthy buyer behind them. The Freedom Council's sole purpose is the defeat of the monarchy and the destruction of the royal family."

"By that you mean they'll try to kill you given half a chance?"

He nodded.

For a second she held his gaze without a word, a thoughtful look in her eyes. Then she squared her slim shoulders. "All the more reason for me to be there."

A pure gesture of courage and loyalty.

He felt an unfamiliar sensation in the middle of his chest. For now, he decided to ignore it.

BELLINGHAM WAS AN AGENT, a go-between man. Berk, the guy they were meeting tonight, was a crew boss, a different animal altogether. Bellingham was a gentleman, using his high standing in society to gain connections, to wheel and deal. He had people for protection and intimidation when necessary. He wasn't the type to get his hands dirty.

Berk was the man in the trenches. He went out on heists and put his neck on the line every time. Lauryn knew his kind only too well. He had a team of rough-and-tough criminals to keep in line, keep from going rogue or trying to take over. Any one of his men could plea-bargain his name if caught, any one could slit his throat to get a bigger share of the loot.

Berk didn't invite them into his home. He insisted on meeting at a neutral location on the Turkish side of the island, at a café near a famous bazaar where he had enough of his armed men watching to make minced meat out of them at the first wrong move. Caution was Berk's middle name. That and shooting first, apologizing later was what kept him alive.

"Does your buyer have a price range?" he asked, drawing from a water pipe. They were sitting over a plate of sweets and strong, unfiltered coffee.

The man had watery brown eyes and a sparse beard that covered only the tip of his chin, the scraggly hairs a few inches long, coming together at the end in a spike. Tattoos of Turkish script covered his lower arms. He wore an eggplant-colored suit and leather loafers that had pointy toes.

"For the right piece, he'd pay the right price," Istvan said as Fernando.

"And the right piece would be something extravagant."

Istvan nodded. "Something truly one-of-a-kind. For a private collection that's never been seen by outside eyes."

"Maybe he has something in mind and would like to commission a job?"

"He's heard about a recent job with several items he might be interested in."

"Commissioned by another collector?"

Istvan shrugged.

"The original buyer would be disappointed if he didn't get what he paid for. Bad business all around."

The two had been talking like that for an hour, hinting much, saying little as Lauryn patiently sat by. The market buzzed around them, people coming and going, shopping, drinking, making deals. Women, too. Some in Western outfits, others veiled. Coming from Turkey, Muslim conservatives were gaining ground on the north side of the island. Only a small foothold, though. Nobody gave her any trouble for her clothes or for sitting with two men, although, knowing what it would be like here, she had added a large, dark blue silk shawl to her outfit. She had draped it loosely over her head and shoulders when they'd arrived.

Directly next to the café was a spice stand, a perfume stand on the other side where scents were mixed on the spot, one-of-a-kind for each customer's taste. Clothing shops took up one full row, silks and damasks in every color of the rainbow. Another alley was dominated by carpet dealers, selling everything from four-hundred-year-old museum-quality pieces to the latest designs. Copper dishes were sold yet in another place. And leather, and everything that can be made from the material, in several shops within sight.

She'd been pretending to pay a great deal of attention to the shopping, leaving the men to talk. But it seemed the talk was going in circles at this stage. She turned her attention to them and snuggled up to Istvan. He ignored her for a while, then pushed her away.

She put on a hurt look, then shrugged and cozied up to Berk, linking one arm through his, smoothing a hand down his lapel. "Can I offer you more coffee?"

He cast an amused look at Fernando/Istvan. Then nodded.

She served him, but didn't pull away when she was done. The thunder in Istvan's eyes looked award-worthy as he pulled a wad of cash from his pocket and tossed the bills at her. "Go shopping."

She bumped into Berk as she slid off her chair, flashed him an apologetic smile. To Istvan she gave a look of defiance, but then took the money and walked away to explore the bazaar.

On her way, she passed a table where Istvan's two bodyguards sat incognito, although she was sure Berk had picked them out as soon as they'd arrived, which was fine.

She went to the candle maker first and bought a chunk of beeswax. Then a length of silk the color of her eyes. Next she visited the leather shop where she selected a supple bodice that laced up in the front, a risqué piece made for tourists. This she took into the dressing room.

She glanced through the crack in the curtain and for a second watched the man who'd been following her all along, one of Berk's goons no doubt. Tall and bulky, he looked the quintessential seedy tough guy, with a scar running along his cheekbone, a bump in his nose where it had healed badly after a fight and greasy hair combed back from his eyes.

She cast the bodice aside, took the keys she'd lifted off Berk and pressed them into the chunk of wax, then cleaned them off to make sure nothing stuck to them. Next came the papers she'd lifted from the man's pocket. She used her cell phone to carefully photograph each page. Then she put everything away and carried out the bodice. She made a show of bargaining, as was expected, but ended up leaving the thing behind.

Her work done, she walked around some more, politely refusing vendors who did their level best to lure her inside their small shops, calling loudly and offering the most incredible deals. She moved within a hundred feet of where Istvan and Berk were sitting, making a game of picking out Berk's men who were standing guard at regular intervals. She found almost a dozen and made a point of remembering their faces. They were his crew, the ones he would send after her and Istvan if something went wrong. It was better to be able to recognize them from afar.

When it looked as if Istvan and Berk were finishing up, she weaved her way back to them, stopped behind Berk and touched his shoulders, smoothed down his lapels, gave the man a sugary smile. "I love your country. Everyone is so nice."

Istvan stood up so quickly that his chair nearly tipped back. "You know how to find me," he told Berk, then grabbed Lauryn's elbow and dragged her along without a word. His steps were controlled, as was the emotion on his face, but enough tension radiated off him to tell everyone who watched that he was displeased with his woman.

The gazes of Berk's men followed them, some looking on with an amused smile.

Then one looked toward Berk's table. Some silent communication must have passed between them because the man began walking down an aisle parallel to theirs, keeping them in his sight.

ISTVAN WATCHED LAURYN come out of their hotel bathroom, again in those sensible pajamas, and go straight to the table to pour herself a glass of water. He was still fully dressed, although resting comfortably, his arms under his head as he reclined on the bed, his legs crossed at the ankles. They'd had a productive day, all in all. They both deserved a break.

He glanced toward the window. The last time he'd checked, Berk's goon was gone. He let the guy follow them back to the hotel. Let Berk have that information, let him think he had the upper hand and that Fernando and his guards weren't as sharp as they thought.

The chunk of beeswax had been picked up by his backup team, the keys already being made. The copies of the two pieces of scrap paper in Berk's pocket lay on the nightstand. On one there was an address. He'd already sent a man there to check it out. A tailor shop, not much more than a small room with a window front, his man had reported after the premises had been entered and searched. Nothing suspicious had been found.

"How did I do as the misbehaving mistress?" Lauryn brought the glass of water over and set it on her nightstand.

"You have misbehaving down pat. The mistress part needs work." He sat up and reached out and pulled her down to the bed.

She moved away from him, putting some distance and a throw pillow between them. "Listen. About this afternoon…"

Thinking about that afternoon put his body on alert and then some. Sitting on the bed with her and thinking about their passionate kisses kicked the heat up another notch. "I agree. It's high time we finished. I apologize for the interruption."

She threw him a look of exasperation. "You know that's not what I was about to say."

His body was buzzing with anticipation. As usual, her seductress act had gone only too well. Her touching him had filled him with need. Her touching Berk had filled him with thoughts of murder.

"Anyway. About this afternoon…" She looked away. "That was a mistake."

"Says who?"

"Reality and common sense."

"Both overrated."

"You can't be involved with someone like me." She turned back to him and folded her arms in front of her. "Think of the press."

He'd already thought of that. Anyone involved with the royal princes came under a magnifying glass. Her past, her family, would never stand up to scrutiny. They'd crucify her. And Chancellor Egon would crucify him for the bad press. More than ever, the monarchy had to be beyond reproach. The Freedom Council stopped at nothing to malign the royal family and turn the people against them, stooping to outright lies if needed. Lauryn's past, even if nothing more than rumors, would be used against them mercilessly.

He rarely railed against the confines of his title, certainly not like Lazlo and some of his other brothers. But he did now. Something to be dealt with later. He swiped the pillow from between them and pulled her close, pulled her down to the bed with him and settled her in his arms, kissed her temple, then the tip of a small, pink ear. "I don't see any press in sight."

She turned her head, but she didn't move away. "You want a temporary mistress."

"I want you, any way you're willing."

"Since when?"

"Since you broke the Brotherhood's code." Probably even before. Possibly from the first moment he'd set eyes on her, but he thought telling her that might give her too much power.

She struggled with a smile as her eyes opened. "You're impossible."

"I've been called worse."

"I bet." She pulled away to pick up the paper that held the information she'd lifted from Berk. The address was a dead end, but she'd also photographed some kind of a drawing.

"What do you think it is?" he asked.

"A map, but of what?" She traced the lines. "Could be roads and hills. Could be a map of the early Christian catacombs right here in Paphos."

"Could be a map of hallways inside a building."

"We need at least one point of reference. Without that, the map is no help whatsoever." She put the paper back, frustration drawing small lines around her full lips, lines he wouldn't have minded kissing away.

He reached out to fold his fingers around her slim wrist and pulled her closer.

"I can't do this," she said, her voice pained.

"Why?"

She looked as if she wasn't going to answer, but then she said, "There is something here." She drew a slow breath, looking away from him. "At least for me there is. If I open this door, it's going to hurt to walk away."

"Then don't." He caught himself as soon as he said the words. What the hell did he mean? Damned if he knew.

"I'll have to. Sooner or later. We live in different worlds."

He hated that she was right. Because, to be honest, there was something here for him, too. A pull he might have underestimated earlier. That she could coolly analyze the situation and so easily walk away from what could be burned him.

"I'm not sleeping on the couch tonight."

She moved all the way to the other side of the bed and turned her back to him. "Suit yourself."

Two hours later, he was still staring at the ceiling, which was just as well. At least his mind wasn't fuzzy from sleep when his phone rang.

The head of the team he'd left at Alexander's estate was on the line. They were following up on a number of things, as Istvan had requested.

"Our man who was following Berk called in. The guy went straight to Canda in Limassol. They hopped into a car and headed off toward the countryside," he said.

Canda was another possible link on Cyprus on their list. "Are they being followed?"

"We have two men on them. The one who shadowed Berk and the one who shadowed Canda. They'll report back to me as soon as there's any change."

"Where are they now?"

"Five kilometers from Dali."

He was dragging his clothes on already. "I'm coming."

"Me, too." Not surprisingly, Lauryn already had one of her Catwoman outfits on, blinking the sleep from her eyes, running her fingers through her copper hair to tame it enough for a ponytail.

He didn't have time to argue as she grabbed the sketchy map and shoved it in her pocket. He rapped on the door to alert his guards in the adjoining suite. They caught up while Istvan and Lauryn waited for the elevators. Probably slept with their clothes on, judging by the wrinkles.

They took two cars for safety. Having backup could come in handy. He turned on the GPS and contacted the man who'd been following Berk. "Anything new?"

"They drove into Dali and pulled into a courtyard. Not sure what happened in there, but they came out with a black van and backup."

"How many?"

"Two jeeps with four men in each. Could be more in the back of the van."

"Heading which way?"

"North."

"Morphou Bay," Lauryn said once he'd hung up.

"Probably." If his asking around spooked the thieves because they had something to hide, they could be getting ready to move the artifacts off the island. He couldn't allow that to happen. Syria was too close, just a boat ride away, so was the African coast. It would be all too easy for the thieves and the crown jewels to disappear forever.

It started to rain, a rare event in the summer. The phone rang. He pushed the on button.

It was one of his men who followed the two crew bosses. "They pulled over and got out. They're walking into the woods."

"Where are you?"

"On the main road to the bay. You'll see the cars. We're going after them."

He hung up, then called the investigative team at Alexander's estate, gave them the location and ordered them to meet him there as soon as possible. Then he stepped on the gas. "There are guns in the glove compartment," he told Lauryn. "Take what you need and get ready."

"I'm not much for weapons." She opened the compartment gingerly.

Great, an ex-criminal who didn't like violence. He should have figured. She was unusual in every other way, as well. And he would have lied if he said he didn't like that about her. She had a lot of layers, a lot of secrets to explore and investigate. He would enjoy discovering what lay at her core, as much as he enjoyed discovering the secrets of the earth. His favorite activity was peeling back layers. He had a feeling he would never be bored with her around.

But to have her around, first they had to survive the night.

He watched as she hesitated over the weapons. "For self-defense," he told her, but she didn't look reassured.

She took the smallest one, handling it in a way that told him there was very little chance of her ever firing it, which was fine. He didn't plan on putting her in harm's way. He would leave her in the car.

Soon the vehicles by the road came into sight. He parked farther down, in the cover of an abandoned shack, then called his men, who were already hidden in the woods, for an update.

Neither of them picked up.

He called again.

Nothing.

The muscles in his shoulders grew tighter and tighter, as he waited. And still nobody answered.

Chapter Eleven

"I'm not staying in the car," Lauryn told the prince before he could have told her to.

"It'd be safer," he argued without any heat, preoccupied with worry because his men weren't answering his calls, and also smart enough to know that nothing could convince her.

Good. She liked smart men. That her feelings for him were rapidly moving beyond "like" she ignored for now.

"As it would be safer for Your Royal Highness to remain safe." She used his official title to remind him who he was and what his life meant not only to himself but to others. She better remember, too, and not sink too far into some imaginary fairy tale that could never be real. "We could wait for backup to get here."

"You should."

She glared at him through the darkness. The headlights had been cut as soon as they'd arrived. The only illumination came from the moon above and little of that with rain clouds drifting through. At least it had stopped drizzling.

There were four of them, including Istvan's two guards. A dozen men would be coming from the estate where the original war room had been set up. Lauryn figured they couldn't be more than an hour behind them.

"Spread out?" she asked.

"Stick together," Istvan answered.

And soon she realized why as the guards took up protective positions around him. They were probably under order not to let the prince out of their sight.

They moved forward quietly through the woods. There was hardly any light at all as they walked, the trees filtering what little moonlight the clouds let through.

"I have a penlight," she offered, digging into her pocket.

"I have my lighter, but even that's too dangerous." Istvan kept moving forward. "We don't want to alert them that we're here."

She could barely make out the tree trunks, let alone the path. Their only chance of finding the men was catching sight of their lights up ahead, but even after long minutes ticked by, they saw nothing.

Then the guard who led the group tripped and swore under his breath. "Careful here." He bent and looked at the boulder in their way. A strange-looking boulder.

Not a boulder at all.

"Man down," the guard clarified.

Istvan stepped forward. "Ours?"

A second passed while the man checked the body, peering closer, tilting the face to the dim moonlight. "Yes."

"We'll come back for him." Istvan's voice was tight.

He took her hand and helped her over the body, and she let him even though it wasn't necessary. She was used to getting around in the dark and moving around obstacles.

"One of the men could escort you back to the car," he offered.

She considered it for a fraction of a second. She'd been a thief, sure. But she'd avoided violence all her life. The sight of it never failed to shake her. She would have to get over that tonight. "No, thanks." She hung on to his hand.

Soon they came to some sort of meadow that was dotted with rocks, some the size of beach balls, others taller than a man. Then the path went from dirt to paved with small rocks. They came to an even flatter area after that. No boulders here, but partially collapsed walls cordoned off by construction tape and a posted sign.

Istvan let her go as he passed his guards and moved up to the sign, then sounded out the letters of the Greek alphabet. "It says the site is protected by the Ministry of Culture."

"A historic ruin," she guessed and looked around, wondering from what period. She spotted an arch that gave it away. "I think Roman."

Due to the economic crisis that hit tourism hard at tourist paradises like Cyprus, many excavations on the island had been halted, awaiting better times and sufficient funds. Many sites stood deserted like this one. They'd seen two on their drive to her uncle a few days before.

Istvan moved ahead, but she grabbed for his arm after a few steps to stop him. She pulled the sheet of paper from her pocket. Of course, they couldn't see anything written on it in the dark.

"All right. Get out that penlight." Istvan directed her toward a partially excavated wall and squatted, pulling her with him. Then he told the men to surround them and block the light as much as they could from the side that wasn't protected by the wall.

She produced the penlight from her shoe. It was about the size and shape of a slim lipstick and cast its light no farther than a foot, but for their purpose, it was perfect.

"If that's the path and this is the boulder and over there is the wall—" Istvan pointed at the marks.

"Then we have to go that way," she finished.

Another thirty minutes or so passed before they found their destination, an excavation shaft they would have never come upon in the dark without the map. A man sat at the hole's mouth, leaning against a pile of stones.

They crouched and waited. Istvan was probably considering how best to rush the guy, Lauryn figured. Waiting didn't bother her. Staying still and silent was one of her specialties.

But the more she looked, the more she realized there was something strange about that guard.

Istvan turned to her with a questioning tilt of his head. She inclined her own. He signaled to one of his men to move forward. The guard did, keeping in the shadows. The others raised their guns to cover him if necessary. The man at the stone pile still didn't move.

Then the guard was there and putting a finger to the man's neck. A couple of seconds passed. The guard came back. "Another one of ours," he whispered.

Both men who'd been shadowing Berk and Canda were dead. And the backup team hadn't arrived yet. Waiting would have been the smartest thing to do. But the sound of an approaching chopper gave them motivation to hurry. The crown jewels, if they were here, could be removed from the site before backup arrived.

"That excavation shaft probably has another exit to an area that's clear and flat enough for the helicopter to land." Istvan moved forward.

Lauryn and the guards followed. He was very likely right. Excavation shafts often had multiple entry points to allow better flow for the carts going down and coming up with rubble, as well as to provide better ventilation for the workers.

The small hill could have covered an entire buried Roman town beyond the single villa that was visible.

They entered the shaft, the guards first, the prince next, Lauryn bringing up the rear. Good thing she wasn't scared of dark places. The first man walked into a wall and swore. She pulled her flashlight and passed it up front; less chance of that giving them away than the noise they made as they bumped into things. The corridor twisted enough to shield the light even as its cavernous length amplified sound.

The shaft soon linked to an ancient hallway that was made of stone from floor to ceiling, probably leading to the villa's cellar, then to a low-ceilinged room with a reinforced-steel door to one side, which was not at all normal at a standard excavation. If the authorities wanted to protect the site, they would have closed off the entrance of the shaft.

She looked at the lock, which was also not standard issue. The keys she'd lifted off Berk would have come in handy, but their copies weren't ready yet.

"Want to give it a whirl?" Istvan asked.

She got out her picks and did her best. Several minutes and some adjustments later, she smiled when she heard the small click.

The look on Istvan's face was conflicted.

"Right. You disapprove on principle." She rolled her eyes at him. "Disapproval duly noted." She opened the door and pressed inside.

An old-fashioned generator hooked to a flood lamp was the first thing they saw. Because it would have made too much noise, they didn't turn it on. Her flashlight was used instead, along with Istvan's lighter.

A dozen or so crates occupied the underground room, some full, some empty. Istvan rushed to the closest, tipping up the lid and lowering his lighter, victory in his voice as he said, "The war chest."

They immediately went to check the rest, not an easy task with what little light they had.

"Most of what was stolen from the treasury is here," he told them after a while, but his shoulders were sagging.

"Except?" she asked in a low voice, standing near him, already suspecting the answer.

"Except what was in the special vault."

So they were still missing the crown jewels.

He left a man with the artifacts and instructions to send the backup team after him and Lauryn once they arrived. Then Istvan, Lauryn and the remaining guard moved on to discover the rest of the shaft and the location of the crown jewels.

When, a few hundred yards later, they saw a dim light up ahead, they extinguished their own and moved more slowly and quietly. But then soon realized that the light wasn't manmade. Moonlight was filtering in up ahead. They reached the end of the tunnel; another few hundred feet would bring them back out into the open. They could even hear the hovering chopper.

They came out on the other side of the hill, and spotted a road nearby with a canvas-top truck and a dozen armed men, rifles outlined in the moonlight. The truck's back was open. Two men were working on lifting a large box, hurrying, keeping one eye on the helicopter.

Those who were not involved in the work held their rifles on the chopper. Whoever was up there was not their friend.

The standoff provided the perfect distraction. Istvan

moved forward, followed closely by the guard and Lauryn.

Then all hell broke loose as gunfire erupted behind them.

She dived to the rocky ground and rolled blindly for cover until she found relative safety in a ditch. A second later Istvan landed on top of her, knocking the air out of her lungs.

The gunfire stopped once the shooters lost their targets.

He poked his head up, not much of a risk given the darkness. "They had a lookout on the hillside. He saw us coming from the cave."

She, too, peeked out and saw Istvan's bodyguard a few feet away, lying in a pool of blood, arms outstretched. Her stomach constricted painfully. "Can we pull him in?"

She could feel Istvan's muscles tighten on top of her as he said, "He's gone."

The men were shouting around the truck, the crate was finally lifted. But then more shouting came from the same direction Lauryn and Istvan had just come from. The backup team. They burst forth from the opening and the men by the truck opened fire, and the chopper stepped into the melee, indiscriminately firing at everyone on the ground.

Istvan took aim at the chopper and missed. She couldn't have contributed if she wanted to. He was lying on top of her and showed no sign of wanting to move.

He took aim again and hit it this time. The rotors gave a grinding noise.

Unfortunately, the gunner had no intention of giving up on the battle.

Half the Valtrian guards were dead on the ground, the other half pulled back into the shaft. Berk's and Canda's men rushed in after them, desperate for cover from the chopper.

The hand-to-hand combat that ensued was bloody and fierce. Istvan kept shooting at the chopper, trying to at least stop the firing. And the bird did come down, even if it didn't crash. The pilot landed it just as the blades came to a complete halt. A half-dozen men jumped off immediately, keeping low to the ground and spreading out as they ran forward.

They were fresh to the fight with plenty of ammunition. They ended the battle at the opening of the shaft within minutes. Then they came looking for whoever had shot down the chopper.

Lauryn pulled her head back in and held her breath, gripping Istvan's shirt, thankful that they were both dressed in black, praying that he would stay very, very still.

HE HAD SECONDS. Istvan grabbed his empty gun and watched as a familiar man got out of the chopper, his face visible in the truck's headlights.

"Stay down no matter what happens," he whispered to Lauryn, then pried her fingers off him and stood from the ditch, threw aside his useless weapon and walked forward, bellowing, "Bellingham!"

"Stand down! Put away your weapons!" the man ordered as he sauntered closer, holding his own pistol in front of him. "Well, well, Your Highness."

He stopped in front of the man and kept his hands up, his mind working furiously as he reassessed their meeting. "You've known all along?"

"Only since Fernando was arrested this afternoon in Buenos Aires." He laughed. "Good show, by the way. I've been asking questions and learned that the Valtrian royal treasures had gone missing. I'm always game, thought I'd track them down and sell them to Fernando for a fair commission. But if it wasn't Fernando who came to breakfast, I had to ask myself, who could it be?"

He motioned Istvan toward the truck. "Maybe someone who wanted to retrieve the treasures? Didn't take much to sort out that Prince Istvan of Valtria hasn't been seen in public in the past couple of days. Turns out his secretary cancelled all his appointments. Once I had that information and your latest media photos in front of me..." He gave an aristocratic shrug.

"Name your commission," Istvan offered. "I'll pay it to have the artifacts back." It was likely the man had no idea exactly what he had captured from Berk and Canda. He hadn't had a chance to open the box yet. He wouldn't dream that it held Valtria's crown jewels.

"If only it were that simple. You see, I already thought about that. And then I thought, if whatever was stolen was important enough for His Royal Highness himself to come after it, how important could it be to your enemies?"

His heart sank. "You contacted the Freedom Council?"

"In a way. Turns out we have friends in common. Imagine my surprise when they said that they in fact would not be interested in the recovery of the treasure as they were the ones who ordered the heist in the first place. Impressive."

"Criminal is another word for it."

"I knew if anyone on the island had anything to do with it, it had to be either Berk or Canda. I had both of them followed all day. The only surprise was that they did the job together. Usually they'd dig each other's eyes out sooner than look at each other." The man shrugged. "I tell you, the power of love has nothing over the power of money when it comes to reconciling people."

"So now you do have the treasure and you can make the Freedom Council pay."

"Oh, here is the good part." Belligham laughed. "What they pay for what's on that truck will look like a small bonus compared to what they'll pay for a Valtrian prince."

Istvan didn't waste his breath protesting. While he'd come forward to protect Lauryn and because he knew Bellingham was too much of a gentleman to shoot a royal prince in cold blood—despite his unsavory occupation—he also knew that he wouldn't hesitate to sell one for the right price to the highest bidder.

The only thing he could do was go with the man and draw him away from the place before Lauryn was discovered.

Except that she seemed to be intent on getting herself killed, as if there hadn't been enough blood already spilled tonight. He caught a small shadow moving along the edge of the woods. He could have strangled her. He looked away on purpose, not wanting anyone to pick up on what he was looking at.

Then hope came, even if it was laced with misgivings.

Belligham had only a half-dozen men. They were hard to miss in the truck's headlights. If she found a decent enough cover, she might be able to pick them off one by one before they rushed her. She had enough bullets.

"I'll match whatever you think the Freedom Council will pay for me," he said to distract Bellingham.

From the corner of his eye, he watched as Lauryn reached a good-size boulder. He was prepared to drop and roll so any flying bullets wouldn't hit him. But Lauryn didn't stop at the boulder.

"If I let you go with the treasure, the Freedom Council will come after me. Nasty people." Bellingham shrugged. "If I give you to them along with the treasure, they'll be my grateful allies forever. At the end of the day, I think I'd feel better not making enemies out of them."

The sound of the truck's engine revving as it was put into gear drew everyone's attention.

"Who the bloody hell is that?" Bellingham whipped around. "Get after him!"

But it was too late. All they could do was shoot at the rear lights as Lauryn hightailed it out of there with Valtria's crown jewels, the heist of a lifetime.

Istvan stared after her, his hands coming down, his mind and body in shock for a moment. Bellingham's men were scrambling around, but he was too stunned to take advantage of the distraction. Then Belligham's gun came up and was aimed right at his chest. Outrage twisted the man's face.

But even the threat of imminent death couldn't stop the prince from breaking out in strangled laughter.

"I wouldn't be laughing if I were you," the man shouted.

"I'm not laughing at you, believe me," Istvan reassured him, looking after the truck. "I'm laughing at what a fool I've been."

"Your partner, then?" Bellingham's mood turned to amused. "Never trust a woman." Then he shrugged. "No bigger fool than I was, thinking the elusive Fernando was coming to my home for a visit. I was not pleased with my associate who vouched for you. My men had a chat with him, and with the old man who recommended you to him."

Istvan surged forward, but was stopped by the gun that was raised to point at the middle of his forehead. Frustration and worry tore through him. Chances were better than good that Lauryn would head straight to her uncle. If Bellingham's men were still there, she would be walking straight into danger.

And despite the fact that she'd just betrayed and abandoned him, he cared.

Chapter Twelve

Her cell phone was nowhere to be found. When Istvan had jumped on top of her in that ditch, he'd probably knocked it from her pocket. And, naturally, there wasn't a house in sight where she could ask to use a landline.

Lauryn drove madly over country roads that were even worse in the hills than elsewhere. She needed a plan. She tried not to think that Istvan might already be dead. Tried to keep in mind that she had to keep the car on the left side of the road if she didn't want to die in a head-on collision.

"What is it with island nations anyway?" she muttered to the steering wheel and smacked it for good measure. "And what is it with princes?"

She refused to worry about Istvan. He could handle himself. He wouldn't want her as backup anyway. He never wanted her as backup, only let her join him after considerable begging each and every time. Because in his arrogant princely mind, he probably saw her as nothing more than a weak woman. And he still didn't trust her, no matter that she'd been as straight as an arrow long before he'd ever set eyes on her. Probably wouldn't trust her in the future either, no matter what she did.

And she wasn't going to waste a lifetime trying to prove herself to him, trying to get something from him that she could never get.

"I'm not going to fall for His Highness, Indiana damned princely Jones," she said into the night. "Not gonna happen."

No matter how good his arms had felt around her.

No matter how well he kissed.

No matter how irresistible he was with all that passion in his voice and eyes when he talked about preserving history, or when they'd talked about great art. Passions they shared.

She was not going to lose all reason and determination, qualities she actually liked in herself, and go fall in love, damn him.

Which didn't mean that she was going to leave the prince at the mercy of his enemies.

Her uncle's monastery wasn't far, so she headed that way. He was the only person she trusted on this island. She needed him to look after the crown jewels while she went back to help Istvan, and she could use his phone to call the embassy and let them know they should send some men ASAP to the Roman ruins.

And, oh, hell, maybe she could talk to her uncle about her mixed-up feelings for Istvan, too, if they had an extra minute. An objective opinion might be what she needed. Someone to tell her that she wasn't falling in love.

She wasn't. She definitely wasn't.

The monastery came into sight at last, along with a shepherd and his flock by the side of the road who settled in for the night. The man had leaned his scooter against a dried-out oil tree. Seemed like a modern guy, probably had a cell phone, too, but now that she was so close to her uncle, she decided to make the call from the monastery where she'd have more privacy.

She pulled the truck right up to the heavy wooden gates, wrapped her head in a rag she found between the seats, making it look like a beat-up skullcap. She rubbed some dirt on her face from the dashboard where dust stood half an inch thick in places. Then she squared her shoulders like a man and beeped the horn.

A monk shuffled forth from the door next to the gate and looked sleepily at the truck, his wide face wrinkled with age. "What is it?"

"Wine delivery," she said, deepening her voice. She knew she spoke the local language with an accent, but that couldn't be helped. There were enough foreign workers on the island so that it shouldn't raise suspicion.

Back in the day, she'd often masqueraded as a boy or young man to get into places, the ruse not entirely unfamiliar or unpracticed. Plus she was inside the cab of a truck, concealed in darkness. She imagined women never drove delivery trucks to this gate. The monk would see what he'd always seen, what he was used to, what he wanted to see.

And he did. He barely paid any attention to Lauryn, eyeing the truck instead. "Nobody said anything about night delivery."

"Wasn't supposed to be night delivery. I had to change a tire. Twice. On a day when my partner is home and I ride alone. Killed my back."

At that, the monk nodded with understanding. He'd probably spent plenty of time on his knees in prayer. The man didn't look a stranger to back pain.

"The office is closed. You can't get paid until morning."

"Fine with me. I'd like to take a look at that tire by daylight before I head back anyway."

"You're welcome at pilgrim's hall. There's water to wash. Prayer's at six, then a small breakfast." He shuffled back through his door, then opened the main gate, letting the truck enter.

"I'll park in the back, by the caretaker's cottage." The familiarity would reassure the man that she had delivered here before, as well as put her closer to her uncle. She had a good idea of the monastery's layout from her uncle's letters. He'd often described his work as well as the renovations going on, financed by donations, progressing little by little.

She drove slowly over the uneven cobblestones, groaning when the cottage finally came into view. What looked like dozens of candles flickered in the windows.

A prayer meeting or some strange ritual? But why not in the chapel? Why in the caretaker's cottage? She'd hoped to find her uncle alone so she could ask for his help immediately.

She cut the engine and let the truck roll all the way to

the rock wall that edged the monastery grounds in the back. Whoever was with her uncle, she didn't want to draw their attention. She crept to the window, prepared to wait for the guest or guests to leave, yearning to see her uncle's familiar face. She'd been toughened up by life, but that didn't mean she never needed a hug, a soothing pat on the shoulder and to be told that everything would turn out okay.

She peeked in the front window and saw several monks at prayer, lit candles filling every available surface. Worry stabbed at her heart. What if her uncle was sick?

She would talk him into taking Istvan's offer and moving to Valtria. If Istvan said he would protect the man, then he would. Her uncle was getting old, he shouldn't live in a spartan hut that didn't even have running water and precious little heat in the winter. He looked much younger than his age, but he was well into his sixties. Too old to work as hard as he still did, keeping the grounds for a place as big as this. At one time the monastery was the only place where he was safe. But now that he had other choices, she wanted him someplace where he could live the rest of his life more comfortably.

At least in Valtria she could visit him anytime and spend time with him. Here, they were restricted to brief visits, the two of them standing outside the gate. She moved toward the back window, which she guessed to be the bedroom.

More monks in there, heads bowed as they prayed

silently in the light of dozens of small flickering flames. The bed caught her eye. Empty. Not sick then, she thought as relief filled her. Then someone moved and she spotted the table that had been dragged in from the kitchen. A long dark cloth covered the top where a body lay dressed in black, the hands folded in prayer.

Her fingers flew to her mouth to stifle the sob that tore from deep in her chest. She didn't have to guess what her uncle had died of. There were enough candles to illuminate his face, which had been beaten bloody. A glimpse was all she had, then her eyes filled with tears and she could no longer see.

Dozens of questions flew through her mind, but only one explanation came. They'd been followed here. Her uncle had been interrogated, then killed. By Bellingham? By the Freedom Council?

She sagged against the wall and cried silently, sobs racking her body. Grief pulled her to collapse to the ground. She'd brought Istvan here. She'd brought trouble to her uncle's doorstep. A cat came around the corner of the cottage and sidled up to her. She pulled the animal onto her lap and buried her face in its soft fur. Part of her wanted to lie down in the dark outside that window and cry herself into numbness. But the bad guys still had Istvan.

She swallowed her tears. She would be damned if she let them do the same thing to him.

"I love you," she whispered to the glass. "I'll always love you. You'll never be forgotten." Then she let go of the cat and as carefully as she'd come, she stole back into the darkness.

Twenty minutes of searching the grounds, moving in the shadows, and she found the office. The lock was as old-fashioned as the rest of the place and proved no impediment at all. She was inside with her usual speed.

She went straight for the phone, called international directory assistance and asked to be put through to security at the Valtrian Royal Palace.

"Security office," a man responded.

"I need to talk with Prince Miklos immediately."

"I'm sorry, ma'am, he's not available, could I help you?"

The patronizing voice made her see red. "I'm not some lovesick teenage fan, for heaven's sake. Prince Istvan's life is at stake. And so are the coronation jewels that were stolen," she added, knowing that wasn't public information.

Another voice came on the line immediately. "Prince Miklos here. Who is this?"

"Lauryn Steler. I have the crown jewels." She gave the name of the monastery. "And I know where the rest of the stolen treasure is, but your brother is in grave danger." She explained the scene the last time she'd seen him.

"We're on our way. I'm requesting local assistance in the meantime. You stay at that monastery and be safe. I'll send an escort for you and the crown jewels."

"Hurry." She hung up and exited the office, leaving everything as she'd found it, locking up behind her. Then she went back to the monastery wall and traced it until she came to a spot that was easily scaled and out of the way enough so she wouldn't be seen by anyone who might come from or go to her uncle's vigil.

Her eyes refused to dry, which made looking for handholds difficult. Half the time she went by feel, but she made it to the top. She paused there, looking toward the cottage and the flickering lights in the windows. She felt more alone than she ever had before.

Her uncle had been the last of her family.

She whispered a prayer for him, then jumped off the wall on the other side and headed straight for the sleeping shepherd.

Her old self would have taken the scooter, not wanting to be seen. She marched straight up to the man instead, not bothering to quiet the dog that immediately ran toward her, barking.

"I need your help," she said in Greek. "It's an emergency. I have to go help a friend. Right now. Immediately." She pulled money from her pocket and pointed at the scooter.

The shepherd wiped the sleep from his eyes and quieted his dog. "Go help your friend." He nodded toward the scooter. "I'll be here when you bring it back."

She thanked him and got on the road, knowing her chances of finding Istvan where she'd left him were one in a million. Hours had passed since she'd left. She didn't know how bad the damage had been to Bellingham's chopper. They might have been able to fix it and get it up in the air. And in any case, there were plenty of cars on the other side of the woods to use as getaway cars, Prince Istvan's and his guards' included.

Tears filled her eyes anew, making it difficult to see the road. She blinked them away. She couldn't bear the thought of losing Istvan, too, of never seeing him again.

And she knew without a doubt why that was. Because despite all her best intentions and protests, she had fallen in hopeless and unrequited love with the prince.

HE WAS IN A CRUMBLING dungeon, part of a half-collapsed fort left from the time of Turkish occupation. He was tied like a hog and suspended from ropes hanging from the ceiling. The result was that his arm was about to fall off and every small move he made to seek a little relief sent him swinging, activating his motion sickness.

He still had the pearl bracelet thing Lauryn had made for him, in his pocket, had been carrying it around for some reason, although he'd meant to give the pearls back to her. Of course, he couldn't reach his pocket.

The room was spinning with him, his stomach in his throat. He was hard-pressed to think of a time when he'd been more miserable, and his physical condition was only half of that misery. He was worried about Lauryn, bursting with anger and frustration that he hadn't been able to get away and go after her.

Bellingham had left with the rest of the royal treasure, giving him over to his goons to be taken away. That had been over three hours ago. He'd had human contact only once since, when the goon's leader came in to tell him that Bellingham had sold him to the Freedom Council, a representative of which was on his way to confirm that he indeed was the prince and witness his killing.

He was no longer mad at Lauryn for leaving. He was glad she'd taken off and hadn't been captured by Bellingham. His most fervent wish was that she hadn't been captured by anyone else either. She might have proven herself a thief at the end, her upbringing proving too difficult to resist, but had she stayed, she would be killed along with him.

He half convinced himself that she wouldn't go to her uncle. She had to know that it would be the first place he'd look for her if he got free.

The door of his prison opened. He twisted his body to look, the motion sending his rope turning in a slow circle. He swallowed the nausea and swore under his breath.

"Not how I imagined our next meeting, Your Highness," the man who'd come in said, shining a flashlight in Istvan's face.

"Richard Kormos," Istvan called him by name. He knew the man by reputation more than personally, although they'd met at receptions given by the Valtrian Business League. Kormos was one of the most prominent businessmen in the country, owning all the most important coal mines in the north of Valtria and several others all over Europe.

Kormos was a short guy with a trim body that spoke of strict discipline, sharp eyes, a beak nose and a forceful voice that went with his forceful personality. The business papers often wrote about his Napoleon complex.

He was not a representative of the Freedom Council, Istvan realized at once. He was one of the three mysterious founding members, all wealthy men whose identity he could only guess until this point.

"What do you want?" he asked the man, already knowing the answer, but wanting to delay until he could figure out how to escape.

"The same thing you do. My own country. Hardly seems fair that I can't have it just because I wasn't born a prince. I mean, other than being born to the right mother, what have you ever done to deserve it, Your Highness?" He spoke the words *Your Highness* like a curse, with a sneer.

The three founding men of the Freedom Council sought to destroy the monarchy, break up the country along ethnic lines and create three small republics that they would rule, adjusting laws and the constitution to their liking.

"I love my country," was Istvan's only response. If he was to be dead soon, that was one of the last things he wanted to say.

"You can guard it from the afterlife," Kormos mocked him.

"You really think you can get away with this?"

"If I didn't, would I have shown you my face?"

That question didn't require an answer, so Istvan said instead, "Harm my family and my people in any way, and I *will* haunt you from the grave."

"We'll cross that bridge when we come to it." He gave a superior grin as the handheld radio clipped to his belt crackled to life.

"We're ready. Over."

"Give me a second to get out. Wait for my word. Over." He backed toward the door as he addressed Istvan again. "A shame these wonderful old sites being abandoned for lack of funding. The weather. The rare earthquake. It's no wonder they're falling down. Take this splendid fort for example, Your Highness. Hardly any of it is standing. Nobody will be surprised if those few remaining walls collapse. We did have that rain. The ground moved. A terrible accident."

He sounded so pleased with his plan that he could barely contain himself from taunting the prince. "I don't imagine the economy will recover anytime soon. When it does, they'll have other things to do first before they return to restoring old piles of stones in the countryside. By the time they find you, if they ever do, there'll be nothing more than bones. They might do DNA testing and it might connect those bones to a prince who'd disappeared years before somewhere on the island. Then again, they might not. By then, your people will have new leaders and you will be forgotten."

He worked the ropes at his wrists furiously, no longer caring about the swinging. "My people will not bend mindlessly to your evil rule. I have faith in them."

"How touching. I've never known this emotional side of Your Highness. I must admit you always looked cold and distant at those state dinners. Anyone else you want to voice your royal love for before I leave?"

It seemed foolish, he didn't even know why he was doing it, but he said, "I love a thief named Lauryn." He wanted those words said if he was about to die, if this was the end.

"Not that I know who you're talking about, but I can—" Kormos stopped talking and fell forward, his head knocking against Istvan's knees. Blood rushed out the back of his head.

Istvan looked up, trying to see who was coming in behind him.

"Take it back," Lauryn said, tossing the bloody stone in her hand. "Or I'm not saving you."

"You don't want me to love you?" He'd never been as happy to see anyone. He felt downright giddy, which didn't mix well with nausea, but he worked with what he had. "Most women would take that as a compliment. You do know I'm a prince?"

"This is a tight place. With your ego and all, I'm not sure there'll be enough room for all of us and I need to come farther in. I wasn't talking about the love part." Her cheeks turned pink.

His head was spinning. "May I inquire, then, what you want me to take back?"

She moved with some impatience as she cut his ropes. "The thief thing."

He rubbed his wrists, turned Kormos enough to grab the man's radio. Then they were heading out through one of the many dark tunnels, but he grabbed her arm and stopped her, turned her to him. "I take it back thoroughly," he said and kissed her.

And realized in that moment that he did love her with a love that didn't slowly creep up on him unnoticed and turn a friendship into something more as he'd always assumed would someday happen to him, as he'd hoped would happen with Amalia at some point.

He barely knew Lauryn, he reflected as they began running again, but he felt as if he knew everything important about her. And he knew without a doubt that he couldn't live the rest of his life without her.

Once they cleared the ruins, they came up to the surface, not far from the Roman villa where he'd been captured. Having major digs side by side wasn't a rarity on the island due to its rich history. Often one invading nation built on the ruins of another, which made Cyprus a paradise for tourists interested in the past.

The radio came on as they sneaked into the woods. "Are you ready? Over."

He looked back over the picturesque view the ruins painted in the moonlight—four hundred years of history. "I killed the bastard myself. No need for the explosives. Over."

"It's all set up," came the protest. "Over."

"He's dead."

"Are you out and clear? Over."

"I am."

The next second, a small charge blew. Not big enough to be noticed with the nearest houses being miles away and people asleep in the middle of the night, but big enough to bring down the already-unsteady structure.

"That was a terrible thing to do." Lauryn looked as if she might cry, staring wide-eyed at the dust cloud that was rising, aghast at the willful destruction.

He felt equally stricken, hating to see history destroyed, but there was nothing they could do now. "Come on." He tossed the radio and took her hand. "We're done here."

But, of course, they weren't. Two men rose from the darkness, guards who'd been securing the perimeters. He was furious enough, after all that had happened, to go after them barehanded. He was fed up, fed up to the limit. He grabbed the rifle of the first and shot the bastard in the head without thinking, and with another well-aimed shot took care of the other even as he heard big trucks coming down the road that led through the woods. He aimed the weapon in that direction.

"Get in cover. And this time, stay there no matter what happens to me," he ordered Lauryn.

"That might be Miklos," she said, staring wide-eyed at the destruction he'd wrought.

"How?"

"I called him before I left the crown jewels at the monastery."

"With your uncle? But I thought—"

She told him what had happened to her uncle then, her eyes filling with tears. She stumbled. He picked her up in his arms.

That was how he met the first truck, with Miklos behind the wheel.

"Need help?"

"I'm good. You've got a chopper?" He thought he'd heard the sound of rotors earlier, figured it might have been Bellingham leaving, but they were high enough now on the hill so he could see Bellingham's bird still on the ground where it had been shot down. He must have called another truck to carry away the treasure.

"Where there are no trees," Miklos told him. "If you're already handled this yourself—" he looked behind Istvan "—I'm going to be very disappointed."

"Cheer up. Bellingham's and Kormos's bastards are running all over the countryside. Go to it."

"Who's Bellingham? Kormos as in head of industry Kormos?" His brother's eyebrows went up. "Never mind. You'll tell me later. No time to waste." And he directed his truck, filled to the brim with Valtrian Royal Guards, around them to tear down the path. The other vehicles followed.

"I'm sorry about your uncle," Istvan said when they were alone again.

"You can put me down. I can walk."

"Mind if I carry you anyway? It brings home the point that you're here with me and safe."

She tightened her arms around his neck and leaned her head against his chest. "Whatever he'd done in the past, he was a good man. He was different from my father. He did have a conscience. He tried to atone for the things he did. He helped me so much in the past couple of years. I have nobody left." Her voice broke.

"You have me."

"All the way to the chopper?" She went for sarcastic, knowing, as he did, that their time together would soon have to come to an end.

And he knew suddenly that he couldn't accept that. Couldn't let that happen.

"All the way to the chopper, then all the way to forever," he said and kissed her again.

Epilogue

Istvan watched Lauryn as she straightened, covered in mud from head to toe, in workman's overalls. She was the most beautiful sight he'd ever seen.

She'd put together the materials for the exhibit for the Getty, but hadn't gone back. Chancellor Egon was traveling with the Valtrian treasures.

She gave a soft grunt. "It's the curse of the Kerkay brides."

"To be loved beyond reason by their husbands?" he inquired.

"To become pregnant the moment they say the words *I do*." She set aside the small pick she'd just broken and reached for another tool in her bucket.

"Pregnancy suits you beautifully. You glow."

"We call that sweat down in the lower classes." She braced her lower back with her hands, her belly protruding from an otherwise slim frame. "I'm as large as a prehistoric whale."

"You're pregnant with twins. They run in my family." He was exceedingly pleased with himself.

"I don't know how much longer I can help you."

He put down his pail and strode over to her. "I'll set up a golden throne for you in the shade and present you with binoculars encrusted with rubies, then you can watch the dig in comfort." They were close to finding the treasure of the Brotherhood, had spent part of their honeymoon deciphering the codes cleverly hidden in the decorative patterns of the royal crown.

"At least you know me well enough not to try to talk me into staying home."

"Soon we'll be one of those couples who finish each other's sentences," he teased her.

"Sickening," she groused, but her grin ran from ear to ear.

"Beyond appalling." He couldn't have been happier. He pulled her to him and kissed her gently.

"I still can't believe they let you marry an alleged thief," she said on a dreamy sigh when they pulled apart.

"I married a heroine. The woman who saved the coronation jewels."

Not one item had been lost, which was a miracle. Miklos was still hunting the last of the bad guys on the island, working with the local authorities, to make sure something like this wouldn't happen again.

Her eyes narrowed. "Are you saying you married me out of gratitude?"

"Having a sense of obligation is a must for a prince."

She kicked him in the shin.

He lifted her into his arms and carried her to the field tent he had set up so she could take as much rest as she needed, not that she ever took advantage of it. He laid her down on the bed. "Is it still safe to—"

"The doctor says it is. You do realize you ask me that question every single day? Never mind. Yes, you may exercise your princely rights when we return to the palace." She acted all put out, but the smile in her eyes betrayed how much fun she was having.

He kissed her again, harder this time, deeper, running his hand down the front of her overalls and undoing the buttons.

"Wait. Here?" She squealed with alarm when she realized that he had no intention of postponing anything until they returned to the palace.

"I'm a born archaeologist. I do my best work in the field."

He gave her a hopeful smile. She pressed closer. And then he proceeded to make thorough love to his amazing wife, a woman he loved above all others, the woman he would love forever. He told her so, too, just to be clear.

"I love you, too." She kissed him. "You're a prince of a man." She giggled.

She was a different person than when they'd met, loosened up a lot, learned to trust, learned to be part of a large family. Learned that she didn't have to check behind her every second because he had her back. She was just as self-assured and tough as ever, but now at times she was also completely carefree, starting to believe that what they had together was good, it was real and it was going to last forever.

When all their clothing had been removed he covered her belly with kisses. Then he moved inside her, gently, slowly centimeter by centimeter, reveling in the pleasure on her face, the way her eyes widened when he pushed all the way in.

They moved together in perfect harmony.

"Who knew we'd be so good together?" She sighed as pressure built.

"I did." He dipped his head to her puckered nipple.

"Liar."

"Insulting a prince to his face is a serious breach of protocol," he said, then proceeded to seduce her thoroughly to make sure he prevented further incidents. Even if she was right. He _had_ fibbed. Never in his life could he fathom that to be truly in love and be married to the right woman could be half this glorious. It seemed insane now that he used to think that being a loner was preferable to all the work it required being a couple.

The pleasure that was building in his body was nothing compared to the joy that filled his heart to the brim.

Afterward, when they lay satiated in each other's arms, he reached for his field bag and retrieved a long velvet case and gave it to her. "I finally got this today. I was going to hold it until the twins were born, as a gift…" He trailed off. He couldn't stand the wait. He wanted to shower her with presents. He

didn't agree with her frequent protests that he was hope-
lessly spoiling her.

"A stainless steel pick?" She'd taken to archaeology
like a duck to water.

He chuckled. "Get your mind out of the ditch for a
second."

She opened the case and gasped as she inspected the
one-of-a-kind string of large pearls. "How old is this
thing?" she asked after a minute.

"About a hundred years, give or take a couple. It was
my great-great-great grandmother's." He took it from
her and fastened it around her neck. The pearls shone
between her naked breasts. He felt desire stir again. Bent
to kiss her. "We might never leave this tent."

"Your Highness," came an urgent call from outside,
ruining his hopes.

"Go away."

"We found a large stone chest."

He exchanged a glance with Lauryn. They broke
records getting dressed. They were back in the ditch
within minutes, supervising as the lid was removed from
the stone chest with the help of a pulley. Then the way
was finally cleared and they could look inside.

Instead of jewels and gold coins, the chest was filled
to the brim with brittle book pages, all handwritten.

"What's this?" Lauryn was pulling on white
gloves.

He'd already put his on and was taking one of the
better preserved books gently into his hands, opening it
to the first page, deciphering the code without trouble.

"The real diary of the Brotherhood of the Crown." He took another book and inspected it. "Along with crucial historical manuscripts that had been thought lost through wars and theft. Looks like at least some of the jewels the Brotherhood had received from their admirers had been used to pay for copying and saving our history. This is—"

"The history of the country," she said misty-eyed.

"The find of a lifetime."

"Real treasure." They smiled in unison.

"We're going to read and document all of this together. And be very careful to keep the pages out of little hands." She patted her belly. "You realize this might take a lifetime?"

He pulled her into his arms and thought about spending the rest of his life with her, working side by side, loving her. "I couldn't think of a life better spent." He kissed her, his hand caressing her swollen belly where their babies were doing backflips.

"Probably impatient to get out of there and start digging. God help the royal gardens if they take after their daddy." She was grinning.

"We'll have to put a full platoon of royal guards into service around them if they take after their mother," he murmured against her lips.

* * * * *

HIS PREGNANT
PRINCESS BRIDE

CATHERINE MANN

To my dear friend and former neighbor
from Louisiana—Karen. Thank you for
all the Mardi Gras cakes and celebrations!

Prologue

"I have to confess, I don't care for the football at all."

Princess Erika's declaration caught Gervais Reynaud off guard, considering they'd spent the past four hours in the private viewing box overlooking Wembley Stadium, where his team would be playing a preseason exhibition game two months from now.

As the owner of the New Orleans Hurricanes NFL team, Gervais had more important things to do than indulge this high-maintenance Nordic princess he'd been seated beside during today's event, a high-stakes soccer match that was called "football" on this side of the globe. A game she didn't even respect regardless of which country played. Had it been sexist of him to think she might actually enjoy the game, since she was a royal, serving in her country's army? He'd expected a military member to be athletic. Not unreasonable, right? She was definitely toned under that gray, regimented uniform decorated with gold braid and commendations.

But she was also undoubtedly bored by the game.

And while Gervais didn't enjoy soccer as much as American football, he respected the hell out of it. The athletes were some of the best in the world. His main task for today had been to scout the stadium, to see what it would be like for the New Orleans Hurricanes when they played here in August. He'd staked his business reputation on the team he owned, a move his financial advisers had all adamantly opposed. There were risks, of course. But Gervais had never backed away from a challenge. It went against his nature. And now his career was tied to the success of the Hurricanes. The media spotlight had always been intense for him because of his family name. But after he'd purchased the franchise, the media became relentless.

Previewing the Wembley Stadium facilities at least offered him a welcome weekend of breathing room from scrutiny, since the UK fan base for American football was nominal. Here, he could simply enjoy a game without a camera panning to his face or reporters circling him afterward.

He only wished he could be watching the Hurricanes play today. He'd put one of his brothers in charge of the team as head coach. Another brother ran the team on the field in the quarterback position. Sportswriters back in the United States implied he'd made a colossal mistake.

Playing favorites? Clearly, they didn't know the Reynauds.

He wouldn't have chosen from his family unless they were the best for the job. Not when purchasing this team provided his chance to forge his own path as more than just part of the Reynaud extended-family empire of shipping moguls and football stars.

But to do that successfully, he had to play the political game with every bit as much strategy as the game on the field. As a team owner, he was the face of the Hurricanes. Which meant putting up with a temperamental princess who hadn't grasped that the "football team" he owned wasn't the one on the field. Not that she seemed to care much one way or the other.

Sprawled on the white leather sofa, Gervais tossed a pigskin from hand to hand, the ball a token gift from the public relations coordinator who'd welcomed him today and shown him to the private viewing box. The box was emptying now that the clock ran out after the London club beat another English team in the FA Cup Final. "You don't like the ball?"

She waved an elegant hand, smoothing over her pale blond hair sleeked back in a flawless twist. "No, not that. Perhaps my English is not as good as I would wish," she said with only the slightest hint of an accent. She'd been educated well, speaking with an intonation that was unquestionably sexy, even as she failed to notice the kind of football he held was different than the one they'd used on the field. "I do not care for the game. The football game."

"Interesting choice, then, for your country to send you as the royal representative to a finals match." Damn, she was too beautiful for her own good, wearing that neat-fitting uniform and filling it out in all the right places. Just looking at her brought to mind her heritage—her warrior princess ancestors out in battle side by side with badass Vikings—although this Nordic princess had clearly been suffering in regal silence for the past four hours. The way she'd dismissed her travel assistant had Gervais thinking he wouldn't even bother playing the diplomat with this ice princess.

"So, Princess Erika, were you sent here as punishment for some bad-girl imperial infraction?"

And if so, why wasn't she leaving now that the game had ended? What held her here, sipping champagne and talking to him after the box cleared? More important, what kept *him* here when he had a flight planned for tonight?

"First of all, I am not a reigning royal." Her icy blue eyes were as cool as her icy homeland as she set down her crystal champagne flute. "Our monarchy has been defunct for over forty-five years. And even if it was not, I am the youngest of five girls. And as for my second point, comments like yours only confirm my issue with attending a function like this where you assume I must be some kind of troublemaker if I don't enjoy this game. I must be flawed. No offense meant, but you and I simply have different interests."

"Then why are you here?" He wanted to know more than he should.

The PR coordinator for the stadium had introduced them only briefly and he found himself hungry to know more about this intriguing but reticent woman.

"My mother was not happy with my choice to join

the military, even though if I were a male that would not be in question. She is concerned I am not socializing enough and that I will end up unmarried, since clearly my worth is contingent upon having babies." Rolling her eyes, she crossed her long, slim legs at the ankles, her arms elegantly draped on the white leather chair. "Ridiculous, is it not, considering I am able to support myself? Besides, most of my older sisters are married and breeding like raccoons."

"Like rabbits."

She arched a thin blond eyebrow. "Excuse me?"

"The phrase is *breeding like rabbits*." Gervais couldn't quite smother a grin as the conversation took an interesting turn.

"Oh, well, that is strange." She frowned, tapping her upper lip with a short, neat fingernail. "Rabbits are cute and fuzzy. Raccoons are less appealing. I believe raccoons fit better," she said as if merely stating it could change a colloquialism on her say-so.

"You don't like kids?" he found himself asking, even though he could have stood and offered to walk her out and be done with any expectation of social nicety.

When was the last time he exchanged more than a few words with a woman outside of business? He could spend another minute talking to her.

"I do not believe I must have a dozen heirs to make a defunct monarchy stable."

Hmm, valid point and an unexpected answer. "So I take that to mean you're no threat to hitting on the players?"

Down on the field, the winning team was being mobbed.

"You assume correctly," she blurted so quickly and emphatically, she startled a laugh from him.

It was refreshing to find a woman who wasn't a sports groupie for a change.

He found himself staying behind to talk to her even though he had a flight to catch. "What do you do in the military?"

"I am a nurse by degree but the military uses my skills as a linguist. In essence, I'm a diplomatic translator."

"Say again?"

"Is that so shocking? Do I not appear intelligent?"

She appeared hot as hell, like a blue flame, the most searing of all.

"You're lovely and articulate. You speak English fluently as a second language. You're clearly intelligent."

"And you are a flatterer," she said dismissively. "I work as a translator, but now that I'm nearing the end of my time in military service, I'll be taking the RN degree a step further, becoming a nurse-practitioner, with a specialty in homeopathic treatments, using natural herbs and even scents, studying how they relate to moods and physiological effects. Stress relievers. Energy infusers. Or immune boosters. Or allergy relievers. Any number of combinations to combine an alluring perfume with a healthier lifestyle."

"Where do you study that?"

"I've been accepted into a program in London. I had hoped to pursue nursing in the military to increase my experience, but my government had other plans for me to be a translator."

A nurse, soon to become a nurse-practitioner? Now, *that* surprised him. "Very impressive."

"Thank you." She nodded regally, a lock of hair sliding free from her twist and caressing her cheek. She tucked it behind her ear. "Now, explain to me what I need to know to speak intelligently about what I saw down on the field with all those musclemen when I return home."

Standing, he extended an arm to her. "By all means, Princess, I know a little something about European football even though the team I own is an American football team."

She rose with the elegance of a woman who'd been trained in every manner to grace high-end ballrooms not ball games. And yet she chose to further her education and serve her country in uniform.

Princess-Captain Erika Mitras wasn't at all what he expected when he'd spotted a foreign dignitary on the guest list. He'd envisioned either a stiff-necked VIP or a football groupie bent on a photo op and a chance to meet the players. He didn't come across many people who dared tell him they didn't like football—European or American. In fact, he didn't have many people in his life who disliked sports. The shipping business might be the source of Reynaud wealth, but football had long been their passion.

How contrary that her disinterest in sports made her all the more appealing. Yes, she aroused him in a way he couldn't recall having felt about any woman before.

And quite possibly some of that allure had to do with the fact that for once in his life he wasn't under the scrutiny of the American media. Perhaps if he was careful, he could do something impulsive without worrying about the consequences rippling through his family's world.

He stepped closer, folding her hand into the crook of his arm, and caught a whiff of a cinnamon scent. "And while I do that, what do you say we enjoy London? Dinner, theater, your choice. Just the two of us."

Flights could be rescheduled.

She paused to peer up at him, her cool blue eyes roaming his face for a moment before the barest hint of a smile played over her lips. "Only if, after a brief outline of the differences in these football sports, we can agree to no football talk at all?"

"None," he vowed without hesitation.

"Then it sounds lovely."

Who knew cinnamon would be such a total turn-on?

One

2 ½ Months Later
New Orleans, Louisiana

Princess Erika Birgitta Inger Freya Mitras of Holsgrof knew how to make a royally memorable appearance.

Her mother had taught her well. And Erika needed all the confidence she could garner striding onto the practice field full of larger-than-life men in training. Most important, she needed all her confidence to face one particular man. The leader of this testosterone domain, the owner of the state-of-the-art training facility where he now presided. Players dotted the field in black-and-gold uniforms, their padded shoulders crashing against each other. Shouts, grunts and curses volleyed. Men who appeared to be trainers or coaches jogged alongside them, barking instructions or blow-ing whistles.

She'd finished her military stint a month ago, her hopes of serving her country in combat having been sidelined by her parents' interference. They'd shuffled her into some safe figurehead job that made her realize the family's Viking-warrior heritage would not be car-ried on through her. She'd been so disillusioned, adrift and on edge the day she attended the soccer game, she had been reckless.

Too reckless. And that weekend of indulgence brought her here. Now. To New Orleans. To Gervais.

Her Jimmy Choo heels sank into the most plush grass ever as she stepped onto the practice field of the New Orleans Hurricanes. She'd assumed this particularly American game was played on Astroturf. And assump-tions were what she had to avoid when it came to her current adventure in the United States.

She had not intended to see Gervais Reynaud again after he left the United Kingdom. Their weekend of dates—and amazing, mind-blowing sex—had been an escape from rules and protocol and everything else that had kept her life rigidly in check for so long. She'd had relationships in the past, carefully chosen and approved. This was her first encounter of her own choosing.

And it had turned out to be far more memorable than she could have ever imagined.

She felt the weight of his eyes from across the open stretch of greenery. Or perhaps he had noticed her only because of the sudden silence. Players now stood still, their shouts dimming to a dull echo.

The rest of the place faded for her while she focused on Gervais Reynaud standing at the foot of the bleachers, as tall as any of the players. He was muscular, more so than the average man but more understated than the men in uniform nearby. She knew he had played in his youth and through college but had chosen a business route in the family's shipping enterprise until he had bought the New Orleans Hurricanes football team. The *American* football team. She understood the difference now. She also knew Gervais's purchase of the team had attracted a great deal of press coverage in business and sports media alike.

He had not told her much about his life, but before she made her trip here she had made a point of learning more about him and his family.

It certainly was amazing what a few internet searches could reveal.

Tracing their ancestry deep into Acadian history, the Reynaud family first built their fortune in shipping, a business that his grandfather patriarch Leon Reynaud had expanded into a thriving cruise ship company. Leon also turned a love of sports into another successful venture when he'd purchased shares in a Texas football team, learning the business from the inside out. His elder son, Christophe, inherited the shares but promptly sold them to buy a baseball team, creating a deep family rift.

Leon passed his intense love of football to his younger son, Theo, whose promising career as a quarterback in Atlanta was cut short due to injury and excess after his marriage to a celebrated supermodel fell apart. Theo

had three sons from his marriage, Gervais, Henri and
Jean-Pierre, and one from an earlier affair, Dempsey.
All of the sons inherited a passion for the game, play-
ing in college and groomed for the NFL.

While the elder two sons broke ties with their father
to bring corporate savvy to the front office of the relatively new team, the younger two sons both continued
their careers on the field. The Reynaud brothers were
especially well-known in Louisiana, where their football exploits were discussed—as much a topic of conversation as the women in their lives. She'd overheard
references to each in the lobby of the five-star hotel
where she'd spent the night in New Orleans.

Would she be the topic of such conversation once
her "encounter" with Gervais became public knowledge? There would be no way to hide it from his football world much longer.

Football. A game she still cared very little about, a
fact he had teased her about during their weekend together, a weekend where they had spent more time undressed than clothed. Her gaze was drawn back to that
well-honed body of his that had made such passionate
love to her.

His dark eyes heated her with memories as he strode
toward her. His long legs ate the ground in giant slices,
his khakis and sports jacket declaring him in the middle of a workday. He stopped in front of her, his broad
shoulders blocking the sun and casting his handsome
face in shadows. But she didn't have to see to know his
jaw would be peppered with the stubble that seemed

to grow in seconds after he shaved. Her fingers—her body—remembered the texture of that rasp well.

Her breath caught somewhere in her chest.

He folded his arms over his chest, just under the Hurricanes logo stitched on the front of his jacket. "Welcome to the States, Erika. No one mentioned your intention to visit. I thought you didn't like sports."

"And yet, here I am." And in need of privacy out of the bright Louisiana sun and the even brighter curious eyes of his team and staff. She needed space and courage to tell him why she'd made this unexpected journey across the Atlantic to this muggy bayou state. "This is not an official royal visit."

"And you're not in uniform." His eyes glided over her wraparound dress.

"I'm out of the service now to begin furthering my studies." About to return to school to be a nurse-practitioner, the career field she'd hoped to pursue in the military, but they would not allow her such an in-the-field position, instead preferring to dress her up and trot her around as a figurehead translator. "I am here for a conference on homeopathic herbs and scents." A part of her passion in the nursing field, and a totally made-up excuse for being here today.

"The homeopathic scents for healing, right? Are you here to share specially scented deodorant with my players? Because they could certainly use it." His mouth tipped with a smile.

"Are you interested in such a line?" Still jet-lagged from the transatlantic flight, she was ill prepared to exchange pleasantries, much less ones filled with taunts at her career choice.

"Is that why you are here? For business before you start your new degree?"

She could not just banter with him. She simply could not. "Please, can we go somewhere private to talk?"

He searched her eyes for a long moment before gesturing over his shoulder. "I'm in the middle of a meeting with sponsors. How about supper?"

"I am not here for seduction," she stated bluntly.

"Okay." His eyebrows shot upward. "I thought I asked you to join me for gumbo not sex. But now that we're talking about sex—"

"We are not." She cut him short. "Finish your meeting if you must, but I need to speak with you as soon as possible. Privately. Unless you want your personal business and mine overheard by all of your team straining to listen."

She definitely was not ready for them to hear she was pregnant with the heir to the Reynaud family dynasty.

She was back. Princess Erika, the sexy seductress who'd filled his dreams since they'd parted ways nearly three months ago. And even though he should be paying attention to the deal with his sponsors, he could not tear his eyes away from her. From the swish of her curves and hips. And the long platinum-blond hair that made her look completely otherworldly.

He needed to focus, but damn. She was mesmerizing. And apparently, every team member on the field was also aware of that fact. From their top wide receiver Wildcard to running back Freight Train.

Gervais turned his attention back to finishing up his conversation with the director of player personnel—Beau Durant—responsible for draft picks, trades, acquiring the right players and negotiating contracts. An old college friend, Beau shared his friend's interest in running a football team. He took a businesslike, numbers approach to the job and wed that with his personal interest in football. Like Gervais, he had a position in his family's multinational corporation, but football was his obsession.

"Gervais, I'd love to stay and chat, but we have another meeting to get to. We'll be in touch," his former college roommate promised.

"Perfect, Beau. Thank you," he said, offering him a sincere handshake. Beau's eyes were on the princess even if he didn't ask the obvious question. Beau was an all-business kind of guy who never pried. He'd always said he didn't want others sticking their noses in his private life, either.

The eyes of the whole damn team remained on the princess, in fact. Which made Gervais steam with protectiveness.

He barked over to his half brother, the head coach, "Dempsey, don't your boys have something better to do than stand around drooling over a woman like pimply teenage boys?"

Dempsey smirked. "All right, men. Back to practice. You can stare at pretty girls on someone else's time. Now, move!" Henri Reynaud, the Hurricanes' quarterback and Gervais's brother, shot him a look of half amusement. But he slung his helmet back on and began to make his way into formation. The Bayou Bomber, a nickname Henri had earned during his college days at LSU, would not be so easily dissuaded from his obvious curiosity.

Dempsey scratched some numbers out on his paper. Absently, he asked, "What's with the royal visit?"

"We have some…unresolved issues from our time in England."

"Your time together?" Dempsey's wicked grin spread, and he clucked his tongue.

He might as well come clean in an understated way. The truth would be apparent soon enough. "We had a quiet…relationship."

"Very damn quiet if I didn't hear about it." Crossing his arms, he did his best to look hurt.

"You were busy with the team. As it should be."

"So you have some transcontinental dating relationship with Europe's most eligible princess?"

"Reading the tabloids again, Dempsey?"

"Gotta keep up with my players' antics somehow." He shrugged it off.

"Well, don't let her hear you discussing her eligibility. She's military. She might well be able to kick your ass."

"Military, huh? That's surprising."

"She said male royals serve. Why not females? She just finished up her time." Which had seemed to bother her. He understood well about trying to find where you fit in a high-profile family.

"Carole Montemarte, the Hurricanes' press relations coordinator, will have a blast spinning that for the media. Royalty for a girlfriend? Nice, dude. And she chased you clear across the ocean. You are quite the man."

Except that didn't make sense. She'd ignored his calls after he left the country. Granted, what they'd shared blew his mind, and he didn't have the time or energy for a transcontinental relationship. So his calls had been more...obligatory. Had she known that? Was that the reason she'd ignored him?

So why show up here now?

He sure as hell intended to find out.

Two

Limos were something of the norm for Erika. Part of the privilege of growing up royal. This should feel normal, watching the sunset while being chauffeured in the limo Gervais had sent to retrieve her from her hotel. Half of her childhood had been spent in the backseat of a limo as she and her family went from one event to another.

But today was anything but normal. As she pulled at the satin fabric of her dress, her mind began to race. She had never pictured herself with a brood of children like her sisters. Not that she didn't want them, but this was all happening so fast. And with a man she wasn't entirely sure of. Just the thought of Gervais sent her mind reeling. The thought of telling him about their shared interest made her stomach knot. She began to wonder about what she would tell him. How she would tell him. News she could barely wrap her brain around. But there were secrets impossible to keep in her world, so if she wanted to inform Gervais on her terms, she would have to do so soon.

Tonight.

And just like that, Erika realized the vehicle had stopped. Reality was starting to set in, and no amount of finery and luxury was going to change that. She had chosen the arctic-blue dress because it reminded her of her heritage. Of her family's Viking past. Of the strength of her small country. She needed these reminders if she was going to face him.

Try as she might, Erika couldn't get the way he looked at her out of her mind. His eyes drinking her in. The memory sent a pleasurable shiver along her skin.

The chauffeur opened the door with a click, and she stepped out of the limo. Tall and proud. A light breeze danced against her skin, threatening her sideswept updo. Fingers instinctively flew to the white-crusted sapphire pin that, at the nape of her neck, not only held her hair together but also had been in her family for centuries.

Smoothing her blond hair that cascaded over one of her shoulders, she took in the Reynaud family compound in the meeting of sunset with the moon, the stars just beginning to sparkle in the Louisiana sky. Though she had to admit, the flood of lights leading up to the door diminished the starlight.

She lifted her gaze to the massive structure ahead of her. Greek Revival with white arches and columns—no other word than *massive*, and a girl who grew up in a palace wasn't impressed easily.

As she walked up the stairs to the home, the sureness from touching her family heirloom began to wane. But before she could lose her nerve and turn back, the limo pulled away and the grand door opened in front of her. This was officially happening.

Though the lights outside had been clinical and bright, the foyer was illuminated by bulbs of yellow. The warmth of these lights reflected on what appeared to be hand-painted murals depicting a fox hunt. American royalty.

A servant gestured for her to walk through the room on the left. Gathering the skirt of her dress, Erika crossed the threshold, leaving behind the foyer and its elaborate staircase and murals.

This room was made for entertainment. She had been in plenty of grand dining halls, and this one felt familiar and impersonal, with wisps of silk that told their secrets to the glass and windows.

Erika had always hated dinners in rooms like this.

Quickly scanning the room, she noted the elaborately carved wooden chair and the huge arrangements of flowers and the tall marble vases. But Gervais wasn't here, either.

She pressed on through the next threshold and found herself in a simpler room. It was clear that this was a family room. The opulent colors of the grand dining room softened, giving way to a creamy palette. The kind of colors that made Erika want to curl up on the plush leather sofa with a good book and some strong tea with milk.

The family room sported an entertainment bar with

Palladian windows overlooking the pool and grounds. But if she turned ever so slightly she could also see an alcove that appeared to lead to a more private section.

The master bedroom and bath? She could envision that space having doors out to the pool, a hot tub, perhaps. She bit her lip and spun away.

It was not as if she was here to gawk at furniture. She had to tell a man she barely knew that they were having a baby. And that the press would have a field day if she and Gervais didn't get a handle on this now.

And there. She saw him. Chiseled. Dark hair, ruffled ever so slightly. His lips parted into a smile as he met her gaze.

Nerves and something else jolted her to life. Pushed her forward. Toward him and that wolfish smile.

She looked around and saw housekeeping staff, but no one else. Erika waved an elegant hand to the expansive room they stood in and the ones she'd already passed through. "Where's the rest of your family?"

"Dempsey owns the other home on the compound grounds, next door. My younger brothers Jean-Pierre and Henri share the rights to the house to the northwest on the lake. Gramps has quarters here with me, since this house has been in our family the longest. It's familiar. He has servants on call round the clock. He's getting older and more forgetful. But we're hoping to hold back time as long as we can for him."

"I am so sorry."

"They make great meds these days. He's still got lots of life and light left in him." A practiced smile pressed against his lips. It was apparent he was hopeful. And used to defending his grandfather's position.

"And where does the rest of your family live?"

"Are you worried they'll walk in on us?" He angled a brow upward, and she felt the heat of his eyes graze across her body. A flush crept along her face, heating her from the inside out. Threatening to set her nerves bounding out of control. She needed to stay calm.

"Perhaps."

"My father's in Texas and doesn't return often. Jean-Pierre is in New York with his team for the season and Henri lives in the Garden District most of the time, so their house here is vacant for a while."

Stepping out onto the patio, he nodded for her to follow. She hastened behind him. Intrigued. He had that way about him. A quality of danger that masked itself as safe. That quality that made him undeniably sexy.

And that, she reminded herself, was how she'd ended up in this situation.

Gervais surveyed the patio. She followed his gaze, noting the presence of a hot tub and an elaborate fountain that pumped water into the pool. The fountain, like the house, was descended from a Greek aesthetic. Apollo and Daphne were intertwined, water flowing from the statues into the pool.

Over the poolside sound system, the din of steel drums competed with the gentle echo of rolling waves on the lakeshore.

"You arranged dinner outside." Erika breathed in the air on this rare night of low humidity. She looked around at the elaborate patio table that was dressed for dinner with lights, fresh flowers, silver and china. Ceiling fans circled a delicious breeze from the slight overhang of the porch.

"I promised you gumbo—" he gestured broadly, before holding the seat out for her "—and I delivered."

She settled into the chair, intensely aware of his hands close to her shoulders. The heat of his chest close to her back. Blinking away the awareness, she focused on the table settings, surprised to realize he planned to serve her himself from the silver chafing dishes. "Your home is lovely."

"The old plantation homes have a lot of character." He slid into the seat across from hers. "I know our history here doesn't compete with the hundreds of years, castles and Viking lore of your country, but the place has stories in the walls all the same."

"The architecture and details are stunning. I can see why you were drawn to live here." When Americans talked about their colonial towns, they always spoke of the old-world charm they'd possessed. But that was selling it short. Cities like New Orleans were the distillation of cultures haphazardly pressed against each other. And that distillation yielded beauty that was so different from the actual Old World.

"If you would prefer a restaurant…" He paused, tongs grasping freshly baked bread.

"This is better. More private." She held up a hand. "Don't take that the wrong way."

"Understood. You made your point earlier."

Seafood gumbo, red beans and rice, thick black

coffee and powdery doughnuts—beignets. It was a spread that sent her taste buds jumping.

"Did you have a nice ride from the Four Winds Resort?"

"I did. The trees heavy with Spanish moss are beautiful. And the water laps at the roads as if the sea could wash over the land at any moment." The languid landscape was so different than her country's rugged and fierce Viking past. She'd liked learning about New Orleans so far.

"You could stay here, you know."

"I did not come here for that." She laced her words with ice even as her body burned with awareness of the man seated across from her.

"Then why are you here after walking out on me without a word or backward glance?"

So that hadn't escaped his notice. She began to prepare the speeches that had replayed in her mind since she had boarded the plane to make the transatlantic journey.

"I'm sorry about that. I thought I was making things easier for both of us. It was a fling with no future, given we live across an ocean from each other. I saved us both a messy goodbye."

At that time she had been thinking about the life she needed to get on track. But all her carefully laid plans were shifting beneath her feet, now that she was pregnant.

"And when I called you? Left messages asking to speak to you?"

"I thought you were being polite. Gentlemanly. And

do not get me wrong, I believe it honorable of you. But that is not enough to build a relationship."

"How much would it have hurt to return one call? If we're talking about polite, I expected as much from you." He cocked an eyebrow.

"You are angry. I apologize if I made the wrong decision."

"Well, you're here now. For your conference, right?"

"Actually, that wasn't the truth." She fidgeted with her leather band bracelet, inspirational inscriptions scrolled on metal insets providing support. Advice. And if ever she was in need of help, the moment was now. "I only said that in case others overheard. I'm here to see you. I want to apologize for walking out on you and have a conversation we should have had then."

"What conversation would that be?"

Oh, what a loaded question, she thought. "How we would handle it if there were unexpected consequences from our weekend together."

He stared at her, hard. "Unexpected consequences? How about you spell it out rather than have me play Fifty Questions."

She dabbed the corners of her mouth as if she could buy herself a few more seconds before her life changed forever. Folding the napkin carefully and placing it beside her plate, she met his dark brown eyes, her own gaze steady. Her hands shaky. "I am pregnant. The baby is yours."

Of all the things that Erika could have said, being pregnant was not what Gervais had been preparing himself for. He ought to say something. Something fast, witty and comforting. But instead, he just looked at her.

Really looked at her as he swallowed. Hard.

She was every bit as breathtaking as that first night they'd met. But there was something different in the way she carried her body that should have tipped him off.

Her face was difficult to read. She'd iced him out of gaining any insights in her eyes. Gervais examined the hair that trailed down her shoulder, exposing her collarbone and slender neck. This was the hairstyle of a royal, so different than the girl who had let her hair run wild over their weekend together.

And what a weekend it'd been. Months had passed since then and he still thought about her. About the way she'd tasted on his tongue.

He had to say something worthy of that. Of her. He collected his thoughts, determined to say the perfect thing.

Despite all of that, only one word fell out of his mouth.

"Pregnant." So much for a grand speech.

Her face flashed with a hint of disappointment. Of course, she had every right to expect more from him. But more silence escaped his lips, and the air was filled not with sounds of him speaking, but with the buzz of waves and boats.

The trace of frustration and disappointment had left her face. She looked every bit a Viking queen. Impassive. Strong. Icy. And still so damn sexy in her soft feminine clothes and that bold leather bracelet.

"Yes, and I am absolutely certain the child is yours."

"I didn't question you."

"I wanted to be clear. Although in these days of DNA tests, it is not a subject that one can lie about." She frowned. "Do you need time to think, for us to talk more later? You look pale."

Did he? Hell, he did feel as if he'd been broadsided by a three-hundred-pound linebacker, but back in his ballplaying days he'd been much faster at recovery. And the stakes here were far higher. He needed to tread carefully. "A child is always cause for celebration." He took her hand in his, as close as he could let himself get until he had answers, no matter how tempted he was for more. "I'm just surprised. We were careful."

"Not careful enough, apparently. You, um, did stretch the condom, and perhaps there was a leak."

He choked on a cough. "Um, uh…I don't know what to say to that."

"It was not a compliment, you Cro-Magnon." She shook her hand free from his. "Simply an observation."

"Fair enough. Okay, so you're pregnant with my baby. When do you want to head to the courthouse to get married?"

"Are you joking? I did not come to the United States expecting a proposal of marriage."

"Well, that is what I am offering. Would you prefer I do this in a more ceremonial way? Fine." He slid from his chair and dropped to one knee on the flagstone patio. "Marry me and let's bring up this child together."

Her eyes went wide with shock and she shot to her

feet. Looking around her as if to make sure no one overheard. "Get up. You look silly."

"Silly?"

For the first time since he'd met her, she appeared truly flustered. She edged farther away, sweeping back her loose hair with nervous hands. "Perhaps I chose the wrong word. You look…not like you. And this is not what I want."

"What do you want?"

"I am simply here to notify you about your child and discuss if you wish to be a part of the baby's life before I move forward with my life."

"Damn straight I want to bring up my child."

"Shared custody."

He reached to capture her restless hands and hold them firmly in his. "You are not hearing me. I want to raise my child."

"*Our* child."

"Of course." He caressed the insides of her wrists with his thumbs. "Let's declare peace so we can make our way through this conversation amicably."

Her shoulders relaxed and he guided her to a bench closer to the half wall at the end of the patio. They sat side by side, shoulder to shoulder.

She nodded. "I want peace, very much. That's why I came to you now, early on, rather than just calling or waiting longer."

"And I am glad you did." He slid his hand up her arm to her shoulder, cupping the warmth of her, aching for more. "My brother Dempsey grew up thinking our father didn't want him and it scarred him. I refuse to let that happen to my child. My baby will know he or she is wanted."

"Of course our child will be brought up knowing both parents love and want him or her."

"Yes, and you still haven't answered my question."

"What question?"

"The *silly* question that comes with a guy getting down on one knee. Will you marry me?"

Three

"Marry you? I do not even know you." Erika's voice hitched. Marriage? She had wanted him to be support- ive, sure. But…marriage? The words tumbled over and over in her head in a disjointed echo.

"We knew each other well enough to have sex. Call me old-fashioned, but I'm trying to do the right thing here and offer to marry you. We can have a civil cere- mony and divorce in a year. As far as our child knows, we gave it an honest try but things didn't work." His voice was level. Calm. Practical.

Her fears multiplied. This seemed too calculated. And she would not land in a family environment that was all for show again. Being raised royal had taught her she was not meant for a superficial existence. She had already chosen a meaningful career. A future where she could make a difference.

Swallowing back the anxiety swelling in her chest, she reminded herself to be reasonable.

"You figured all that out this fast? Or have you had practice with this sort of business before?" The notion cut her with surprising sharpness. She did not want to think about Gervais involved with other women after the way they'd been together.

"I am not joking." His hand inched toward hers.

She scrutinized his face, studied the way his jaw jutted. The play of muted lights on his dark hair, the way it was thickest on top of his head. Even now, he was damn attractive. But that fact wasn't enough to chase reason from her mind.

"Apparently not."

"I'll take that as a no to my proposal." Retreating his hand, he leaned forward, elbows on his knees.

"You most certainly can. It is far too soon to speak of marriage. And have you forgotten? I have plans to pursue my education in the UK."

Tilting his head, he lowered his voice. It became soft. Gentle. "You won't even consider my offer? Not even for the baby's sake? Let me take care of you while you're pregnant and recovering, postpartum and such. You can get to know my family during the football season. Afterward, we can spend more time with yours."

Even if the monarchy was defunct, she was a royal and sure of herself. She shot to her feet. "Do I get any say in this at all? You are a pushy man. I do not remember that about you."

He stood and stepped closer, very close, suggestively. His hips and thighs warm against hers. "What do you remember about our time together?"

"If you are trying to seduce me into doing whatever you want—" Erika needed to focus. Which was tougher than ever with him pressed up against her and that smolder in his eye setting her on fire.

"If? I must not be working hard enough." He slid his hands up her arms.

Her eyes fluttered shut, and for a moment she felt as if she could give in. But thoughts of her future child coursed through her mind. A ragged breath escaped her lips, and she reopened her eyes.

She clasped his wrists. "Stop. I am not playing games. I came here to inform you. Not demand anything of you. And certainly not to reenact our past together."

His hands dropped and he scowled. "Let me get this straight. If I hadn't wanted anything to do with the baby, you would have simply walked away?"

"You never would have heard from me again." The words escaped her as an icy dagger. She would have no use for such a man. And she had to admit that even if his proposal felt pushy, at least Gervais was not the sort of person to walk away from his child.

"Well, not a chance in hell is that happening this time. You may have brushed me off once before, but not again."

Had he genuinely wished to see her again after their weekend together? She had been afraid to find out at the time, afraid of answering his call only to discover that his contact was a perfunctory duty and social nicety. After what they had shared, she was not sure she could bear hearing that cool retreat in his voice. Now, of course, she would never know what his intentions had truly been toward her.

She took a deep breath. Regrouped.

"And you cannot command me to your will," she warned him, her shoulders stiff with tension. "I will not be forced into marriage because you think that is the best plan. I have plans, as well."

How many people had underestimated her resolve over the years because she had that label of "princess" attached to her? Her commanding officers. Teachers. Her own parents.

She would simply have to show Gervais her mettle.

"I understand that," he murmured, his voice melting into the sounds of waves and steel drums. "Now we need to make plans together."

Some of the tension in her eased. "Nice to know you can be reasonable and not just impulsive."

With a shrug, he began again. "In the interest of being reasonable, let's spend the next four weeks—"

"Two weeks," she corrected him. She had already disrupted her life and traveled halfway across the globe for him.

He nodded slowly. "Two weeks getting to know each other better as we make plans for our child. You could stay here in my home, where there are plenty of suites for privacy. I won't make a move that isn't mutual. We'll use this time to find common ground."

"And if we are not successful in your time frame?"

This felt like a business deal. But the time frame might be enough to bring him to reason.

"Then I guess I'll have to follow you home. Now, how about I call over to the hotel for them to send your things here? You look ready to fall asleep on your feet."

"You're honestly suggesting I give up my plans completely and stay here?" She gestured back toward the house. Two weeks. Together. Under the same roof.

That part sounded decidedly *less* like a business deal. The very idea wisped heatedly over her skin.

"Not in my bed—unless you ask, of course." He smiled devilishly. "But if we're going to make the most of these two weeks, it's best we stay here. There are fantastic graduate school programs in the area, too, if you opt for that later down the road. And I can also provide you with greater protection here."

"Protection?" What in the world did she need his protection for? And from what? And what was this later-down-the-road notion for her plans?

"We're a professional NFL family. That brings with it a level of fame and notoriety unrivaled in any other business domain. The fans are passionate. And while most of them are supportive, there is a segment that takes the game very personally. Some of the more unstable types occasionally seek revenge for what they perceive as bad decisions." His jaw flexed. "Since your child is my child, that puts our baby at risk as a Reynaud. If you won't stay here for yourself, then stay for our child. We are safe here."

He had found the one reason she couldn't debate. But she needed to be careful. To give herself time to think through the consequences of what she was agreeing to, and she couldn't do that now when she was so tired.

"I am weary. It has been a long, emotional day. I would appreciate being shown to these guest suites that you speak of and I will consider it."

"Of course." He picked up his phone and tapped the screen twice before setting it down. "You'll find all the toiletries you need at your disposal. I'll have someone show you to a room and make sure you have everything you need."

Before he finished speaking, a maid had arrived at the door, perhaps summoned by his phone.

Apparently, Gervais was serious about giving her some space if she elected to stay in the house with him. And while she appreciated that, she was also surprised at his easy efficiency. Hadn't her pregnancy announcement rattled this coolly controlled man even a little?

"Thank you." She looked at him, her breath catching at the raw masculinity of the man. She backed up a step, needing boundaries. And sleep.

"And I'll have a long Hurricanes jersey sent up for you to sleep in." His eyes remained on hers, but his voice stirred something inside her.

The last time they had slept under the same roof, there hadn't been much sleeping accomplished at all. And somehow, as she took her leave of him, she knew that he was remembering that fact as vividly as she did.

The door closed behind her, and she loosed a breath that she didn't realize she'd been holding.

This was…different from what she had grown up

with. The billowy sheer curtains thinly veiled a view of Lake Pontchartrain. Heels clacked against the opulent white marble as she made her way to an oversize plush bed. Instinctively, she ran her hand over the white comforter as she took in the room.

A grand, hand-carved mahogany-wood nightstand held a score of toiletries.

It was luxurious. She unscrewed the lid on one of the lotion bottles, and the light scent of jasmine wafted up to her. She set it down, picked up the shampoo, popped the lid and breathed in mint and a tropical, fruity flavor.

This house was old, not as old as her castle, of course, but it still had history. And such a different feel than her wintry homeland. This was grander, built more for leisure than practicality.

Plopping onto the bed, Erika was somewhat surprised to note the bed was every bit as comfortable as it looked. The bed seemed to wrap her in a hug.

And she needed a hug. Everything in her life was undergoing a drastic change. Untethered. That was where she was. Her career in the military was over. It left her feeling strange, adrift. The past few years, her path had been set. And now? A river of conflicting wants and obligations flooded her mind.

Yes, she wanted to pursue her dream. She wanted to be a nurse-practitioner and pursue her studies in the UK, wanted that so badly. But that dream wasn't as simple as it had been a couple months ago.

Even now, thousands of miles away, she felt the tendrils of familial pressure. When they learned she was going to have a child, they would be pressuring her.

Probably into marriage. And Gervais seemed to have the same ideas. How was she supposed to balance all of it?

In her soul, she knew she'd be able to take care of her child. Give her baby everything and have her dreams, too. But the weight of everyone's expectations left her feeling anxious. First things first, she needed to figure out what she wanted. How she would handle all of this. And then she could deal with the demands of her family and Gervais.

Lifting herself off the bed, she made her way to the coffee table where a stack of old sports programs casually dressed the table.

Dragging her fingers over the covers, she tried to get a feel for Gervais. For his family. The Greek Revival hinted at wealth but shed little on his personality. Though, from her brief time in the halls, she noticed how sparsely decorated the place was. On the wall, directly across from where she stood, were some photos in sleek black frames. They were matted and simple. The generic sorts of photographs that belonged more in a cold, impersonal office than a residence.

She walked over to investigate them further. The two images that hung on the wall were formal portraits, similar to the kinds she and her family had done. But whereas her family bustled with Viking grace and was filled with women, these pictures were filled with the Reynaud men.

The sons stood closer to the grandfather. Strange. A man who looked as if he could be Gervais's father was on the edge of the photograph, an impatient smile curling over his face.

Gingerly, she reached out to the frame, fingers finding cool glass. Gervais. Handsome as the devil. A smile was on her lips before she could stop it. She dropped her hand.

No, Erika. She had to remain focused. And figure out how to do what was best for her—their—child that didn't involve jumping into bed with him. Again.

Pulling at the hem of the jersey that cut her midthigh, a jersey she'd found on her bed and couldn't resist wearing, she resolved to keep her hands off him. And his out from under her jersey. Even if that did sound…delicious.

Father.

The word blasted in his mind like an air horn.

Gervais tried to bring his mind back to the present. To the meeting with Dempsey, who had stopped by after Erika retreated to a vacant suite for the night. Just because Erika was pregnant didn't mean his career was nonexistent. He needed to talk with his brother about the Hurricanes' development. About corporate sponsorships and expanding their team's prestige and net worth.

But that was a lot easier said than done with the latest developments in his personal life.

He swirled his local craft beer in his glass, watching the mini tornado foam in the center as he made himself comfortable in the den long after dinner had ended. Back when this house had still belonged to his parents, most of the rooms had been fussy and full of interior decorator additions—elaborate crystal light fixtures that hung so low he and his brothers broke a part of it every time they threw a ball in the house. Or three-dimensional art that spanned whole walls and would scrape the skin off an arm if they tackled each other into it.

The den had always been male terrain and it remained a place where Gervais felt most comfortable. The place where he most often met with his brothers. Dempsey had headed for this room as soon as he'd arrived tonight.

Now, sipping his beer, Gervais tried like hell to get his head focused back on work. The team.

Dempsey took an exaggerated sip from his glass and set it on the table in front of them. Cocking his head to the side, he settled deeper in the red leather club chair and asked, "What's the deal with the princess's arrival? She damn near caused Freight Train to trip over his feet like a first-day rookie."

"She came by to see me." Gervais tried to make it sound casual. Breezy.

"Because New Orleans happens to be right around the corner from Europe?"

"Your humor slays me." He tipped back his beer. Dempsey was a lot of things, but indirect? Never.

"Well, she obviously came to see you. And from what I'm starting to hear now from the gossip already churning, the two of you spent a great deal of time together in the UK. Are you two back together again? Dating?" A small smile, but his eyes were trained on Gervais. A Reynaud trait—dogged persistence.

"Not exactly dating."

"Then why is she here?" He leaned forward, picking up his glass. "And don't tell me it's none of my business, because she's distracting you."

He wanted to argue the point. But who the hell would he be kidding?

Instead, he dropped his voice. "This goes no further than the two of us for now."

"I'm offended you have to ask that."

"Right. Well, she's pregnant. It's mine."

"You're certain?" Dempsey set his glass on the marble side table, face darkening like a storm rolling out.

Gervais stared him down. Not in the mood for that runaround.

"All right. Your child. What next?"

"My child, my responsibility." He would be there for his child. That was nonnegotiable.

"Interesting choice of words. *Responsibility.*" Something shifted in Dempsey's expression. But Gervais didn't have to wonder why. Dempsey was Gervais's illegitimate half brother. Dempsey hadn't even been in the picture until he turned thirteen years old, when Yvette, Dempsey's mom, had angled to extort money from their father, Theo, at which point Theo brought Dempsey to the family home.

To say the blending had been rough was generous. It was something that felt like the domestic equivalent of World War Three. Gervais's mother left. Then it was just a houseful of men—his brothers, Theo and Gramps. And it was really Gramps who had taken care of the boys. Theo was too busy shucking responsibilities.

"I'm sure as hell not walking away." He'd seen too

well the marks it left on Dempsey not knowing his father in the early years, the sting of growing up thinking his father didn't care. Hell, their father hadn't even known Dempsey existed.

Not that it excused their father, since he'd misled Dempsey's mother.

"I'm just saying that I understand what it feels like to be an inconvenient mistake. A responsibility." His jaw flexed, gaze fixed over Gervais's head.

"Dad loves you. We all do. You're part of our family."

"I know. But that wasn't always the case."

"We didn't know you then."

"He did. Or at least he knew that he'd been with women without considering the consequences." Dempsey's eyes darkened a shade, protectiveness for his mother obvious, even though the woman had been a negligible caregiver at best. "Anyhow, it took us all a long time to come back from that tough start. So make sure you get your head on straight before this baby's born. Better yet, get things right before you alienate the child's mother. Because if you intend to be in the kid's life, you're not going to want to spend years backtracking from screwing up with words like *responsibility* at the start."

The outburst was swift and damning. Dempsey shot up and out of his seat. He began to storm away, heading for the door.

Gervais followed.

"Dempsey—wait, I…" But the words fell silent as he nearly plowed into his brother's back.

Dempsey had halted in his tracks, his gaze on the

staircase in the corridor. Or, more accurate, his gaze on the woman now standing on the staircase.

Erika. In nothing but his jersey that barely reached midthigh. And she looked every bit as tantalizing as she had in her dress.

Gervais's eyes traced up, taking in her toned calves, the slope of her waist. The way her breasts pushed on the fabric. That wild hair of hers... She was well covered, but he couldn't help feeling the possessive need to wrap a blanket around her to shield her from his brother's gaze.

"I heard noise and realized there was someone wandering around." She drifted down a step, gesturing toward a shadowed corner of the hallway outside the den, where Gervais's grandfather stood. "I believe this is your grandfather?"

Gramps must have been wandering around again. Leon Reynaud was getting more restless with the years, and forgetful, too. But it was Erika who concerned him most right now. Her face was emotionless, yet there was a trace of unease in her voice. Had she overheard something in their conversation in the den?

Gramps Leon shook a gnarled finger at them. "Somebody's having a baby?" He shook his head. "Your father never could keep his pants zipped."

A wave of guilt crashed against him. For years he had tried to avoid any comparisons between himself and his father. Purposely setting himself on a very different path.

His father had been largely absent throughout his childhood and teen years. Theo Reynaud was a woman chaser. Neglectful of his duties to his children, his wife and the family's business.

Gervais would make damn sure he'd do better for his child. Even if Erika wasn't on board. Yet. He'd be an active presence in his future child's life. Everything his father failed to be.

Dempsey moved toward their grandfather, face slightly flushed. He stood and clapped Leon on the shoulder. "Dad's not expecting another child, *Grandpère*."

"Oh." Leon scratched his sparse hair that was standing up on end. "I get confused sometimes. I must have misunderstood."

Dempsey looked back at Gervais, expression mirroring the same relief Gervais felt. Crisis avoided.

His brother steered Gramps toward the door. "I'll walk with you to your room, Gramps." He gave Erika a nod as they passed her, though his focus remained on Leon. "I programmed some new music into your sound system. Some of those old Cajun tunes you like."

"Thank you, boy, thank you very much." They disappeared down the hall. Leaving Gervais alone with Erika.

Her arms crossed as she met his gaze. Unflinching bright blue eyes.

"You look much better in that jersey than anyone on the team ever did." God, she was crazy sexy.

"Whose jersey is this?" She traced the number with one finger, tempting him to do the same. "Whose number?"

He swallowed hard, a lump in his throat. "It's a retired number, one that had been reserved for me if I joined the team. I didn't." He shook off past regrets abruptly. He'd never played for the team, so he'd bought it, instead. "So shall I escort you back to you room?"

He couldn't keep the suggestive tone from his voice. Didn't want to.

She tipped her haughty-princess chin. "I think not. I can find my own way back."

That might be true enough. But they weren't done by a long shot. He wouldn't rest until the day came when he peeled that jersey from her beautiful body.

Four

She was really doing it. Spending two weeks with Gervais in his mansion on the shores of Lake Pontchartrain. She'd slept in his house and now that her luggage had been sent over from the hotel, she had more than a jersey to wear. She tugged at the hem, the fabric surprisingly soft to the touch, the number cool against the tips of her breasts.

This was actually happening. Last night had been more than just an overnight fluke. True to his word, Gervais hadn't been pushy about joining her here. But she felt his presence all the same.

And she was here to stay. A flutter of nerves traced down her spine as she fully opened the pocket doors to get a better look at the guest suite. She crossed the threshold from the bedroom to the sitting room, clothes in hand.

But she paused, toes sinking into the rich texture of the red Oriental rug. The way the light poured through the window in the sitting room drew her eye. Stepping toward the window, she took a moment to drink in the twinkled blue of Lake Pontchartrain.

The morning sun warmed her cheeks, sparking prisms across the room as it hit the Tiffany lamps. Glancing at her reflection in the gilded-gold mirror that was leaning on the mantel of the fireplace, she tucked a strand of hair behind her ear.

Mind wandering back, as it had a habit of doing lately, to Gervais. To the way his eyes lingered on her. And how that still ignited something in her…

But it was so much more complicated than that. She pushed the thought away, moving past the cream-colored chaise longue and opening the cherrywood armoire. As if settling her belongings in drawers gave her some semblance of normalcy. A girl could try, after all.

Her hand went to her stomach, to the barely perceptible curve of her stomach. A slight thickening to her waist. Her body was beginning to change. Her breasts were swollen and sensitive.

And her emotions were in a turmoil.

That unsettled her most of all. She was used to being seen as a focused academic, a military professional. Now she was adrift. Between jobs. Pregnant by a man she barely knew and with precious little time to settle her life before her family and the world knew of her pregnancy. She had a spot reserved for her in a graduate nursing program this fall, and she wanted to take coursework right up until her due date. But then what?

A knock on the door pulled her back to the present. She opened the paneled door and found a lovely, slender woman, wearing a pencil-thin skirt and silky blouse, tons of caramel-colored hair neatly pinned up. A large, pink-lipstick smile revealed brilliant white teeth.

She extended her hand. "Hello, I'm Adelaide Thibodeaux. Personal assistant to Dempsey Reynaud—the Hurricanes' coach. Gervais asked me to check in on you. I just wanted to make sure, do you have everything you need?"

Erika nodded. "Thank you. That is very kind of you to look in on me."

"I've been a friend of Dempsey's since childhood. I am happy to help the family." She wore sky-high pumps that would have turned Erika into a giantess—exactly the kind that she enjoyed wearing when she wasn't pregnant and less sure-footed.

"Did you have my things sent over?"

Adelaide's brow furrowed, concern touching the corners of her mouth. "Yes, did we miss anything?"

"Everything is perfect, thank you," she said, gesturing to the room behind her. "The home is lovely and comfortable, and I appreciate having my personal belongings sent over."

"We want you to enjoy your stay here in the States. It will be a wonderful publicity boon for the team to have royalty attending our games."

Erika winced. The last thing she wanted was more

attention from the media. Especially before she knew how she was going to handle the next few months.

Adelaide twisted her hands together, silver bracelets glinting in the sunlight. "Did I say something wrong?"

"Of course not. It is just that I am not a fan of football, or competitive sports of any kind." It was a half-truth. Certainly, no matter how she tried, she just didn't understand the attraction of football. But she couldn't tell Adelaide the real reason she didn't want to be a publicity ploy.

"And yet clearly you're quite fit. You must work out."

"I was in the military until recently, and I do enjoy running and yoga, but I have to confess, team sports have never held any appeal for me."

"No?" Adelaide frowned. "Then I am not sure I understand why you are here— Pardon me. I shouldn't have asked. It's not my business."

Erika searched for a simple answer. "Gervais and I enjoyed meeting each other in England." Understatement. "And since there is a conference in the area I plan to attend, I decided to visit." Okay, the conference was a lie, but one she could live with for now.

"Of course." Understanding lit her gaze, as if she was not surprised that Gervais would inspire a flight halfway across the world. "If you need anything, please don't hesitate to ask."

"Thank you. I appreciate your checking on me. But I am independent." She had always been independent, unafraid of challenges.

"I wasn't sure of the protocol for visiting royalty," Adelaide said, her voice curling into a question of sorts.

As if a princess couldn't fend for herself. "You are a princess."

"In name only, and even so, I am the fifth daughter."

"You're humble."

"I have been called many things, but not that. I am simply...practical."

Pink lips slipped back up into a smile. "Well, welcome to New Orleans. I look forward to getting to know you better."

"As do I." She had a feeling she was going to get to know everyone exceptionally well. Erika's thoughts drifted back to Gervais. She certainly wanted to get to know him better.

Adelaide started to leave, then turned back. "It might help you on game days if you think of football as a jousting field for men. You were in the military and come from a country famous for female warriors. Sure, I'm mixing time frames here with Vikings and medieval jousters, but still, if you see the game in the light of a joust or warrior competition, perhaps you may find yourself enjoying the event."

The door closed quietly behind her.

A joust? She'd never considered football and jousting. Maybe...maybe she'd give that a shot.

Her gaze floated back to the window, back to Lake Pontchartrain. It stretched before her like an exotic promise. Reminded her she was in a place that she didn't know. And it might be in her best interest to find any way into this world.

To make the most of these days here, to learn more

about the father of her child, she would need to experience his world.

And that meant grabbing a front-row seat.

Yet even as she plucked out a change of clothes, she couldn't help wondering… Had Adelaide Thibodeaux welcomed many other women into this home on Gervais's behalf?

Today was quite the production. Gervais watched the bustle of people filling the owners' suite at Zephyr Stadium for a preseason game day. Tickets for special viewing in the owners' box were sold at a premium price to raise money for a local charter school, so there were more guests than usual in the large luxury suite that normally accommodated family and friends.

His sister-in-law Fiona Harper-Reynaud was a renowned local philanthropist, and her quarterback husband was the golden boy of New Orleans, which added allure to her fund-raising invitation. Henri—beloved by fans as the Bayou Bomber—was the face of their franchise and worth every cent of his expensive contract. He was a playmaker with the drive and poise necessary to make it in the league's most closely dissected position.

The fact that female fans loved him was a bonus, even though it must be tough for Fiona sometimes. But she seemed to take it in stride, leveraging his popularity for worthy causes. Today her philanthropic guests sat casually on the dark leather chairs that lined the glass of the owners' suite. Half-eaten dishes with bottles of craft beer peppered the table in front of them as the clock ticked down the end of the second quarter that saw the Hurricanes up by three points.

Yet Gervais's eyes sought only one person. Erika.

He'd been busy greeting guests and overseeing some last-minute game-day business earlier, so he hadn't gotten to spend any time with her yet. She was tucked away, in a leather sofa by the bar, sipping a glass of sparkling water with lemon, wearing a silky, fitted turquoise dress that brushed her knees and caressed her curves with understated sex appeal. He knew full well where those enhanced curves came from.

From carrying his baby inside her.

She scrunched her toes in her heeled sandals, reaching down to press her thumb along the arch of her foot. The viewing box was cool—downright chilly. But was the New Orleans heat bothering her? The climate was a far cry from where she lived. He wanted to help her feel more comfortable, to love his home city as much as he did so they wouldn't be forced into some globe-hopping parenting situation. He wished they could have had a private breakfast to talk, but he'd been called away to the game. Thank goodness Adelaide had offered to check on her personally. Dempsey's assistant and long-time friend remained the one good thing that had come from Dempsey's early years spent living a hardscrabble life before their father had found him.

Adelaide had texted Gervais this morning, assuring him that Erika had everything she needed.

Now he watched Erika eyeing the food the servers carried. Caviar nachos and truffles pizza. Delicious delicacies, but she declined the offerings whenever the waitstaff stopped in front of her. Though she certainly looked hungry.

"Is the food not to your liking?" He stepped toward her, smoothing his tie and wondering if he should look into the foods native to her homeland. "We ordered a special menu for the event today, but we can have anything brought in."

Nearby, a group of women cheered as Henri connected with one of the rookie receivers running a slant route down on the field. No doubt, it would be one of Henri's last big plays of the game, since they needed to test the depth of the quarterback position with some of the backup talent.

Erika stood, moving closer to him, the scent of magnolia pulling his focus away from the game and slipping under his guard, making him recall their weekend together. Making him remember the view of her long legs bared just last night in a jersey that had covered her only to midthigh. He'd barely slept after that mouthwatering visual.

"Gervais, this is all incredible and definitely far more elaborate than I would have expected at a football game. Thank you."

Her response had been polite, but he could see something tugging at her. So he pressed, gently, "But…"

She took a few steps toward the glass, gesturing to the seats below, where fans were starting to crowd the aisles as halftime neared. "Honestly? My mouth is watering for one of those smothered hot dogs I see the vendors selling. With mustard and onions."

"You want a chili dog?" He couldn't hide a grin.

Right from the start she'd charmed him with the unexpected. She was a princess in the military. A sexy rebel. And despite all the imported fare weighing down the servers' trays, she wanted a chili dog.

"If it is not too much trouble, of course." She frowned. "I did not think to bring my wallet."

"It's no trouble." He wouldn't mind stepping out of the temperature-controlled suite into the excited crowd. How long had it been since he'd ventured out from behind the tinted-glass windows during a game? It had been too long.

He leaned to whisper in her ear, hand bracing her on the small of her back. "Pregnancy craving?"

She blinked quickly, her breath quickening under his touch. "I believe so. Mornings are difficult with nausea, but then I am starving for the rest of the day. Today has been difficult, with all the travel yesterday and jet lag."

"Then I will personally secure an order for you." He smiled. "I have to say I wouldn't mind having one for myself." He touched her shoulder lightly, aching to keep his hands on her. "I'll be right back."

Erika moved closer to the glass and took a seat, looking down into the field, her eyes alert.

There was no fanfare in yoga or running, so Erika looked on at the halftime show with a sense of wonder. LSU's band performed in tandem with a pop star local to the area, sending the fans into wild cheers as a laser light show sliced the air around her. The scents of fog and smoke wafted through the luxury suite's vents, teasing her oversensitive nose.

This box was quite different from the Wembley luxury suite where she'd met Gervais. The Reynaud private domain was decorated with family memorabilia, team awards and lots of video monitors for comfortable viewing in the back of the box right near the bar.

But she enjoyed her front-row seat, watching intently.

So this really did have a form of old-world pageantry mixed with a dash of medieval jousting. Her military training made her able to pick out various formations on the field below, the two teams forming and re-forming their lines to try to outwit one another. Viewing the game this way had been a revelation—and definitely not as boring as she'd once thought. And she couldn't wait to taste one of the chili dogs once Gervais returned.

Fiona Harper-Reynaud, the quarterback's wife and Gervais's sister-in-law, if Erika remembered correctly, tilted her head to the side. "Princess Erika, you look pensive."

"I have been thinking about the game, trying to understand more about what I've seen so far, since I am actually quite a neophyte about the rules. My sisters and I were not exposed much to team sports."

A few of the other women laughed softly into their cocktail napkins, eyeing Erika.

Fiona smiled, crossing her elegant legs at the ankles. "What an interesting choice, then, to spend time with Gervais when you're not a football enthusiast."

"I am learning to look at the game in a new light." She would read more about it now that she knew her child would be a part of this world.

She couldn't allow her son or daughter to be unprepared for their future, and that meant football. She could not sit in this box overflowing with Reynauds and fail to realize how deeply entrenched they were in this sport.

"How so?" Fiona traced a finger on her wineglass, her diamond wedding ring glinting in the light from a chrome pendant lamp.

Erika pointed down to the field, where the head coach and his team were now returning to the sidelines. "Adelaide Thibodeaux suggested I think of this as a ritual as old as time, like an ancient battle or a medieval jousting field. The imagery is working for me."

"Hmm." Fiona lifted one finely arched eyebrow. "That's quite a sexy image. And fitting. Armor versus shoulder pads. It works. I'll have to spin that for a future fund-raiser."

"That sounds intriguing." And it did. If it helped Erika to appreciate the game more, it could certainly appeal to someone else.

"Perhaps I should rethink the menu, too, as I may have overdone things with this event." She picked up a nacho and investigated it.

"The food is amazing. Quite a lovely, fun spread," Erika offered, smiling at her.

"But you want a chili dog—or so I overheard you say."

"I hope you did not take offense, as I certainly did not mean any." Erika fought the urge to panic. She bit down her nerves—and a wave of nausea. This was easily explainable. "I am in America. I simply want to experience American foods served at a regular football game."

A server walked by with another fragrant tray of caviar nachos—too fragrant. She pressed her hand to her stomach as another wave of indigestion struck, cramping her stomach.

Fiona's eyebrows rose but she stayed silent for a moment. "If you need anything, anything at all, please don't hesitate to ask."

Did Fiona know somehow, even though she didn't have children? There seemed to be an understanding—and a sadness in her eyes.

For a brief, fleeting moment, she wondered if Fiona had ever found herself in Erika's situation. Not the pregnant-with-a-handsome-stranger situation, but the other one. The one where she was an outsider who shouldered too much responsibility sometimes.

The weight of that thought bore down on her, making her stomach even more queasy. She fought back the urge, praying she could get to her feet and to the ladies' room before she embarrassed herself.

Erika bit her lip, shooting to her feet, only to find the ground swaying underneath her. Not a good sign at all, but if she could just grab the back of her seat for a moment to steady herself… There. The world righted in front of her and she eyed the door, determined. "I will be right back. I need to excuse myself."

And the second she took that first step, the ground rocked all the harder under her, and she slumped into unconsciousness.

Five

Gervais pushed through the crowds, eyes set on the chili dog vendor. As he weaved in and out, he saw recognition zip through their eyes.

The media had done a nice job planting his image in the minds of the fans even though he would have preferred a quieter role, leaving the fame to the players. But the family name also sold tickets and brought fans to their television screens, so he played along because he, too, loved the game and would do whatever was needed for the Hurricanes.

Many of the fans smiled at him, nudged a companion and pointed at Gervais. He felt a little as if he was in a dog-and-pony show. And while part of him wouldn't mind pausing to speak to a few fans and act as an ambassador for the team, he really just wanted to get Erika that chili dog. Pronto.

So he flashed a smile as he continued, stopping in front of the food vendor, the smell of nacho cheese and cayenne peppers sizzling under his nose. Of all the things Erika could have asked for, he was strangely intrigued by this request. It was the most un-princess-like food in the whole sports arena. He loved that.

Gervais's phone vibrated. He juggled the two chili dogs to one hand as he fished out his cell while taking the stadium steps two at a time. He glanced at the screen and saw his sister-in-law's name. Frowning, he thumbed the on button.

"Yes, Fiona?"

"Gervais—" Fiona's normally calm voice trembled "—Erika passed out. We can't get her to wake up. I don't know—"

"I'm on my way." Panic lanced his gut.

His hand clenched around the hot dogs until a little chili oozed down his fingers as he raced up the steps faster, sprinted around a corner, then through a private entrance to the hall leading to the owners' viewing box.

A circle of people stood around a black leather sofa, blocking his view. A cold knot settled in his stomach. He set the food on the buffet table and shouldered through the crowd.

"Erika? Erika," he barked, forgetting all about formalities. He dropped to his knees beside the sofa where she lay unconscious. Too pale. Too still.

He took her hand in his, glancing back over his

shoulder. "Has anyone called a doctor? Get the team doctor. Now."

Fiona nodded. "I called him right after I called you."

He brushed his hand over Erika's forehead, her steady pulse throbbing along her neck a reassuring sign. But still, she wasn't coming around. There were so many complications that could come with pregnancy. His family had learned that tragic reality too well from his sister-in-law's multiple miscarriages.

Which made him wince all the more when he needed to lean in and privately tell Fiona, "Call the doctor back and tell him to hurry—because Erika's pregnant."

Erika pushed through layers of fog to find a group of faces staring down at her. Some closer than others.

A man with a stethoscope pressing against her neckline while he took her pulse must be a doctor.

And of course she should have known that Gervais would be near. He sat on the arm of the sofa at her feet, watching her intently, his body a barrier between her and the others in the room staring at her with undisguised interest.

Curiosity.

Whispering.

Oh, God. Somehow, they knew about the baby and she hadn't even told her parents yet.

"Gervais, do you think we could have some privacy?"

He looked around, started, as if he hadn't even realized the others were still there. "Oh, right, I'll—"

Fiona stepped up. "I've got this. You focus on Erika."

She extended her arms, gesturing toward the door. "Let's move to the other side of the box and give the princess some air…"

Her voice faded as she ushered the other guests farther away, leaving behind a bubble of privacy.

She elbowed up, then pressed a hand to her woozy head. "Doctor, what's going on?"

The physician wearing a polo shirt with the team's logo on the pocket said, "Gervais here tells me you're pregnant. Would you like him to give us some privacy while we talk?"

She didn't even hesitate with her answer. "He can stay. He has a right to know what is going on with the baby."

The doctor nodded, his eyes steady and guarded. "How far along are you?"

"Two and a half months."

"And you've been to a doctor?"

"I have, back in my homeland."

"Well, your pulse appears normal, as do your other vital signs, but you stayed unconscious for a solid fifteen minutes. I would suggest you see a local physician."

Gervais shot to his feet. "I'll take her straightaway."

Erika sat up, the world steadier now. "But you will miss the rest of the game."

"Your health is more important. We'll take the private elevator down and slip out the back." He shifted his attention to the physician. "Doc, can you send up a wheelchair?"

She swung her feet to the ground. "I can walk. I am not an invalid. I simply passed out. It happens to pregnant women."

"Pregnant women who don't eat," Gervais groused, sliding an arm around her waist for support. "You should take care of yourself."

Even as she heard the grouchiness in his voice, she saw the concern in his eyes, the fear. She wanted to soothe the furrowed lines on his forehead but knew he wouldn't welcome the gesture, especially not right now.

So she opted to lighten the mood instead. Heaven knew she could use some levity after the stress she had been under. And how strange to realize that in spite of being terrified, she felt safer now with Gervais present.

She looked up at him and forced a shaky smile. "Don't forget my chili dog."

Gervais paced the emergency room. The hum of the lights above provided a rhythm to his pacing. He tried to focus on what he could control.

Which was absolutely nothing at this point. Instead of being in the know, he was completely in the dark. He couldn't start planning, something he liked to do.

Sitting still had never been his strong suit. Gervais wanted to be in the midst of the action, not hanging on the sidelines. That was how he'd been as a football player, how he dealt with his family. Always engaged. Always on.

But now? No one would tell him anything. He wasn't a family member. Not technically, even though that was his unborn child.

God, he hated feeling helpless. Most of all he hated feeling cut off from his family. His child.

What the hell was taking the doctor so long?

Sure, the place was packed with weekend traffic. To his left was a boy with what appeared to be a broken arm and a cracked tooth. His sister, a petite blonde thing, wrinkled her nose in disgust as he shoved his arm in her face.

The man on his right elevated a very swollen ankle. He was in the ER alone, sitting in silence, hands rough with calluses.

Gervais could hear snippets of the conversation going on in the far corner of the room. A young mom cooed over her baby, holding tight to her husband's hand. They were probably first-time parents. Nervous as hell. But they were tackling the problem together. As he wanted to with Erika, but the lack of information was killing him.

The whole ride over, Erika had been woozy and nauseated. He tried to tell himself that fainting wasn't a big deal. But he wasn't having much luck calming down his worries.

The possibilities of what could be wrong played over and over again in his head. He hated this feeling. Helplessness. It did not sit well with him.

A creak from the door called his attention back to the present moment. Snapping his focus back to the ER. And to the two men heading for him. His brothers Henri and Dempsey. Henri's sweat-stained face was grave as he caught Gervais's eye. Hell, he knew time had passed. But that much? And he hadn't even watched the rest of the game on the waiting room television.

He charged over to his brothers.

Henri hauled him in hard and fast for a hug, slapping him on the back. Smelled of Gatorade. Heavily.

The leftover jug must have been poured over his head, signifying victory. "What's the news?"

"I'm still waiting to hear from the docs." He guided both of his brothers over to the privacy of a corner by a fat fake topiary tree. "We won?"

Dempsey didn't haul him in for a brotherly hug, but he thumped him on the back. They were brothers. Not as close as Henri and Gervais, but the bond was there. Solid. "Yes, by three points. Even though we sidelined most of our starters to test depth at various positions. Henri's backup did a credible job marching the offense downfield for one more TD in the closing minutes. But that's not what matters right now. We're here for you. Is everything okay?"

Gervais shrugged. "We don't know yet. Nobody's talking to me. I'm not tied to her in any legal way."

Dempsey's voice lowered till it was something barely audible. He looked squarely into his brother's eyes. "Do you plan to be there for your child?"

"Yes." Gervais didn't hesitate. "Absolutely."

Henri shifted his weight from foot to foot. The three Reynaud men stared at each other, no one daring to utter so much as a syllable for a few moments.

Dempsey nodded. "Good. You know what? I'm going to get coffee for us. Who knows how long we will be here. ER visits are never short."

"Great. Thanks," Henri said as Dempsey walked back toward the doors. "Is she considering giving the baby up for adoption?"

"I didn't bring that up." Truth be told, he hadn't even

thought of that as a real option. It was his child. He wanted to provide for his child.

"Did she?" Henri crossed his arms, voice lowered so only they could hear each other.

"No. I'm not even sure how the royalty part plays into this." God, what if his power, prestige, money, wasn't worth jack and she took his child away altogether? "She discussed shared parenting."

Henri shrugged. An attempt at nonchalance that fell flat. "I just want you to know that if things change, Fiona and I are willing to raise the baby as our own."

Gervais looked over at his brother quickly, thinking of all the miscarriages his brother and sister-in-law had been through, the strain that had put on their marriage. This baby news had to be hitting his normally happy-go-lucky brother hard. "Thank you, my brother. That means a lot to me. But this is my child. Not some mistake. Not just a responsibility. My child."

Henri nodded and hooked an arm around his brother's shoulders. "I look forward to meeting my niece or nephew. Congratulations."

"Thank you." Gervais noticed how Henri's face became blank. Distant. "Are you and Fiona okay?"

"Sure, we're fine," Henri replied a bit too quickly.

"We need your total commitment to the season. If you're having any problems, you can come to me." And he meant it. He wanted to be there for his brother. For his whole family. They meant everything to him.

Henri shook his head, looking his brother in the eyes. Offering a smile that refused to light his cheeks or touch his eyes. "No problem."

Gervais shook his head, raising an eyebrow at him. "You never were a good liar."

Wasn't that the truth? When they were kids, Henri always cracked under pressure. His eyes would widen when he fibbed.

"No problems that will distract me from the game. Now stop being the owner of the team and let's be brothers."

Gervais was about to protest, but suddenly the ER waiting room was alive with movement. Dempsey strode back over to them, cups of coffee on a tray. A damn fine balancing act going on.

And following closely on his heels was a doctor. The same old, frazzle-haired doctor that had been treating Erika. His gut knotted.

The doctor cleared his throat. "Mr. Reynaud— Gervais Reynaud," he clarified. The whole town knew the Reynauds, so no doubt the doctor recognized them. "Ms. Mitras is asking for you."

All he could do was nod. Deep in his chest, his heart thudded. Afraid. He was afraid of what was wrong with Erika and his child.

The doctor opened a thick pinewood door to a small exam room and gestured for Gervais to enter.

In the center of the room, Erika was hooked up to a smattering of machines. Lights flashed from various pieces of equipment. Her blond hair was tied back into a topknot, exposing the angles of her face. Somehow making her seem impossibly beautiful despite the presence of the machines.

Within moments he was at her side. He wanted to

show her he was here. He was committed to their child and would not abandon her. Stroking her hand, he knelt beside her. "You're okay? The baby's okay?"

Her face was pale, but she smiled, her eyes serene. "We are fine. Absolutely fine."

"This child is important to me. You are important to me." She was damn important. He had to make her see that.

"Because I am the baby's mother." The words spilled from her mouth matter-of-factly. As if there was no other reason he'd be here right now.

"We had a connection before that."

A dramatic sigh loosed from her pink lips. "We had an affair."

"I called you afterward." She'd been imprinted on his brain. A woman he could not—would not—forget.

"You are a gentleman. I appreciate that. In fact, that was part of what drew me to do something so uncharacteristic. But it was only a weekend."

"A weekend with lasting consequences." A weekend that had turned him inside out. Given time, he could make her see that, too.

"More than we realized," she said with a shaky laugh.

"What do you mean?" Head cocking to the side, he tried to discern the cause of the uneasy laughter.

She gestured to the ultrasound machine next to her. "I am pregnant with twins."

Gervais tore his gaze from Erika, focusing on the screen. Sure enough, there were two little beans on the ultrasound. He and Erika were going to have twins.

Six

Exhausted, Erika relaxed back into the passenger seat of Gervais's luxury SUV. The leather seat had the smell of a woodsy cologne, a smell she distinctively recognized as Gervais. It was oddly comforting, a steadying moment in a day that had been anything but stable.

As the car pulled away from the hospital, she glanced out the window, craning to see the collection of Reynaud brothers who stood at the entrance. Her sisters would swoon over the attractive picture they presented, those powerful, broad-shouldered men. They had all come rushing to the hospital, filled with concerns. And likely, with questions.

But they had been polite in the lobby after her release. They didn't press for information—the conversation had been brief. They'd wanted to know if she was okay. And neither Gervais nor Erika had offered any information about twins. That was something that they still had to discuss together. Something she still hadn't processed.

But how should she broach this new development in an already emotionally charged day? How in the world could she bring up everything in her whirring mind? Her eyes remained fixed out of the car, even though the scene of the hospital had faded from vision, framed by wrought-iron fences and thick greenery. Now the vibrant pinks and yellows of the old French houses populated her view.

Glancing at an elaborate wood-carved balcony, she let out an emotional sigh. What had happened today had left her shaken. She'd never passed out like that before, never felt so disoriented in her life. She'd been blessed with good health, and she had pushed her physical endurance to the limit during her military training. Yet this pregnancy was only just beginning and it had already landed her flat on her back. But, thanks to Gervais's quick action, she and her children—*children*, plural, oh, God—were safe.

It was all that mattered. That her children were okay. The twins were fine. *Twins.* She turned the word over. Was it possible to love them both so much already, even though she'd just learned about them? And yet, she did. In spite of her nerves, in spite of not having a plan figured out. Sure, she was scared about the future, about having to deal with her family…but she was overwhelmed with a deep love for her children already.

She peered over at the man in the driver's seat beside her. Perhaps he felt her eyes on him, because soon Gervais's throat moved in a long swallow. "Twins?" he mused aloud. "Twins."

The simple utterance seemed to linger on his tongue and echo through the quiet interior of the luxury vehicle. Not that she could blame him for being overwhelmed by the news. There was a lot to take in. Still, even under Gervais's audible processing of the fact that he was about to be a father not to one but two children, she could hear a glow of pride in his tone. A protectiveness that caught her attention.

Of course, the raw, masculine appeal of his muscular body taking up too much space beside her might have something to do with how thoroughly he held her notice. How easy it would be to simply lean closer. Lean on him. She could almost imagine the feel of his suit jacket beneath her cheek if she laid her head on his shoulder and curled up against his chest.

She forced herself to focus on the conversation they needed to have instead. On their children.

"Yes, there are two in there. I even heard the heartbeats." Her heart fluttered with joy as she remembered the delicate beating of her—*their*—children. The sound had made her spring to life in a way she didn't know was possible. She felt bad he'd missed that. They were his children, too, and he'd deserved to have that same feeling of awe. Looking at him sidelong, she said cautiously, "Next time you can come with me if you wish."

"I wish." There was no mistaking the sound of his commitment.

"Then you should be there." She couldn't hold back

the smile swelling inside her as she drank in his eyes alight with honest excitement. "It is too early to distinguish the sex, you know."

He shrugged, clearly unconcerned. "That doesn't matter."

"It did in my family." It came out in a whisper, something almost like a secret. And each word hurt.

He glanced over at her briefly before turning his eyes back to the road as they drove west toward his home. "Be clearer for me."

She smoothed the skirt of her dress, wrinkled beyond recognition after being crumpled into a hospital bag during her exam. If only she could smooth over her past as easily. This was knowledge she carried every day. Knowledge that ate at her and had her entire lifetime. "A line of girls was always cause for concern in my home. The monarchy is technically inactive, but even so there is no provision for a female ruler. There are no male heirs. I am afraid…"

"Oh, no. No way in hell is anyone taking my children away." His brow furrowed, anger simmering in his eyes, the joyous warmth gone.

"Our children. These are our children." She felt all the same protective instincts he did, and she felt them with a mother's fierce love.

"And we can't afford to forget for even a moment how important it is that we work together for the children. If there's a chance we can have more than a bicoastal parenting relationship, don't you think it's worth figuring that out as soon as possible?" The look he gave her was pointed. Sharp.

But Erika wasn't about to back down. She hadn't decided how to handle whatever was between them. And that meant she had to think a bit more. She wouldn't be rash and impulsive. One of them had to think through their actions.

"I will let you know when I schedule my doctor visit. I will want to visit the doctor again before returning home."

He scowled. "Can we not talk about you leaving? We're still settling details."

"You know I do not live here." New Orleans was lovely, with its vibrant history, loud colors and live music that seemed to drift up from every street corner. But it was not home. Not that she really knew where home was these days…

"One day at a time. And today we are dealing with a big change, the reality of two children. I know that happens. I just never expected…" His voice trailed, his words ebbing with emotion.

"I have twin sisters." She had always envied them their closeness, like having a built-in best friend from birth. "Twins—how do you say?—walk in my family."

"Run in your family. Okay."

She blinked at him, filing away the turn of English phrasing that brought a funny image to her mind of twins sprinting through her family tree. This was all happening so fast, she'd never stopped to consider the possibility of twins. There was so much to figure out still. "My oldest sister also has twin girls. I should have considered this possibility but I have been so overwhelmed since I realized I was expecting."

"Thank you for coming to tell me so soon." He covered her hand on the center console. "I appreciate that you didn't delay."

"You are the father. You deserve to know that." Erika lifted her chin up, tilting her head to the side to get a better look at him. He was a good man. She knew that much.

"We're going to make this work." He lifted her hand and kissed the back, then the inside of her wrist over her rapidly beating pulse.

The press of his mouth to her skin was warm and arousing, stirring memories of their weekend together. The air crackled between them now as it had then. Her emotions were already in turmoil after the scare at the game. She ached to move closer, to feel his arms around her. To have those lips on her body again. Everywhere. Arousing her to such heights her head spun at the thought. How quickly she could simply lose herself in what he could make her feel.

But doing so would take away any chance of objectivity. And now she had twice the reason to tread carefully into the future.

The silver stain of moonlight washed over the lake. The water was restless. Frothy. Uneasy. A lot like the restlessness inside Gervais. But he had to pull it together in order to make this phone call.

He thumbed through his phone, finding his father in his contact list. How long had it been since they'd spoken? Months, no doubt. The bright screen blared at him.

He knew he had to call him about Erika's pregnancy.

Theo was in Paris for the week with his latest girlfriend. Which was, in some ways, fortunate. This way, Gervais had gotten to talk to Erika privately before his father had a chance at royally screwing the dynamic up.

But it also meant he had to make this call. Which was something he never looked forward to doing. Years of neglect and dysfunction had their way of clinging to their current relationship. Another lesson of how not to treat children brought to you by Theo Reynaud. Dear old dad loved football and his family, but not as much as romancing women.

Before he could think better of it, Gervais pressed Send on the screen. Feeling the pinch of nerves, he poured himself a glass of bourbon from the pool-deck bar, staring at where a few kids messed around with a stand-up paddleboard. Beyond them, the lights of gambling boats winked in the distance and even farther behind those he could see the bridge that spanned the lake.

Gervais wasn't sure why he felt the need to talk to his dad other than doing him the courtesy of making sure he didn't hear via the grapevine. Discretion wasn't Theo's strong suit. But if Gervais spun the news just right, maybe he could keep a lid on it a bit longer. Erika would appreciate that.

And tonight making Erika relaxed and happy felt like the first priority on a quickly shifting list in his life. But knowing that she carried his children had brought things into sharp focus for him today.

"Hello, son." His father's graveled voice shot through the receiver, yanking him from his thoughts.

Might as well cut to the chase.

"Dad, you're going to be a grandfather."

"About damn time. Damn shame Henri is still carrying a grudge and didn't tell me himself. The divorce was a long time ago."

In the background of the call, the sound of violin music and muted chatter combined with the clink of glasses. The sounds of a bar scene.

Gervais ignored the mention of his parents' dysfunctional marriage. "Henri and Fiona aren't expecting. I'm the one about to make you a gramps."

News about the twins could wait. One step at a time. He was still reeling from that news himself.

"With who? You didn't knock up some groupie looking for a big payoff from the family?" His voice crackled through the phone from across the Atlantic.

"Dad, that's your gig. Not mine." And just like that, he was on the defensive. Gervais was not his father. He would never be like his father. And the fact that his father thought he had that in his nature sent him reeling.

"No need to be disrespectful." Bells chimed in the background of the call, an unmistakable sound of a slot machine in payoff mode.

So much for keeping the subject of his parents' divorce off the table. "You destroyed your marriage with your affairs. You ignored your own sons for years. I lost respect for you a long time ago."

"Then why are you here now telling me about this baby?"

Gervais closed his eyes, blotting out the lights from the distant boats on the lake, listening to the sound of the water. With his spare hand, he pressed on his eyes, inhaling deeply. Exhaling hard, he opened his eyes, resolve renewed.

"Because this news is going to go viral soon and I want to make sure you understand I will not tolerate any inappropriate or hurtful comments to the mother of my child." That was something he absolutely would not allow. From anyone. Least of all his father. He would protect Erika from that.

"Understood. And who might this woman be?" An air of interest infused his words.

"Erika Mitras." He sat down, inspecting his ice cubes as he waited for his father to make some sort of off-color remark.

"Mitras? From that royal family full of girls? Well, hell, son. It's tough to find someone not out for our money, but kudos to you. You found a woman who doesn't need a damn thing from you."

The words cut him, even though, for once, his father hadn't meant any harm by them. Erika had said as much about not needing Gervais's help. But he wanted to be there for his children. For her. Seeing those two tiny lives on that monitor today had blown him away.

And knowing that Erika was already taxed from travel and devoting her beautiful body to nurture those children made him want to slay dragons for her. Or, at the very least, put a roof over her head and see to her every need.

"Thanks. That wasn't forefront in my mind at the time."

"When you were in England, I assume?"

"Not your business."

"You always were a mouthy bastard." Smug words from the other end of the receiver.

"Just like my old man." He downed half of his glass of bourbon. "Be nice."

"The team's winning. That always puts me in a good mood."

"Nice to know you care." Not that his father owned a cent of this team. The Hurricanes belonged to Gervais and Gervais alone.

"Congratulations, Papa. Name the little one after me and I'll give—"

"Dad, stop. No need to try so hard to be an ass."

"I'm not trying. Good night, son. Congrats."

The line went dead. So much for father-son bonding time.

Gervais tossed his cell phone on a lounge chair and tipped back the rest of the ten-year-old bourbon, savoring the honey-and-spice finish in an effort to dispel the sour feel left by the phone call. He didn't know what he'd expected from his old man. That he would magically change into…what? A real father? Some kind of reassurance that maybe, just maybe, he himself could be a good father to not just one but two babies?

Foolishness, that. Theo remained as selfish as they came.

Regardless, though, he knew one thing for certain. He was not going to ditch his responsibility the way his father had.

Tucked in the big guest bed in Gervais's house, Erika snuggled deeper beneath the lightweight comforter, hugging the pillow closer as sleep tugged her further under. She was exhausted after the hospital visit and the strain of pregnancy that seemed to drain all her physical resources. She would feel better after she rested, and she couldn't deny taking extra pleasure at sleeping under the same roof as Gervais.

During her waking hours, she did all in her power to keep the strong attraction at bay so she could make smart decisions about her future. Her children's future. But just now, with sleep pulling her under, and her body so perfectly comfortable, she couldn't resist the lure of thinking about Gervais. His touch. His taste…

Her memories and dreams mingling, filling her mind and drugging her senses with seductive images…

The press of Gervais's lips on hers sparked awareness deep in Erika's stomach. He pulled back from the passionate kiss, and she surprised herself when she was disappointed. She wanted his lips on hers. And not just there. Everywhere.

But he led her toward the couch in his den.

His den?

A part of her brain realized this was not a memory. She was in Gervais's house. In Louisiana. She could smell the scent of the lake mingling with the woodsy spice of his aftershave as he drew her down to the leather couch, tossing aside a football before he landed on the cushion while she melted into his lap. And it felt right. Natural. As if she belonged here with him.

Her heart slugged hard in her chest, the strength and warmth of his so incredible she could stay for hours. Longer. She wanted this. Wanted him. She'd never felt so alive as during those days when she'd been in his bed, and she couldn't wait to feel that spark inside her again. The hitch in her breath. The pleasure of sharp orgasms undulating through her body, again and again.

Now he tilted her chin up, searched her eyes for something. A mingle of nerves, anticipation and desire thumped in her chest as he kissed her forehead. Her lips. Her neck. She trembled as he touched her, her whole body poised for the fulfillment he could provide.

Her eyes closed, and the muted noise of a football game on a television behind them began to fade away until only the sound of their mingled breaths remained.

"Erika," he whispered in her ear before kissing her neck again. The heat of his breath on her skin made her toes curl.

"Mmm?" A half question stuck on her lips.

"Stay here with me." His request was spoken in clips between kisses, then a nip on her earlobe.

His hands tugged at the heavy jeweled collar around her neck. He removed it from her, the metal crown charms clanking against the coffee table. How good it felt to set that weight aside.

"Let me take care of you. Of them." Wandering hands found her shoulders, slipped underneath the thin straps of her dress. She burst to life, pressing into him with a new urgency. A want and need so unfamiliar to her.

As he kissed her, he rocked her back and forth. The scent of earthy cologne seemed to grow stronger. Demanded more of her attention...

"Erika?" a deep voice called, a man's voice.

Gervais.

Opening her eyes, she had a moment of panic. This was not the hotel room.

As the suite came into focus, she realized where—and when—she was. This was Gervais's house, his guest bedroom. She wasn't in London, but rather in Louisiana. Still, the memory pounded at her mind and through her veins.

She wanted to go back there now. To her dreamworld in all its brilliant simplicity.

But Gervais himself stood in the doorway of the guest suite.

His square jaw flexed, the muscles in his body tensed, backlit from a glowing sconce in the hall.

"Erika?" He crossed the threshold, deeper into the room, his gaze intense as he studied her. "I heard you cry out. I was worried. Are you okay? The babies?"

The mattress dipped as he sat beside her, stirring heated memories of her dream.

"I am fine. I was, um, just restless." The sensuality of her dream still filled her, making her all the more aware of his hip grazing hers through the lightweight blanket. The electricity between them was not waning. If anything, she felt the space between them grow even more charged. More aware.

"Restless," he repeated, eyes roving her so thoroughly she wondered what she looked like. Her hair teased along her bare shoulder, her silk nightdress suddenly feeling very insubstantial, even though the blanket covered her breasts.

Images from her dream flitted back into her mind,

and she bit her lip as her gaze moved down his face, to his hands reaching up to her exposed shoulders. Looking back at him through her eyelashes, she could tell he sensed the charged atmosphere, too. But his hands didn't move. Not as she'd expected—and wanted—them to. There was something else besides hunger in the way he held her gaze. Something that looked a bit like worry.

"Gervais, I truly am all right. But are *you* all right?"

He ran his hand through the hair on top of his head, eyes turning glossy and unfocused. "I called my dad tonight to tell him about the pregnancy. Not the twin part. Just…that he's going to be a grandfather. I didn't want him to hear it in the news."

She thought of how the day had gone so crazy so fast simply because she passed out. "I wish we could have told your family together."

"You didn't include me when you told your family."

She looked away, guilt stinging her. And didn't that cool the heat that had been singeing her all over?

"You've told your family, haven't you?" he asked, his eyes missing nothing.

"I will. Soon. I know I have to before it hits the news." She wanted to change the subject off her family. Fast. "What did your family have to say? Your brothers were quiet at the emergency room."

"My brothers are all about family. No one judges. We love babies."

Erika raised her eyebrows, unsure how to take the casual tone of what felt like a very serious conversation. She noticed he didn't include his father in that last part.

"That is all?" she asked, knowing she had no right

to quiz him when she hadn't shared much about her own family.

"That's it. Now we need to tell your parents before they find out."

"I realize that."

"I want to be with you, even if it's on the phone in a Skype session." His jaw flexed in a way she was beginning to recognize—a surefire sign of determination. He slid his arms around her and said, "I want to reassure them I plan to marry their daughter."

Seven

"You have forgotten we have *no* plans to get married. I have plans—other plans. Our plans are in flux."

Erika pulled out of Gervais's arms so fast he damn near fell off the bed. He wasn't sure why he'd raised the issue again, other than not wanting to be like his father, and certainly the timing of his proposal hadn't been the smoothest. But the least she could do was consider it, since they hadn't taken time to seriously discuss it that first night.

Time to change that now. He shifted on the bed so they were face-to-face. And promptly remembered how little she must be wearing under that blanket. A bare shoulder peeked above the fabric, calling his hands to rake the barrier down and away.

To slide between those covers with her.

"Why not even consider?" he ground out between clenched teeth, determined to stay on track with this talk. "We have babies on the way. Even if we have a civil ceremony and stay together for the children's first year." From the scowl on her beautiful face he could see he was only making this worse. "Erika?"

"I came here to tell you about being pregnant, see if you want to be an active father, and then make plans from there. I didn't come for a yearlong repeat of our impulsive weekend together."

He swallowed. Had his carnal thoughts been that obvious? No sense denying that he wanted her.

"And what would be so wrong with that?"

"I have a life in another country."

"You're out of the military now. So work here. You have more job flexibility than I do."

Red flushed into her cheeks, making her look more like a shield maiden and less like a delicate princess in need of saving. "You are serious?"

The more he thought about it, the more it felt right. A marriage of convenience for a couple of years. He stroked her hair back and tucked it behind her ear, the silky strands gliding along his fingers. "We have amazing chemistry. We have children on the way. You're already staying in my home—"

"For two weeks," she said, finality edging her voice.

"Why not longer? Things have changed now with the twins. Two babies at once would be a lot for anyone to care for."

He needed to be involved. A part of his children's lives.

"I have plans for this fall. A commitment to my career. You are thinking too far into the future." She shook her head, a toss of silvery-blond hair in the moonlight. "Please slow down."

She angled an elbow against a bolster pillow, reclining even as she remained seated. And damn, but he wanted to be the one she leaned against, the one who supported her incredible body through the upcoming months while she carried this burden for them.

"We don't have that option for long. And you yourself said you were concerned about the babies being boys and being caught up in the family monarchy as next in line. If they're born here and we're married here in the States…" He wasn't exactly sure what that would mean for the monarchy, but it certainly would slow things down. Give them time to become a family. And to figure out how everything would work together.

She clapped a hand over his mouth. "Stop. Please. I cannot make this kind of decision now."

The magnolia scent of her lotion caught him off guard. He breathed in the scent, enjoying the cool press of her skin on his lips. Would have said as much if he hadn't noticed the glimmer of tears in her eyes.

A raggedy breath before speaking. "Can we please think about our future rationally? When I am rested and more prepared?" Though she did her best to look past him, every inch a regal monarch in that moment, he could see the strain in her cheeks.

She'd had a helluva long day. Fainted. Found out she was pregnant with twins. And she still had not gotten her damn chili dog.

There was a lot going on.

He could cut her some slack, give her space to collect herself. It was no use pushing so hard while she was emotional. And she had every right to be. Hell, he'd been upset tonight, too, uncharacteristically irritated with his father.

So he would revise his approach until cooler heads prevailed. This tactic to get her to stay was not the right one. She'd dismissed it out of hand.

Who could blame her, though? He'd given her no real reason to stay. And, as much as he hated to admit it, Erika Mitras was a woman who did not need him for anything. She could afford the best care and doctors for her pregnancy the same as he could. She would have highly qualified help with day-to-day care in her homeland.

But what she hadn't realized yet was that they were so damn good together. There was something between them, a small spark that could be more. And they had the children to consider.

Rather than insist she stay, he'd convince her. Which meant she was in for some grade A romancing. That was something he could give her that she couldn't just find in a store.

He would win her the old-fashioned way. Because like hell if he was losing his children. Missing out on the lives of his offspring simply wasn't an option. He'd make sure of that.

The next evening Erika still could not make sense of what had happened the night before. But no matter which way she spun Gervais's actions in her bed last night, nothing made sense. She'd been so sure that he wanted her. That he felt that same sharp tug of attraction between them, but his decision to simply walk away and let her go to bed alone had left her surprised. Confused. Aching. Wanting.

He hadn't mentioned the baby issue at all the whole day, then he surprised her with this dinner date, a night out in the city they called the Big Easy.

Draping an arm along the white-painted wrought-iron railing of the patio, her hand kept time to the peppy jazz music playing. She hadn't realized her head nodded along to the trumpet until Gervais flashed her a smile.

Heat flushed her cheeks as she turned her attention away from the very attractive man in front of her. She pushed around the last bite of her shrimp and andouille sausage, a spicy blend of flavors she'd quizzed their waiter about at length. Every course of her meal had been delicious.

Attention snapping to the present, she caught a whiff of something that smelled a lot like baked chocolate and some kind of fruit. Maybe cherries, but she couldn't be sure. All she knew was that her senses were heightened lately.

As were her emotions.

What was Gervais up to with this perfect evening? Was he trying to charm her into changing her mind without discussing the logistical fact that he still moved too fast?

Setting her fork down, she inclined her head to the meal. "Dinner was lovely. Thank you."

His dark eyes slid over her. One forearm lay on the crisp white linen tablecloth, his tanned hand close to where hers rested. He made her breath catch, and she felt sure she was not the only woman in the vicinity who was affected. She liked that he didn't notice. That his gaze was only for her.

"I'm glad you enjoyed yourself. But the evening doesn't have to end now." His hand slid closer to hers on the table.

Her tummy flipped. Did he mean—

Standing, he folded her palm in his. "Let's dance."

She was relieved, right?

Oh, heavens, she was a mess.

She took his hand, the warmth of his touch steadying her as he guided her over to the small teak dance floor. Briefly they were waylaid by an older couple who congratulated Gervais on the Hurricanes' win the day before. But while he was gracious and polite, he didn't linger, keeping his attention on her.

On their date and this fairy-tale evening that Gervais had created for her.

Beneath the tiny, gem-colored pendants, he pulled her into him as the slow, sultry jazz saxophone bayed. With ease, his right hand found the small of her back, and his left hand closed around her hand. As they began to sway, he tucked her against him, chest to chest underneath the din of the music and the lights.

The scents and sounds were just a colorful blur, though, her senses attuned to Gervais. The warm heat of his body through his soft silk suit. His fingers flexing lightly on her back, his thumb grazing bare skin where a cutout in her dress left her exposed.

She swallowed. Each fast breath of air she dragged in pressed her breasts to the hard wall of his chest, reminding her how well her body knew his. What would it be like to be with him now, with her senses so heightened? It had been incredible two and a half months ago.

She couldn't hold back a soft purr. She covered by saying, "The music is beautiful."

"It's the heartbeat of our city. The rhythm the whole place moves to."

He whirled her past the bass player, where the deep vibrations hummed right through her feet.

"There's so much more about my hometown to show you beyond our sports. So much history and culture here. And of course, some amazing food."

Which she could still smell drifting on the breeze. The scent of spices thickened the air, making the heat of the evening seem more exotic than any of the places she'd ever been to during her stint in the military.

"I cannot deny this Big Easy fascinates me." She could lose herself in these brick-and-wrought-iron-laced streets, the scent of flowers heavy in the air. "But I want to be clear, as much as I enjoyed the food tonight, or how much I might like the sound of jazz, that is not going to make me automatically change my mind about your proposal. We have nothing in common."

His voice tickled in her ear, a murmur accompanying the jazz quartet. "Sure we do. We both come from big families with lots of siblings."

A shiver trembled along her skin, and she reminded

herself it was just the pregnancy making her so suscep-
tible to him. It had to be. No man could mesmerize a
woman so thoroughly otherwise. Her hormones simply
conspired against her.

"I guess your family does qualify as American royalty." She held up her end of the conversation, hoping
he could not see the effect he had on her. "So that is
one thing we have in common. Just minus the crowns."

"True. No tiaras here." His head dipped closer to
speak in her ear again. "Although thinking of you in
a tiara and nothing more—that's an image to die for."

She knew he joked. That did not stop her from imagining being naked with him.

"An image that will have to remain in your mind
only, since I do not pose for pictures. After what happened to my sister because of the sex tape with the
prime minister," she said, shuddering, "not a chance."

Gervais almost missed a step, though he recovered
quickly enough.

"Your sister was in a sex tape?"

"You must be the only person in the world who did
not see it." That snippet of footage had almost ruined
her family. The publicity was all the more difficult to
deflect, since their monarchy was both defunct and not
particularly wealthy. They'd had precious few resources
to fight with.

"Never mind." Gervais shook his head, dismiss-
ing that conversation. "That's beside the point. First, I
wasn't speaking literally. And second, I would never,
never let you be at risk that way."

Her neck craned to look at him, eyes scanning his

face. There was no amusement in her eyes. "Perhaps more to the point, I will not put myself at risk."

"You're an independent princess. I like that."

"Technically, I am a princess in name only. The monarchy doesn't have ruling power any longer."

"Fair enough."

Gervais spun her away from him. There was a moment before she returned to the heat of his body that left her with anticipation. She wanted him to keep touching her, to keep pressing his body against hers.

After they resumed their rhythmic swaying, he said softly into her ear, "You are pretty well-adjusted for someone who grew up in a medieval castle surrounded by servants and nannies."

"What makes you think we had servants and nannies?"

A smile played with his sexy mouth. "That princess title."

She rolled her eyes. "The castle was pretty crumbly and we had some maintenance help, since we opened part of the palace to the public, and tutors volunteered just to have it on their résumé that they'd taught royalty. But definitely no nannies."

"Your parents were the involved types." Somehow they had gotten closer, lips barely a breadth away from each other. The thought of how close he was made it hard for Erika to concentrate. So she pulled back a bit, adjusting her head to look out over the crowd, toward the band.

"Not really. After class we had freedom to roam. We were quite a wild pack of kids. Can you imagine having your own real-life castle as a playground? We had everything but the unicorn."

"You make it sound fun."

"Some days it was fun. Some it was lonely when I saw the kids on tour with their parents." She hesitated. The last thing she wanted from Gervais was sympathy. She'd accepted what her family was and was not a long time ago. So she continued, "And some days were downright dangerous."

"What do you mean?"

"My sisters and I wanted a trampoline for Christmas." Which sounded perfectly normal. Except for the Mitras clan, there was no such thing as normal.

"Okay. And?"

"You do not get those on royal grounds. It does not fit the historical image, and without the tours we didn't have money. So, we made our own."

"Oh, God." A look of horror and intrigue passed over his face.

"We pulled a couple of mattresses down the stairs, stacked them under a window... And we jumped."

Gervais's eyes widened. "From how high?"

She shrugged. "Third story. And the ceilings were high."

"You're making me ill."

"It was only scary the first time when one of my sisters pushed me." And, later, when another sister broke an arm and the game ended for good.

"Pushed you?" Disbelief filled his voice. Surely his brothers had done equally dangerous things as forms of entertainment when they had been younger.

She'd seen the Reynaud males up close, and there was an air of confidence and arrogance about all of them that didn't exactly coincide with a sheltered upbringing.

"I was the test dummy," she informed him. "As the youngest and the lightest, it was my job to make sure the mattress had been placed correctly and had enough bounce."

"And did it?"

"We had to add some duvets and pillows."

"So it hurt."

"Probably no more than playing football without shoulder pads."

Tucking a loose strand of her hair behind her ear, he whispered, "You're such a badass. I expected a story like that from a family of boys, but not girls."

Not all girls were the descendants of female warriors. And that was usually the justification for their shenanigans as children. "We considered it our gym class. It was more interesting than lacrosse."

"Lacrosse, huh? I didn't expect that." He brushed his lips across her temple, his breath warm, his brief kiss warmer.

Her body even warmer still with want.

Just when she thought she would grip his lapels and melt right into him, he stepped back.

"I should get you home, Princess. It's late."

And just like that, the fairy-tale book was closing. She felt close to him all evening, physical distance aside. And every time it seemed as if there was something more between them, he pulled back.

While part of her was relieved that he'd stopped pushing for more, a larger part of her wanted him. She had to weigh her options. Had to be strong for her unborn children and make the wisest decision possible. It wasn't just her life in the balance.

After a sleepless night dreaming of Gervais's touch, Erika hadn't awoken in the best of moods. And now she had to make the phone call she had been dreading. The one that had sent her on edge all morning long until she found her courage and started dialing.

Erika sat on the chaise longue in the guest room as she hugged the device to her ear and listened to the call ring through on the other side of the world. She needed to speak with her parents and tell them that she was pregnant. With twins. There was no sense in avoiding the inevitable any longer.

Her mother answered the phone. "Hello, my love. What brings about this lovely surprise of a call?"

"Um, does there have to be a special reason for me to call you?"

"There does not have to be, but I hear a tone in your voice that tells me there is a reason. Something important perhaps?"

Her mother's surprise intuition tugged at her already tumultuous emotions.

"I am pregnant. With twins." The words tumbled out of her mouth before she had even had a chance to respond to the pleasantries with her mom.

So much for the long speech Erika had outlined and perfected. Glancing down at the piece of paper in front of her, she noted that her talking points were basically for show. There was no going back now.

Silence fell from the other end of the receiver for what seemed like an eternity.

"Mother?" she asked, uncertainty creeping into her voice.

"Twins, Erika? Are you certain?"

She nodded, as if her mother could see. "Yes, Mother. I'm certain. I went to the doctor two days ago and heard the two distinct heartbeats with my own ears. The tradition of twins lives on in the Mitras family."

"Who is the father?" Her mother's interest pressed into the phone.

"Gervais Reynaud, the American football team owner—" she began, but her mother interrupted.

"A son of the Reynaud shipping empire? And Zephyr Cruise Ships? What an excellent match, Erika. American royalty. The press will love this."

"Right, but, Mother, I wanted to—"

"Oh, darling, have you considered what this could mean for the family? If you have boys, well…the royal line lives on. This is wonderful, my love. Hold on, let me get your father."

Rustling papers and some yelling came through over the phone. Erika's stomach knotted.

"Your father is on speakerphone. Tell him your news, my love." Her mother cooed into the phone, focused on all the wrong things.

"I'm going to have twins, Father. And I'm just—"

"Twins? Do you know what this means? You could have a boy. Maybe two."

Erika nodded dully into the phone, the voices of her parents feeling distant. As if they belonged in someone else's life. The way they had when she was a child. The image of the royal family always seemed more important than the actual well-being of the family itself.

They weren't interested in hearing what she had to say but were already strategizing how to best monetize this opportunity. The press was about to have an all-access pass to her life before she even knew how she was going to proceed.

"Mother, Father," she said, interrupting their chatter, "I've had quite the morning already." They didn't need to know how much it taxed a woman to daydream about Gervais just when he'd decided to pull back. "Do you mind if I call you later, after I've rested?"

Tears burned her eyes for a variety of reasons that shouldn't make her cry. Pregnancy hormones were pure evil.

"Of course not, my love."

"Not at all, my dear," her father said. "You need your rest if you are going to raise the future of the royal line. Sleep well."

And just like that, they were gone, leaving her cell phone quiet as the screen went dark. They had disconnected from the call as abruptly as they often did from her life, leaving her all alone to contend with the biggest challenge she'd ever faced.

"Well, we're surprised to see you so early, that's all," Dempsey said from a weight bench, his leg propped up on a stool. He pressed around his knee, fidgeting with the brace. An old injury that had cost him his college football career. It was flaring up again. Most days, it didn't bother him. But then there were days like today.

Gervais understood Dempsey's position. He'd been sidelined from the field, as well. One too many concussions. But quite frankly, he enjoyed the business side of owning the Hurricanes.

There were new challenges, new ways of looking at the game and new styles of offense to develop as players came up stronger and faster than ever before. And he was still involved in football, which had been his ultimate goal anyway. This had just been another way to get at the same prize.

As an owner, he would not only strategize how to field the best possible team, he would also make the Hurricanes the most profitable team in the league. Corporate sponsorships were on track to meet that goal in three years, but Gervais had plans that could shorten that window to two. Maybe even eighteen months. The franchise thrived and the city along with it.

"I'm not sure what you two find so fascinating about my night out with Erika." Gervais curled the dumbbells, sweat starting to form on his brow as they worked out in a private facility within the team's training building.

The team lifted in a massive room downstairs, but Gervais had added a more streamlined space upstairs near the front offices.

"We just want to know what's going on in your life. With the baby. And you," Henri, their father's favorite, added. Theo had high hopes that Henri would one day wear a Super Bowl ring for the Hurricanes and continue in the old man's footsteps as a hometown hero.

The whole family was here, with the exception of their father and their brother Jean-Pierre, who played for a rival team in New York and didn't get to Louisiana much during the season.

And while Henri technically worked out with the team, he never minded putting in some extra hours in the upstairs training center to try to show up his older brothers in the weight room.

"That offer still stands, by the way, if you want it to," Henri said, his voice low enough so only Gervais could hear. Gervais knew that things had been hard for Henri and his wife since they hadn't been able to conceive. It affected everything in their marriage. But Gervais wasn't about to give them his unborn children. He wanted to raise them, to be an active part of their lives. To be the opposite of their father.

"Hey now, secrets don't make friends," Dempsey snapped, his face hard. Henri rolled his eyes but nodded anyway.

"So, Pops—" Dempsey shot him an amused grin "—have you decided what you are going to do?"

"Yeah, how are you going to handle fatherhood in the public eye with a princess?" Henri teased, huffing out pull-ups on a raised bar.

"I told you both, I'm taking care of my children." And Erika, he added silently. His main goal as they got ready for the game in St. Louis was to show her that they could be together. That they were great together. An unconventional family that could beat the odds. He was prepared to romance her like no other. And he might have shared that with Henri and Dempsey, if not for the man that rounded the corner, stopping in the entrance to the weight room.

From the door frame, a familiar booming drawl. Theo. "I'm here to meet the mother of my first grandchild."

Eight

As the limo driver faded from view, Erika sped into the Hurricanes' office building. She moved as fast as her legs would carry her, feeling less like royalty and more like a woman on a mission.

Twenty minutes ago, Gervais had called her. Urgency flooded his voice. He needed her in the office stat.

Pushing the heavy glass door open, she took a deep breath, feeling ever so slightly winded. The humidity was something she had yet to fully adjust to, and even small stints outside left her vaguely breathless. The rush of the cool air-conditioning filled her lungs as she crossed the threshold, a welcome chill after the New Orleans steam bath. Striding beneath the black-and-gold team banners hanging overhead, she struggled to figure out what was wrong that he needed her here.

Taking the stairs two at a time, she made it to the second floor and hung a right. Headed straight for the glass wall and door with an etched Hurricanes logo.

The secretary smiled warmly at her from her desk. Adjusting her glasses, she stood. "Princess Erika, Mr. Reynaud is expecting you—"

Extending a manicured hand, she gestured to another door and Erika didn't wait for her to finish. Hurrying forward, she reached the polished double doors made of a dark wood. And heavy. She gave one side a shove, practically falling into the huge office of the team owner.

Currently an empty room.

Erika looked around, heart pounding with nerves. And, if she was being honest, disappointment.

Spinning on her heel, she practically ran into the secretary. Grace was not on her side today.

"My apologies, ma'am," the secretary started in a quiet voice. "Mr. Reynaud will be back in a few minutes, but please make yourself comfortable. Can I get you anything while you wait? We have water, soda, tea. And of course enough Gatorade to fill a stadium."

"Thank you." As the words left her lips, she settled down. Slightly. "I'm just fine, though."

"Of course." The secretary smiled, exiting the room and closing the door with a soft click.

So she was here. In his office without him. While not ideal, it did give her a chance to feel out what sort of man he was. At least in the business sense.

A bank of windows overlooked the practice field below, the lush green grass perfectly manicured with the white gridiron standing out in stark contrast. Silver bleachers glimmered all around the open-air facility with a retractable dome. Funny they didn't have the stadium roof on today when it was so beastly hot outside, but perhaps the practice had been earlier in the day as there were no players in sight now.

Turning from the wall of windows, she paced around the office. She noted the orderly files, the perfectly straightened paper stacks on the massive mahogany desk. The rows of sticky notes by the phone. The walls were covered with team photos and awards, framed press clippings and a couple of leather footballs behind glass cases. The place was squared away. Tight.

Not too different from the way she kept her own living quarters, either. Impersonal. Spit-shined for show. They might not have done a lot of talking in London, but clearly they had gravitated toward each other for reasons beyond the obvious. After last night she felt as if they had more in common than they realized.

A tightness worked in her chest. So desperately did she want to trust him now that they found themselves preparing to be parents together. But trust came at a high cost. It wasn't a commodity she candidly bestowed. It was earned—her most guarded asset. Years of being royalty had taught her to be suspicious.

Shoving her past aside, she approached a picture on the farthest corner of his desk. It was different than the rest. It seemed to have nothing to do with the Hurricanes. Or football, for that matter.

The photograph was faded, old—probably real film instead of digital. But she would have recognized him anyway. Gervais. His brothers. A woman. His mother, she assumed. But no Dempsey. Which struck her as odd.

She would have continued to stare at the picture as if it could give her the answers she was after if she didn't hear a man clearing his throat behind her.

She glanced over her shoulder, through the blond strands of her hair. Gervais stood in the doorway. And he looked damn sexy.

He was disheveled. Not nearly as put together as his office. His hair was still wet from a shower, and his shirt was only half buttoned. For the quickest moment she had the urge to finish undoing it. To kiss him—and more.

The urge honestly surprised her. She had promised herself yesterday that after a good night's sleep, she would be levelheaded today. She needed logic to prevail while she figured out if he could be trusted. Only then could she decide what to do next.

Leaning against the desk, and looking at his lips with feigned disinterest, she asked as casually as possible, "What is the emergency? Is something wrong?"

He shook his head, closing the door behind him. "Not really. I just wanted to speak with you privately about—" he hesitated "—a…uh…new development."

Her smile faded. He was leaving. People always did. Her parents, who never remained in town with their kids for long. The vast majority of her friends who hung around only because she was royalty. The dozens of tutors who only helped for long enough to get a good reference before moving on to an easier job than five hell-raising sisters.

Schooling her features to remain impassive, she sat

down in a leather wingback chair. She needed the isolation that chair represented. She didn't need him tempting her by sitting next to her on the sofa or walking up to her to brush against her. Touch her. Weaken her resolve.

"Tell me." She met his gaze. Steeled herself.

"Remember that I told you I called my father a couple of days ago to tell him about the baby?" His dark eyes found hers for a moment before he stalked toward the wall of windows and looked down at the field. "Apparently, he decided to make a surprise visit."

"Your father is here? In the building or in New Orleans?"

The tight feeling in her chest returned, seizing hold of her. Erika was as unsure of how to deal with his family as she was her own. Selfishly, she had hoped they would have alone time together—without family making plays and demands—to figure out how to handle their situation. And to figure out if there was something there between them, after all.

"He was in the building but he's taking his girlfriend out to lunch before coming to the house later. I wanted to warn you in person and couldn't leave work."

More confirmation she didn't want to hear. But she felt compelled to hear it anyway. "Why do I need warning?"

"He's not a good person in spite of being charming as hell when he wants to be. I just want to make sure you're prepared. Feel free to steer clear of him."

"I can take care of myself. If he becomes too much to handle, I will flip him with Krav Maga I learned in the military." The warrior blood boiled beneath her skin. She would not be taken for a fool.

"You're pregnant."

"I am not incapacitated. But if you are concerned, I will simply pretend I do not understand his English." Uncrossing her arms, she gave him a wickedly innocent grin. Eyes wide for full effect. "It worked on almost half the tutors who showed up at the Mitras household prepared to teach the rebellious princesses."

"Good plan. Wish I'd thought of that as a kid."

A laugh escaped him and he turned toward her, a good-natured smile pushing at his cheeks. Funny how that smile slid right past her resolve to let logic prevail. To be levelheaded. That shared laugh stirred a whole wealth of feelings that had been building inside her ever since she'd stepped onto the practice field to face Gervais Reynaud.

Thinking back to the photograph on the desk, she had to admit, she was curious about him. His past. What it was like growing up in New Orleans. She had so many things to learn about him that it could take a lifetime. And wasn't it perfectly *reasonable* of her to learn more about him when her children would share his genes?

Emboldened by the rationalization, she thought she might as well begin her quest to know him better right now. "But you did not need to arm yourself with elaborate schemes to outwit the grown-ups around you as a child. You and your brothers are so close—or the three of you I've met."

The faintest pull of unease touched his lips. "We weren't always. Dempsey didn't come to live with us until he was thirteen. Our dad… Maybe you already know this."

"No, I do not."

"That's right." He shifted away from the windows to move closer to her, taking a seat on the edge of the desk. "You're not a big follower of football and the players."

"I am learning to be. You make me curious about anything that relates to you." Leaning forward, she touched his arm gently.

"I'm glad." A small victory. She could see him struggling with his family history, despite the fact that it was, apparently, public knowledge.

"Why did Dempsey come to live with you later?"

"We have different mothers."

"Your parents got divorced? But—" That certainly did not seem strange.

He met her gaze, his expression tight. "The ages don't match up. I'm the oldest, then Dempsey, followed by Henri and Jean-Pierre. Dad slept around on Mom, a lot."

"Gervais, I am so very sorry." She touched his arm lightly, which was as much sympathy as she dared offer without risking him pulling away or shutting down.

"My father used to go to clubs with his friends. Remember, this was before the internet made it possible to stalk your date before you'd ever met." He took another breath, clearly uncomfortable.

Erika's eyes widened, realizing that he was opening up to her.

"All families have…dead bones in the closet," she said quietly.

A smile pushed against his lips. "You mean skeletons?"

"Is that not the same thing?" She ran her hand over his.

"More or less, I suppose. Anyway, he hooked up with Dempsey's mom, Yvette, at a jazz club. She got pregnant. Worked a lot of jobs to raise Dempsey, but never found my father, since he hadn't even been honest about who he was, apparently. Until his image was blasted all over the sports page and she recognized his face. Yvette thought it was her ticket out of the slums. She arranged a meeting with my father. But he insisted Dempsey become part of the family. And Dempsey's mother agreed. For a price."

How horrible for Dempsey. And, from Gervais's perspective, how horrible it must have been for him to assimilate a new brother almost his own age when they were both young teens. She avoided focusing on him, however, guessing he would only shift gears if she did.

"That had to be strange for your mother," she observed lightly.

He bit back a bark of a laugh. "Strange? She wasn't much of a motherly type. After one more kid got added to the mix, she left."

"That is so much change for children." Her heart swelled with sympathy for him. She had no idea that there was so much struggle in the Reynaud family.

"We didn't handle it well. I was jealous. Henri was my shadow, so he followed my lead. We blamed Dempsey for breaking up our parents, which was ridiculous from an adult perspective. But kids can be cruel."

"What happened?"

He looked at her sidelong. "We were living in Texas then. Staying at our grandfather's ranch while our father chased our mother around, trying to work things out. Anyway, I dared Dempsey to ride a horse. The biggest, meanest horse on the ranch."

"Oh, my."

"You don't sound horrified."

She shrugged her shoulders. "Remember? My sisters threw me out a third-story window. I know how siblings treat each other even when they have grown up together."

"True enough." He nodded. "Of course, he had no idea how to ride—not even a nice horse. So he was… completely unprepared for a high-strung Thoroughbred used to getting her own way."

"That's scary. What happened?"

"She threw him clear off, but he landed awkwardly and broke his leg. We both almost got trampled while Henri and Jean-Pierre ran to get help."

"You did not mean to break his leg." Ah, sibling cruelty was something that existed in all countries.

"Things were difficult between us for a long while, even once we all made up. I don't want my children to live in a fractured family. Not if I can help it. I want them to have a firm sense of belonging, a sense of being a Reynaud."

"And a Mitras," she reminded him.

"Yes. Both." He reached out to take her hands in his and squeezed. "I want your strength in our children. They will need it."

His words warmed her even more than his touch, and that was saying a lot when a thrill danced over her skin.

Too breathless to answer, she bit her lip, unwilling to allow a dreamy sigh to escape.

"Erika, please stay here with me for a while. We need more time to get to know each other." He drew her to her feet, his eyes pleading with hers at a time when her resolve was at an all-time low.

Her heart beat wildly, her lips parted. Anticipating the press of his mouth to hers.

He rubbed her arms, sliding them up until his hands tangled in her hair. They kissed deeply, with open mouths and passion. Tendrils of desire pulsed through her as he explored her mouth with his tongue, tasting her as she tasted him right back. She had not been passive in their lovemaking before, and she could already feel the urge to seize control driving her to the brink now.

It could have gone on like that for hours, for days even, if not for the sound of the door opening. She pushed back. Looked down. Away. At anything else but him.

While Gervais spoke in a low voice to his secretary, Erika used the time to collect herself. Straighten her dress. Find her purse. She had to figure this out soon. It was apparent there was chemistry simmering hot just beneath the surface. But now there was also a tenderness of feeling. An emotional connection. How would she ever forget that look in Gervais's eyes when he told her about the guilt of seeing Dempsey hurt? Of course she understood why he wanted to keep his own family intact. His children connected.

That was admirable, and a deeper draw for her than the sensual spell he cast around her without even trying. It had been difficult enough resisting just one.

How would she ever keep her wits about her with both those persuasive tools at his disposal?

On the private plane to St. Louis later that week, Erika replayed the kiss in Gervais's office over and over again. Of course, she had already relived that moment in her mind more than once, awake and asleep. Every look between them was filled with so much steam she could barely think, much less trust herself to make logical decisions around him.

At least they were on different planes today, so she could avoid temptation for a few hours. All the wives and girlfriends traveled first-class, while the team went on a chartered craft. Gervais had a meeting in Chicago first, something to do with corporate sponsorship for the Hurricanes. But he would arrive in St. Louis at the same time she did.

With any luck, she could use this flight to get her bearings straight.

But even as she tried to focus on being objective, her mind wandered back to the kiss in the office. A kiss that hadn't been repeated despite the fact that they'd spent time together over the past few days. It felt as though he was always on the clock, managing something for the team or overseeing business for one of the other Reynaud family concerns. So he was a bit of a workaholic; not a flaw in her opinion. In fact, she respected how seriously he took his work. He expected nothing to be handed to him in life.

And when they were together, he was fully present. Attentive. Thoughtful. He'd even helped deflect

an awkward run-in with his father and his father's girlfriend because she hadn't felt ready to face Theo after
what she'd learned about him. And knowing how little
his own son trusted him.

Erika's instincts had seldom failed her. In London,
there had been something between them. Something she
hadn't imagined. And the more she thought about the
past few days, the more excited she was to be with him
again. To have another kiss. To throw away caution as
quickly as clothes peeled away in the heat of passion.

To make love again and discover if the fire burned
as hot between them as she remembered.

Erika clutched a long silver necklace in her hand,
running the charm back and forth. Just as she did as
a child.

Fiona, Henri's wife, gently touched her arm. "You
know, we have a book club to help pass the time when
we're on the road with the guys."

"A book club?" She glanced at the row across from
her, to where Gervais's father's girlfriend stared intently
at a fashion magazine.

Fiona scrunched her nose. "I should have asked. Do
you like to read?"

"Which language?"

Fiona laughed lightly. "No need to get all princess-sy
on me."

"I apologize. That was meant to be a joke. Sometimes
nuances, even though I speak all those languages, get
lost. Tell me more about the book club."

"We choose books to read during all those flights

and then we have one helluva party while we discuss them."

"Party?"

Fiona nodded. "Spa or five-star restaurant or even the best room service we can buy."

"Did Gervais ask you to sit here and use the time to convince me it is fun to be on the road?" Try as she might, Erika couldn't keep the dry sarcasm out of her voice.

"I am simply helping you make an informed decision. It's not just about partying. We have homeschooling groups for families with children, as well." Shadows passed briefly through her eyes before Fiona cleared her throat. "It's amazing what you can teach a child when your field trips involve traveling around the country. Even overseas sometimes for the preseason. Our kids have bonds, too. There are ways to make this kind of family work. Family is important."

Damn. That struck a chord with her. Maybe Fiona had a point. She had just dismissed the women of the group without bothering to really get to know them. And that certainly was not fair.

Maybe she could strengthen her ties to Gervais's world this way. She already knew she wanted to explore their relationship more thoroughly—to take that first step of trust with him and see where indulging their sensual chemistry would lead. But in the meantime, why not work on forging bonds within his world? If things between them didn't work and they ended up co-parenting on opposite sides of the world, she would need allies in the Reynaud clan and in the Hurricanes organization. Growing closer to Fiona would be a good thing for her children.

All perfectly logical.

Except that a growing part of Erika acknowledged she wasn't just thinking about a rational plan B anymore. With each day that passed, with every moment that she craved Gervais, Erika wanted plan A to work. And that meant this trip was going to bring her much closer to the powerful father of her children.

There was nothing Gervais hated more than a loss. It rubbed him the wrong way, sending him into a dark place, even though he knew that a preseason loss didn't matter. The preseason was about training. Testing formations. Trying out new personnel. The final tally on the score sheet didn't count toward anything meaningful.

Opening the door to his suite, he was taken aback by what he saw on the bed. Erika in a Hurricanes jersey. On her, it doubled as a dress, hitting her midthigh. Exposing her toned legs.

His mind eased off the loss, focused on what was in front of him. "I wanted to catch you before you went to bed."

She closed the book she'd been reading and uncurled her legs, stretching them out on the bed. "I am sorry about the game."

"I won't lie. I'm disappointed we lost this one. But I'm realistic enough to know we can't win every time, especially in the preseason when we don't play all of our starters or utilize our best offensive strategies. The whole point of the preseason is like a testing ground.

We can create realistic scenarios and see what happens when we experiment." He told himself as much, but it didn't soothe him when he saw a rookie make poor decisions on the field or watched a risky play go up in flames.

"You have a cool head. That is admirable."

Her head tilted sympathetically.

Gervais was floored. Unsure of what to make about Erika's behavior. For the first time since her arrival in the United States, it felt as if she was opening up to him. But could that be?

She'd been so adamant on keeping distance between them, urging logic over passion. She was probably just being polite to him. After all, they would have to be civil to each other for the sake of the children. She had said as much more than once.

Still, damn it, he knew what he saw in her eyes, and she wanted him every bit as much as he wanted her. Back in his arms.

In his bed.

"Thank you. I'm sorry I've been so busy the past few days." He had taken a red-eye to Chicago to be there this morning for a meeting to secure a new corporate sponsor for the team. He was exhausted, but the extra hours had paid off, and he was one step closer to making the Hurricanes the wealthiest team in the league.

"You have been very thoughtful." She leaned forward, her posture open, words unclipped.

Her gaze was soft on him. And appreciative, he noticed. So maybe he hadn't been so off base. "I was concerned you would feel neglected having to fly in a separate plane."

"I understand you have other commitments. And I had a lovely conversation with Fiona—in case you were wondering, since you made sure we had seats beside each other." Erika raised her eyebrows as if daring him to deny it.

"Are you angry?" He couldn't help that he wanted to give her reasons to stay in New Orleans. But he knew she did not appreciate being manipulated.

He'd never met a more independent woman.

"Actually, no. She was helpful in explaining the logistics of how wives blend in to the lifestyle of this team you own."

He hadn't expected that.

"She answered all of your questions?"

"Most…" Shifting on the bed, she crawled toward him. "I had cats when I grew up."

All of his exhaustion disappeared.

His eyes couldn't help but watch her lithe form, the way her breasts pushed against the jersey he'd given her. An unforgettable vision.

And the sensory overload left him dumbly saying, "Okay."

"We had dogs, too, but the cats were mine."

Trying his damnedest to pull his eyes up from the length of her exposed legs, he stumbled over the next sentence, too. Focusing on words was hard. And he had thought that tonight's loss had left him speechless. That was nothing compared to the sight in front of him. "Um, what were their names?"

Erika's lips plumped into a smile as she knelt on the bed in front of him. "You do not need to work this hard or pretend to woo me."

"I'm not pretending. I am interested in everything about you." And he was. Mind, spirit…and body. He tried to keep his mind focused on the conversation. On whatever she wanted to talk about.

"Then you will want to know the real reason why I mentioned the cats. I loved my cats. And yet my children—our children—will not be able to have pets when they are traveling all over the country to follow this team that is part of their legacy." She gave him a playful shove, her smile still coy.

"Actually, I have a baseball buddy whose wife travels with her dog." He deserved a medal for making this much conversation when she looked like that. "I think the guy renegotiated his contract to make sure she got to have her dog with her."

"Oh," Erika whispered breathily. Moved closer to him, hands resting on his arms. Sending his body reeling from her touch.

"Yes, oh. So what other questions went unanswered today? Bring it. Because I'm ready."

"I do have one more question I did not dare to ask your sister-in-law." Her hands slid up to his neck. Pulled him close. Whispered with warm breath into his ear. "Will it mess up your season mojo if we have sex?"

Nine

Erika's heart hammered, threatening to fall right out of her chest as she stared at Gervais. All the time on the plane and waiting for him tonight had led her here. To this moment. And while the direction of her life may have been still uncertain, she knew this was right.

This was exactly where she needed to be. There was a closeness between them, one she had been actively fighting against.

Gervais's eyebrows shot upward. "What brought on this change?"

"I desire you. You want me, too, if I am not mistaken." Direct. Cool. She could do this.

"You are not mistaken. I have always wanted you. From the moment I first saw you. Even more now."

"Then we should stop denying ourselves the one

thing that is uncomplicated between us." And it was the truth. Everything was happening so fast, but it was undeniable that there was an attraction between them. In her gut, she knew that he would be there to support their babies. But it was more than that.

It was a deeper connection between them. When she had boarded the plane for New Orleans, she hadn't expected much from him. People had a nasty habit of leaving her, using her for the minimal privileges her royal status awarded her. She'd never expected to be welcomed and treated so well. In the past, her friends were dazzled by the idea of her world, rarely seeing beyond the outer trappings to the person beneath.

She also hadn't thought his family would be so accepting. It had scared her a bit, how many people were in the Reynaud clan. The number of people suddenly fussing over her and trying to get to know her had been overwhelming.

But they had also been kind. And maybe, just maybe, she'd be able to see past her preconceived notions about family. She had no real idea how to make a family anyway. But with Gervais…

"You're sure?" His forehead furrowed as he scrutinized her face. The look said everything. This was as far as he'd go without confirmation from her.

"Completely certain." She wanted to take a chance on him. On them. To give them an opportunity to be a couple.

And now that she'd made the decision after careful reasoning, she could finally allow her emotions to surface. She felt all her restraints melting away in the heat of the passion she'd been denying.

Even as she felt those walls disintegrate, she could sense a shift in Gervais. Like shedding a jacket and tie, he seemed to set aside his controlled exterior as a look of pure male desire flashed through his gaze. He closed the distance between them, his brown eyes dark and hungry while he raked his gaze over her.

He peeled the jersey up and over her head. She shook her hair free in waves that fanned behind her, leaving her rounded breasts bared to his devouring gaze. Heat pulsed through her veins—and relief. She had missed him since their incredible time together two and a half months ago, and she'd worked so hard to keep her desire for him in check for the sake of her babies so that she could make a smart decision where he was concerned. Now it felt so amazing to let go of those fears and simply fall into him.

She'd wondered what he would think of the subtle changes pregnancy had brought to her body. Her full breasts had fit in his palms before; now she knew they would overflow a hint more.

But Gervais's eyes were greedier for her than ever, and he stared at her with need he didn't bother to hide. Lowering her to rest on her back, he followed her down to the bed, his touch gentle but firm. His woodsy scent familiar and making her ache for him.

He hooked his thumbs in the sides of her pale blue panties, tugging gently until she raised her hips to accommodate. He slipped the scrap of satin down and off, flinging it aside to rest on top of the discarded Hurricanes jersey. His throat moved in a slow gulp. "That incredible image will be seared in my brain for all time."

He rocked back for a moment, his eyes roving over her.

Then his gaze fell to rest on the ever so slight curve of her stomach. The pregnancy was still early, but now she realized that the twins had been the reason her pants had grown a little snug faster than she would have expected.

A glint of protectiveness lit his eyes. "Are you sure this is safe? You passed out just last week. I don't want to do anything that could risk your health."

She thought she might die if he did not touch her, actually. But she kept that thought locked away.

"The doctor said I am healthy and cleared for all activities, including sex. Well, as long as we do not indulge in acrobatics." A wicked memory flashed through her brain. "Perhaps we should not re-create that interlude on the kitchen table in your London hotel room."

His heart slugged hard against his chest. Against hers. She wanted to arch into his warmth like a cat seeking the sun.

"No acrobatics. Understood." He trailed kisses beneath her ear and down her neck. "I look forward to treating you like spun glass."

A shiver tripped down her spine, her skin tingling with awareness. Tingles of heat gathered between her legs, making her long for more. For everything.

"I will not break," she promised, needing the pleasure only he could bring her.

He skimmed a fingertip down the length of her neck.

"Oh, careful, light touches can be every bit as arousing as our more aggressive weekend together."

She licked her lips. Swallowed over her suddenly dry throat.

"I look forward to your persuasion—once you take those clothes off." She ran her hands down his chest and back up his shoulders. "Because, Gervais…" She savored the feel of his name on her tongue. "You are seriously overdressed for the occasion. Undress for me."

His brown eyes went molten black with heat at her invitation, and his hands went to work on his tie, loosening the knot and tugging the length free, slowly, then draping the silver length over the chaise at the end of the bed. And oh my, how she enjoyed the way he took his time. One fastening at a time, he opened his white button-down until it flapped loose, revealing his broad, muscled chest in a T-shirt. In a deliberate motion he swept both aside and laid them carefully over his tie.

Her mouth went moist and she bit her bottom lip. She recalled exactly why she hadn't bothered with light, teasing touches the last time they were together. His body was so powerful, his every muscle honed. She hadn't been able to hold herself back the last time.

He winked at her with a playfulness that she didn't see in this intense man often.

She could not stop a wriggle of impatience, the Egyptian cotton sheets slick against her rapidly heating flesh.

Then all playfulness left his eyes as swiftly as he took off his shoes and pants, leaving his toned body naked and all for her.

The thick length of him strained upward against his

stomach. Unable to hold back, she sat up to run her hands up his chest, then down his sides, his hips, forward to clasp his steely strength in his hands. To stroke, again and again, teasing her thumb along the tip.

With a growl of approval and impatience, he stretched over her while keeping his full weight off her. He braced on his elbows, cupping her face and slanting his mouth along hers. His tongue filled her mouth and she knew soon, not soon enough, he would fill her body again.

His hands molded to her curves, exploring each of her erogenous zones with a perfection that told her he remembered every moment of their time together as much as she did. His hard thigh parted her legs, the firm pressure against her core sending her arching closer, wriggling against him, growing moist and needy. She clutched at his shoulders, breathy whispers sliding free as she urged him to take her. Now. No more waiting. He'd tormented her dreams long enough.

Then the blunt thickness of him pushed into her, inch by delicious inch. He was so gentle and strong at the same time. She knew she would have to be the one to demand more. Harder. Faster. And she did. With her words and body, rocking against him, her fingers digging into his taut ass to bring them both the completion they sought.

Her fingers crawled up his spine again and she pushed at his shoulders, nudging until he rolled to his back, taking her with him in flawless athleticism. His power, his strength, thrilled her. She straddled him, her sleek blond hair draped over her breasts, her nipples just peeking through and tightening. Gervais swept aside her hair and took one pink peak in his mouth. He circled with his tongue, sending bolts of pleasure radiating through her. Sighs of bliss slipped from between her lips. She rolled her hips faster, riding him to her completion. Wave after wave of her orgasm pulsed through her.

She heard his own hoarse shout of completion, the deep sounds sending a fresh wash of pleasure through her until she melted forward onto his chest. Sated. Every nerve tingling with awareness in the aftermath.

The swish of the ceiling fan sent goose bumps along her skin. The fine thread count of the sheets soothed her.

But most of all, the firm muscled length of him felt so good; the swirls of his body hair tempted her to writhe along him again.

If she could move.

And just like that, Erika realized how utterly complicated being with him was. Because like it or not, she had feelings for him. Feelings that were threatening to cloud her judgment.

And while this may have felt right for her, she needed to be sure it was right for him, too.

Gervais poured the flowery-scented shampoo into his hand. Her magnolia scent filled the steam and teased his senses as they stood under the shower spray in a vintage claw-foot tub. The sheer plastic curtain gave both privacy and a view of the room filled with fresh flowers he'd ordered sent up especially for her.

There was so very much he wanted to do for—and to—this incredible woman.

Drawing Erika close to him, he kissed her neck, nuzzled behind her ear, savored the wet satin of her skin against his bare flesh. Already he could feel the urge building inside him to lift her legs around his waist and surge inside her. To bring them both to completion again, but he was determined to take his time, to build the moment.

And yes, draw out the pleasure.

He lathered her hair, the bubbles and her hair slick between his fingers as he massaged her scalp. Her light moan of bliss encouraged him on, filling him with a sense of power over fulfilling all her needs. He continued to rub along her head, then gently along her neck, down to her shoulders in a slight massage. He wanted to pamper her, to show her he was serious about her and the babies.

She leaned into his touch but stayed silent. Feeling her let out a deep sigh, he decided he wanted to really get to know this beautiful, incredible woman. Sure, they'd spent some time together…but there was still so much he could learn about her. That he wanted to learn about *her*. Everything, not just about her beautiful body, but also about that magnificently brilliant mind of hers.

Such as why she had chosen a career in the military after growing up as royalty.

"So tell me about your time in the service. What did you really do?"

"Just what I told you that day we met."

"Truly? Nothing more? Not some secret spy role? Or dark ops career no one can ever know about?"

"How does the saying go in your country? I could tell you but then I would have to kill you."

He laughed softly against her mouth. "As long as we go while naked together, I'll die a happy man."

She swatted his butt playfully, then her smile faded. "Truthfully, there is nothing more to tell. I was a translator and handled some diplomacy meetings."

"I admire that about you." It had been a brave move. A noble, selfless act.

Shrugging, she tipped her shampooed head back into the water. Erika closed her eyes, clearly enjoying the feel of the steamy water. The suds caught on her curves, drawing his gaze. She was damn sexy.

"Why are you so dismissive of your service to your country?"

Eyes flashed open, defensive. He could tell it in the way she chewed on her lip before she answered, "I wanted to be a field medic and go into combat zones. But I was not allowed."

He nodded, trying to be sympathetic. To understand the complication of letting a princess, even from defunct royalty, into an active war zone.

"I can see how your presence could pose a security risk for those around you. You would be quite a high-value captive."

Her half smile carried a hint of cynicism. "While that is true, that was not the reason. My parents interfered. They did not want me to work or join at all. They wanted me to marry someone rich and influential, like I was some pawn in a royal chess game from a thousand years ago."

"Still, you made your own way. That's commendable. Why a field nurse and not in a military hospital?" He respected her drive. And her selfless career choices. She wanted to help people. Something told him she would have been a good field medic. Strong, knowledgeable, fearless.

"I did not want special treatment or protection because of my family's position. And still, I ended up as a translator not even allowed anywhere near a combat zone." Her voice took on a new determination. A tenacity he found incredibly attractive.

"So you made plans to continue your education after your service was finished." He knew she'd registered for coursework that would begin next month in the UK but had assumed she would ask for her spot to be held until after the children were born.

"I will not be deterred from my plans because of my family's interference." Eyes narrowed at him. Every bit a princess with that haughty stare. "I can support myself."

"Of course you can." He brought his negotiating skills to the conversation, hoping to make her see reason. "This is about more than money, though. You have a lot on your plate. Let me help you and the babies while you return to school."

"That makes it sound like I am incapable of taking care of myself the way my parents always said." Bitterness edged back into her voice. And something that sounded like dulled resignation.

"This isn't just about you. Or me. We have children to think of. You know I want you to marry me. I've made that clear. But if your answer is still no, at least move in with me. Make this easier for all—"

She pressed her mouth to his, silencing him until she leaned back, water dripping between them again.

"Gervais, please, this time is for us to get to know one another better. This kind of pressure from you about the future is counterproductive."

One thing was for sure—she had been opening up. Maybe asking her to marry him again was too much too soon. But he could feel the connection between them growing. So he would back off. But not forever. He just had to figure out a way to show her how good they were together. "Then how about we find food?"

Her smile was so gorgeous the water damn near steamed off his skin. "Food? Now that is music to this pregnant woman's ears."

The strands of Erika's hair fell damp against the cloth of the jersey. They sat in the suite's kitchen. She was on the countertop, cross-legged, peering over at Gervais's back.

He'd retrieved an assortment of ripe fruit—pitted cherries, chocolate-dipped strawberries, pineapple slices and peach slices. At the center of the platter was a bowl of indulgent-looking cream.

Stomach growling, she looked on in anticipation. He brought it next to her and pulled up a bar stool so that they were eye level.

Extending her hand to grab a cherry, he stopped her. "Let me, Princess." With a playful smile, he lifted a cherry to her lips. Inside, she felt that now-familiar heat pulse. He was tender, charming.

A threat to her plan of objectivity, too.

She popped a chocolate-dipped strawberry into his mouth. He licked the slightly melted chocolate off her fingertips, sending her mind back to the shower. Back to when she had thought this was uncomplicated.

Needing to take control of the situation, Erika cleared her throat. Her goal was the same as before. To get to know him. "What did you want to be as a little boy growing up?"

Finishing chewing, he tilted his head to the side. "Interesting question."

"How so?" It had seemed like a perfectly reasonable question. One she had been meaning to ask for a while now.

"Everyone assumes I wanted to be a pro football player."

To Erika, Gervais had seemed like the kind of man who wasn't nearly as cut-and-dried as that. He might live and breathe football, but it didn't seem as if it was the only dimension to him. Childhood dreams said a lot, after all. She'd wanted to be a shield maiden from long ago. To protect and shelter people. Her adult dream was still along those lines.

A nurse did such things. "And you did not want to be a football player like the rest of your family?"

"I enjoy the game. Clearly. I played all through elementary school into high school because I wanted to. I didn't have to accept the offer to play at the college level. I could afford any education I wanted."

"But your childhood dream?" She pressed on, before taking the cream-covered peach slice he'd offered her. She savored the taste of the sweetness of the peach against the salty flavor of his fingers.

Looking down at his feet, then back at her, he smiled sheepishly. "As a kid, I wanted to drive a garbage truck."

Her jaw dropped. Closed. Then opened again as she said, "Am I missing something in translation? You wished to drive a truck that picks up trash?"

"I did. When my parents argued, I would go outside to hide from the noise. Sometimes it got so loud I had to leave. So I rode my bike to follow the garbage truck. I would watch how that crusher took everyone's trash and crushed it down to almost nothing. As a kid that sounded very appealing."

Thinking of him pedaling full-tilt down the roads as a child put an ache in her heart she couldn't deny. "I am sorry your parents hurt you that way."

"I just want you to understand I take marriage and our children's happiness seriously."

His brown eyes met hers. They were heated with a ferocity she hadn't seen before.

This offer of a life together was real to him. His offer was genuine, determined. And from a very driven man. She needed to make up her mind, and soon, or she could fast lose all objectivity around Gervais.

Ten

It had only been three days since he'd gotten home from the loss in St. Louis. He needed time to think of his next strategy. And not just for the Hurricanes. With Erika, too.

Which was exactly why he'd pulled on his running shorts and shirt. Laced up his shoes and hit the pavement, footsteps keeping him steady.

Focused.

Sweat curled off his upper lip, the taste of salt heavy in his mouth. The humid Louisiana twilight hummed with the songs of the summer bugs and birds.

This always set his mind right. The sound of foot to pavement. Inhale. Exhale. The feel of sweat on his back.

He'd been quite the runner growing up. Always could

best his brothers in distance and speed. Especially Jean-Pierre, his youngest brother.

Jean-Pierre had to work harder than all his older brothers to keep up with them as they ran. Running had been something of a Reynaud rite of passage. Or so Gervais had made it out to be. He'd always pushed his brothers for a run. It was an escape from the yelling and fighting that went on at their home. Whether the family was at the ranch in Texas, on the expansive property on Lake Pontchartrain or on the other side of the globe, there was always room to run, and Gervais had made use of those secured lands to give them all some breathing space from the parental drama.

Slowing his pace, he stopped to tighten his shoelace. Looking at the sparkling water of the lake, he realized it had been too long since he talked to Jean-Pierre. Months.

Gervais knew he needed to call him…but things hadn't been the same since Jean-Pierre left Louisiana Tech to play for the Gladiators in New York. Sure, Jean-Pierre maintained a presence on the family compound, sharing upkeep of one of the homes where he stayed when he flew into town. But how often had that been over the past few years? Even in the off-season, Jean-Pierre tended to stick close to New York and his teammates on the Gladiators. When he did show up in New Orleans, it was to take his offensive line out on his boat or for a raucous party that was more for friends than family.

How Jean-Pierre managed to stay away from this quirky, lively city was beyond Gervais. When they were younger, the family had spent a lot of time in Texas. Which, make no mistake, Gervais loved, but there was a charm to New Orleans, a quality that left the place rarified.

He wanted to share those things with Erika. The cultural scene was unbeatable, and the food. Well, he'd yet to take her to his favorite dessert and dancing place. He pictured taking her out for another night on the Big Easy with him. She'd love it if she'd give him a chance to show her.

And though they'd fallen into a pattern over the past few days, he felt as distant as ever and all because she wouldn't commit even though they had children on the way. Sure, they made love nightly now. And he relished the way her body writhed beneath his touch. But it wasn't enough. He bit his tongue about the future and she didn't say anything about leaving.

Or staying.

And he wanted her to stay. Starting to run again, he picked up the intensity. Ran harder, faster.

He didn't want her to leave. He didn't want a repeat of London. Before he'd even woken up, she'd packed her things and let herself out of the hotel suite. Though it had been only one weekend, he had fallen for her. Now they'd spent days together.

Rather blissful days. Mind wandering, he thought to the last night in St. Louis when they'd explored the rooftop garden that was attached to their hotel suite. There'd been a slight chill in the air, but things between them had been on fire. In his memory, he traced the curves on her body.

Though she might be pumping the brakes on the future, he was getting to know her. To see past her no-nonsense facade to the woman who was a little sarcastic, kindhearted and generous.

The thought of her just leaving again like in London... it made his gut sink.

Rounding the last corner on his run, he didn't hold back. He sprinted all out, as if that would allow him to hold on to Erika.

This was damn awful timing, too. He knew he needed to focus on his career. To turn the Hurricanes into a financial dynasty to back the championship team Dempsey assured them they had in place. And this thing with Erika—whatever it might be—was not helping him. Sure, he'd nabbed that sponsor in Chicago. But every day he spent with her was a day that he wasn't securing another sponsor that would make the Hurricanes invincible as a business and not just a team. They'd been teetering on the brink of folding when he'd purchased them, and he'd reinvigorated every facet since then, but his work was far from done to keep them in the black.

But damn. He could not. No. He *would* not just let her leave as she had before. This wasn't just about the fact they were having a family, or that they were amazing together in bed.

Quickening his pace, he saw the Reynaud compound come into sight. The light was on in Erika's bedroom.

His grandfather had taught him a few things when he was a kid. Two of the most important: *build your dream* and *family is everything.* Two simple statements. And he wanted Erika to be a part of that. To create the kind of home that his own kids would never want to run from.

Sitting cross-legged on a cushioned chair in the massive dining room, Erika absently spread raspberry jam on her puffy biscuit. Try as she might, she couldn't force her mind to be present. To be in the moment.

Instead, her thoughts drifted back to Gervais and last night. He'd knocked on her door after his run. She'd opened the door, let him in. And he'd showered her in determined, passion-filled kisses. There was an urgency, a sincerity in their lovemaking last night. A new dimension to sex she had never thought possible.

Last night had made it even harder for her to be objective about their situation. She wanted Gervais. But she also wanted what was best for them both. Balancing that need seemed almost impossible.

A motion in the corner of her eye brought her back to the present. She found Gervais's grandfather filling his plate at the buffet with pork grillades and grits, a buttered biscuit on the side.

Gracious, she could barely wait for the morning to wane so the queasy feeling would subside and she could indulge in more of the amazing food of this region. Everything tasted so good, or perhaps that was her pregnancy hormones on overload. Regardless, she was hungry but didn't dare try more for a couple more hours yet.

She looked back at Gervais's grandfather, keeping her eyes off the plate of food. Leon hadn't gone with them to St. Louis, but Gervais had explained how travel anywhere other than from his homes in New Orleans and Texas left the old man disoriented.

He took his place at the head of the table, just to the left of her, and poured himself a cup of thick black coffee from the silver carafe. "So you're carrying my first great-grandchild—" He tapped his temple near his gray hair. "Grandchildren. You're having twins. I remember that. Some days my memory's not so good, but that's sticking in my brain and making me happy. A legacy. And if you won't find it disrespectful of me to say so, I believe it's going to be a brilliant, good-looking legacy." He toasted her with his china coffee cup.

"Thank you, sir. No disrespect taken at all. That's a delightful thing to say, especially the smart part." She gave him a wink as she picked at her biscuit. Praise of her intelligence was important. Erika had worked hard to be more than a pretty princess. Wanted her worth and merit to be attached to her mind's tenacity. To realize her dreams of setting up a nurse-practitioner practice of her own someday, one with an entire section devoted to homeopathic medicines and mood-leveling aromatherapy.

"That's important." He sipped more of his coffee before digging into his breakfast. "We have a large family empire to pass along, and I want it to go into good hands. I didn't do so well with my own children. But my grandkids, I'm damn proud of them."

"Gervais will make a good father." Of that she had no doubt. He was already so attentive.

"He works too much and takes on too much responsibility to prove he's not like his old man, but yes, he will take parenthood seriously. He may need some books, though. To study up, since he didn't have much of a role model. He sure knows what not to do, though." A laugh rasped from the man's cracked lips and he finished more of his coffee.

"I believe you played a strong part in bringing up your grandchildren." She reached for the carafe and offered to refill his cup, even though she wasn't drinking coffee. She stuck to juice and water these days.

He nodded at her, eyes turning inward as if he was reading something she couldn't see. "I tried to step in where I could. Didn't want to bring up spoiled, silver-spoon-entitled brats again." His focus returned to her. "I like that you went into the military. That speaks well of your parents."

Her mother and father had pitched an unholy fit over that decision, but she would not need to say as much. "It was an honor to serve my country."

"Good girl. What do you plan to do now that your studies are on hold?"

Technically, they weren't. She would be back in university in autumn.

"When I return to school, I will undertake the program to become a nurse-practitioner, even as a single mother." And she would. No matter how long it took.

"Really? I didn't expect you to, um—"

"Work for a living? Few do, even after my military service." Her voice went softer than she would have liked.

"You'll take good care of my grandson when I'm

gone?" His question pierced her tender heart on a morning when her emotions were already close to the surface.

"Sir, you appear quite spry to me."

"That's not what I mean and if you're wanting to be a nurse-practitioner, you probably know that." He tapped his temple again. "It's here that I worry about giving out too soon. The doctors aren't sure how fast. Sometimes I prefer the days I don't remember talking to those experts."

"I am so very sorry." She hadn't spent a lot of time with Leon Reynaud. But she could tell he was a good man who cared a lot about his family. And the stories Gervais told her only confirmed that.

"Thank you. Meanwhile, I want to get to know you and spend time with you so you can tell my great-grans all about me." He pointed with his biscuit for emphasis and she couldn't help but smile.

"That sounds delightful," she said to Gramps, but her eyes trailed over his head. To Gervais, who strode into the dining hall.

Sexy. That was the only word that pulsed in her mind as she looked at him. Dressed in a blue button-down shirt, he looked powerful.

"Don't mind me," he mumbled, smiling at her. "Just grabbing some breakfast before heading to the office. You can go back to telling embarrassing stories about me, Gramps."

Gramps chuckled. "I was just getting ready to tell my favorite."

Gervais gave him a faux-injured grin, swiping a muffin and apple from the table.

He stopped next to her. Gave her a hug and a kiss. Not a deep kiss or even lingering. Instead, he gave her one of those familiar kisses. A kiss that spoke of how they'd been together before. That they knew each other's bodies and taste well. She bit her bottom lip where the taste of him lingered, minty, like his toothpaste.

As he walked away, everything felt...right. Being with him seemed so natural, as if they had been doing this for years. It'd be so easy—too easy—to slide right into this life with him.

And that scared her clean through to her toes.

It had been a long day at the office, one of the longest since their return from St. Louis. Gervais had tried his best to secure a new technology sponsor for the Hurricanes, a west coast company with deep pockets that was currently expanding their presence in New Orleans. The fit was perfect, but the corporate red tape was nightmarish, and the CEO at the helm hadn't been as forward thinking as the CFO, whom Gervais had met on another deal the year before. Not everyone understood the tremendous advertising power of connecting with an NFL team, and the CEO of the tech company had been reluctant. Stubborn. It had been a hellish day, but at least the guy hadn't balked at the deal. Yet.

Gervais had left work midday to talk with some of Gramps's doctors. They were discussing treatment plans and some of the effects of his new medicines. All he wanted to do was give the best he could to his family.

Family. Gramps. Hurricanes. Jean-Pierre. Work and Reynaud business had swirled in his mind all day. The only thing he wanted to do this evening was see Erika. The thought of her, waiting at home for him, had kept him fighting all day. Besides, he had a gift for her and he couldn't wait to present it to her.

Walking into her room, he felt better just seeing her. She was sitting on the chaise longue, staring blankly at her suitcase.

Her unzipped suitcase.

That fleeting moment of good feeling vanished. Was she leaving? If he had come home later, would she have already been gone, just like London?

Taking a deep breath, he set aside his gift for her and surveyed the room. The two arrangements of hydrangeas and magnolias were on her dresser alongside an edible bouquet of fruit. He'd had them sent to her today while he was at work. For her to think about their time in St. Louis together.

As he continued to look around the room, he didn't see any clothes pulled out. So they were all either in the drawers or in her bag.

He hoped they were still in the drawers. Gervais didn't want her to go. Instead, he wanted her to stay here. With him. Be part of his family.

Tapping the suitcase, he stared at Erika "That's not full, is it?"

He tried to sound light. Casual. The opposite of his current mental state.

She looked up quickly, her eyes such a startling shade of blue. "No, of course not. Why would you think that?"

"You left once before without a word." He wanted to

take her in his arms and coax her into bed for the day, not think about her leaving.

"I promised you I would stay for two weeks and I meant it. After that, though, I have to make a decision."

He tensed.

"Why? Why the push?"

"I need to move forward with my life at some point." Chewing her lip, she gestured at the suitcase.

"I've asked you to marry me and move in with me, yet still you hold back. Let me help support you while you make a decision, with time if not money, wherever you are." He would do that for her and more.

She looked at him with a steady, level gaze. "Seriously? Haven't we had this discussion already? We have time to make these decisions."

"The sooner we plan, the sooner we can put things into place."

"Do not rush, damn it. That is not the way I am. My parents learned that when they tried to push me into their way of life, their plans for me." Her gaze was level, icy.

"So you plan to leave, just not now?"

"I do not know what I am planning." Her voice came out in a whisper, a slight crack, as well. "I am methodical. I need to think through all of the options and consequences."

"Is that what you did the morning you left me? Stayed up and thought about why we needed to turn our backs on the best sex ever?" Dropping onto the edge of the bed across from her, he caught her gaze. Looked at the intensity of her blue eyes. She was damn sexy.

Beautiful. And he wasn't going to let her walk away as if this was nothing.

"Best sex ever? I like the sound of that." She licked her lips seductively, leaned toward him, her breasts pressing against her glittery tank top.

So tempting. And definitely not the direction he needed to take with her.

He raised his brow at her. "You're trying to distract me with your beautiful body."

"And you are using flattery. We need more than that." Crossing her arms, she scrutinized his face.

"I've made it clear I understand that. That's what our time together has been about. But I am willing to use everything I have at my disposal. I am not giving up."

"Everything?" She gestured to the flowers, the candy and a small jewelry box.

He'd forgotten about the gift he'd brought for her.

Pushing off the bed, he approached her, leaned on the arms of the chaise longue. He kissed her forehead, one arm around her, the other still cradling the box. "Flattery, which is easy because you are so very lovely. Charming words are tougher for me because I am a businessman, but for you, I will work so very hard with the words. And, yes, with gifts, too. Will you at least open it?"

She took the box from his hands, eyes fixed on his. Her fingers found the small bow. Gently, she slowly pulled the white bow off. The Tiffany box was bare, undressed now.

Erika lifted the lid, let out a small gasp. Two heart earrings encrusted in diamonds glinted back at her.

Gervais's voice dropped half an octave. "It made me think of our children. Two beautiful hearts."

He tucked a knuckle under her chin and raised it to see her face. Tears welled in her eyes.

Pulse pounding, he put his arms around her, held her tight to his chest. "I didn't mean to make you cry."

She shook her head, her silky blond hair tickling his nose. "It is sweet, truly. Thoughtful. A wonderful gift."

Kneeling in front of her, he wiped the tears off her pale cheeks. He'd wanted to get her something meaningful. Drawing her hands in his, he kissed the back of each one, then the insides of her wrists in the way he knew sent her pulse leaping. He could feel it even now as he rubbed his thumbs against her silky skin. "I want this to work. Tell me what I can do to make that happen. It is yours."

Her eyes flooded with conflicting feelings. It was as if he could see into her thought process where she worked so hard to weigh the pros and cons of a future. Somehow he knew she was at the precipice of the answer she'd been looking for. One he was scared as hell to receive.

And, cursing himself for his weakness, he couldn't resist this one last chance to sway the outcome. To make her want to stay. So he kissed her deeply, ebbing away the pressure of speech to make room for the pleasure they both needed.

Eleven

Gervais had Erika in his arms and he wanted that to go on for… He couldn't think of a time he wouldn't want her. Every cell inside him ached to have her. So much so his senses homed in to her. Almost to the exclusion of all else. Almost to the point where he lost sight of the fact he'd left the door ajar.

And now someone was knocking lightly on that door.

With more than a little regret, he set her away from him and struggled to regulate his breathing before turning to the door to find…a security guard?

Hell. How could he have forgotten for even a second that his family's wealth and power carried risk? They needed to stay on watch at all times.

Security guard James Smithson stood on the other side of the half-open door, his chiseled face grave.

Gervais had always liked James—a young guy, athletic and focused. James had almost made the cut for the team. The poor kid was in an interesting position; he'd declined a college football scholarship when his high school girlfriend became pregnant. James attended an online school while helping raise their son, but he'd shown up at a couple of Hurricanes training camps with impressive drive, even though his stats weren't quite strong enough.

So before Dempsey could send him home, Gervais had taken him aside and found out he had skills off the field, too. He'd offered him help forming his own security company, making him a part of the Hurricanes family.

"Sorry to disturb you, sir, but we have some unexpected company."

"I don't accept unexpected guests. You know that." Gervais stared at the guard. Who, to be fair, was doing a damn good job at not looking at Erika in her tight-fitting sparkly tank top that revealed her killer curves. Even so, he found himself wanting to wrap her up in a sheet. Just to be safe.

"I understand that, sir," James assured him. "But…"

Erika looked back and forth between the guard and Gervais. "I'll leave the two of you to talk." She closed the jewelry box and clutched it to her chest. "If you'll excuse me."

James held up a hand. "Ma'am, I believe you'll want to stay."

Ericka's face twisted in confusion. "I'm not sure how I can be of help—"

James scrubbed his jaw awkwardly. "It's your family. Their limos are just now coming through the front gate."

Gervais blinked slowly. "Limos?" Plural?

"My family?" Erika stammered, color draining from her skin. "*All* of my family?"

James gave a swift nod, his gun just visible in a shoulder harness under his sports jacket. "It appears so, ma'am. Both of your parents, four sisters, three of them married and some children, I believe?"

Gervais scratched the back of his head right about where an ache began. Talk about a baptism of fire meeting all the in-laws at once. So many. "I think we're going to need to air out the guesthouse."

The pressure of a headache billowed between Erika's temples. As she stood in the grand living room, attention drawn outside, past the confines of this room, she felt everything hit her at once. First, her conflicting feelings for Gervais, and now this.

Her entire family, down to her nieces, was here. Now. Her eyes trailed past the bay windows to where Gervais, her father, Gervais's brothers and his grandfather stood on the patio. Having drinks as if this was the most casual affair ever. As if this was something they had done together for years. Gervais had a gift with that, taking charge of a situation and putting everyone at ease.

She'd spent so much time focusing on the reasons to hold back, she forgot to look for the reasons they should. There was a lot to admire about this man. His obvious love of his family. His honorability in his standing up to care for his children. And the way he handled his business affairs with a mix of savvy and compassion. Her heart was softening toward him daily, and her resolve was all but gone.

And of course there was the passionate, thorough way he made love to her. A delicious memory tingled through her. She tore her eyes from him before she lost the ability to think reasonably at all.

Her father, Bjorn Mitras, slapped his knee enthusiastically at something Gervais had said. So they were getting along.

The mood inside the living room was decidedly less jovial. She could feel her sisters and mother sizing her up. Determining what Erika ought to do. And if she had to bet, getting her Master's in Nursing wasn't even on the table anymore. They'd never supported her ambitions. And if she was carrying a male child…well, they'd certainly have a lot of opinions to throw at her.

For the first time since learning she was pregnant, Erika felt alone.

She had hoped for an ally in Fiona, but Fiona hadn't come to meet everyone. She wasn't feeling well. Erika was not feeling all that great herself right now. Her family overwhelmed her in force.

Turning reluctantly from the bay windows, she studied her mother. Arnora Mitras had always been a slight, slim woman. Unlike other royals, she recycled outfits. But Arnora was a friend of many fashion designers. She was always draped in finery, things quite literally off the runway.

Her four sisters—Liv, Astrid, Helga and Hilda—stood in the far corner, discussing things in hushed tones. The twins, Helga and Hilda, both had the same nervous tic, tracing the outline of their bracelets. It was something that they had both done since they were little girls. Erika squinted at them, trying to figure out what had them on edge.

But it was Astrid who caught her gaze. Blue eyes of equal intensity shone back at her. Astrid gave a curt nod, her honey-blond bob falling into her face.

It was a brief moment of recognition, but then Astrid turned back to the conversation. Back to whispering.

Three of her sisters had married into comfort, but not luxury. Not like what the Reynauds offered. And they lived across Europe, leading quieter lives. No male heirs, no extravagance. A part of Erika envied that anonymity, especially now.

Of course, Gervais had seen to every detail. And in record time. He called in all the staff and security. Arranged what looked like a small state dinner in record time. He even had nannies brought in for her nieces.

Beignets, fruit and pralines were decadently arranged into shapes and designed. It looked almost too beautiful to eat. Erika watched as her sisters loaded their plates with the pastries and fruit, but they eyed the pralines with distrust. They weren't an open-minded bunch. They preferred to stick to what they knew. Which was also probably why they skipped over the iced tea and went straight for the coffee. That was familiar.

"Mother—" the word tumbled out of Erika's mouth "—some advance notice of your visit would have been nice."

"And give you the opportunity to make excuses to put us off? I think not."

Sighing unabashedly, Erika trudged on. "I was not putting you off, Mother. I was simply..."

"Avoiding us all," Helga finished for her as she approached. The rest of the Mitras women a step behind her.

"Hardly. I wanted time to prepare for your visit and to ensure that every detail was properly attended to."

Helga gave a wave to the spread of food and raised her brow. She clearly didn't believe Erika's protest. "This place is amazing. You landed well, sister."

"I am only visiting and getting things in order for our babies' sake." Erika's words were clipped, her emotions much more of a tangle.

"Well, you most certainly have something in common. Relationships have been built on less. I say go for it. Chase that man down until he proposes." The last word felt like nails on a chalkboard in Erika's ears. She schooled her features neutral, just as she had done when she was a translator. No emotions walked across her face.

Erika stayed diplomatically quiet.

Her mother's delicately arched eyebrow lifted, and she set her bone china coffee cup down with a slow and careful air. "He has already proposed? You two are getting married?"

"No, I did not say we are getting married."

"But he *has* proposed," Hilda pressed gently.

"Stop. This is why I would have preferred you wait to meet him. Give Gervais and me a chance to work out the details of our lives without family interference, and then we will share our plan."

Liv waggled her fingers toward the French doors leading to the vast patio. "*His* family is here."

"And they are not pushy," Erika retorted with conviction. She wasn't backing down from this. Not a chance.

"We are not pushy, either. We just want what is best for you." Hilda's porcelain complexion turned ruddy, eyes widening with hurt and frustration like during their childhood whenever people laughed at her lisp. She always had been the most sensitive of the lot.

Smoothing her green dress, Liv—always the prettiest, and the most rebellious, the infamous sex tape being the least of her escapades—took a deep breath and touched her hair. "I think all of this travel has made me a bit weary. I shall rest and we will talk later."

And with that her mother, Liv, Helga and Hilda all left the grand living room, heels clacking against the ground.

But Astrid didn't leave. She hung back, eyes fixed on Erika.

Anger burned in Erika's belly. Astrid was her oldest sister. The one who always told her what to do. She had been the sister to lecture her as a child. Erika fully anticipated some version of that pseudo-parental "advice" to spill out of Astrid's lips.

"Keep standing up for yourself. You are doing the right thing."

Gaping, Erika steadied herself on the back of the tapestry sofa. "Seriously? I appreciate the support but

I have to say it would be nice to have with Mother present."

Astrid shrugged. "She is frightening and strong willed. We all know that. But you do understand, you are strong, too. That is why we pushed you off the balcony first."

"Wow, thanks," Erika grumbled, recalling the terrifying drop from balcony to homemade trampoline.

"You are welcome." Astrid closed her in a tight embrace. In a half whisper, she added, "I love you, sister."

"I love you, too." That much of life was simple.

If only the other relationships—her relationship with Gervais—could be as easily understood. Or maybe they could. Perhaps the time had come to stop fighting her emotions and to embrace them.

Starting with embracing Gervais.

With the arrival of Erika's family, work for the Hurricanes had taken a backseat. Not that he would have had it any other way. They were his children's aunts and grandparents. They were important to him. He had to win them over—particularly her father, the king, not that King Bjorn had shown any sign of disapproval.

But important or not, they were the reason he was just now getting to his charts and proposals in the wee small hours of the morning.

Gervais pressed Play on the remote. He was holed up in the mini theater. He had a few hours of preseason games from around the league to catch up on. This was where he'd been slacking the most. Hadn't spent much time previewing the talent on the other teams yet. Because while Dempsey would fine-tune a solid fifty-three-man roster from the talent currently working out with the team, Gervais needed to cultivate a backup plan for injuries and for talent that didn't pan out. That meant he needed to familiarize himself with what else was out there, which underrated players might need a new home with the Hurricanes before the October trade deadline.

A creak from the door behind him caused him to turn around in his seat. Erika was there, in the doorway. A bag of popcorn in one hand, with two sodas in the other.

She certainly was a sight for his tired eyes. He drank her in appreciatively, noting the way her bright pink sundress fit her curves, the gauzy fabric swishing when she walked. The halter neck was the sort of thing he could untie with a flick of fabric, and he was seized with the urge to do just that.

As soon as possible. Damn.

"I thought this could be like a date." She gave him a sly smile, bringing her magnolia scent with her as she neared him, a lock of blond hair grazing his arm.

He took the sodas from her and set them in the cup holders on either side of the leather chairs in the media room.

"Well, then, best date ever."

"That seems untrue." Worry and exhaustion lined her voice. "I am sorry about my family arriving unexpectedly. And for how much time they are taking out of your workday."

"It's no trouble at all. They are my children's grandparents. That's huge." Pausing the game, he gave her a genuine smile, conceding that he wouldn't be giving the footage his full attention now. But he had notes on the talent across the league, of course. As an owner, he didn't run the team alone.

And right now nothing was more important to him than Erika and his children.

Settling deeper into the chair beside him, Erika flipped her long hair in front of one shoulder and centered the bag of popcorn between them.

"I also appreciate how patient you have been. And my sisters loved the tours through New Orleans." Erika leaned on his shoulder, the scent of her shampoo flooding his mind with memories of London. St. Louis. And last night. Making love, their bodies and scents and need mingling, taking them both to a higher level of satisfaction than he'd ever experienced.

Damn. He loved that. Loved that this smell made her present in his mind.

"Of course." He breathed, kissed her head, inhaled the scent of her hair and thought of their shower together.

Her breath puffed a little faster from her mouth. She nibbled her bottom lip and gestured to the screen. "May I ask what you are doing?"

Gervais hit Play, a game springing to life. "Well, I have to get a feel for who is out there. I have a team to build. So I may have to replace my current rookies with some of these guys."

Erika nodded. "And why is this so important to you? Why do you spend so much time on football when, according to the press, they are worth only a fraction of your overall portfolio?"

"Someone's been doing her research," he noted. Impressed.

"I was not joking when I told you that I am trying to figure out where to go from here. I am thinking through all possible paths." Her blue gaze locked on him. "Including the one you have proposed."

His chest ached with the need to convince her that was the best. But he restrained himself. Focused on her question.

"Why the focus on football?" he repeated, reaching into the popcorn bag for a piece to feed her. "My family is a lot like yours. They come with expectations. But I have my own expectations, and I've always wanted to carve out something that was all mine within the vast Reynaud holdings. Some success that I made myself, that was not handed to me. Does that make any sense?"

He presented her with the popcorn and she opened her lips. His touch lingered a bit longer than necessary against her soft mouth.

She chewed before she answered. "You want to stand on your own two legs?"

Gervais smiled inwardly. Her idiom use was so close. "Something like that. If I can stand on my own two feet, make this team into something…" His mind searched for the correct words.

"Then no one can take that away from you. It is yours alone."

Gervais nodded, stroking her arm. "Exactly. I imagine that's why you want your Master's in Nursing so badly. So that is holistically yours."

"Mmm," she said, tracing light lines on his chest.

"Very wise of you. You have been listening to me, I see."

Her touch stirred him. Heat rushed through his veins as he set aside the remote.

"We are more alike than you think." He curled an arm around her shoulders and drew her closer, his fingers skimming through her silky hair to the impossibly soft skin of her upper arm.

"Because we are both stubborn and independent?" She slid her finger into the knot of his tie and loosened the material.

"It's more than that." He wrenched the tie off, consigning the expensive Italian silk to the floor.

"We are both struggling to meet the expectations of too much helpful family?" She arched a pale brow at him, all the while fingering open buttons on his shirt.

The hell with waiting.

He slid an arm under her knees and lifted her up and onto his lap, straddling him. Her long sundress spilled over her thighs, covering her while exposing just the smallest hint of satin panties where she sat on his thighs.

"And we both need to lose ourselves in each other right now." His fingers sifted through her hair, seeking the ribbon that secured the halter top of her sundress.

"You are correct," she assured him, edging down his thighs so that their hips met.

Her breasts flattened to his chest.

A hungry groan tore from his throat.

He kissed her hard, his control fractured after so many days of thinking through every move with her, of strategizing this relationship like the most important deal of his life. Because while it was all that and more, Erika was also the hottest, most incredible woman he'd ever met, and he wanted her so badly he ached.

She met each hungry swipe of his tongue with soft sighs and teasing moans that threatened to send him right over the edge. Already, her fingers worked the fastening of his belt, her thighs squeezing his hips.

"This day has been too much," she admitted, her whispered confession one of the few times she'd confided her feelings. "I need you. This."

And he wanted to give it to her. Now and forever.

But he knew better than to rattle her with talk of forever. Understood she was still coming to terms with a future together. So he forced himself to be everything she needed right now.

Flicking free the tie at her neck, he edged away from the kiss just enough to admire the fall of the gauzy top away from her beautiful breasts. Her skin was so pale she almost glowed in the darkened theater, his tanned hands a dark shadow against her as he cupped the full weight of one breast.

Molding her to his palm, he teased his thumb across the pebbled tip, liking the way her hips thrust harder against his as he did. She was more sensitive than ever, the least little touch making her breath come faster. Making her release quicker.

Just thinking about that forced him to move faster, one hand skimming down her calf to slip beneath the hem of her long dress. He stroked her bare knee. Smoothed up her slender thigh. Skimmed the satin of panties already damp for him.

She cried out his name as he worked her through the thin fabric, coaxing an orgasm from her with just a few strokes. Her back arched as the tension pulsed through her in waves, her knees hugging him until the spasms slowed.

He didn't waste time searching out a condom, since they no longer needed one. He let her go just long enough to shove aside the placket of his pants and free his erection.

She took over then, her fingers curling the hard length and stroking up to the tip until his heart damn near beat its way out of his chest. He kissed her deeply, distracting her from her erotic mission, leaving him free to enter her.

And oh, damn.

The slick heat of her squeezed him, the scent of her skin and taste of her lips like a drug for his senses. He gripped her hips, guiding her where he wanted. Where he needed. And looking up at her in the half-light reflected from the dim screen, he could see that she was as lost as him. Her plump lips were moist and open, her eyes closed as she rode him, finding her pleasure with as much focus and intensity as him.

He must have said her name, because her eyes opened then. Her blue gaze locked on his.

And that did it.

More than any touch. Any kiss. Any sexy maneuver in the dark. Just having Erika right there with him drove him over the edge. The pleasure flared over his skin and up his spine, rocking him. He held on tight to her, surprised to realize she had found her own peak again right along with him, their bodies in perfect sync.

After the waves of pleasure began to fade and the sweat on their bodies cooled, he stroked her spine through that long veil of her hair, savoring the feel of her in his arms, her warm weight so welcome in his lap. He wanted her every night. Wanted to be the one to take care of her and ease her. Pleasure her.

But even as his feelings surged, he could tell she was pulling back. Throwing up a seemingly impenetrable wall of ice as she edged back and tugged her dress into place. Her family's arrival had shaken her. Awakened an instinct to define herself in opposition to their expectations.

A part of him understood that. And was damn proud of her, too. But that same urge that motivated her to stand her ground, meet her parents and family dead-on, might also be the reason he felt frozen out.

The more he thought about it, the more real seemed the idea of losing not just his children, but her, too.

And as if she sensed his thoughts, she got to her feet. "Gervais, my family's here, so I would appreciate it if we didn't sleep together with them nearby."

"Seriously?" He propped himself up on his elbows.

"I know it may seem silly with the babies on the way, but...them being here? I need space."

He studied her face, her platinum-blond hair tumbling around her shoulders. "Damn it, Erika, all I've done is honor your need for space, taking cues off you."

"A few short days. Less than a month. And you call that space? Time?" Her throat moved. "Clearly we have very different ideas about taking our time. Maybe we don't understand each other nearly as well as you think."

Frustration fired inside him as he felt victory slip away word by word. He tugged on his pants, all the while searching for the right words and coming up short.

Not that it mattered, since before he could speak, she'd left the room. The click of that door made it clear.

She was running scared and he wasn't welcome to join her now.

If ever.

Twelve

The excitement of the fans at the home Hurricanes game was dwarfed in comparison to the buzz going on in the owners' box.

Erika sat against the leather chair, taking it all in, her heart in her throat after the way she'd left things with Gervais last night. But the way he made her feel scared her down to her toes. He made her want too much at a time when she had to be more careful than ever about protecting her heart and her future.

Gramps Leon called out to the Mitras clan. "Did Erika tell you how the Reynauds came into their fortune?"

"No, Leon, she hasn't shared much of anything with us. We'd love to know. American origin stories are so fascinating," Hilda said darkly, shooting her a daggered look across the spread of shrimp gumbo and decadent brownies. Erika rolled her eyes, moving closer to the glass to get a look at the field. Somehow, this game she had disliked so much was starting to make sense to her.

"Grampa Leon, we all know that story," Fiona said with a light laugh, her hands wringing together. She was nervous but Erika couldn't tell why.

"Yes, but the beautiful princesses and queen haven't. And they want to. Who am I to deny them that?" he said with a wink at Hilda, whose face was already turning into a toothy grin.

"It was a high-stakes poker game. My surly old Cajun ancestor was sweating as he stared at his hand of cards. The stakes were incredibly high, you see," Gramps Leon began, leaning on his knees.

"What were the stakes, Leon?" Queen Arnora asked, on her best behavior, since Erika had been emphatic with her mother that histrionics would not be tolerated. The babies were Erika and Gervais's, not potential little royal pawns.

Arnora had vowed she simply wanted to bond with their expanding family and was thrilled over impending grandparenthood.

"If my riverboat grandpa won, he would get a ship out of the deal. But if he lost, he would have to sign a non-compete. And stay working for the tyrant captain who kept him away from home for months on end. Needless to say, the cards laid out right for him and he won the first ship in the fleet. The Reynaud family empire was born. Just like that." He snapped his fingers, eyes alight with a new audience to entertain. "The rest is history. The family has been successful ever since. Especially my grandboys."

King Bjorn inclined his head. "You feel responsible for your grandchildren's success?"

"Yessir, King Bjorn. I'm proud of all of those boys. Feel like I practically raised them myself. Though I kind of did," Gramps Leon wheezed, eyes drifting to Theo, who shrank in the back corner, "My son almost made it big…eh. No matter. My grandboys did. That's what matters in the end."

Erika watched as Theo fidgeted with his drink, balling up a cocktail napkin in his right fist. She knew he hadn't been the best father, but a small part of her felt sympathy for him.

"And what did all your grandchildren do?" Arnora asked lightly, swirling the champagne in her glass.

Erika had often wondered how her mother had such ease with others but not as much with her children. Her mom took her role as a royal, a liaison to the world, seriously. Erika looked around at the Reynaud family and saw their bond, but not only that. She saw their relaxed air. The way they kept life…real. Connected. She wanted that for her children, as well.

And yet she'd pushed her babies' father away the night before out of fear of living like her parents.

Gramps Leon's dark eyes gleamed with pride and affection. "Well, you know Gervais bought his own team. I figure they'll make it big soon the way that boy works. And Dempsey is the youngest coach in the league's history. Henri is already a franchise quarterback looking for his first championship ring. Even Jean-Pierre is doing good things as a quarterback for that northern Yankee team. Where is he again?"

Theo cleared his throat. "New York. Jean-Pierre is the starting quarterback for the New York Gladiators." Pride pierced his words, and he lifted his eyes to meet Leon's. So he did care, Erika thought. It was just masked.

She wished it was that easy to tell what was going on with Gervais. Nothing he'd said so far betrayed any level of an emotional depth. Just sex. But that wasn't enough for her. And that was the reason she hadn't been able to help but pull away the night before.

Last night when she'd gone to him, she'd believed he might really care for her. Sure, the sex was great and he wanted to provide for their children. But she'd started to think that he also genuinely liked her, sex and children aside.

Before then, she'd been so sure of him. Of the decision she was close to making.

As she sat in the owners' box again, she realized she couldn't stop replaying seeing the bed empty when she woke up, knowing it was her fault for pushing him away but not knowing what she could have done differently. Erika would have continued to analyze the situation if it wasn't for the approach of Liv, her sister. The one that had been through the sex tape fiasco.

The scandal had almost cost Liv everything.

Liv narrowed her gunmetal eyes at Erika, pinning her. She sat next to Erika, hands firmly grasping the wineglass's stem. The smell of alcohol assaulted Erika's sense of smell, turning her stomach sour.

"Sister," she said lazily, "this family…"

Erika straightened, finishing the sentence for her. "Is filled with wonderful, loving people."

Liv nodded solemnly. "Yes. And how do you say— American royalty?"

Erika's eyes remained out toward the field, toward where Gervais stood with a reporter giving an interview, players and photographers around them. She would not be dignifying her sister's comment with a response.

"All I am trying to say, dear sister, is that you need to be here. You could be royalty for real if you did." Liv's words, spoken in a hushed tone, had a bit of a slur to them.

"That's not what matters to me. What matters is—" But the words caught in her throat as she watched Gervais get hit by two men locked in a tackle. Gervais was on the sidelines, knocked to his feet, his bare skull slamming back into the ground. Hard. Tackled on the sidelines with no equipment.

She barely registered what the Mitrases or the Reynauds were doing. In an instant, the panic that stayed her breath and speech was replaced by a need to move. A need for action. The damn need to get to his side.

Pushing her way to the door that led down to the stands, she ran smack into James, the security guard who had first alerted them that the whole Mitras clan was arriving. He stood at the door to the tunnels leading through the bowels of the stadium and out onto the field. His credentials were clipped to his jacket, a communication piece in his ear. "Princess, I am afraid I can't allow you onto the field. Please wait here. I promise to keep you updated about Mr. Reynaud."

James put a hand on her shoulder. Consoling? Or to restrain? Either way, it didn't matter to her because this man kept her from Gervais.

Years of practice drills during her time in the military pressed her muscles into action. Without sparing a second thought, she grabbed his hand and bent back his pinkie. A minor move but one that could quickly drive a man to his knees if she pushed farther. "James, I am a nurse, but I am also former military. I can flip you onto your back in a heartbeat and you cannot—will not—fight me because I am pregnant. Now, we can do this simply or we can make this difficult, but one way or another, I am going to Gervais."

James's eyes narrowed, then he exhaled through gritted teeth. "I could lose my job for this." He shook his head, rolling his eyes. "But come with me. You'll need my credentials to get through to the field."

She bit her lip hard in relief. "Thank you."

"Um, ma'am, could you let go of my pinkie?"

"Oh." She blinked fast, having forgotten she'd even still held him pinned. She released his hand and stepped back.

Wincing, he shook his hand. "Follow me."

She followed him through the corridors, urging him to go faster and barely allowing herself to breathe until she saw Gervais with her own eyes. He waved off his personal security team as soon as she came into sight, his face twisted in pain as the team doctor shone a small flashlight in front of his eyes, checking his pupils.

Her medical training came to the fore and took in his pale face. He sat on the ground, upright, and was not swaying. His respiration was even, steady. Reassuring signs. Her heart slowed from a gallop. He would need a more thorough exam, certainly, but at least he was conscious. Cognizant.

"Gervais? Are you okay?" Erika knelt beside him, then turned to the team's doctor, her voice calm and collected now. "Is he all right?"

On the field beside him, the game continued, the fans cheering over a play while Erika's focus remained on Gervais and all that mattered to her.

"I'm fine," Gervais growled, then winced, pressing his hand to the back of his head.

The doctor tucked away his flashlight into his bag. "He's injured, no question, given the size of that goose egg coming up. Probably a concussion. He should go to the emergency room to be checked over."

"Then let us go." She barked the command at the doctor. Meanwhile, the game had resumed playing, and she trailed behind him.

As she stepped out of the arena with Gervais, leaving her family behind, reality crashed into her. Her heart was in her throat for this man. He was the father of her children. But she barely knew him and already he'd turned her world upside down. She felt as if she, too, had taken a blow to the head and her judgment was scrambled. How could she care so much so soon?

What was she doing here? She had started to love him, but maybe she just loved the surface image. Maybe she'd done what her family had done—just looked at the surface. After all, he'd offered no feelings, no emotions to her. Just convenient arrangements for their children and sex. His marriage proposal had never included mention of love.

And she couldn't settle for less than everything from him, just as she wanted to give him her all.

What if in spite of all logic, she had fallen in love with him and he could never offer her his full heart?

There were only a few times in his life that Gervais had felt extreme elation and intense concern all at the same time. This was certainly being added to that tally.

Later that night as he stretched out in his own bed, Erika hovering, he was still replaying that moment Erika had rushed out to him. His head throbbed but his memories were crystal clear.

Watching Erika care enough about him to rush to his side filled him with a renewed purpose. He'd been blown away and more than a little unnerved watching her rush to his side, somehow having persuaded James to let her through security and out onto the field.

Make no mistake, he always wanted her there. By his side. But he didn't want any harm to come to her or their children, either. The thought of harm befalling her or their children by her own rash actions gnawed at him. The security was there for a reason. God, she was everything to him. Everything. And he wasn't sure how he could have missed out on realizing the depth of that.

They could be so good together, but it also seemed as if the risk of her pulling back was at an all-time high. All of her interactions with him since the CT scan came back had been rigid. Formalized. As if she was a nurse doing a job, not a woman tending to her lover.

That reaction clapped him upside the head harder than the wall of a football player that had crashed into him. Her reactions didn't add up. She had been so upset on the sidelines, so freaked out about what was happening to him. And now she was answering in snippets of sentences. He didn't want to upset her more, or keep her awake all night. But his family had been in and out of the room for hours. It was nearing morning before he finally had a moment alone with her.

His head throbbed far more from this situation than his minor concussion.

Propped up on the bed, he quietly said, "How did you get James to let you join me on the field?"

She flushed the most lovely shade of pink, her hand fidgeting with her blond hair draped over her shoulder. "I used some of my military skills to persuade him. Nothing extreme, given my condition, of course, just a small but painful maneuver."

"Seriously? Apparently, I need to have you train my security."

"And give away my secrets?" She gave him a princess-like annoyed scoff. "I think not. Besides, he should not have tried to keep me from you."

"While I find that sexy on one level, you have to be careful and think about the babies. What if you had been hurt?"

She shrugged, looking him square in the eye. "I was careful. You are the injured one. Now, relax. You may not be stressed but you have to stay awake. Do as the doctor instructed or I am taking you back to the hospital."

He felt the prickles of her emotions. Had to change the direction. Bring it back to breezy. Shooting her a sly smile, he said, "We could have sex. That would keep me awake."

"You're supposed to rest." Eyes narrowing with annoyance, Erika crossed her arms.

"Then take advantage of me. I'll just lie back and be very still." He closed his eyes, then half opened one of them to look at her. Hoping to elicit some sort of response out of her. Hoping to see that radiant smile spread across her face. Damn. He loved that smile.

"Oh, you think you are funny. But I am not laughing right now. You are injured and I am here to make sure you take care of yourself."

"You could tie me up so I don't get too…boisterous."

"Boisterous? Now, that's an interesting word choice and a challenge. But sadly, for your own health, I will have to hold strong against your boisterous charms. Let us play cards." There was no jest in her voice.

"Cards? Strip poker, maybe."

"No, thank you."

"Then I'll pass on the cards. I gotta confess, my vision is a little blurry." He held up his hand, trying to focus on his fingers. A dull ache pulled at him.

Turning, practically out the door to the room, Erika said, "I should get the doctor."

"The doctor has checked me. I've had an X-ray and MRI and CT scan. I'm fine. Concussed, but nothing the players don't face all the time. I'm not going to be a wimp in front of my team."

"They wear helmets."

"I have a thick head. Just ask anyone I work with. Or those I don't work with." He tried his best to crack that smile wide-open, but Erika's face was as solemn as ever. She was shutting him out and he didn't understand why.

"I'm not laughing."

"You want to be serious? Then let's be serious. Erika, I want you to move in with me. Hell, to be honest, I want you to marry me, but I will settle for you moving in here. Go to school here. Let's be together. Life is complicated enough. Let's enjoy more popcorn dates and sex in the screen room and every other room in this place. And in my cars. I have many, you know." The declaration was earnest. He wanted her. For now. Forever. And not just because they were having children together.

Erika slammed her hand on the desk, a quiet rage burning in her fine, regal features. "I am still not laughing, Gervais. We cannot build a relationship on sex. I need something meaningful. I have fought so hard to build a life for myself, to be seen as someone more than ornamental. A royal jewel in the crown meant to bear an heir to the line, defunct or not."

"Erika. It's not like that. I don't think of you as a crown jewel." Gervais searched her face, trying to understand her.

"All you have done since I told you I was pregnant is press for marriage. I have worked hard to gain my independence, my happiness, and I will fight for my children, as well. They deserve something more."

"Erika, I—" Gervais, the man who always had a plan, stammered, fighting for words.

Tears glistened in her eyes, but she stood tall, her shoulders braced as she backed away. "I will wake one of your brothers. It is morning anyway." Erika turned, was already to the threshold and then gone before he could even think of words to delay her.

He had botched this chance to win her over. And what a helluva time to realize just how much he loved her, this proud, strong woman. He loved her intelligence, her passion, even her stubbornness. He adored every hair on her head.

He loved her so deeply he knew any fear of repeating his father's mistakes would not happen. Gervais loved Erika. Real love. The kind that he knew damn well was rare in this world.

And in rushing her, he may have ruined his chance to have her.

As Erika let her feet dangle over the edge of the dock, she focused her attention out on the lake's waters. The late-afternoon sun cast golden shimmers on the surface of the water.

She felt as if the whole day had been a training exercise. Nothing had felt real to her. Since she stormed out of Gervais's room last night, Erika had felt disoriented.

The problem was simple. Despite logic and reason, she was madly in love with Gervais. These past few days had proved how easy it would be to fall into a routine together.

But they had also shown her how difficult it would be for them to become more than…well, whatever this was.

A breeze stirred her loose blond hair, pushing strands in front of her eyes. Though it was humid, and the bugs played a loud symphony, she was comforted by the noises, smells and sights of this foreign land. It was starting to feel a bit like home. Another confusing feeling to muddle through.

The wind gusted stronger, stirring the marsh grass into a beautiful shudder. Boats zipped a ways off from the dock, and she watched the wakes crest and crash into each other.

It was practically silent, except for the boats and bugs. Everyone had gone. She'd packed her family into their limos, watched from the dock until the landscape of New Orleans swallowed them up.

The Reynauds were gone on a day trip. Theo's idea, actually. He'd even taken Gramps with them. All the Reynaud men, save for Jean-Pierre, on one trip in one spot. Probably something that didn't happen too often.

Inching backward on the dock, she pulled her knees to her chest. Erika was at a complete loss of what to do.

If only it could be as simple as the word *love*. She loved her children. She loved their father. But she still didn't know if he loved her back. On the one hand they hadn't known each other long, yet she was certain of her feelings. She needed him to be just as sure.

Her head spun with it all.

And her heart twisted.

She knew what she wanted, but it didn't make sense. She wanted to say to hell with logic and stay here with Gervais. To move in. To love him. To build their family together and pray it would all work out.

Footsteps echoed along the dock, startling her an instant before she heard Gervais's deep voice.

"You did not leave with your family."

Whipping her head up, she took him in. Fully. And a lump formed in the back of her throat.

"Did you think that I would do that without saying goodbye to you?" She would never have done something so cruel. Not after what she felt for him and all they'd been through together.

His chin tipped, the moonlight beaming around him. "Is this your farewell, then?"

"I am not going home with them."

He pressed further, drawing near to her. "And to school in the UK?"

Decision upon decision. Layer upon layer. "Do you think I should?"

"I want you to stay here but I cannot make this decision for you. I don't want to rush you."

His answer surprised her. "I expected you to try to persuade me."

"I've made my wishes clear. I want you to stay. I want us to build a life. But I can see you're afraid. I'll wait as long as you need." He knelt to her level, touched her face with his steady hand.

She bristled. "I am not afraid. I am wary. There is a difference."

"Is there?"

She churned over his words. "If you want to mince words in translation, then all right. I am afraid of making the wrong choice and having our children suffer because of it."

"And you think we are the wrong choice?"

"I think that I love you." There. It was out there. This was how she'd make her decision. Let him know exactly where she stood.

"I know that I love you."

She swallowed hard and blinked back tears, barely daring to believe what she was hearing. "You do?"

"I absolutely do. No question in my mind." His voice wrapped around her heart like a blanket, soothing and private and intimate all at once. He was…everything.

"I believe you and I want so very much to believe that will be enough."

"Then be willing to challenge that warrior spirit of yours and fight for what we feel for each other."

Fight? Erika had been used to fighting for the things that mattered to her. Maybe this battleground wasn't so foreign, after all. "Fight."

"Yes, stay here. Get to know me. Let me get to know you. And every day for the rest of our lives we'll get to know more and more about each other. That's how it works."

"I will move in with you?" The idea was tantalizing this time and she wondered why she had dismissed it so readily before. Out of pride? The thought of losing herself in her family again reminded her how hard she had fought for her freedom to live her life. And truth be told, she wanted to live here, in this fascinating town with this even more fascinating man. She wanted to give her children a family life like the Reynauds.

She wanted Gervais.

Looking over his shoulder, her eyes took in the mansion.

"Yes. If that is what you wish."

"I can go to school here?" She hadn't even looked into programs around here, but she could. There were ways to make this work. Now that she knew, beyond a shadow of a doubt, that he loved her.

"Yes. If that is what you wish," he said again, those final words making it clear he understood her need for control over her life.

"We bring up our children here?"

"Yes, and in your country, too, whenever possible, if you wish. And most of all I hope that you'll do all of that as my wife." He squeezed her hand, brought her to a standing position.

Erika looked up at him, reading his eyes. "As simple as that?"

Pulling her into him, he shook his head. "Not simple at all. But very logical."

"Love as a logical emotion?" The idea tickled her.

"The love I feel for you defies any logic it's so incredible. It fills every corner of me. But I do know that my plan to work harder than I've ever worked at anything in my life to make you happy? Yes, that will be a plan I'm not leaving to chance. I will make that a conscious choice. But if you need time to decide—"

She cupped his face in her hands. "I do not need any more time at all. Yes."

"Yes?" Lines of excitement and relief tugged at his face.

She breathed in the scent of him, feeling balanced and renewed. Sure, for the first time in weeks, that this was where she was supposed to be.

"Yes, I love you and I will move in with you. I will go to school here. I will have our children here. And most of all, yes, I will marry you."

He gathered her closer, a sigh of relief racking his big, strong body. "Thank God."

"How did I ever get so lucky to meet and fall for such a wonderfully stubborn man?"

"We knew that day we met."

"In spite of logic."

"Instincts. With instincts like ours, we will make a winning team—" he rested his mouth on hers "—for life."

* * * * *